THE LOVEDAY LOYALTY

THE LOVEDAY LOYALTY

Kate Tremayne

<u>headline</u>

First published in 2006
by HEADLINE BOOK PUBLISHING

1

Cataloguing in Publication Data is available from the British Library

ISBN 0 7553 2871X

Typeset in Bembo by Palimpsest Book Production Limited,
Polmont, Stirlingshire

Printed and bound in Great Britain by
Mackays of Chatham plc, Chatham, Kent

HEADLINE BOOK PUBLISHING
A division of Hodder Headline
338 Euston Road
London NW1 3BH

www.headline.co.uk
www.hodderheadline.com

To the people of Cornwall for their warmth and friendliness during my many visits, and their help with my research.

To the Team at Headline, especially Jane Morpeth and Alice McKenzie for their support and encouragement, and who have brought the Loveday series to such a wide readership.

The Lovedays are such a huge part of my life and their characters are as dear to me as my own family. When I worry over their escapades, adventures and heartaches, my wonderful agent Teresa Chris is always there to inspire me and to dare the Lovedays to reach for the stars and achieve far more than I ever dreamed possible.

And a very special acknowledgement to all the loyal Loveday fans who write and email me at my website www.katetremayne.com. That you all care so deeply for the Lovedays and share your hopes and fears for them is a constant inspiration for me. It is always a pleasure to hear from you. Thank you all.

To my own Aussie connection – my brother Alan and his family. So many happy memories and so much fun and laughter. Writing about Japhet in *The Loveday Pride* and *The Loveday Loyalty* has kept our wonderful time with you in Australia alive.

Also to very dear friends, Vera and William Pearce. And thank you, Bill, for the marvellous portraits of myself and my husband. Your talent inspires us every day.

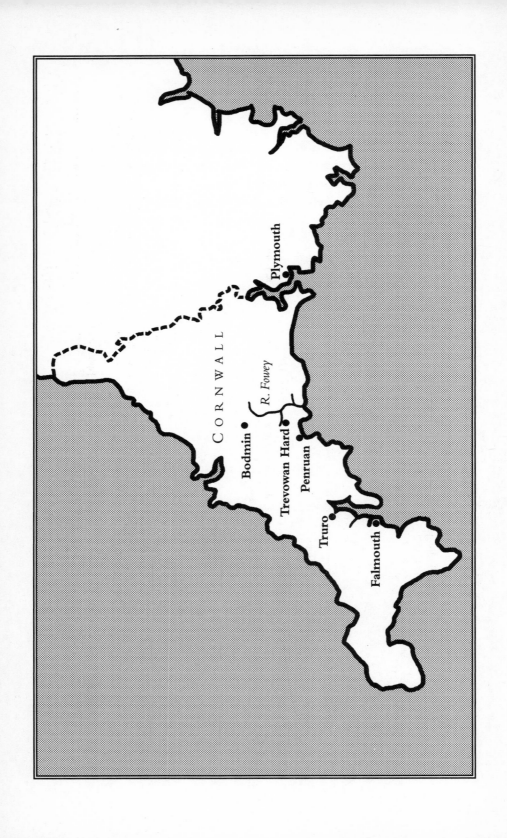

CORNWALL

Plymouth

R. Fowey

Bodmin

Trevowan Hard

Penruan

Truro

Falmouth

THE *LOVEDAY FAMILY*

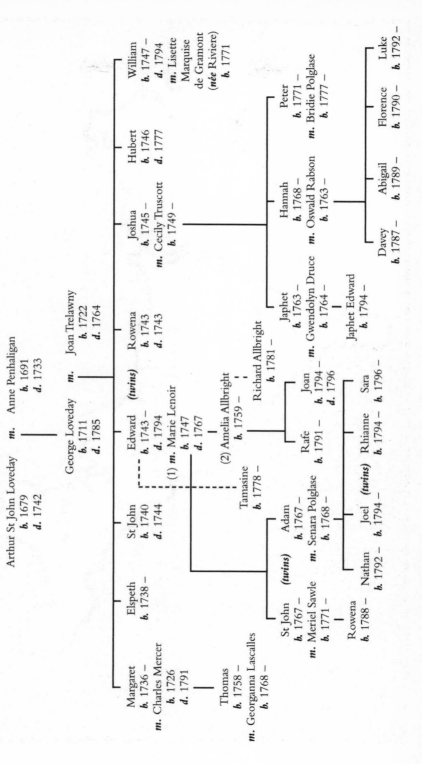

Arthur St John Loveday
b. 1679
d. 1742

m.

Anne Penhaligan
b. 1691
d. 1733

George Loveday
b. 1711
d. 1785

m.

Joan Trelawny
b. 1722
d. 1764

Margaret
b. 1736 –
m. Charles Mercer
b. 1726
d. 1791

Elspeth
b. 1738 –

St John
b. 1740
d. 1744

Edward **(twins)**
b. 1743 –
d. 1794
(1) **m.** Marie Lenoir
b. 1747
d. 1767
(2) **m.** Amelia Allbright
b. 1759 –

Rowena
b. 1743 –
d. 1743

Joshua
b. 1745 –
m. Cecily Truscott
b. 1749 –

Hubert
b. 1746 –
d. 1777

William
b. 1747 –
d. 1794
m. Lisette
Marquise
de Gramont
(**née** Riviere)
b. 1771

Thomas
b. 1758 –
m. Georganna Lascalles
b. 1768 –

Tamasine
b. 1778 –

Richard Allbright
b. 1781 –

Adam
b. 1767 –
m. Senara Polglase
b. 1768 –

Rafe
b. 1791 –

Joan
b. 1794 –
d. 1796

Japhet
b. 1763 –
m. Gwendolyn Druce
b. 1764 –

Japhet Edward
b. 1794 –

Hannah
b. 1768 –
m. Oswald Rabson
b. 1763 –

Peter
b. 1771 –
m. Bridie Polglase
b. 1777 –

St John **(twins)**
b. 1767 –
m. Meriel Sawle
b. 1771 –

Rowena
b. 1768 –

Nathan
b. 1788 –

Joel **(twins)**
b. 1792 –
b. 1794 –

Rhianne
b. 1794 –

Sara
b. 1796 –

Davey
b. 1787 –

Abigail
b. 1789 –

Florence
b. 1790 –

Luke
b. 1792 –

Chapter One

1797

The russet and amber streaks of sunset fringed the clouds over Rabson Farm. With the shortening days of early December Hannah was aware that there were never enough hours to complete her tasks.

She loved the farm, but as the light began to fade she had an encroaching feeling that there was hidden menace lurking in the shadows. A shiver sped down her spine, compounding her instinct. It sharpened her stare as she gazed across the fields.

It was unsettling to realise that the farm was unusually deserted of workers. Sam Deacon, her overseer, had not returned from Launceston market. He had been accompanied by Aggie, the housemaid, to sell the cheese, butter and surplus milk. Mark Sawle, her groom, was also absent, having taken some broken implements to be repaired by the blacksmith at Trevowan Hard, her cousin Adam's shipyard. Dick Caine, who should be feeding the horses, had sloped off and was nowhere in sight, and his wife Mab had also made herself scarce.

Hannah shook off a sense of vulnerability. It had been a long and busy day and she would not allow her tiredness to conjure fears that danger was near at hand. She was no faint-heart and was a match for any man in a verbal battle. She was also far from defenceless. She touched the dagger she had taken to wearing at her waist since her husband's death. She was adept at using it and was a practised shot with a pistol or shotgun. But she had reason to be wary of her safety. There had been several unsettling incidents in recent months involving local smugglers, and their leader, an enemy of her family, ruled the surrounding communities by intimidation and violence.

She was not frightened by the smuggler's threats and had confronted the free-traders on several occasions. Her family were too influential for them to risk harming her, but neither did she underestimate them.

She channelled her disquiet instead into anger at the advantage the Caines were taking of her generosity. She had been too lenient with them. No longer would she tolerate their laziness. She marched to their tied cottage to give them a final warning. The couple were growing more lax in their duties. They would never have taken such liberties when her husband Oswald was alive, and Hannah would not stand for it now.

When she pushed open the door the cottage was empty. It was also filthy. Cobwebs draped the rafters, dirty dishes were piled in the sink, and clothes and belongings were strewn on every chair, table and chest. Hannah shook her head in disgust. The house stank of mouldy food, unwashed clothes and bodies. She guessed the couple had walked the mile to the nearest kiddley — an ale house on the road to Trewenna — to avoid their evening tasks on the farm. As she turned to leave, she saw a keg of brandy on the floor by a rickety chair next to the unlit fire. She shook it. It was full.

Her anger against the couple mounted. Dick could never afford a keg of brandy. It was payment for his work with a smuggling gang, and she had forbidden him to consort with them. Many of her neighbours turned a blind eye to the free-traders, but not Hannah, at least not since her uncle Edward Loveday had been killed because of their activities on his land.

Hannah crossed the farmyard to do the work Dick Caine should be attending to. The three dairymaids had finished the milking and were taking the cows to the lower meadow to graze. They were giggling and talking about men. The young women always had romance on their minds.

The horses were still in the paddock and had to be stabled. To leave them out to pasture could mean the smugglers would use them for pack horses for the night. Four of the six mares belonged to her elder brother Japhet, who intended to use them as brood mares. Each had produced a thoroughbred foal that year.

Hannah was pleased to discover that her children had already penned the chickens and geese for the night. She could hear the youngsters playing hide and go seek in the farmhouse. Her heart swelled with love and pride. They were good children and never complained at the tasks they were set. It was important that they had their time for play before bedtime. The rabbit pie they would have for their supper was cooling on the kitchen table and the apple dumplings were simmering on the Cornish range. In an hour they would be in bed and Hannah would read to them from *Gulliver's Travels* before completing her evening tasks of mending clothes and house linen. She welcomed the long hours of work, which kept her grief at bay.

As she crossed the farmyard, the farm dogs barked from a distant field. The sound rose in cadence, a sign they had encountered a stranger. The hairs at the back of Hannah's neck prickled. She had the feeling of being watched. If anyone had been studying her they would have seen no ordinary farmer's wife, but a woman of poise and beauty. Her figure was slim despite the four children she had borne in ten years of marriage, and the fading rays of the sun burnished her thick dark hair with fiery copper tints. A fire that was echoed in her blood and feisty temperament.

There was battle in her hazel eyes when she spun round to scan the track to the house and the surrounding fields. Although the dogs continued to bark, she could see no one. Her gaze narrowed as it lingered on a coppice on the far side of a field. The barking came from that direction. It could be a poacher, or worse a smuggler. The free-traders had once used that copse for storing contraband without permission. Tomorrow she would get Sam to search it. Harry Sawle, their leader, had been warned that if he used Loveday land to hide his contraband, the authorities would be informed and the illicit goods confiscated.

Again her skin prickled and she breathed deeply to combat a rush of unease incurred by thoughts of Harry Sawle. She had stood up to him in the past but he was an evil and vengeful man. She pushed the memories of those encounters aside. They were too unsettling.

Harry Sawle had not been in the district for three months since taking possession of his new ship *Sea Mist*. It had been built in her cousin Adam Loveday's shipyard and Adam had suffered with his conscience for taking on the work when the family believed that Harry was partly responsible for Edward's death. But without the commission the yard would have had to close. It had cost Adam dear to swallow his pride, but he had been right. Sometimes it was necessary to dance with an enemy for a greater cause to be won. In time Sawle would pay for his treachery.

Her mood remained uneasy as she rounded up the horses. They were skittish and uncooperative and she was flagging with tiredness by the time the last one was in its stall. When she passed four pheasants hanging on a hook outside the tack room, her anger returned. Mab had been instructed to pluck and gut them while the dairymaids were at their evening milking so that the birds would be ready to be cooked tomorrow.

As Hannah fed and watered the horses the dogs continued to bark from the direction of the copse. The sun was sinking lower in the sky and her disquiet increased. Conscious of being alone in the outbuilding, she picked up a pitchfork for protection. Her fingers gripping the wooden handle were slick with perspiration.

The most frightening incident with Harry Sawle had been in this very barn. After Oswald's death she had woken during a gale with the sound of the barn door banging, and not wishing for the children to be disturbed had gone out to close it. As she neared the building Sawle had grabbed her and dragged her inside. The memory of how he had forced his kiss on her and threatened that her family would suffer if she did not permit him to use her property to store contraband, made her flesh cringe. She had fought him, terrified he intended to inflict more than a kiss upon her. Harry had laughed at her struggles but to her relief had not attempted to assault her. He was arrogant enough to believe she would eventually yield willingly to his attentions.

She had vowed she would die rather than submit, and his evil laugh following her defiance now echoed sinisterly in her ears. But Sawle had needed Adam Loveday to build his ship and he would not risk crossing her cousin until the vessel was finished. Even then Hannah doubted the smuggler would be the victor in any encounter. He had come off second best in previous confrontations with Adam. There was also Adam's twin St John to deal with. Sawle and St John had once been partners, at the time when St John had been married to Sawle's sister, Meriel. Sawle had callously betrayed St John and framed him for a murder that he himself had committed. Following St John's trial Meriel had run off with a rich lover.

The Lovedays had been united in their loyalty to St John and he had been acquitted of the murder. Meriel had soon been abandoned by her lover and had died last year. It had resurrected Sawle's vengeance against the Lovedays. Shortly after that incident Sawle had shown how dangerous it was to defy him. The overseer on her brother Japhet's property, Tor Farm, had been murdered and the housekeeper had disappeared. The land had been used for storing contraband whilst Japhet was out of the country. The authorities had found no evidence or witnesses against Sawle, but Hannah knew that he was responsible. It had been a warning to the Lovedays that they were not invincible against him.

She knew Adam would be furious that she had not told him of Harry Sawle's intimidation that night in the barn. But Adam had his own worries at the yard. The year since his father's death had not been easy. He had also moved into the house at Boscabel – the estate he had purchased. The house had been a partial ruin and had needed extensive renovation. If those were not problems enough, there had been the feuding between Adam and his twin. St John had inherited the family home of Trevowan, but after Edward's death he had reverted to his wastrel ways. The old rivalry between the twins had flared once more, this time worse than ever, and now there was no Edward Loveday to intercede between his warring sons.

Hannah wrapped her shawl closer around her body and suppressed a shiver of apprehension. The last of the sunlight was fading. The dogs had finally stopped barking, and to her relief she heard the wagon and horses returning with Sam and Aggie. She breathed more easily.

The children came running into the yard, Sam's son Charlie with them. Their excitement made Hannah collect her thoughts. Sam would be hungry after a long day at the market and she had prepared a meal for him and Charlie to eat in their cottage. The farmhouse was in darkness and she hurried inside to light the candles and cut the rabbit pie into slices.

An hour later the children were abed, and Aggie had finished her chores and gone to the room in the barn she shared with the dairymaids. Hannah settled down to darning the children's hose, a task she deplored, though it kept her mind from wandering to the happier evenings she had spent with Oswald.

Such memories were not easily suppressed. She had loved her husband with a passion. Oswald had inherited the farm in his late teens. His mother had died of consumption when he was seven, and his father after neglecting a chill he had contracted in a thunderstorm when he had ridden all night to round up his milk herd that had escaped on to the moor through a broken gate. Hannah had married Oswald on her eighteenth birthday.

Her choice of husband surprised many, for she had several beaus calling at her father's rectory. Oswald might not have been conventionally handsome, but his wit and interest in diverse topics had spurred her own lively intellect. Their evenings were never dull as they discussed the issues of the day, both local and political, or played chess, and Oswald had been an amusing raconteur. His humour had captivated her and their marriage had been happy.

The candle spluttered and Hannah brushed aside a tear. She refused to feel sorry for herself. Her thoughts returned to the problems facing her cousins. The volatile temperament of the Lovedays was so often their downfall. In the past, family loyalty had overcome their misfortunes. That loyalty ran strongly through Hannah. She was indebted to Adam for his support throughout Oswald's illness. She had not wanted to trouble him with her problems with the smugglers, but there was much bad blood between Harry and the twins. It was time her cousins were reconciled. If their rivalry continued, it could destroy them all.

She prayed the brothers would come to their senses and bury their rivalry. Now more than ever family loyalty was important.

Chapter Two

It had become a tradition with the Loveday family to dine at Boscabel after attending Joshua Loveday's service at Trewenna church. In Edward's lifetime the meal had been at Trevowan, but St John was seldom at the estate, preferring to spend time with his libertine friends rather than with his family.

Today everyone except St John was present. Hannah insisted that she contribute her share of the meal. Adam might be master of his own shipyard, but the family was large and his finances were straitened. She had brought pears from her orchard and potatoes from her crop. Adam's stepmother, Amelia, had brought a large goat's geese from the village of Penruan, and Aunt Elspeth had insisted that the cook at Trevowan bake Adam's favourite spiced apple cake and had also supplied a jar of her special blackberry preserve. Hannah's father always provided two quarts of cider made from apples from the rectory orchard.

'There is no need for you all to go to so much trouble,' Adam insisted.

'Would you spoil our pleasure in contributing to a family gathering?' Hannah laughed aside his protest. 'And Senara has enough work of her own without worrying about feeding such a ravenous horde.'

The family was gathered in the old hall at Boscabel. They made an impressive group. The younger Lovedays were all dark-haired, with striking features. A large log burned brightly in the vast fireplace. The old hall had been a draughty and unsociable room with its high timber-beamed ceiling, but before Adam had moved into the house he had lowered the ceiling and created two extra bedrooms above. Now the hall, with its ancient tapestries on the walls, had a cosy feel about it whilst still able to seat twenty at its long Jacobean oak table.

Today when they rode back from morning service there had been a sharp bite of frost in the air and hot toddies of mulled wine greeted the family on their arrival. Both Adam and Hannah had four children, and with St John away from Trevowan, Aunt Elspeth had brought her

7

great-niece Rowena to play with her cousins. Adam's young half-brother Rafe clung shyly to Amelia's skirts.

There was no formality amongst the family, and Tamasine, her lovely cheeks glowing from the cold, rounded up the nine children to take them to the nursery where they would have their meal. The young woman was at ease with her nephews and nieces. Even dressed in her finery, she would sit on the floor and play with them. Perhaps it was her way of making up for the lack of fun in her own lonely childhood. Not that Tamasine showed any outward sign of that difficult time. In two years she had become so much a part of the Loveday family that it was rare for one of them to remember that she was Edward's Loveday's love-child.

Hannah glanced at Amelia. Since Edward's death she had lost weight, and her auburn hair was now streaked with grey under her lace head-dress. There was aloofness in her eyes if they alighted on Tamasine, whose presence had caused a rift in her marriage in the last years of Edward's life. That Tamasine was to be married in the early summer had eased Amelia's resentment towards the young woman. Amelia was accomplished at putting a brave face on unpleasantness. The trials and scandals in the family since her second marriage had sorely tested her.

The sound of Tamasine's laughter narrowed Amelia's eyes. Her step-daughter was chasing Adam's younger son Joel, who refused to follow his twin sister Rhianne and older brother Nathan to the nursery.

'Must you encourage that young scamp?' Amelia snapped, quick to criticise. 'He must learn to do as he is told.'

Tamasine caught Joel in her arms and tickled him until his cheeks grew pink and his cries of protest turned to giggles.

'Adam could be spirited as a child,' Elspeth responded. 'You are lucky that Rafe is so well mannered, since you take exception to the wild-ness in the Loveday blood, Amelia.'

'Joel is a handful,' laughed Hannah's mother Cecily. 'Tamasine has a way with him. Adam will miss her when she weds.'

'We will all miss her,' Hannah replied.

She watched her cousin herd the children up the stairs. Tamasine had the blue eyes and dark colouring of her Loveday blood, and friends and neighbours accepted her as a distant relative. 'Tamasine is good with the children.' Hannah addressed Cecily. 'Even Rafe, who is usually so shy, adores her.'

'She has become a beauty. Edward would have been proud of her ...' Cecily dabbed a tear from the corner of her eye. She was plump as a pigeon and tiny in comparison to her children and husband. 'And she will marry well. Better than even Edward would have wished. She was fortunate to meet a good man who did not hold her birth against her. Mr Deverell adores her.' Cecily glanced across at her sister-in-law, who was chatting with Amelia. 'I thank God that Amelia has accepted Tamasine now. Though it has not been easy for her, especially when her own daughter died last year, and Joan no more than a toddler.'

'It is never easy to accept the death of a child,' Hannah replied. 'Peter took Bridie's miscarriage badly. It has made my brother more fervent in his preaching. That does not always go down well with his parishioners at Polruggan. Bridie is more resilient.'

'Bridie is a good wife,' Cecily replied. 'She takes after her sister and has Senara's common sense. She will be Peter's salvation. Senara has been a stabilising force behind Adam. To see the two sisters now, you would never suspect their gypsy blood.'

'Only Senara's father was a gypsy,' Hannah reminded her mother. 'Bridie's birth was even more unfortunate.'

'I do not like to think of that. Bridie is not to blame for the brutality of the attack on her mother and her own conception. Blessedly, she has all Leah's sweetness.'

Hannah nodded. 'All in all we are a motley brood. Beneath the veneer of respectability and gentlemanly blood, the Lovedays remain as unconventional as their buccaneering forebears.' She stooped to kiss her petite mother's cheek. 'Despite his two respectable marriages, Uncle Edward kept secret his affair with Tamasine's mother, even though it took place while he was a widower.'

'But the Lady Eleanor was a noblewoman married to a cruel, uncaring husband. Edward would have wed her had she been free.'

'I am sure he would. He had learned to curb his wilder ways. As did Papa! He married an angel in you, Mama.'

Cecily blushed. 'I was a simple parson's daughter. Joshua was the younger son – who had led a far from exemplary youth.' She patted her daughter's cheek. 'You have the Loveday fire, my dear. It will drive you to do well for your children despite your untimely widowhood.'

Her mother squeezed her hand, but Hannah did not want her sympathy. She found it unnerving as it could slip beneath the guard she had erected around her emotions and grief.

'I will go and help Senara. She has disappeared into the kitchen. And I will try and convince Leah to take her place at the table. Even though Bridie and Senara persuaded her to move to the parsonage at Polruggan, she refuses to dine with the family, insisting it is not fitting.'

'Leah knows her place,' Cecily said gently. 'She is ill at ease amongst the gentry. She is happy to help with the children and make herself useful. Her daughters understand that.'

'Then I will not interfere. But I would not have Leah think that I do not accept her within the family.'

Cecily watched Hannah walk away. She had accepted Bridie as her sister-in-law without reservation. Bridie was a sweet girl and Cecily admired her for learning to read and write and then becoming the teacher at the school at Trevowan Hard. But though she had tempered Peter's pious fervour, Cecily still wondered if the marriage could be truly happy. Bridie was a child of nature, like her sister Senara. Senara had not been at church this Sunday nor did she attend regularly. Cecily suspected that she had a heathenish streak inherited from her gypsy father. She had been taught the lore of herbs and remedies by her gypsy grandmother which she used to tend the sick who could not afford a physician's fees.

Cecily suppressed a sigh. Adam did not judge his wife, but her youngest child, Peter, was different. The Bible was his code of law and conduct. In his youth he had been a fanatic and his cousins had called him Pious Peter. Bridie had always been a challenge to her son. She had been a pure maid with an elfin beauty. There was an earnestness about her and a willingness to please. That Peter had married her was to his credit, though Cecily doubted that Adam would have tolerated his cousin and sister-in-law becoming lovers. It worried Cecily that the couple's personalities were so different. Peter had believed Bridie to be young and malleable, but his wife had a will of iron. She had proved that by starting up a cottage lace-making industry in her husband's parish. She might look waif-thin and fragile, her twisted back and short-ened leg giving her an appearance of vulnerability, but she had over-come so many prejudices in the past it proved she had an exceptional constitution and strength of will. Heaven forfend that her son and his wife ever clashed! As a good wife Bridie might compromise on some issues, but never on anything that questioned her integrity.

'You are wool-gathering, Cecily,' Elspeth Loveday boomed in her ear. 'Joshua gave an exemplary sermon. Kept it short and to the point – which is important. I wish I could say as much about that whipper-snapper Peter. I had trouble staying awake through evensong the other week, which he virtually ordered us to attend when Amelia and I called at the parsonage. And he insisted on lengthy prayers before we partook of our luncheon. A simple grace would have sufficed.'

'He takes his role of shepherd to his flock seriously,' Cecily defended.

'A mite too seriously. Joshua keeps his sense of propriety and never allows religion to get in the way of a sensible pleasure. I told Peter, I don't need no preachifying of a weekday. I leave it to Joshua to be the guardian of my soul on a Sunday. But Amelia wished to attend. And I may add that Leah did not look too happy at being forced to join us. She never was much of a churchgoer. For all Bridie's good intentions, her mother is not happy living with them.'

'I will get Joshua to have a word with Peter. Though my son has his own idea about what is right for his flock and has lectured his father before now on what he considers Joshua's laxity.'

'Then if he does not take warning, he will end up preaching in an empty church. The parishioners will not stand for it and will go elsewhere for their service.'

'How is Amelia? She is looking pale.' Cecily changed the subject before she lost her temper with Elspeth. The older woman had a sharp and critical tongue.

'The death of a child is hard to bear.' Elspeth peered over the top of her pince-nez, her voice terse with disapproval as she continued. 'But she should not neglect her friends. I've tried to get her to hunt, but she rarely joins me, just shuts herself away in the Dower House at Trevowan.'

Cecily shook her head. 'That cannot be good for her. I should make more time to visit her.'

The men had left the women to their gossip and as the weather remained fine had walked to the wood on the estate. Joshua and Peter were soberly dressed in their clerical black. Adam looked a typical country gentleman in his cream breeches, navy cut-away jacket and gold-embroidered white waistcoat. His long hair was tied back with a ribbon and his dark side-whiskers emphasised his swarthy complexion. Rabbits and squirrels darted across the dirt track in front of them. Joshua was concerned to see dark circles under Adam's eyes.

'I fear, nephew, that you work too many hours in the yard. Is it not secure now with the order for the new merchantman?'

'Before so large a ship can be built I have to design it to suit our needs. For the voyage to Botany Bay she must have ample hold space, but she needs to carry cannon to protect her from privateers or our enemies at sea. I would not lose another cargo to the French.'

'I thought you said she was to be built on the lines of the Dutch East Indiamen?' Peter remarked.

'I was fortunate enough to observe such vessels during my time in the navy. During a shore leave in Holland I visited a shipyard and saw the lines of a hull and could guess at her measurements. The calculations must be right for her ballast below decks to ensure she is stable in the water, and she must also be fast under sail. We have laid down the keel in the yard but I am not satisfied with the interior design. We will also be carrying settlers and convicts to the new penal colony. And there is a shortage of good English oak, with so many warships being built. Oak takes a hundred to a hundred and twenty years to mature for such a vessel, and then when it is cut down the wood must be seasoned for several years. The large ship-yards are importing oak from Russia to meet their demands. I have enough stored at the yard to complete the brigantine and build the merchantman's hull, but I need hundreds of mature trees to complete her. It is a huge outlay to import the stock required. But the final payment for the Guernsey cutter will meet the cost and restock the yard.'

Adam broke off and shook his head. 'I will not bore you with the yard's problems.'

Peter had dropped back. His head was bent and his wavy hair fell forward across his face, beneath which his expression was tense as he dwelt upon some inner struggle. Peter's piety warred constantly with a wilder side to his nature. Uncle Joshua paused to pick up a sturdy stick to walk with. 'With such a ship comes vast responsibility. I know the designs for the brigantine *Pegasus* and also the cutters *Challenger* and *Sea Mist* were yours, and they have proved most successful. But then you had your dear late father with whom you could discuss any concerns that arose.'

'I worry that I am overreaching myself and also the yard with this new project. I do not even know if *Pegasus* has made the voyage to and from Botany Bay safely. There are so many unknown risks in this venture to trade with the new colony. Perhaps it is madness.'

'Do you doubt your capabilities?' Joshua studied his nephew intently.

Adam shrugged, and then laughed. 'I believe she will be a great ship and become the pride of the yard. But much is at stake. It is not only the security of my family, but vast investments of others.'

'If it was your money alone, would you doubt the ship to be seaworthy?'

'No.'

'Then keep your faith.'

Adam knew his uncle was right. He had spent months working on the plans and rechecking his calculations. He must not think of failure. Too much depended on success.

A gong sounded from the direction of the house, summoning them for their meal.

★   ★   ★

When Hannah entered the kitchen she found the cook and maid busy serving the food into tureens. Senara was crouched on the floor bathing a cut on the paw of Adam's cross-breed spaniel, Scamp. The dog limped over to the warmth of the range and was ordered outside by the cook. Senara poured fresh water from a ewer into a bowl and washed her hands.

'Go and enjoy the company of your family, Hannah,' Senara chided. 'Everything is prepared here.'

'I find it difficult to sit with my hands idle.'

'This is your day to rest. You work too hard.' Senara tucked a stray wisp of earth-brown hair behind her ear and smiled. 'I had better tidy myself. I cannot appear before my husband's family looking like a gypsy ragamuffin.'

'No one thinks of you as a gypsy.' Hannah sensed Senara's tension. Adam's wife was not so at ease in this grand house as she had been in the cottage at Trevowan Hard. 'You have earned your place by Adam's side. Your manners are those of a lady.'

She turned to Leah, who was sitting in a chair by the window watching the cook lift a saddle of lamb from the range and place it on a china serving plate for Adam to carve at the table. Leah's face was drawn with pain, her fingers swollen and gnarled. She sipped on a mug of ale.

'You must be very proud of your daughters, Mrs Polglase,' Hannah remarked.

'Happen I be, thank you kindly, Mrs Rabson.'

Senara removed her apron. 'Are you sure you will not join us, Ma?'

'I know my place. I be content here in the warm. I wouldn't know what to say to gentry folks. And I will sit awhile in the nursery. That young Joel needs a firm eye watching over him.'

'An army of servants could not control him,' Senara returned with a laugh. 'I am fortunate that his twin is an angel. Joel will be leading Nathan and Rafe astray. How do you keep your children in order, Hannah?'

'Davey takes control.' Hannah's voice softened with her pride in her offspring. 'Their tasks on the farm and attending the school help to tire them. When yours are older there will be more to occupy them. Nathan is only four and the twins fifteen months younger.'

'I look forward to more tranquil days. Though when was life in a Loveday household peaceful?'

Hannah wandered into the panelled corridor leading to the stairs. It must once have been a gloomy place, but Adam had enlarged a window above the entrance door and the oak panelling now glowed golden in the sunlight that was also reflected on the wooden floor.

Tamasine appeared at the head of the carved Elizabethan staircase and ran down the stairs. For a moment her lovely face looked sad, until she saw Hannah waiting for her. Instantly she painted on a bright smile. Hannah was not deceived.

'What is amiss, Tam?'

The young woman shrugged. There were faint shadows under her eyes and her raven-black curls were pulled high on her head in a Grecian style. 'Nothing.'

Hannah was not convinced. Something was clearly troubling her. 'And the plans for your wedding, are they going well?'

Was that panic she saw in the younger woman's eyes? Hannah continued more gently. 'It is natural to have misgivings about marriage. Mr Deverell is a remarkable man.'

'Yes, he is. I cannot fault him.'

'But . . .' Hannah persisted.

Tamasine shook her head. 'There is no but. He is truly a wonderful man.'

'Indeed. The family all sing his praises.' She was concerned at Tamasine's pallor. 'Are you having second thoughts?'

'I have given my word. I respect Mr Deverell greatly. He is so like my father and Adam – both of whom I adore.'

'You talk of respect but not of love.'

The panic again flashed in Tamasine's eyes, then she lowered her lashes. Hannah took her arm. 'A man like Max Deverell is easy to love. You have seen so little of him in recent months. His estate is in Dorset.'

'I thought I loved Rupert Carlton, but he betrayed my love and trust. I have great affection for Max, but I have known so little love in my life. I would marry for love or prefer to stay single.'

'That is not always a happy option within our society. These are just nerves talking. I saw you with Max – you made a perfect couple. He would never betray you. He is an honourable man.'

Tamasine did not argue. 'Yes, he is. I am being foolish. Marriage is a vast step. And I have spent so little time with my new-found family. I shall miss you all dreadfully.'

Even to Tamasine the words sounded hollow. There had been no time to get to know Max properly. She admired and respected him. Throughout her childhood, when her mother's family had shut her away in a ladies' academy, she had never known what it felt like to love and be loved by another in return. She was young, not yet seventeen, and her heart craved to find fulfilment within her marriage.

Hannah squeezed her arm in reassurance. 'Max adores you. You will be happy. Has he not promised that you will visit your family regularly?'

Tamasine wished she could believe her cousin. There had been so many uncertainties in her life. Had she been too impulsive in agreeing to this marriage? Had she done it to please her family? She cared for Max. He was handsome, intelligent and brave. Had he not rescued her from abduction in the most romantic manner? But did she love him? That was the fear that haunted her most.

Chapter Three

After the meal the men of the family adjourned to the solar, where they could smoke in comfortable padded chairs and relax in front of a log fire. The women joined the children in the nursery for an hour.

'How goes work at the yard, Adam?' Joshua asked. 'The weather has been kind to us so far this winter.'

'It progresses well on the cutter for the Guernsey merchant. Delivery will be in three months.'

'Huh! Your customer is no merchant, he is more like a free-trader,' Peter snorted. 'You bring disrepute to the yard by working for such customers.'

Adam curbed his irritation at his cousin. 'Would it be more commendable for the yard to close and the shipwrights and their families starve through the winter?'

'Smuggling is the scourge of our community. The rivalry between the gangs can be intense and bloody at times.' Peter refused to back down.

'It has been going on for centuries,' Joshua interceded. 'It is best if we turn a blind eye. It is for the authorities to deal with.'

'They bring in brandy, which leads to drunkenness and debauchery,' Peter continued. 'Where is the reverence in attending service of a Sunday when the men are nursing sore heads and fall asleep through the sermon?'

'Then keep the sermon short.' Joshua shrugged. 'The tubmen who work for the free-traders earn little enough labouring in the tin mines, on the farms, or as fishermen. They need the extra money to provide for their families.'

'That makes wasting their money on drink a sin.' Peter stood up to pace the floor. Lines of bitterness were carved into his face around his eyes and mouth.

'Sit down, Peter,' his father groaned. 'Can we not enjoy a peaceful

Sunday afternoon for once. We have tended to the souls of our parishioners this morning. We cannot dictate every aspect of their lives.' He turned to Adam, ending the conversation with his son before he lost his temper. 'St John was not at church again. Neither does he attend at Penruan. I've called at Trevowan twice in the last month and he has been absent.'

Anger darkened Adam's eyes. 'If St John did not learn his lesson at losing the last harvest from his negligence, it is not for me to remind him of his duties.'

'Then you still have not resolved your differences?' His uncle voiced his displeasure. 'This rivalry must end. He is master of Trevowan and there is nothing you can do about it. St John must also accept that the shipyard is yours and that the two incomes are no longer joined.'

'He would have brought the yard to ruin as well as the estate. He is a wastrel and does not deserve Trevowan.' The old antagonism simmered too close to the surface for Adam not to retaliate.

'He was the heir,' Joshua declared. 'And this last year has not been easy for your brother.'

'It has not been easy for any of us.' Adam snapped. 'However, we do not all act the victim of fate and use it as an excuse for laziness and ineptitude. He brought any problems on his own head by his disreputable conduct. And he would have brought me to ruin by his betrothal to another whilst his wife still lived.'

'We are all sinners.' Peter gripped the open front of his black jacket in a pious posture. 'Our salvation is in the Lord.'

Joshua puffed on his clay pipe before answering. 'That is as maybe. But we are all responsible for our actions. St John is now a widower. And if he has any sense, this time he will marry a woman of fortune.'

'If any woman is foolish enough to take him. His reputation for gambling is becoming notorious.' Peter sniffed his disapproval. He had refused a long-stemmed clay pipe and tobacco from Adam.

'He needs support from the family, not condemnation,' Joshua advised. 'I had great respect for your father, Adam. Edward always believed that family loyalty would see us through any crisis.'

'Where was St John's loyalty when in a jealous rage he set fire to my haystacks? There was enough there to feed the herd at Trevowan, as well as my cattle here. His spite cost him dear, as he now has to buy in winter feed.'

'He swears he did not set fire to the hay.' Joshua shook his head. 'I am inclined to believe him. He is angry that we have all condemned him.'

'The facts speak for themselves. He was found drunk and unconscious by the ricks with a burnt-out torch by his side.' Adam set his own pipe aside in his agitation.

'You have been too busy at the yard to see how he has suffered over this rift.'

'And he hopes to win us over by drinking and gaming!' Adam could not contain his sarcasm.

'If he has been wrongly accused . . .' Joshua let the statement weight the air. 'It has been three months. There is much speculation amongst our neighbours that you are at loggerheads. It does no good to either of your reputations.'

When Adam continued to look unrepentant, Joshua sat forward in his chair, his manner stern. 'There has been mischief afoot here. St John has many faults, but he is no coward. He would confront you over an issue of contention. Your frequent fights as youths proved that. He would not set fire to your haystacks to spite you. I could think of others who might. Men who have grudges against our family. Men who have been warned the authorities will be informed if they store contraband on Loveday land.'

Adam stood up to light a taper from the fire and set the flame against the bowl of his pipe to re-ignite the tobacco. He puffed a cloud of blue smoke into the air before replying. 'There has been no sign of Harry Sawle in these parts for months.'

'He has men to do his dirty work for him. Men who have their own grievances against our family. What of Mordecai Nance? He was thrown out of his cottage at Trevowan by St John and now works for Sawle in the Dolphin Inn. There has been gossip that St John tried to seduce Nance's wife.'

'My brother was always a fool over women,' Adam returned. 'Etta Nance leads Mordecai a merry dance and has had a string of lovers since they wed. St John should know better than to fool around with the wives of his workers. Nance has an evil temper.'

Joshua picked up the tobacco jar and refilled his pipe. 'Nance is not a man to let a grudge go unavenged. And Sawle has no love for St John, even though your brother wed his sister.'

'And Sawle was the one most likely responsible for the murder of Japhet's overseer at Tor Farm,' Peter expounded. 'Hannah said he has even threatened her.'

Adam rounded on his cousin. 'I had no idea Sawle had threatened Hannah.'

'At the time she did not want you worried,' Peter replied. 'You had problems at the yard. She found evidence that goods had been stored at Tor Farm and informed Sir Henry Traherne as Justice of the Peace, and the authorities have been keeping a watch on the place.'

'Thank God she had the sense to do that. But she should have come to me.'

'You know how independent Hannah is.' Peter looked offended. 'She did not even mention the matter to me. I learned of it from Sir Henry. I am her brother. It is for me to protect her. Sometimes, Adam, you take too much upon yourself.'

Joshua steepled his fingers and regarded his son with a resigned air. 'With respect, Peter, you are no swordsman or crack shot. You would stand no chance against the likes of Sawle.'

'I would not see my sister in danger.' Peter struck a self-righteous pose. 'I may not brawl in the street, but I—'

'You are not a coward either, Peter,' his father placated. 'But Sawle is a brute. He has no ethics or morals. He would shoot you in the back without a qualm.'

Peter's eyes darkened with injured pride. 'I do not fear Sawle. I would defend my sister with my life. Though killing goes against the Lord's teaching, I would not fail her.'

Adam nodded. He could only guess at the complexities of his cousin's nature. Peter's blood was no less wild than Adam's own, but he repressed it – and that could not be easy or even good for him. Peter's passion had been channelled into his piety.

'No one doubts your valour, Peter,' Adam said. 'I will speak with Hannah, though. I need to know what has been happening with Sawle. I vowed he would be brought to justice for his crimes when my father was shot. He had an alibi then. My hands were tied whilst we built his ship. Not so now.'

'But the second cutter – the one commissioned by Sawle's Guernsey agent – they could cancel their order if Sawle commands them.' Joshua became concerned. 'That could bankrupt you. If you lose the yard then he would have triumphed over us.'

'The Guernsey agent has paid half of the cost of the ship. They are in too deep to back out. They need the speed of the cutter to outrun the revenue ships. Only *Challenger*, which we built for the revenue office, can match it in speed.'

'This dealing with smugglers sits ill with me,' Joshua frowned.

'Father did not scorn their money,' Adam reminded him. 'He built other cutters for the trade.'

Joshua spread his hands in acceptance. 'And it all ended badly. Did nothing come of the tender you gave the Admiralty to improve their revenue fleet?'

'Not as yet. They are more concerned with building ships for the war with France. Unless Harry Sawle tries to intimidate Hannah again, I can wait until the cutter is delivered before dealing with him. But he will pay for his part in Father's death. The reckoning is long overdue.'

Adam sought out Hannah and found her staring out of a window in the long gallery on the top storey of the house. The room ran the entire length of the building and had been used in past times as a place to stroll on cold or rainy days. It was still unfurnished and there were no hangings yet at the long windows. No fires had been lit in the two hearths, and he rubbed his hands together on encountering the chill air.

'It is warmer in the solar. What brings you up here?'

She smiled at him, shrugging off the air of sadness that had settled on her. 'This is a lovely house, Adam. You have worked so hard to renovate it. You deserve it. Senara mentioned that the view from here was quite magnificent. You can see for miles out across to the moor and the church towers of four villages. I could not resist exploring.'

He sensed that Hannah had wanted a quiet moment of reflection. The demands of her young family and the farm must give her little time for peace. He could not help worrying about her. He adored her. She was beautiful, with a wilful, stubborn streak. In courage she was the equal of any man. But he hoped she was not too proud to ask him for help if she needed it. 'Peter told me that you have been visited by Sawle. Is he causing you problems?'

'Nothing I cannot handle.'

He saw the uncertainty flicker into her eyes and the defiant tilt of her chin. He hooked his arm through hers. 'This should be discussed. Join your father, Peter and me in the solar. I need to know what has happened. Sawle is a dangerous enemy. He hates our family.'

She walked beside him for several moments before answering. 'He was prowling on our farm one night last summer and I sent him away.' She spoke softly, and deliberately did not mention the incident in the barn. If Adam knew the extent of Sawle's threats he would throw caution to the wind to deal with the smuggler without delay. That could have fatal consequences. She went on, to divert his attention away from herself, 'Then there was the murder of Japhet's overseer at Tor Farm. It must have been Sawle's men. There were signs that contraband had been stored there. Sir Henry has informed the authorities and the farm is being watched.'

'So Peter informed me.' Adam sensed that his cousin was not telling him everything. 'Sawle does not take kindly to informants. Has he approached you since?'

They had reached the solar and Hannah needed also to reassure her father and brother, who had heard Adam's comment. 'Once or twice we have passed on the road. And before he left these parts I often had the feeling of being watched.'

'You must go nowhere without Sam Deacon to safeguard you,' Joshua insisted. 'If Japhet was here, Sawle would not dare approach you, or use your brother's land.'

'Japhet thought only of himself when he took to highway robbery,' Peter sneered. 'He did not deserve his lovely wife, who stood by him when he was transported.'

'Japhet paid dearly for his recklessness,' Joshua snapped. 'He has been pardoned. And I pray daily that he will soon return to the bosom of our family. You judge him too harshly.'

Peter did not take his father's criticism well. His expression darkened. 'Is it wise to have Mark Sawle working as your groom, sister? Sawle always bullied his younger brother.'

'Mark hates his brother. He has proved his loyalty,' Hannah defended.

'I shall take responsibility for supervising Tor Farm until Japhet returns,' Peter declared. 'I should have done so before this. And I do not judge my brother harshly. I am angry that he has caused such suffering to my mother and his wife. And now the repercussions of his crimes are rebounding on Hannah.'

Hannah bit her lip to stop a sharp retort. Peter carried his own pain concerning his older brother. All his life he had lived in Japhet's shadow. Japhet had been the gallant one, devil-may-care and charming. Peter had envied his brother for his spirited nature and had never been able to match him in daring or charm. His envy had turned to jealousy and his jealousy to a need to prove that piety won more respect than devilry. He knew he had failed abysmally.

'You have the duties of your parish,' Hannah reminded him.

He put out a hand to halt her words. 'It will not jeopardise the welfare of my flock to ride to Japhet's farm twice a week. It cannot be long now before he returns to England. I put family loyalty before consideration of the needs of my parishioners.'

'That will be a great help to us all.' Adam nodded approval. 'I'll have a word with Isaac Nance. If his nephew has some vendetta against St John for throwing him out of his cottage, I need to know that our bailiff's allegiance is not divided. His job demands that his fealty is first to us. He worked for Father for twenty years, and his son Dick is Trevowan's gamekeeper.'

'All the more reason for you and St John to sort out your own differences,' Joshua advised.

'I agree.' Hannah nodded. 'Our family has never been divided. We need a united front to bring Sawle to justice. And this has to be done by the letter of the law and with no personal grievances that could end with another Loveday facing trial for murder.'

'To avenge my father's death I would willingly give my life,' Adam proclaimed.

'And what good would that do your widow and four children?' Elspeth had come to the door, her cane silent on the wooden floor. She could move with surprising stealth when she chose. 'There have been too many deaths in our family in recent years, some like my brother William under suspicious circumstances. I want you to promise, Adam, that you will not tackle Sawle on your own.'

'I can make no such promise, Aunt. Honour forbids it.'

'Men and their honour.' Elspeth sniffed her disapproval. 'I never thought I would say this, but it is time the Lovedays curbed their wild blood. No good ever came of feuding.'

'Adam wishes to protect me, Aunt,' Hannah defended. 'Harry Sawle has tried to intimidate me with threats.'

'Did he succeed?' The older woman's stare was fierce.

Hannah jutted her chin in a stubborn line. 'No.'

'You have great courage, niece, but you are but a woman and therefore vulnerable, however brave a front you present to the world,' Elspeth curtly informed her.

Adam saw a fierce glitter in his aunt's eyes that he had known better than to challenge as a youth. Like Hannah she was a stalwart and formidable woman, but no woman and few men were the match for Harry Sawle and his vicious henchmen.

Chapter Four

Five days later Adam learned that St John had returned to Trevowan. He left the yard that afternoon, resolved that for the good of the family he would end the discord with his twin. The mist along the coast had not dispersed all day and the leafless branches of the trees were twisted and bent from years of being buffeted by the winter gales that swept in from the Atlantic.

He paused on the road before turning into the long drive of his childhood home. He could hear the waves crashing on to the dark granite rocks of Trevowan Cove. Out to sea he could just make out the dark outlines of a dozen fishing sloops with their single triangular sails headed back to Penruan harbour. The church clock struck the half-hour, a guide for the fishermen in such weather.

Adam turned towards the house set back from the cliff. The mist distorted the outline of the tall chimneys and gables, and the local stone of the walls looked dark and unwelcoming. His eyes narrowed. He had never felt that way about his childhood home before and it saddened him. With a critical gaze he noted the beef herd grazing in the meadow. Their number was depleted. Had St John been selling off the cattle to pay his debts? A foolhardy scheme. The prime herd had taken years to establish. At least he could see two fields had been sown with winter crops, and he recognised Dan and Ned Holman, who lived in tied cottages, repairing a dry-stone wall. As he approached the house he noted that the gardens had been tended and were tidy. It was three months since Adam had last been here. At least his brother was no longer allowing the estate to show neglect, but in the gloom of the mist there was still an air of lethargy and desolation. The house was protected from the worst of the winter storms as it had been built in a protective fork at the side of a wooded hill. Smoke trailed from four of the chimneys and the scent of the burning pine logs hung in the air. It brought a lump to Adam's throat, reminding him of the carefree winters of his childhood.

There was also smoke rising from the Dower House, set further back in the grounds. Aunt Elspeth and Amelia had taken up residence there, preferring its seclusion to the rowdy gaming sessions St John now indulged in at the main house. His anger at his brother returned. What right had St John to drive his aunt, who had been born in the main house, and his father's wife to the smaller residence? Trevowan House was large enough for them all.

There would be no time today to see the women. No doubt when Elspeth learned that he had called at Trevowan without visiting them he would be given a dressing-down. After an interview with St John, he doubted he would be fit company. On his way home he intended to take a long gallop across the moor to clear his head. The meeting was bound to be stormy.

At the sound of Adam's approach Jasper Fraddon appeared from the stable yard. He was sprightly on his bow legs and his walnut-creased face lit with pleasure.

''Tis a welcome sight you be to my old eyes, Cap'n Loveday.'

Adam did not take offence at the familiarity. The head groom, like many of the locals, continued to address him as captain, though his sea-going days as captain of his ship *Pegasus* had ended with his father's death. Fraddon and his wife Winnie, who was the cook at Trevowan, had served the family for thirty years. Adam leapt to the ground and threw him Solomon's reins. 'This is a short visit. Do not trouble to unsaddle Solomon – just loosen his girths and give him some water.'

The old servant tipped his forelock to Adam, who was already striding towards the house. The front door was never closed in daylight hours and Adam waved aside the maid when he passed her in the hall. The sound of his boots resounded on the black and white marble floor.

'I will announce myself, Jenna.'

She bobbed a curtsey. 'Master St John be in Mr Edward's study, Cap'n Loveday.'

The door to the study was ajar. St John was staring out of the window, twirling a quill pen, his expression drawn and haggard. The sight made Adam halt before entering. The book-lined room and large mahogany desk, now cluttered with papers, had for so long been his father's domain. His twin looked too much at home at the desk for the image to settle comfortably within Adam.

'So, you have returned,' he announced by way of greeting.

St John started; lost in his daydreaming, he had not heard Adam's approach. Then his eyes hardened as he swivelled round and scowled. 'Who let you in? You are not welcome here.'

24

Adam unbuttoned his greatcoat and stuck his thumbs in the waist-band of his black breeches. He regarded his brother with disdain. St John had become more foppish in his attire since he had come into his inheritance. The twins had never been identical, and now the difference in their appearance was more marked. St John's complexion was pallid and his handsome features were becoming bloated from his excessive drinking. He had grown long side-whiskers and his brown hair was cut short and his fringe flopped over his brow. Adam was lean and hard-muscled. His dark hair had ebony streaks and he wore a gold earring in one ear, a habit from his seafaring days.

St John held his brother's stare but his nervousness showed in the way he twisted the quill in his fingers. The swan's feather became mangled. 'If you have something to say, out with it and leave. But remember I am master here. I am sick of the family comparing me to Father.'

Adam bit back a scathing retort. He drew a calming breath before replying. 'No one could step easily into Father's shoes.'

St John digested this and a tense silence stretched between them. 'I suppose you consider that you have done so at the yard. The talk of the neighbourhood is how it prospers. Though you took Judas silver to save it. Father would turn in his grave that you accepted Sawle's money.'

'His coin was as good as anyone else's. I would not risk losing the yard.' He battled to control his sliding temper. St John was being deliberately provocative. Attack was the first form of defence for a guilty man.

'How are you meeting your debts, brother? Gambling is a fool's solution. You lose more than you win in the long run.'

'What the devil has that to do with you?'

'In as much as it affects the reputation of our family. But I am not here to judge you.'

'Then keep your opinions to yourself.'

St John remained sullen. Despite Adam's resolve to remain calm, his brother's manner goaded him to rap out, 'Did you set fire to my hay ricks?'

'Would you believe me if I said no? You condemned me readily at the time. I no longer care what you think.'

'The evidence pointed to you. You were drunk. The burnt-out torch was by your side. You then ran off before anyone had risen the next morning to avoid questioning. Not the action of an innocent man.'

'Who would listen to me? They were on your side. That was obvious from what I remember of the fire.'

'No one wanted to believe such ill of you. I admit I was angry.

25

Justifiably so, since the loss of the hay cost me dear. But such an act was petty. It was unlike you. Our quarrels have always been open. We fought often but never stooped to stab each other in the back.'

'Yet the family judged me.' St John's face flushed with anger.

'Because you disappeared in so guilty a manner.'

St John dropped his gaze, his mood truculent. 'You had your grand celebrations for moving into Boscabel. Everyone was congratulating you on the success of the yard. Even cousin Tom and Aunt Margaret came from London to celebrate. And Tom had got some of his bank clients to invest in your scheme to trade with the colony at Botany Bay. I was in debt and had to go cap in hand begging him for a loan.'

Adam realised how much pride St John had had to swallow to do that. He made an attempt to placate his twin's resentment. 'The family were naturally pleased at the success I had made of the yard after the years of work Father had put into expanding it.'

His attempt had backfired. St John bared his teeth and said accusingly, 'And they did not fail to call me to account for my failures.'

Adam sighed. His brother's petulance stemmed from jealousy. Adam's own antagonism had been due to the unfairness of being the second-born twin. St John was the heir to the house he adored. He had worked so hard to renovate Boscabel and get it established as a home for his wife and children, but it would never be Trevowan. It would always be second best.

'Thomas would not refuse you a loan,' he said more gently. 'And it was that same loyalty to our family that made him promote my venture in the new colony.'

'Our cousin subjected me to a damned long lecture before he agreed to it. If I had not been so desperate I would have told him what he could do with his blasted money.' St John flushed with outrage. 'It will take me five years to pay it back. You even got that brat Tamasine out of your hair and her future husband was toadying up to the family by investing in your crackpot scheme.'

'You should be delighted that our half-sister is to marry so well.' Adam put his knuckles on the desk and leaned towards his brother. 'But she would have been welcome at Boscabel for as long as she wished to stay with us. And Max Deverell, for your information, toadies to no man. He knows a good investment when he hears it.'

St John rose to face him, his stare hostile. 'How is it that you can afford to buy into it? Boscabel must have taken all your money. I doubt you made much profit on Sawle's ship. The yard soaks up money like a sponge.'

'My contribution is to build a merchantman to sail to the South Seas. My partners will provide the cargo and the profit will be split between us.'

'It costs a great deal of money to build a ship and pay the ship-wrights.'

'It does indeed, and I work for every penny that I plough back into the yard and estate.'

Again the tension simmered. St John stepped back and folded his hands across his chest. Adam straightened. Old resentments ricocheted unspoken between them. Both were on guard. Both defensive. The silence lengthened and Adam lost patience. He had done his best and St John was being bloody-minded as usual. He was about to spin on his heel and walk out when his glance fell on a favourite paperweight of their father's. It was a wooden ship carved by their grandfather. Edward often used to rub his fingers along its sides when deep in thought. It reminded Adam of the purpose of this visit.

'Father would be ashamed of the way we are behaving,' he said. 'I do not want to be your enemy, St John.'

His brother's shoulder's sagged, but his eyes remained condemning. 'I did not set fire to the hay. I was hit on the head from behind and knocked out cold. That is the truth.'

'I believe you,' Adam conceded. 'Then it must be Sawle who was behind it.'

'You've met your match there, brother.' St John did not hide his smirk.

'Are you so riddled with jealousy that you cannot see Sawle means to bring us all to ruin?' Adam bristled and stepped closer to his brother, his hands itching to shake some sense into St John. 'Sawle will not have taken kindly to you moving his sister's body from the Loveday vault. He'd take that as an insult.'

'I'll not have that whore desecrating our ancestors' resting place.'

'Then you should not have married her. She died a Loveday and is the mother of your daughter.'

Fury darkened St John's eyes at the mention of Rowena. Adam realised his mistake. There was still the unsettled question over the parentage of Meriel's child. To get her final revenge on her husband, on her deathbed she had proclaimed that it was Adam who was Rowena's father, not St John. Adam knew that it was possible. In the days before Adam had met Senara they had both been rivals for Meriel's affection. On his return from a naval voyage Adam had been shocked to discover St John wed to her and Meriel heavily pregnant.

27

St John snapped the quill in two and threw it on to the desk. 'The whole county knows Meriel ran off with Lord Wycham and abandoned her marriage and child. She made a cuckold of me!' His voice rose and his cheeks flushed with anger. 'And you let her come back here whilst I was in America.'

'She was dying. I could not turn her out to die in the poorhouse. That would have shamed us all.'

'She should have rotted in the London gutters where she belonged. She ruined everything.'

The harshness of the statement showed the depth of St John's hatred for his wife. The marriage could not have been an easy one. Adam knew he was blessed in his union with Senara. It mellowed his anger and he continued in a more conciliatory tone.

'When our blood runs high mistakes are made and the consequences have to be faced. You did not always act with honour, especially in America.' He referred to St John's betrothal to a wealthy widow whilst Meriel still lived. It had all blown up in his face when she arrived unexpectedly in England. Fortunately that scandal had not become public knowledge or they would now be ostracised by society and friends. There was no point in raking over and becoming embittered by the past.

'If you are in debt then now is the time to find an heiress to wed. Trevowan is no small prize and our family is an old and revered one.'

If his brother had an opinion on remarrying, from the clamped set of his lips he was keeping it to himself.

Adam continued, 'It is Sawle who is our enemy, not each other. He has struck at Japhet by killing his bailiff and tried to intimidate Hannah into allowing her to store contraband at Tor Farm. She refused, of course.'

'Then he must be stopped.' St John was outraged, for he was fond of Hannah. 'But he is more sly than a fox. It is not him but his henchmen who do his dirty work.'

'It is Sawle I want to bring to justice to pay for Father's death.'

The twins locked stares, Adam fierce and determined; St John more guarded. Slowly he nodded his head. 'Sawle must be dealt with.'

'Then we must end this rivalry between us.' Adam held out his hand to his brother.

St John took it. 'Japhet should have received his pardon in Botany Bay by now and will be on his way home. Sawle will not be so ready to pick a fight then.'

'The voyage takes several months. We cannot delay dealing with Sawle. Though he has kept away from us in recent months.'

His twin had not asked Adam to be seated or offered him refreshments. Adam strode to the door. He held out a further olive branch. 'Will you then join the family after church next Sunday?'

'If I am here. I have business in Truro.' St John had sat down at the desk and pulled some papers towards him.

His insolence caused Adam's blood to boil. St John was more intent on gaming with his friends than healing family rifts. But at least they had taken the first steps towards resolving their differences. His parting shot was a warning. 'Your selfishness has driven our stepmother and Aunt Elspeth to live in the Dower House! If Sawle thinks our family is at odds with each other, he will pick us off one by one. We are invincible only when we are united.'

Chapter Five

St John was not pacified by his twin's visit. He remained in the study long after Adam had left, scowling at the pile of papers that demanded his attention. Then he shoved them aside and poured himself a large brandy and tossed it back. He did not even taste its fine quality, but its heat was an old friend that eased the tribulations that continued to dog him.

His expression became mutinous as he recalled his twin's sanctimonious visit. He had seen through the hollow words of reconciliation. In Adam's controlled manner he had observed arrogance and condescension. His brother did not believe in his innocence. He was acting a part, showing forgiveness for the sake of family unity. That made St John resent him even more. His anger deepened. It was so unjust. He *was* innocent. He did not want his family to patronise him. He expected them to trust him – to have faith in his honour.

Did no one understand him? Since the trial, and the trauma of facing charges of murder, he had felt unjustly persecuted. His life had become a series of disastrous events. First Meriel had miscarried of his son, and then she had cuckolded him, making him a laughing stock by running off with her lover. His flesh flushed with the humiliation of the further disgrace he had suffered by being sent to Virginia by his father until the scandal of the trial had died down. Edward should have supported him, not sent him away. But then Edward's mealy-mouthed new wife was having a fit of the vapours over what had happened. No one had considered how he felt at the prejudice of it all. Had he not been proved innocent? That should have been enough to restore his reputation.

His mood soured. Nothing went right for him. For a time in Virginia he had thought his luck had changed. His father's cousin, Garfield Penhaligan, had no surviving children and wanted to make him heir to his large tobacco plantation. He had also met and fallen in love with Garfield's niece, Desiree Richmond.

He saw no wrong in his subsequent declaration of his feelings for Desiree. He deserved the love of a beautiful and wealthy woman. In his mind Meriel, the faithless whore, was dead to him. His future was in America — where his past involvement with smugglers was unknown, and he was admired and respected. As Garfield's heir he was fêted and popular. It was another world — another life. He had deluded himself that he could marry Desiree, convinced that Meriel would end her days diseased and in rags. In that at least he had been proved right. But his wife did not die without wreaking her vengeance on him, blighting his romance and his future in America when Garfield and Desiree had unexpectedly travelled to England.

What a cruel twist of fate that had been! The foulest of bad luck. And destiny had continued to mock him. His luck at the gaming tables had turned and he had amassed a fortune in debts. Drink was his solace, and egged on by his wastrel friends he took his pleasures wherever he could find them without thought of the consequences.

He reached for the brandy decanter again and poured himself a generous measure. His bitterness was fuelled by the liquor. Why must his family persecute him? Where was their forgiveness? If it had been the saintly Adam who had transgressed, they would have rallied to support him. His father had even forgiven him for marrying a gypsy. Consumed with outrage, St John ignored the fact that Edward had also forgiven St John himself for marrying beneath him.

His grievances against his family mounted as he scowled into the empty brandy goblet. All he received from his relatives were reminders that he was a failure, or lectures on his responsibilities as master of Trevowan. He could feel their censure that he did not fill his father's shoes. But who could? Edward had been a remarkable man, loved and revered by everyone.

He poured another brandy to console himself. His father's virtues were too numerous to mention. But dammit! He was not Edward, and it was not fair for the family to expect him to follow doggedly in his footsteps.

The injustice of it consumed him. He was a victim of fate. Had he not done his best to recoup his gaming losses, convinced that Lady Luck would again smile on him? But the debts had mounted. And while he battled with despair, he was expected to sit back and applaud his brother's good fortune.

Another brandy added to his sense of persecution. He would not give Adam the satisfaction of thinking his attempt at peacemaking had succeeded. He certainly did not intend to dine at Boscabel, where his brother would gloat over the success of his new estate, that matched Trevowan in size. He was still seething at Adam's suggestion that he had driven his aunt and stepmother from their home. The two women had chosen the tranquillity of the Dower House after the death of his infant half-sister. And he recalled with indignation that the Dower House had been his place of residence during his marriage to Meriel. If it had been good enough for him for seven years, it was good enough for them now.

In his righteous reasoning his selective memory abandoned the fact that he had preferred the seclusion of the Dower House so as to escape the notice of his father and servants when he had been a partner with Harry Sawle in their smuggling days. That income had funded his gambling.

St John resented any curtailment of his pleasure. Trevowan, which should have provided him with full coffers to indulge his degenerate lifestyle, had instead become a millstone round his neck. He begrudgingly admitted that Adam was right in one thing. To put his estate and fortune in order he needed a new wife – and an extremely wealthy one.

Suitable women were few on the ground. He wanted not only a wealthy bride but also a malleable one. He'd had enough of Meriel's greed and shrewish ways to last him at lifetime. He did not expect to marry for love either. He had loved Meriel and she had betrayed him. But she had been exceedingly comely and voluptuous and he had an eye for beauty. Providing that a prospective wife was not unattractive, he would view the fortune she brought to the marriage bed with favour.

He considered the eligible women he knew. Most of good family were already settled. Perhaps he should cast his net wider than Cornwall. Here both his trial for the murder of Thadeous Lanyon, the leader of a rival gang of smugglers, and his reputation as a gambler went before him. He would not be known elsewhere.

The trial had been a dark time in his life; some of the memories were almost too painful to recall – the horror of incarceration, and the fear during the trial itself. Those terrors could still invade his dreams. Although his innocence had been proven, no culprit had been found for Lanyon's murder. The obvious candidate must be Harry Sawle, but as usual the blackguard had hidden his tracks well and had a ready alibi.

Harry Sawle had played St John for a gullible fool, and that rankled far deeper than any other resentment. Sawle must be taught a lesson. For the sake of getting even with the smuggler, he would agree to a truce with his twin. St John grimaced. The old jealousy towards his brother resurfaced. It was now an obsession with him. He would show his family and his enemies that he was his brother's equal. More than that, he would prove that he was the worthy heir of Trevowan.

But that was in the future. First there was a week's gaming to be had with Basil Bracewaite and his cousin in Bodmin, and Lord Fetherington had a hunt ball planned at his estate the following week. Adam no longer mixed with the Fetheringtons as his lordship's wife had refused to accept Senara into her social circle. Whereas the Honourable Percy Fetherington was a close friend of St John. It was a pity that Aunt Elspeth would also be present to put a dampener on the four days. He would have to curb any extravagance at the card tables. His aunt's passion for hunting would never allow her to miss such an occasion. It would also be an ideal opportunity for him to take note of what heiresses were on the marriage market.

On leaving his brother Adam was caught by Elspeth in the stables. She was fussing over one of her mares that had shown signs of coming up lame when she had ridden her earlier.

'Have you spoken some sense to that twin of yours?' She left the mare's stall to question him as Fraddon went to fetch Solomon.

Half the stalls in the stable were empty. And Adam noted that St John still had not replaced the two shire horses needed for the ploughing. The four carriage horses were there, paid for by Amelia from the income of her property in London. Their stepmother seldom rode, even though Elspeth urged her to accompany her more often. Even Elspeth was down to three mares instead of five. The others had been sold during an earlier financial crisis. His father's hunter was still here, exercised by Elspeth. Adam would have bought it himself if St John had tried to sell it to pay off a gaming debt. There was also his brother's gelding. Enough horses to keep Fraddon and another groom busy in the stables, though the cost of feed would be high.

'I spoke to him,' Adam replied. 'Whether he will heed me is yet to be discovered.'

The steeliness in his voice brought her head up to regard him sternly. 'Have you ended this foolish rivalry?'

'On my part, yes. What St John chooses to do . . .' He spread his hands. 'Your guess is as good as mine.'

'I suppose you quarrelled as usual.'

'We are united in our hatred for Sawle and our desire to bring him to justice.'

She shook her head. 'Another feud is not what this family needs.'

Adam refused to be drawn further on the subject. As he had walked through the house he had noticed several changes. 'What has happened to the Chinese vases and bowls in the hall, and the porcelain my grandmother prized so much?'

'They've been sold to pay his debts.' At the flicker of anger on Adam's handsome face Elspeth raised her finger in remonstrance. 'Better they were sold than the land. He would have sold the coach and horses if Amelia had not bought them from him for her own use.'

'They are hers to use by right.' Adam glanced towards the house, a muscle pumping along his jaw.

'Amelia is a wealthy woman from her first marriage. She is to return to London next week until Tamasine's wedding. She does not wish to be in Cornwall for Christmas without Edward.'

'Will you join her, Aunt?'

'Indeed not. I have my hunting. I have no liking for London.'

'But you will be alone in the Dower House. You should be in your old rooms in the main house.'

'Rowena often sleeps there when her father is away. I entertain little. I meet my friends at the hunt not in the living room. I have my books and Rowena and her cat Bodkin for company. My needs are small. I would not be an encumbrance upon my family.'

'You are welcome to make your home at Boscabel.'

She waved a hand dismissively. 'This is my home. I have Lord Fetherington's hunt ball to look forward to.'

'So you have taken up dancing,' he teased.

She flashed him a look of exasperation. 'Dancing is for the young and frivolous. The hunting is what is important. I shall keep an eye on St John, though. He will earn a tongue-lashing from me if he goes near the gaming tables.'

Adam grinned and kissed her cheek. 'Don't ever change, Aunt Elspeth.'

'Why should I change? I am too set in my ways.' Irony was often lost on her. 'And don't you and that stubborn twin of yours allow your hot blood to blind you to reason. You are old enough now to control it. Leave Sawle to the authorities.'

But Adam had no faith in the local forms of justice, however well-intentioned they were. Harry Sawle was too clever for them.

Chapter Six

On the far side of the world Japhet Loveday was facing his biggest challenge yet. Two months ago the arrival of Adam's ship *Pegasus* in Sydney Cove had opened up new horizons for him, but like all new ventures it was fraught with problems. When Adam had invested in the voyage he could not have known about the corruption of the military, who ran a monopoly on all goods arriving in the colony. They had wanted to seize the cargo, pay Adam a low rate, and then charge extortionate prices for selling on the farm implements and stock. Usually all such provisions were sent by the British government to help establish the settlement and the militia made a vast amount of money. Japhet was not about to allow Adam and his investors to be cheated of their profits.

He had asked for an interview with Governor John Hunter. Originally Hunter had arrived with the fleet serving under the first governor, Arthur Phillip, but had returned to England in 1792. When Phillip resigned his post in 1793 Hunter was appointed in his place and returned to the colony in 1795. Japhet had found him to be a compassionate man but ineffectual in controlling the military.

Japhet came straight to the point. 'The ship *Pegasus* which has recently arrived in port is owned by my cousin. The New South Wales Corps will not allow her to be unloaded unless they have control of the sale of her cargo.'

Hunter spread his hands in apology. 'What can I do? The officers disregard my edicts on such matters when I have tried to stop their profiteering in the past. It appalls me that the very men sent to uphold law and order in this land are little better than felons themselves.'

'This cargo is the property of private investors. The Corps controls the government provisions arriving in the colony. If you allow them to take control of *Pegasus*'s cargo, news will get back to England that there are no profits to be made here and no private investors will support the colony. Word like that also spreads to respectable people who might

35

otherwise wish to settle here but who will see it as a barbaric and lawless place.'

'The government has need of such settlers, but I have tried to reason with the officers and failed.'

Japhet bit back his anger at the man's ineffectiveness. 'Grant me a licence to be my brother's agent and sell his goods here. I will only deal with the Loveday ships to ensure that their investors are not cheated.'

'You will be persecuted by some officers who would not lose their hold on the monopoly,' Hunter warned.

'I am not prepared to allow their corruption to steal my cousin's profits. I will fight for my rights.'

'That could be dangerous. In the years between Governor Phillip's resignation and my arrival here, the militia ruled the colony. Many of the laws passed in those days were in their favour. Any man who strikes a soldier is immediately arrested and could be hanged. They rule the convicts by brutality and the emancipists little better and have no high regard for the settlers.'

'I will take my chances.'

'Then take care you give them no opportunity to strike against you.'

'I will fight for the rights of all settlers to succeed and make their fortune in this land with honesty and dignity,' Japhet proclaimed.

'Then I wish you well. You have my support.' The governor looked relieved that Japhet would be fighting an important battle for him. 'Your wife has influential relatives in England, and if any man can take on the corruption of the Corps then I believe it is you, Mr Loveday.'

Japhet presented his letters of concession to act as sole agent for the Loveday ships to Major Grose, the officer in charge of the Corps. Sir Gregory Kilmarthen, who had accompanied Gwen on her voyage and was a friend of the family, would be returning to England on *Pegasus*. He had been shocked at the lack of law and order in the colony and had insisted on attending with Japhet when he met Major Grose.

In the months since his release, Japhet had advised Grose when some of the horses had been ill. He had known all along that he needed to trade skills to have some sway with the militia. Grose was ambitious and knew that in the expansion of the colony lay the potential for great riches.

'Many of my officers will resent that you would take what they believe is theirs by right,' he said.

'I want no part of government stores, just to sell goods from my cousin's ships. Ships with high-ranking and important investors, I should add. If they make a profit here, others will follow. This is a young colony, with great potential for any enterprising man to make his fortune. The officers of the Corps would be short-sighted if they thought they could sell all the cargoes arriving in this land.'

Grose cast a wary eye upon Sir Gregory. 'What is your interest in this venture?'

'I am an investor. Indeed, it was partly my idea. I would not like to see it fail as I gave my word that it was an honourable venture. I will report back to my associates and also to the government of my find-ings here. I worked for some years for Mr Pitt. He trusts any informa-tion I pass on to him.'

A tightening of the major's jaw showed his displeasure that the Lovedays had so much influence in England. 'I cannot see that the future consignments arriving from your cousin's investors will be viewed unfavourably by my men. They are only interested in how lucrative their monopoly is whilst they are stationed here. Eventually they will be recalled to England or will serve elsewhere.' Grose had always been wary of Japhet's reputation in the colony. He was a rare breed of settler who mixed easily with both the convicts and the new colonists. His knowledge of livestock, horses and farming and his carpentry skills had made him many friends.

'There are no spirits on *Pegasus*,' Japhet stated. 'It is the rum trade which your men are most interested in.' Drink was more highly prized than food amongst the convicts, and most of them regularly drank them-selves into oblivion.

'And if I do not agree to uphold the Governor's grant once Sir Gregory has sailed?' Grose challenged. 'What would you do, Loveday?'

'I want no fight with the Corps. But I have never given way under threats. I will fight them by any means in my power.'

Grose laughed. 'You can try, I suppose. But if a soldier is harmed, then you will answer with your life.'

Japhet realised he was being tested. The major would turn a blind eye to any retaliation by his men if they chose to challenge him over the sale of the cargo.

'As long as we understand each other, Major Grose.'

'It is scandalous the way he thinks he can appropriate all imported merchandise,' Sir Gregory said when they had left. 'It will be mentioned in a report to Mr Pitt, but it will be a year and a half before any action

37

can be taken upon it. That is a long time to be in contention with the militia here, Japhet.'

'There are riches enough in this land for any man who seeks his fortune. I intend to return to England in a few years a very wealthy man indeed.'

Japhet did not deny the wisdom in his friend's words. He had left the meeting with Grose with the uncomfortable feeling that this was just the first round in many potentially lethal confrontations with the soldiers.

Aware that the livestock and provisions aboard *Pegasus* could be stolen once they were landed, Japhet had ordered that they remain on the ship until he had decided how best to sell them. He had inspected the cattle, goats and horses on board. They would be ferried ashore in a week and sold by auction. He then spent a week visiting the settlements along the Hawkesbury River and around the growing towns of Parramatta and Sydney, informing the farmers of the goods on board. His friend Silas Hope had given him sound advice when he had arrived at his farm on the first of his calls.

'The military will make any auction as difficult as possible. They will intimidate the settlers against bidding. They will then make a low offer and sell the livestock at a profit.'

'But the settlers are free men. The Corps have no jurisdiction over them.' Japhet frowned.

'They have more power than is good for them. Many of the soldiers are brutal. They can trump up charges against a settler and his family and have them put in gaol. They may need the livestock and farm implements to improve their farm, but life is hard enough for them without making an enemy of the militia.'

'I will not allow my cousin to be cheated on these goods. This was a huge gamble for him.'

'But have you considered the danger of taking on the soldiers?'

Japhet fixed Hope with a forthright stare. 'I have dealt with the scum of the London underworld. I know how to take care of myself.'

'But these men can turn the law against you, Japhet. I beg you to reconsider.' Silas knew of Japhet's past, but he had also seen the soldiers beat senseless a settler who had stood against them.

'My cousin would do the same for me.'

Silas could see his friend would not change his mind, but his stomach curled at the thought of the violence and persecution Japhet could face. He asked, 'How had you intended to sell the dry goods and household wares?'

'I will have to build a warehouse in Parramatta with a shop attached. This is but the first of my cousin's ships to sail here. But that will take time. However, I intend to have it ready before a second ship arrives. I was hoping that for now David Baxter, who has started a livery stables there, will rent me half of the stables. I will pay him with one of the horses. He has already said he wants three more horses. With Parramatta growing, the outlying farmers will hire a hack and wagon to take their goods back to their farms until they can afford to buy them for themselves.'

Silas nodded approval. 'You have a good business head, and the courage to face the consequences of the military over this. As to the livestock, why not set a price for the animals and sell them to the farmers before they are brought ashore? You've inspected them and they are healthy. You could then deliver them to each farm, with an armed guard if need be. You could also do this for the ploughs and heavier farm goods.'

'That makes sense. Thank you, Silas.'

'I need a plough, and after you told Eliza of the success Keziah Sawle had had selling her goat's cheese in Penruan, she wants some goats to try this for herself. So I will take half a dozen of the goats and one of the more gentle mares for Eliza to ride.'

Japhet had followed his friend's advice, and though it had been an exhausting two weeks of unloading and delivering the livestock, they had all been sold, and also all the ploughs on board. David Baxter had agreed to Japhet's proposal and had rented him a third of his stables. Japhet had built shelving to display the bales of material, dry foods and house and farm utensils. He had also selected the provisions and tools needed at his own farm, for which Gwendolyn had written a banker's note for Adam to cash in England.

To his relief he had met no opposition from the militia. As the livestock had already been sold, there was no need for an auction, and the farmers took the animals directly to their farms. Several convicts had escaped and gone into the bush and the militia had been ordered to track them down. Because he had avoided a confrontation this time, Japhet expected some form of retaliation from them in the future.

Sir Gregory had sailed on *Pegasus* when she continued her voyage to the East Indies, where Captain Matthews had been given the name of an agent known to Max Deverell. They hoped for a cargo of spices to take back to England and further increase their profits. Sir Gregory had taken the payment received from the livestock and farm tools and Gwendolyn had written a second bank draft for the goods to be sold in the livery stables.

On the day of the opening of the store Gwendolyn had accompanied Japhet to Parramatta. It had been decided that she would lodge with a couple in the town and attend the stables every day for a month until most of the goods were sold. Japhet could not afford to leave the farm for so long and had engaged a one-eyed ex-convict, Patch Evans, to protect her. Patch had been transported for theft, but from his story it was obvious that he had been set up. He had fallen out of a hayloft when he was a child and landed on a pile of broken chairs, and the leg of one of them had taken out his eye. He and his younger brother had been orphaned a year later and taken in by an uncle. The brother regularly stole from their uncle, and when some possessions were found to be missing they were planted under Patch's mattress and he was the one arrested for theft. He had come to Japhet's farmstead looking for work. Gwen had been kind to him and he tended to follow her round like a devoted dog. He was a big man with a temper, and he adored Gwen enough to attack anyone who tried to harm her.

On the first day the shop had been constantly busy, though it was obvious that many of the settlers had little money spare for luxuries. Japhet saw how the men cast envious glances over the saws and pick-axes that would make their lives so much easier, then choose small sacks of dried peas and flour to feed their families. He decided that he would take a chance of allowing them a certain amount of credit against their next harvest on the goods they needed.

'What if we canna pay? Many farmers lost their crops in the flooding last winter,' one asked, and it became a common question.

Japhet thought quickly. He had many plans on ways to make his fortune in this land. 'Instead of credit you can pay me by working off your debt. A half-day or a day at a time. I need a shop and warehouse built.'

'You can use convict labour.' They remained suspicious.

'I could, but I would rather have loyal men who would work for the good of the community. Most of the convicts put little effort into their work and need constant watching.'

The solution suited the farmers, who would rather work off their debt, while Japhet would have the labour he needed to expand his business.

★   ★   ★

The first week had been a success. When *Pegasus* sailed she would carry on board a coffer full of money for Adam's investors. Most of the dry goods had sold quickly, and from his profits Japhet had paid a carpenter to start work on the store and warehouse in Parramatta. He intended to return to his farm tomorrow, leaving a ticket-of-leave couple who had served their time helping Gwen in the livery stables. He wanted a proper house on his land and it was still only half built, and to accommodate the livestock he had purchased more trees would need to be felled.

The stables were empty of customers and Gwendolyn finished counting up the money they had taken. 'All our hard work has been worth it. Adam will be pleased with his profits. It will make so much difference to our own circumstances here.'

Japhet gave a wry smile. 'I had never thought to see myself as a shop-keeper.'

'It is a very different dream than the one we had of breeding race-horses. Are you sure this is what you want to be doing?'

'Selling the goods and livestock for Adam and his investors ensures my cousin's and our future. The farm merchandise was sold before it was unloaded, and once the bulk of the stores here are sold, the shop will only be open one day a week. There is always the threat from the militia, trying to close us down. But so far the profits have been worth it.'

As though on cue, an officer and three men in uniform strode into the stables. David Baxter, who had been mending a harness, scurried out of the back door. Japhet moved behind the counter, where he kept a musket.

Sensing the tension, Gwendolyn smiled at the officer. 'It is Captain Haughton, I believe. We met at the Governor's house one evening. How may we help you, sir?'

'We are not here to exchange pleasantries, Mrs Loveday. I have business with your husband. You should leave.'

'I will not be ordered from our shop, Captain.' She kept her voice polite but her heart was thudding with fear that they intended to cause trouble. Haughton had shown himself to be a bully in the colony, and was too quick to use the lash on convicts.

He nodded to one of the soldiers to remove Gwendolyn from the shop. Japhet brought up the shotgun and pointed it at the officer. 'Anyone who touches my wife will be shot. I suggest you and your thugs back off and find someone else to annoy.'

Captain Haughton's thin lips twisted into a sneer. 'Shoot and you're a dead man, Loveday. It is a hanging offence to strike or shoot a soldier.'

'Not if they threaten my family. My wife is no convict and her family is a prestigious one with connections at court.'

'That cuts no ice here, Loveday. We are the law. Now, you've cost us a packet with this enterprise. I reckon you owe us.'

'I owe you nothing. *Pegasus* has sailed with the bulk of the takings. My commission was taken in goods. But what I did earn I earned honestly with the blessing of the Governor.'

Gwendolyn was appalled at what she was witnessing. Japhet would never allow a man like Haughton to threaten him, but her husband was being deliberately provoking. This was the fearless Japhet she loved, but his attitude held the seeds of his undoing. How could he put all their dreams and all they had worked for at risk?

Haughton laughed. 'You didn't have *our* blessing. Now pay up or face the consequences.'

Japhet kept the shotgun trained on the officer. 'What you are demanding is extortion, or would you class it as protection money? Both are hanging crimes in England. You dishonour your rank by your demands.'

'You are the convict here, Loveday. Not I.'

'My husband was pardoned, sir.' Gwendolyn disliked the officer's arrogance. 'You have the manners of a guttersnipe, not an officer and a gentleman.'

'Madam, your airs and graces may have served you in England, but not so here.'

Japhet moved between Gwendolyn and the officer, 'Careful how you speak to my wife. I've called men out for less. Are you man enough to face me in a duel?'

Baxter had returned with Patch Evans and three other male settlers who were men of high status in the colony. Japhet pressed his challenge. 'Which of your men will act as your second? Choose swords or pistols. I have fought duels with both in the past.'

Gwendolyn stared at her husband in horror. Why must he always be so hot-blooded, so fiercely antagonistic towards any who would challenge him? Haughton was looking to rouse Japhet's anger. If her husband struck him he could have him arrested and would find a way to confiscate merchandise from the shop.

'I didn't come here to challenge you to a duel,' Haughton sneered. 'Rather to show you who runs the trading here.'

'Not man enough then to face me!' Japhet lifted a mocking brow. 'That fits with what I have heard of you.'

'Will the two of you please stop this nonsense,' Gwendolyn intervened. She felt sick with fear that this would turn into a fight.

Japhet lowered the shotgun but there remained a brittle challenge in his eyes. 'Captain Haughton was just leaving. And I've witnesses now who have heard his threats should anything untoward happen to my business or my family. Governor Hunter may not be able to curb the profiteering of the New South Wales Corps, but he could banish an officer or soldiers who threaten the livelihoods of decent settlers to a tour of duty on Norfolk Island.'

The three men accompanying Haughton blanched. 'I reckon there's been a misunderstanding, Captain,' one blustered. He had been eyeing Japhet warily throughout the exchange. He had been on the ship Japhet had sailed on and knew his reputation. He had also lost half his pay at cards when they had gambled together after Japhet had obtained his release from the hold to care for the captain's livestock on board. Japhet had waived the debt, though in truth as a convict the soldier could have refused to honour it and Japhet would have had no redress for payment. But the soldier had been grateful and it had left him beholden to Japhet.

Also, Norfolk Island was a thousand miles off the mainland, and re-offending convicts or troublemakers were exiled there. It was a soldier's dread to be sent there.

Haughton scowled. 'This cargo may be yours, but I will not forget today.'

Gwendolyn did not want a feud to start between her husband and the officer. 'Is there not profit enough for all? My husband only deals with his cousin's ships and I doubt there will be more than two arriving in a year. Is that so unreasonable, Captain? A man of such refinement as yourself would set much store by the loyalty my husband shows to his family in this matter.' She was offering him a way of saving face before his men.

He turned to her and she could smell the sweat of his fear. With so few men to support him, he would not risk a fight. 'You are both gracious and beautiful, Mrs Loveday. We will let this incident pass for the moment.' He bowed to her, and when his back was to Japhet mouthed a kiss in her direction.

Gwendolyn disliked his audacity and moved to stand at Japhet's side as the soldiers marched from the stables. It was not an end to the matter. Haughton would bide his time and make trouble for them.

When they disappeared she let out a relieved sigh. 'Thank God that did not turn unpleasant. Japhet, how could you provoke him? If we are to make a success of our time here, we need the support of the military, not their enmity.'

'You cannot give a man like that an inch or he will destroy you. Trust me, my love.'

'It was a vendetta against a man too frightened to face you openly that led to your downfall in England. Japhet, I beg you, do not let your anger against Haughton bring about your destruction here.'

Chapter Seven

The sound of laughter echoed through the parlour of Polruggan parsonage. The women of the village were gathering for their lace-making lesson. They met four times a week in the early afternoon, and they were now producing strips of lace one or two inches wide of a quality that would be bought by a haberdasher in Bodmin. Two of the women who were more competent than their companions had become ambitious and were working on lace collars. Their teacher, Maura Keppel, worked rapidly at her own work and was at the side of anyone who had a problem. The money from the lace once it was sold brought a welcome income to the women for their families. Many of the village men had lost their work in Sir Henry Traherne's tin mine when he had been forced to close it earlier in the year, and there was little labour available on farms until the spring. At two of the weekly meetings the workers were joined by women from Trewenna and Trevowan Hard who were also eager to be part of the new venture.

By introducing the lace-making, Bridie had become accepted by the villagers. Although she was the schoolteacher at Trevowan Hard of a morning, and there was no maid at the parsonage to help with the housework, she laboured more diligently than any of her husband's parishioners. Peter's stipend was meagre and her two incomes enabled them to live in a greater degree of comfort.

Today the mood of the women was jovial. There were dozens of yards of lace packed in the basket for Maura to take to Bodmin to sell next week.

Leah Polglase sat at her spinning wheel by the hearth. Her fingers were too swollen and clumsy to make the delicate lace, but she enjoyed spinning the thread. At moments like this she felt a rare contentment in being part of a community. For most of her adult life she had lived in isolation. She had run away from her drunken, abusive father when her mother died and married her handsome gypsy lover. After her husband's death, her eldest child, Caleb, had stayed with the gypsies, but Leah no longer had the heart for travelling.

To survive she had taken many menial jobs, but with two daughters to feed it had never been easy. A woman living alone was always viewed with suspicion that she would become a burden on the parish, and she had lost count of the times the family had been stoned and run out of villages. When she learned of her father's death she had returned to the Polglase cottage. The isolation had never troubled her, but after Bridie married she found that she missed the companionship of her daughters, although she never complained of her loneliness. She had her pride and she knew her place. Her daughters had married well. She had no wish to shame them with her country speech and manners. A bad fall in the summer had made her an invalid for some weeks, and only reluctantly had she agreed to move to the parsonage.

There had been many mixed blessings in those months. She had repaid Bridie's generosity by comforting and helping her daughter after her miscarriage. For all Bridie's stoical spirit, her constitution had never been strong. Being a preacher's wife meant that she was at the beck and call of the parishioners of three parishes night and day. Bridie never stinted in her duties. She wanted to be the helpmeet of her husband, but her diligence had cost her the child.

Leah did not like or approve of Peter's religious fervour. Praying several times a day sat uncomfortably with her. The women of the village gave her a grudging respect but she did not feel at ease here. Whenever she raised the subject of returning to her cottage, though, Bridie was horrified.

'I need you, Ma. There is so much to be done. I thought you were happy here. You've made new friends.'

How could she tell her daughter that the women Bridie saw as her mother's friends were not interested in her but only wanted a link with the Loveday name? However, there were compensations, Leah acknowledged. The animals from her homestead now resided in the parsonage's barn. Daisy the milk cow and her heifer; Hapless the cantankerous old donkey, and the chickens and ducks. The milk, eggs and meat provided by those animals released any feelings of guilt from Leah that she was a financial burden to her daughter.

Now to hear Bridie laughing was better than any tonic. She smiled at her youngest child, proud of all she had achieved. Bridie laughed seldom since her miscarriage. Leah hoped that at last the pain was lifting – that she may yet even be expecting another. Leah began to hum a popular ditty. It was taken up by the other women as they worked.

The front door to the parsonage was banged loudly shut. The singing stopped and Leah glanced at Bridie. The young woman's elfin face had lost its animation and she was staring guiltily at the door. Peter Loveday, dressed in a sober black suit and white Geneva bands, stood inside the parlour clutching his Bible.

'Good women of the parish, there is much unseemly merriment this day as you work.'

'It be no sin to sing, Parson,' Gertrude Wibbley challenged. Her expression was antagonistic as she regarded the preacher. Her ample figure dwarfed the sturdy wooden chair; her thin lips were topped with a down of black hair. Most of the villagers stood in fear of her. Peter did not even flinch as her gimlet eyes regarded him with scorn.

'You would be better served by listening to a Bible reading.'

'This be a lace-making meeting, not a Bible class, with respect, Parson Loveday,' Leah interceded. 'We do start with the Lord's prayer like you suggested. Some of the women here be Methody. Our work is for the good of the community as a whole. That in itself be the Lord's work, to my mind.'

Peter flushed.

Bridie put aside her work and poured a mug of weak ale for Ma Wibbley, and cast a pleading look towards her husband. 'Had you come in earlier you would have heard us lifting our voices in praise. There are no women from the chapel present today. We have been practising our carolling. The festive season will soon be upon us.'

'Our Lord's birth is a time of reverence,' Peter began.

Gert Wibbley helped herself to a walnut from a bowl. The nuts grew on three trees in the parsonage garden. She cracked the shell with her teeth and spat the fragments into her hand before eating the nut.

Bridie hurried to Peter's side, 'You must be hungry, husband. We have saved you a slice of Maura's fine apple cake that she brought to share with us. I will brew you a fresh pot of tea.' She went into the kitchen, willing Peter to follow her. He hesitated by the parlour door.

Jenny Pascoe, who was much in awe of their new parson, said slyly, 'We shall show Parson how well we sing.' She led them: 'God rest you, merry gentlemen, let nothing you dismay . . .'

The others joined in. 'Remember Christ our saviour was born on Christmas day.'

Bridie placed a slice of cake before Peter, who continued to frown. 'The women mean no harm by their singing.'

'This is a parsonage and must be respected as part of God's house.'

'It was a little light relief. It is taxing work; some of the patterns are complicated.'

His handsome face darkened. 'Singing the praise of the Lord should have been uplifting enough.'

'Not when we are trying to sing in harmony and some had forgotten the words.' She lowered her voice to add with a smile, 'Ma Wibbley has a voice like a stuck pig.'

Peter did not return her smile. He looked tired, his cheeks sunken. He had been eating badly and pushed himself too hard. In the early days of their marriage he would have laughed at her jesting. It troubled her how fervent he had become in his religious devotions. He had been like that years ago and had mellowed in later years until her miscarriage. She loved him fiercely, but this was a side to him that disturbed her.

The song had ended. 'Enjoy the cake, my dear. It was kind of Maura to bring it for us.'

Peter folded his hands together to say grace. His dark head was bent and Bridie saw the hollowness to his cheeks and the weariness in his movements. Her heart ached to comfort him. But this was not the time or the place. When they first married it had been easy to make him laugh. He had changed with the death of their unborn child. If only she could conceive again, all would be well.

Every day she prayed to the Lord Jesus and also to the old fertility goddess to bless them with a child. She felt a pang of disloyalty to her husband for still revering the old ways, but like her sister she had kept her faith in the gods of nature and ancient sacred places. She had been brought up to respect all life, whether animal or human, and had been horrified after learning to read to discover that so many wars were fought in the name of religion. How could that be right when from what little she had learned of other faiths they all spoke of God's love and compassion towards their fellow men?

Bridie acknowledged that her education was sparse on such matters, but something within her believed there was but one creator – the source of all prophets, gods and goddesses whether ancient or new. She would have liked to discuss her reasoning with her husband, but Peter would be appalled at such heresy. She therefore kept her beliefs to herself and outwardly showed her love for her husband by conforming to his faith.

When she returned to the parlour the women were talking in low voices. The friendly atmosphere in the room had changed. Gert Wibbley put aside her work and wrapped it in an old piece of calico to protect it. 'Sitting here won't get my ironing done.'

The other women took their cue from her and packed away their own work. Before they could leave Peter appeared at the door. Several of the women exchanged irritated glances.

'God bless you all.' Peter stepped back from the door to allow them to leave.

'Happen this lace will be more holy than holey,' Gert Wibbley snorted.

'You get above yourself if you think you have no need for prayers,' Peter returned.

'I didn't come here to be insulted.' Gert's glare was belligerent. 'I can work as well at home. Lace will get done faster without stopping every time the mood takes you to pray, preacher.'

Bridie saw from the other women's faces that Ma Wibbley had touched a nerve. Peter towered over Gertrude, but the woman remained defiant and held his glare. He rapped out, 'I will not neglect the welfare of the souls of my flock.'

'A good shepherd knows—' Ma Wibbley began.

Bridie cut across her protest. She did not want Peter criticised before them all. 'Come, ladies. It has been a long day. Think of the profit to be made from the lace when it is sold. It will provide a fine feast for your families this Christmas.'

The women broke out into excited chatter at the thought of the money they would make and the benefits it would bring to their homes. Bridie sighed as the last of them left.

'That woman is an evil influence on the others,' Peter announced. 'She will mend her ways or not attend these meetings in future.'

'You cannot ban her. Ma Wibbley is not so bad. But was the lecture absolutely necessary? You will set the women against this venture.'

'Only the ungodly—'

'Oh, Peter.' She burst into tears. 'Why are you so harsh and condemning? I could not help losing the baby. It was not their fault. It was I who failed you.'

He stared at her in astonishment. 'I do not blame you for that. It was God's will. It was I who had failed Him . . .' The anguish was torn from him.

She moved to take him in her arms and was shocked at how thin he had become. He held her tight and she could feel his inner tension. Then, with a harsh intake of breath, he kissed the top of her head and gently put her from him, saying, 'I have a sermon to write.'

Bridie's heart ached to be held and comforted. Peter had been so loving in the early days of their marriage. Each week he was becoming more zealous, his emotions channelled into the work of the Lord. Could he not see how much she needed his affection and support? He was becoming a stranger, far removed from the loving man she had married.

Chapter Eight

Washday was always busy on the farm. Today Hannah had to abandon her own tasks to help in the laundry. After ten days of rain, when it had been impossible to dry the washing, it had turned mild and sunny. With nearly three weeks' laundry to be done, it would take all day. Hannah had been up since dawn. The animals had to be tended first and the cows milked. She had sent Mark to the Caines' cottage to ensure that Mab collected the wood and lit the fire under the stone laundry tub. Then the groom had gone to do the weekly check at Tor Farm. Hannah had leased two fields to a neighbouring farmer to use for his sheep until her brother returned to England. The income would be of help to Japhet and she hoped that the presence of the shepherd living in one of the cottages would further deter the smugglers from using the land. Another servant had also been engaged to do general maintenance on the farm. Until he proved his worth a watch needed to be kept on him that he was doing the work he was paid for.

Before setting out to take her three older children to the school at Trevowan Hard, she gave her own servants their tasks for the morning. When she returned she was greeted by the smell of the fresh bread Aggie had put in the oven. The cows by now should have been milked and put in the far meadow to graze, and she frowned to see that the animals were still in the milking shed.

Exasperated at the delay, Hannah went to investigate and found Fanny and Bessie coughing, their flushed faces leaning wearily against the cows' sides as they tugged at the udders. The milkmaids were clearly far from well and her irritation turned to concern.

'You both look like you should be in your beds.' She put her hand to Fanny's brow and found it red hot. 'You're burning up, Fanny. You too, Bessie.'

'My throat hurts awful bad, Mrs Rabson,' croaked Bessie, the younger

51

of the two. 'Truly we've done our best to get the cows milked and you need us to work in the laundry today.'

'Neither of you looks well enough for that.' As she spoke, Bessie's face darkened to purple and she coughed so violently that she startled the cow she was milking and it kicked out, knocking the pail of milk over, then put its hoof down on Bessie's foot. The dairymaid burst into tears.

Hannah slapped the animal's rump to move the beast. 'You have a fever from the looks of it, Bessie. Get to your bed. You too, Fanny. Fortunately I have some of Mrs Loveday's cough remedy and some feverfew tincture to bring down your temperature. If you take them and rest you may be able to do the milking this evening.'

Bessie wiped her eyes and shuffled to the door. Fanny looked guilty. 'But there still be four more cows to milk, Mrs Rabson.'

'I will help Tilda. You cannot work when you are so ill and I do not want the children coming down with a fever.' She turned to the third woman. 'Is your throat sore, Tilda?'

'No, Mrs Rabson. I be fine. I can do Bessie and Fanny's work. I will milk the rest of the cows. You've your own duties.' The woman was buxom, her sandy hair scraped back under her mobcap. Her apple cheeks were rosy but this was her natural complexion and was not caused by a temperature. She grinned good-naturedly. Though Tilda was rather slow-witted, she made up for it in her enthusiasm to please.

'Thank you, Tilda. I appreciate your hard work. You had better make a bed up for yourself tonight in the farmhouse attic. I can't have all my servants ill at once.'

'Yes, Mrs Rabson.'

'Dick Caine can take the cows to the far meadow. I shall need you to help with the laundry. I do not want to waste such a good drying day as today.'

Dick Caine grumbled as he entered the milk shed to lead out the cows. He scratched listlessly at his armpit, his shirt grey with dirt and his jerkin greasy from several years' wear. Under a battered slouch hat his greying hair and straggly beard were matted. From his louse-ridden clothing wafted the perpetual smell of cabbage soup.

'Bain't my job to do dairymaids' work,' he protested.

Hannah was helping Tilda muck out the hay before the floor was swilled down. She lifted her broom and shook it at Dick.

'It is your job to do whatever I tell you. You and Mab are on your last chance. If you will not work I will find someone who gives me an honest day's labour. There are out-of-work miners aplenty who would be glad of your job and cottage.'

Dick scowled and shouted at the cows, shoving them to get them on their way. He ambled after them, making no effort to hurry.

'When you are done with the cows, get the milk delivered to Penruan and the rest of the round,' Hannah ordered. 'And no malingering. I expect you back here in two hours. There's wood to be chopped. That is another job you have been shirking, Caine. By now the winter wood pile should be twice as high as it is.'

'I do me best. I've only got one pair of hands.'

'And you use them too often to lift a quart of ale on the milk round. Mark does it in half the time you take.' Hannah increased the pace of her sweeping. The list of the day's work to be completed seemed endless.

He grumbled under his breath as he shuffled away. She had halved his pay last quarter day because of his laziness and it still had made no difference. If anything he complained more and did less.

Tilda took hold of Hannah's broom to halt her work. 'You shouldn't be doing this, Mrs Rabson. I'll finish here and be over to help with the laundry as soon as I can.'

'Thank you, Tilda. If I do not check on Mab she will have slunk off somewhere.'

The day had begun badly. Short of two servants, she would be rushed off her feet. It would be an hour before Mark returned from Tor Farm and Sam would not be back until tomorrow evening. Unexpectedly, he had asked for four days' leave after receiving a letter from a lawyer in Bodmin. He had said he needed to attend to some business.

'It must be important business to involve a lawyer,' she had joked.

'It's a funeral.' A guarded look had come into his eyes, and puzzled, she had not pressed him. Sam rarely used his monthly day off to leave the farm. Her curiosity was pricked, but he was a private man and she did not pursue the matter. He would tell her his business in his own time. 'I'm sorry for your loss, Sam. You are owed the time. If you wish to leave Charlie with me, you are welcome. A young boy could be diffi-cult to keep entertained on a long ride.'

'I'll take Charlie with me, but thank you for the offer.'

'Then you must use one of Japhet's mares. It will exercise her.'

'In that case I will accept.'

She was struck by his unwillingness to take any charity. Sam was an enigma. He spoke too well to be a common labourer. From their conver-sations she had realised he was as well educated as her brothers and cousins, though he often took pains to play this down. He might dress like a farm worker, but there was no mistaking his gentlemanly bearing. When he gave orders to any migrant workers it was with the authority of a man who expected to be obeyed without question.

There was a stern set to his features that prompted her to add, 'If for any reason you need to take more time over this matter, please do so. I value your work and experience, but Mark can take on your everyday jobs. And if there is anything I can do . . .' She let the sentence drift, feeling suddenly awkward in his presence.

'I appreciate your kindness, Mrs Rabson, but four days should be sufficient.'

He had left that afternoon. His absence intrigued her and she realised how little she knew about her overseer. On the few occasions she had questioned him about his family or past he had said little. Though she did know that Charlie was not his son but the child of his sister, who had been seduced by a cousin who had then abandoned her. After giving birth she had hanged herself, unable to face her shame. Sam had found Charlie in an orphanage. Sam never spoke of his parents or his background. His past was his own affair and she valued his work and reliability too much to risk offending him.

When she entered the laundry room she noted that the fire had been lit under the washtub. The sheets were soaking in the hot water, and petticoats and aprons were in the dolly tub. Mab was sitting on a three-legged stool rubbing her back. She was as unkempt as her husband. Hannah had never known the older woman to wash, and her clothes did not see the washtub from one month to the next.

'Where be those lazy sluts?' the slatternly servant complained. 'They should be doing this. I can't do the heavy sheets with my back.'

'Then set to work in the dolly tub. Bessie and Fanny both have a fever. I have sent them to their beds.' There was nothing wrong with Mab's back. It was just an excuse that was used too often to get out of work. Senara had examined the woman twice and found nothing wrong.

Mab groaned and pressed a fleshy hand to her temple. 'I be near cut in two with a pain in the head. And I be hot. Reckon I should be back in my cottage. Fever you say they have. Reckon I do have the fever meself.'

Hannah glared at her and snapped, 'You've the fever no more than I. Tilda will be here to help us soon. Once Aggie has finished her work in the house she will also help.'

Hannah tossed the older woman a bar of soap to use on the sheets. She glanced around at the washing that Tilda had sorted into piles before starting the milking. Amongst the servants' pile she could see nothing of Mab's or Dick's.

'Did you forget to bring your washing, Mab?' Her anger at the woman's laziness made her harsher in her judgement. 'That bodice could do with a change. You have not had it off your back for two months. Sleep in it, do you? I expect my servants to take pride in their appearance.'

'I washed this last week,' Mab brazenly lied and gave an affronted sniff. 'I don't want my clothes muddled up with those sluts'. Don't know where they've bin. Could catch any manner of nasty disease.'

'Laziness is the only disease that you suffer from,' Hannah snapped. The toll of running the farm had sapped her patience. 'Go and change your clothes. You stink like a midden and Dick is no better. I find it offensive.'

'Offensive! I bain't been so insulted in all my born days. No one in their right mind washes their clothes in winter. Gentry do get some uppity ideas. Bit of dirt don't harm no one. Protects you, it does, from the cold.'

'That is nonsense, Mab.'

'First I offend you. Now I talk nonsense.' Mab glowered. 'You be turning mighty pernickety since the master died. It bain't right the way you talk to us. Jus' because we don't have no rights. Being beholden to you for a roof over our heads don' mean you can work us like slaves.'

Hannah put her hands on her hips. 'Then you had better get yourself to the hiring fair and find work better suited to you both. I have been tolerant long enough of your idle ways. I will not stand for your insolence.'

Turning her back on the servant, Hannah bent over the washtub and scrubbed at a sheet on the washboard. She heard Mab shuffling about near the dolly tub with much sighing and groaning.

'Still here, Mab?' she challenged. 'There is a hiring fair in Launceston in three days. Time enough for you and Dick to walk there and find more suitable employment.'

'Happen I was hasty with me words, Mrs Rabson. It be the pain in me back. Ceaseless it be. I'm a martyr to it. Makes me say things I don't mean. Sam be away, and with those lazy sluts taking to their beds, it wouldna be right for me to leave you short-handed.'

'Then you and Dick must mend your ways. And I meant what I said about taking more pride in your appearance. Many a week I've been tempted to put you both in the washtub after the washing. A bit of soap certainly would not go amiss. Your clothes, skin and hair are rotten with dirt. Your cottage is a disgrace. Wash and keep yourselves and the cottage clean, or you will be dismissed.'

Mab's mouth opened and shut but no words came forth when she saw the determination in Hannah's stance.

The older woman peered resignedly at her filthy bodice and shirt. 'I'll go change. Happen it be grief at losing the master has made us let things slip. He were a good man. We do miss him. There be a bit of Dick's washing could be done as well.'

'Mourning is no excuse for slatternly behaviour. And do not take your time. I am losing patience with you both.'

Mab moved faster than she had in months and was back in the laundry within minutes, having changed her skirt and bodice and carrying a pile of clothing. She did not utter another complaint all morning, although there were frequent groans of pain theatrically put on to try and win some sympathy.

Hannah ignored her. The couple had to go but she felt guilty turning them out just before Christmas. She hoped they would mend their ways, but doubted that they would.

Tilda appeared, humming tunelessly, and joined Mab to wring out the sheets. Aggie, having finished her housework, kept them supplied with a steady stream of buckets of water drawn from the well. She had brought with her Hannah's youngest son Luke, who played happily, stamping in the puddles of water forming on the laundry room floor.

Each sheet in turn was lifted out of the hot water and put into a wooden vat filled with cold. Once rinsed, Aggie and Tilda took them outside and twisted them until the water ceased to drip from them, then hung them on the ropes stretched across the yard to dry. Luke joined in, eager to pass the pegs to help the women in their work. The aprons and petticoats were next on the lines, then the darker clothes.

Hannah's blouses and the children's clothes needed more care, and she washed these herself, not trusting Mab with the more delicate garments. When all the washing was on the lines to dry, Hannah ordered Mab and Tilda to empty the water from the tubs and ensure that everything was left clean and tidy.

Mark had returned from Tor Farm and gone to a far meadow where the ditch needed cleaning to avoid flooding in the winter. Dick should have returned from delivering the milk an hour ago but there was no sign of him or the cart in the yard. He was clearly taking advantage of Sam being away and had stopped at a kiddley for ale.

Tired from the heat of the washtubs and from the extra work she had been doing, Hannah's temper got the better of her. She returned to the laundry room and rounded on Mab.

'Dick has not returned. If he is too drunk to work, that is the last straw. I warned him before he left not to visit the kiddley. The pair of you will go first thing in the morning.'

'He wouldna touch a drop,' Mab defended with indignation. 'Something must have happened to delay him. The recent rain churns up the road powerful bad.'

'If I smell a hint of drink on his breath, then you go. If he is sober I still expect the wood to be chopped even if he has to work all through the night.' Her patience with the couple was at an end. She needed loyal, competent workers to manage the farm. She had been lenient with the Caines too long.

Hannah returned to the house to cut the bread and give Luke a bowl of pottage. Once she had eaten she must collect the other children from school. The dogs set up a racket barking in the lane, and she went outside to investigate, half hoping it was her brother Peter, able to give her a couple of hours' work on the farm. He had started to repair a dry-stone wall last week. She was grateful for any time he could spare.

The distant rider was not Peter, with his distinctive wide-brimmed parson's hat. The thick-set figure sent a shiver of alarm through Hannah. It looked uncomfortably like Harry Sawle, and Mark was too far away to call for assistance. Though she doubted that the groom was any match for his bullying brother.

She spun round, her gaze searching for her son, and saw him playing by the door with one of the farm kittens. 'Come inside, Luke. It is time for your lunch.' She propelled the lad into the kitchen. 'I want you to sit at the table until you have finished your meal. We have a visitor. Now you be a good boy and I will let you ride on Abigail's pony when the man leaves.'

With Luke safe out of the way she hurried to Oswald's old den at the back of the house where he had worked on the farm accounts and kept his fishing rods and guns. The blunderbuss hung on two hooks high on the wall out of reach of the children. She had kept it primed and loaded since the night Sawle had come to the farm in the spring. Now she took it down and put it under her arm. She heard Sawle's horse in the yard and had no intention of allowing him to enter the house. She met him before he reached the door. She had paused to whip off her dirty wet apron and push a tendril of hair back under the white linen kerchief tied over her hair. Even for a man like Sawle she would not appear dishevelled or at a disadvantage. She never forgot she was a Loveday and a gentlewoman.

He glanced at the gun tucked under her arm and raised a brow in mockery. 'Is that any way to greet a friend who be making a neighbourly call?' The jagged blue-stained scar on his cheek distorted his face, blighting his once handsome looks. He was dressed in a brown linsey-woolsey suit and scarlet waistcoat. He had not troubled to remove his hat, but then he had the manners of a guttersnipe, which no amount of finery could eradicate.

'You are not a friend and have never done a neighbourly act in your life.'

'I make an exception for a beautiful woman.'

There was a chilling arrogance in Sawle's manner and she forced herself to breathe evenly and still the rapid pounding of her heart. The cold gleam in his eyes emanated menace, and she refused to show that she was intimidated.

'State your business, Sawle, and be on your way. I have a farm to run. But you know my views on anything to do with smuggling.'

His stare ran critically over her work dress and the lace-up boots that were practical for her daily tasks. It was galling to be wearing her oldest skirt. The hem had been turned twice and it swung above the ground and around her ankles.

'You may talk with fine airs, but if I passed you in the street you'd be mistaken for a servant. You work as hard as one.'

'I see no shame in that.' She was defiant in the face of his ridicule but inwardly she cursed the work-reddened hands that gripped the blunderbuss. 'It is honest work and I am proud of our family farm.'

'You could do much better. Live in comfort and style.'

'As you can see, I am busy. If you have nothing to say, then please leave.'

His eyes narrowed, and as he took a step forward she brought up the gun, pointing it at his midriff. 'Stay where you are! I know how to use this and I am also a crack shot with a pistol. Japhet taught me.'

'And how be your convict brother? You look down on me for earning a living as a free-trader, but he be no better. By comparison my trade be honest. I bain't no highwayman. I don't rob people. Perhaps you should learn to mend your manners and show respect where respect be due.'

'Respect is earned, it is not demanded. My brother is worth a hundred of you. Now get on your horse and leave.'

'Or you'll do what?' Sawle licked his lips in a salacious manner. 'You be alone here. Deacon left three days past. Has he found more profitable work?'

The knowledge that he knew so much chilled her to the core. She was being spied on.

He laughed and continued to taunt her. 'You weren't going to call on my little brother to defend you, were you? I've thrashed Mark to an inch of his life afore now. He bain't no match for me.'

'You do not impress me with your bully's tactics.'

'You've spirit. That be what I admire in you, Hannah. I like a woman with fire in her blood.'

Nausea churned in her stomach and threatened to rise to her throat. She swallowed hard; his conceit and her disgust for him roused her bravado. 'And I despise you and all you stand for. Now leave before I forget my breeding and shoot you for trespass.'

The blunderbuss was heavy but she held it firmly, her aim unwavering. 'I shall count to five. If you have not mounted your horse I will shoot. One . . . two . . . three . . .' His glare challenged her, the scarred cheek taut with anger, and there was malice in those cruel eyes. Her spine stiffened with resolve. 'Four . . . Fi—'

He backed away. 'Whoa there! This be but a friendly call.' He put his foot in the stirrup and swung into the saddle, whilst her gun remained trained on him. 'Looks like you're gonna take more courtin' than I thought.'

'Until hell freezes over!' The absurdity of his words goaded her anger. 'Get off my land. Set foot on it again and you will be shot on sight for trespass.'

'No one threatens me.' Menace loaded the words. 'You take too much upon yourself, Hannah sweetheart. But you will learn who be your master.'

She was tempted to fire the blunderbuss over his head to startle his horse into a bolt. But if he controlled the gelding she would then be unarmed and at his mercy. 'Get off my land.'

With a mocking bow Sawle tipped the brim of his hat to her. 'Until we meet again, sweet Hannah.'

He wheeled his horse and trotted away. Relief hit her like a battering ram. Her knees buckled and she gripped the door post for support. Her victory was hollow. It had but earned her a reprieve.

This was the second time she had escaped him. Her flesh crawled as she remembered the time he had waylaid her in the barn. Until now he had taken no more than an unwilling kiss, but he would not stop at that. He wanted revenge on the Lovedays for many past slights.

Hannah knew she could take precautions: never travelling without Sam or Mark accompanying her, and always carrying a pistol. But Sawle was sly and unremitting as a demon in his evil quest. One day she knew he would find her unprotected and unguarded and his hatred for her family would seal her fate. She must never slacken her vigilance. She would be safe only when he was dead or behind bars.

Chapter Nine

The quayside of Penruan harbour was noisy with the chatter of the fishwives gutting the day's catch. Around their feet the terns and seagulls screeched and squabbled as they fought over the discarded entrails.

The fishing sloops were lined up along the harbour arm, the men sluicing down their decks or sorting through their nets. The clock in the square church tower struck one, and half a dozen children ran down the headland cliff past the first of the thirty cottages set into the hillside. They were too young to sail with the fleet but they had been scouring the beach for anything useful that had been washed up.

The Reverend Mr Snell left the rectory with his Bible clasped under his arm to visit a sick parishioner. His portly wife accompanied her husband for some way, then turned towards the three almshouses with a basket of food that was allocated to the poor every week.

The women on the quayside kept one eye on the younger children playing in the streets and the other on their work. They were wrapped in shawls that were crossed over their chests and tied at the back of their waists. Their purple-mottled hands were streaked with blood and raw from the sea salt and cold. As they worked they shifted their weight from one foot in its heavy clog to the other to ease the ache in their swollen knees and ankles. Their usual ribald laughter was missing today and their conversation was terse, their voices lowered to a whisper accompanied by furtive glances across to the Dolphin Inn on the far side of the quay. Only one topic occupied them. Harry Sawle had returned.

His ship *Sea Mist* was moored at the end of the harbour arm in the deepest water. The cutter was an impressive vessel that dwarfed the fishing sloops. It proclaimed Sawle to be a man of substance – a man to be reckoned with.

Not that the women needed reminding of the fear Sawle could

instil. The villagers hated him. Most of the men worked as tubmen on smuggling runs for Sawle, but he pushed them into taking unnecessary risks. More than one fishwife had been made a young widow because of Sawle's greed. Fights amongst rival gangs were not uncommon and heads and ribs were cracked in the mêlée. The diligence of the revenue men added to the hazards of the trade. They would shoot indiscriminately if they came across free-traders transporting a cargo inland. If a villager refused to work for Sawle he would find his fishing sloop scuppered and his only other means of income taken from him.

'Did you see how he strutted, thinking 'e be cock of the roost?' Nell Rundle pursed her lips primly. There was a sourness about her ageing features that would curdle milk. The eldest of her six girls, Ivy, was helping her mother. She didn't speak, afraid that her mother would give her a clout about the head to make her ears ring. The young pimpled lass kept her head bent over her work, a trail of mucus dripping from her nose. Nell hawked and spat on to the flagstones of the quay. 'Now that devil be back in these parts, that will be the end of my Barney having his nights to himself.'

'Happen you bain't averse to spending the money Barney brings home,' Dot Warne grunted. 'Or drinking an illicit packet of tea.' She had been a widow for ten years and shared a cottage with her daughter-in-law Moira and son George, none of whose three children had survived infancy.

'They bain't worth my Barney risking life and limb,' Nell returned. 'He be a decent man. He don' spend all his wages in the pub, like some I could name.'

'He be too scared to come home if he did.' Molly Biddick sniggered. She was the mother of Jenna, who worked at Trevowan, and her body was stooped and old before its time, her thin face scored with lines of worry and deprivation. She lived next door to the Rundles. 'Your Barney drinks like a fish. You be always rowing, and how many times have you laid him out cold with a skillet for coming home drunk?'

'You calling me a liar? You nosy cow.' Nell yanked on Molly's hair, and the other fishwives, anticipating a fight to lighten the boredom of their work, egged them on. Dot Warne, however, threw a bucket of entrails over Nell and dragged Molly back to her bench. 'Get on with your work. The jowters will be here soon with their ponies to take away the catch. They won't buy what bain't been gutted.'

Nell and Molly continued to snipe at each other as they worked. Dot was more conscientious than the others. 'Winter storms be upon us now,' she said, not losing her rhythm in gutting the herring. 'Men won't be out much of a night now till spring.'

'They will if Sawle has his way. That grand ship of his will weather most storms. He don't respect the lives of his men, long as he gets his profit.'

'My Barney near lost a leg last winter when the rowboat they were bringing goods ashore in overturned and he were smashed against the rocks,' Nell said. 'Thank God his leg were saved. But it were ten weeks afore he could take his sloop out. And us with no money coming in and seven kids to feed. If it hadna been for the fishermen giving us a fish or two from their catches we would have starved.'

Tess Biddick listened to the talk and it made her blood run cold. She knew last winter had been a hard one for the fishermen. The catches had been small and over half of Sawle's cargoes had been confiscated by the revenue men. When the goods were taken, the tubmen weren't paid. Tess hoped this winter would not be so dire. She rubbed the small of her back, the child in her belly heavy in her seventh month of pregnancy. Tess was seventeen and still viewed with suspicion as a newcomer by many of the villagers. She had come here from Polmasryn when she married John Biddick. There were a dozen Biddick cousins in the village and even some of them remained reserved towards her.

Her brow furrowed in concentration. The fish were slippery and she was far from accomplished in her work and often cut her fingers with the sharp knife. Dot Warne was her neighbour and had taken pity on her in the early days of her pregnancy when she couldn't stop being sick both day and night.

Tess spoke quietly. 'In Polmasryn, Sawle's name was used to frighten children who wouldn't do as they were told. I were more scared of him than I were of being carried off by a pixie.'

Dot held up two fingers in a sign to ward off evil. 'Don't mock the pixies, my lovely, or Sawle – both could ill-wish you and you'd vanish without trace.'

Tess winced as the knife slipped and sliced into her knuckle. She sucked it and drew a piece of rag from her pocket to bind it before continuing her work. Harry Sawle had bought himself a house a mile from the coast, but she had seen little of him since her arrival in the village. She knew his elder brother Clem, though. His cottage was further up the steep side of the coombe and his wife kept goats and sold their cheese. She lifted her eyes to the skyline and could make out Keziah's sturdy figure sweeping out the goat shed, her wiry amber hair blowing around her like writhing eels in the wind. The cottages higher on the coombe were not so sheltered as those by the harbour. The trees in the gardens tilted at crazy angles from the constant buffeting and winter gales.

'Clem keeps himself to himself and troubles no one. His wife Keziah be really nice.' Tess was moved to speak up for her neighbour. She admired the buxom woman who was fearless as a man and strode through the village uncaring what anyone thought of her. 'She were the first one to make me feel welcome in the village.'

'She be an outsider herself,' Nell barked. 'And she be a fearsome woman to cross. She don't hold with smuggling. She made Clem swear to give it up afore she agreed to wed him. Strange for such as he, he's abided by his word.' The older woman gave a coarse chuckle. 'He has no part of his brother's doings and be an honest fisherman. Though I wouldn't get the wrong side of his temper. Kezzie never managed to tame that. He don't drink much now, but if he does, he's a demon with his fists.'

'Clem be a big bear of a man. I doubt Harry would want to cross him,' Tess replied.

Nell rubbed her nose in a sign of caution. 'Harry Sawle don't do his own dirty work. It be his henchmen you have to watch out for. I wouldn't trust Mordecai Nance, who runs the Dolphin for Sawle. It were run by Reuban Sawle for years before Nance took it over.'

'I remember Reuban,' Tess said. 'Lost his legs, didn't he? Always drunk and abusive. Died sudden like. And his wife left the pub before his body were cold in its coffin.'

'Nance moved in too quick to my way of thinking. Not that I would say a word against him.' Nell leaned closer as she threw a gutted fish into a wicker basket. 'Folk could get a nasty beating if wind of it got to him. They say Reuban choked on his vomit when drunk.' Her lips mouthed the next words in silence. 'Or were choked to death by someone who stood to gain a lot.'

Tess rounded her eyes in astonishment. 'You mean Nance killed him?'

'Never let no one hear you say that.' Nell cast furtively around her to ensure they had not been overheard. Fortunately the other fishwives were intent on their own conversations.

Nell loved to gossip, and with so avid a listener she expanded. 'That wife of Nance's bain't no better than she should be. They've got two new girls in the tavern and it bain't just ale they serve to the men, so I heard. It be a knocking shop and I won't have my Barney go near the place.'

There was a shout from the village general shop and a ragged youth ran out. A thin woman with bright brassy hair appeared at the door and aimed a rotten apple at the lad's head. He yelped as it hit his ear. 'Don't you come sniffing round in here again, Jimmy Warne. I'll have your guts for garters if I catch you thieving again.'

Dot Warne whirled round. 'You watch your mouth, Goldie. My son bain't no thief.'

Goldie put her hands on her narrow hips. There had been little comfort in her life before she came to Penruan, and her thin face was pinched and hard. 'Then you can pay for the pie he stuffed in his gob.'

Another woman appeared at Goldie's side. They were two of the wealthiest women in the village but their money had brought them little happiness. This one was still beautiful, her reddish hair partially hidden under a lace cap. She was young and well dressed but there was also a harshness to her face that marred her beauty. She carried a toddler on her hip.

'There be another who bain't no better than she should be,' Nell stated. 'That child be the image of Harry Sawle, and her wed to Lanyon afore he were murdered. That be another killing that don't bear too close a minding. Her and Sawle were lovers. But Sawle ditched her fast enough when Goldie turned up with proof she were wed to Lanyon years past and he realised Hester wouldn't get a penny of his money.'

'I like Goldie. She's got a tart tongue but she bain't so bad,' Tess ventured. 'She's always got a pleasant word for me.'

'She be another newcomer here herself. Though I'll give her her due. She took in Hester when she were in labour and her family had thrown her out.' Nell nodded towards the chandler's shop on the corner of a side street. 'Moyle's Hester's father, and the uppity Dr Chegwidden's wife, Annie, be her sister. Hester always were a minx. She'd been Harry's lover for years, but he wouldn't wed her. They say Lanyon scared her into wedding him. Sawle never forgave her. He used her as his whore to get back at Lanyon.' Nell draw a sharp breath, the air steaming from her mouth in the cold. 'That Thadeous Lanyon were an evil cove – worse than Sawle in some respects. He had two other wives in Penruan and they both died young. And him all that time wed to Goldie. She's done right by Hester and they be partners in Lanyon's shop and business.'

'How does Sawle get away with murder and the like?' Tess shuddered.

'Bribes, I reckon,' Nell whispered. 'But one day he'll go too far. There's been too many deaths that he's benefited from. People don't forget that. Justice can only be mocked at one's peril.'

Chapter Ten

Another week of gaming had emptied St John's purse, and he returned to Trevowan in a disgruntled mood. Nothing had gone right for him. How the devil was he to find four hundred guineas by the end of the week to meet an IOU? Honour demanded that he pay without delay or face being ostracised by his friends and barred from future gaming sessions.

What madness had driven him to gamble again? He had drunk enough to be reckless. A chance remark at how well Adam prospered had fired him to rebellion against the constraints of his financial troubles. He had wagered indiscriminately, and had written out his IOU believing he could win a final pot of a thousand guineas. But his three kings had been beaten by a royal flush. The loss had sobered him instantly, leaving him sick to his gut. The coffers at Trevowan were empty, the remaining half of the loan from his cousin gambled away.

He shut himself away in his father's study and dropped his head into his hands. Three months' wages were also due for the servants and farm hands. If he did not pay them, word would spread. He could not face that shame.

His pride rebelled. There had to be something he could sell. Articles that would not be noticed too readily by his family. He feared ridicule from them most of all. They would delight in being proved right that he was an unworthy heir and shake their heads at how he had failed his father.

He rubbed his hands across his face, cursing the hold gambling had upon him. It was a temptation he could neither resist nor curb. He would try and limit himself to twenty guineas and in the heat and thrill of the game would lose all caution and wager indiscriminately, convinced he could not lose. But lose he nearly always did.

He had no stomach for the meal Winnie Fraddon had prepared for him, and placing a brandy decanter on the study desk he dismissed the servants for the night. The house servants slept in the attic of the little-used east wing. The estate workers had their own cottages and the stable lad slept behind the tack room. There would be no prying eyes watching over him as he prowled the house searching for anything that would be easy to sell and would fetch a good price.

He carried a candelabra to light his search and avoided the main rooms. Elspeth had eyes like a hawk and would miss anything of value from the living quarters. He had already sold the porcelain and silverware collected by Meriel, and some odd pieces of silver and four miniature paintings from the guest rooms. There were three porcelain figurines left and some silver candlesticks, but they could be missed. He paused outside his father's old bedroom. Amelia had removed her own possessions to the Dower House.

St John entered and held the candlestick aloft. The shutters were closed to prevent any sunlight fading the window and bed hangings, and dust covers had been put over the furniture. He had searched the room before and knew that the drawers and chests were empty. There was a French gilt and enamel clock that was worth a great deal, but it was too large and too easily recognisable to be sold. A table stood empty where once four gold snuffboxes belonging to his grandfather had lain.

In his will, Edward had bequeathed one each to his brothers, Joshua and William, and one each to Adam and St John. Joshua and Adam had taken theirs, and St John had sold his months ago. Only William's remained in the house. His uncle had died mysteriously last year, his body later being washed up on a beach. His will had left all his possessions to his young French wife Lisette. But she and her brother Etienne had disappeared about the same time as William died.

St John suspected that Lisette had run off with her brother. She could have quarrelled with William and Etienne killed him. They were a volatile pair, and capable of such an act – at least Etienne was. They had not been seen or heard of since and no one knew for certain what had happened. St John pocketed the snuffbox to sell. If Lisette ever returned, she had money of her own and would not miss it.

He frowned. The mystery of her disappearance had long puzzled the family. If Uncle William's death had been by foul play, it could not go unavenged. The family had employed an agent to track down Lisette and Etienne and learn the truth. He had discovered no new information. They had certainly left Trevowan in a hurry. Lisette had left her clothes behind. They were still in Uncle William's old room.

St John walked up a flight of stairs to his uncle's chamber. It suddenly struck him that if Lisette had abandoned her clothes, she could have left behind something of value. When she had fled France during the Revolution it had been with a fortune in jewels sewn into her petti-coats. Most of them had been put into a bank vault for safe keeping.

The room smelt musty. The shutters were closed as they had been in his father's room. He opened a casket on a walnut table. Inside was his uncle's silver hunter and watch chain, a gold ring and two stock pins, one emerald and one diamond. He hesitated. Would they be missed? Elspeth was bound to remember them. The watch did not work. It had been found on William's body and had been in the sea too long. But the silver casing still had value. He pocketed it, and one of the stock pins. Hopefully he would not need to sell the other pin and the ring. He had been fond of his uncle and he felt guilty at taking his things.

He turned to a closet that was full of dresses. He searched these. Lisette had spent a fortune on her fashionable clothes and there must be a market for such garments of the finest embroidered silk, taffeta and damask. Yet they were cumbersome to handle and were bound to raise questions as to why he was trying to sell them. However, some of the garments had large seed pearls sewn into the embroidered flowers on the bodices. These he sliced off with his dagger. A velvet pelisse was fastened with large garnet and pearl buttons, which he also removed. One dress still had attached to the bodice a diamond brooch in the shape of a lover's bow. He pulled this off and pocketed it with satis-faction. If Lisette had forgotten the brooch she could have forgotten other jewellery.

He snatched the dust covers from the dressing table. There was no sign of her jewel casket or ring stand. He swore roundly. But then Adam or his uncle Joshua would have ensured that any such valuables would be put in the bank vault for Lisette's future use. He cursed his family and the fact that he had been in Virginia when his father and uncle had died.

But Lisette was devious. She would be capable of hiding jewels from her husband. They had frequently quarrelled over the fact that she was selling them to buy expensive gowns. St John spent half an hour ransacking the clothes chests, running his hands along the seams and hems of her petticoats and gowns. Sewn inside a hidden placket in a boned bodice he found twenty guineas. That was more like it. His good mood did not last long, as no further money was to be found.

His stare hardened as he regarded the room. The lack of light irri-tated him, but he dared not risk a search during daylight in case the servants came upon him. A red and blue Persian rug covered a third of the floor space from the foot of the bed to the hearth. He kicked it aside, searching for any evidence that the floorboards had been tampered with. They showed no sign of having been disturbed, but then that could be too obvious a place. Lisette was more cunning than that. He studied the floor of the clothes closet. Again nothing was out of place. He thrust his hand into a dozen pairs of shoes and high-laced boots, without success, though he tore the pearl-encrusted buckles from a pair of red satin shoes, and also removed two pairs of silver buckles. He wrapped the ruined shoes in a linen chemise. They would have to be burnt in secret, as they had been too obviously mutilated and would arouse suspicion.

Convinced that there was still more booty to be found, his gaze lifted to the heavy drapes of the canopy over the four-poster bed. He stood on the mattress and ran his hand over the folds above his head. It was another fruitless search and he was about to abandon it when his fingers touched something cold and hard in a deep pleat of the fabric. His heart raced with anticipation as he strained to get a purchase on the object, but his fingers were clumsy where Lisette's had been petite. The candlestick was hampering his search and the precarious angle of his body made the flame touch a tassel that trimmed the drapes. A thin thread of flame sprang into life. In a panic he gripped it with his hand to smother it before it got out of control. His flesh seared but the flame was doused.

Swearing roundly, and now panting heavily, he put the candlestick down on a chest, and ignoring the pain in his blistered hand probed deeper into the pleat. This time his fingers closed round the object and he drew out a ruby and diamond pendant.

He sat on the bed, cradling his prize, and grinned triumphantly. His financial problems were over. His debts would be settled and he could pay the wages and still have money to spare.

He winced as he placed the pendant in his pocket. His hand was throbbing with pain. He took out a handkerchief and bound it. Then caution took over. The maids did not clean this room, but he did not want to rouse any suspicion that someone had been in here. The items he had taken still belonged to Lisette. Even if she was dead, the conditions of his uncle's will would apply, and that would split his estate equally between all the Loveday cousins.

For a moment his conscience troubled him. Then he pushed it aside. Without the sale of his plunder he would have to sell Trevowan land. He told himself that the end justified the means. Trevowan could remain intact.

He patted the bulge of jewels in his pocket with satisfaction. His family would never know that he had taken them.

His fingers were becoming more painful by the moment. He raised himself on to the mattress again and lifted the candlestick to examine the damage to the bed canopy. The dark burn mark was small and he managed to twist the material in a way that would hide it from any but the most observant. Even if it was discovered, no one would think the master of Trevowan had been responsible.

He smoothed out the Persian rug and replaced the dust sheets he had moved. The room looked just as it had when he entered it. All he had to do now was decide where to sell the trinkets he had found. He would get the best prices in Bodmin or Truro but his face was too well known in those towns.

He groaned at the thought of the festive season. Several of his friends had hinted that they would escape their families and spend Christmas at Trevowan. He had been tempted by the thought of several days of cards, hazard and hunting. But this last gambling debt had sobered him. All year luck had been against him. He had had a narrow escape this time and was resolved to learn from it.

The next morning St John was relieved to find the sky clear, with no sign of rain or mist. He ordered his horse to be saddled after breakfast, intending to ride to Fowey and obtain passage on a ship sailing to Plymouth. He would return to Trevowan before the end of the week. Whilst enjoying his breakfast of kippers and eggs he was annoyed to hear Aunt Elspeth's uneven tread in the hall. She was talking to Uncle Joshua, who must have arrived earlier at the Dower House without him noticing.

Instantly he was suspicious of their visit. Whatever their reasons for seeking him out, St John suspected it would be to his detriment. He swore under his breath, resenting this intrusion and hoped they would not stay long.

'Nephew, how fortunate that we find you up and about your business so early,' Joshua said by way of greeting.

'I have some pressing engagements and must be on the road in an hour. But it is always a pleasure to have your company, Uncle. And Elspeth too. A rare treat.'

His sarcasm was not lost on his aunt. 'Off on your travels again? You have been back less than two days. What mischief do you pursue this time?'

'It is business, Aunt.'

'What business is this? Edward did not spend days away at a time on

70

business.' Her piercing stare told him she did not believe him. He refused to be troubled by her censure. He was master here and she lived on the estate on his sufferance.

'I do not have to explain myself to you.' He voiced his irritation. 'Have you come to enquire about my welfare? As you see, I am in good health. I have no time for lectures.'

'Your welfare is always our concern.' Joshua spoke to cut across his sister's expected tirade. This meeting needed diplomacy, and Elspeth's sharp tongue would antagonise their nephew, which would gain them nothing. 'You have a heavy burden of responsibility. The family are here to help you.'

'I have experienced little of that in the past.' St John rose from the table. 'It will be more comfortable to talk in the orangery. We will adjourn there. A fire has not been made up in the winter parlour as I planned to leave early.'

The glass panes of the orangery reflected the wintry sun, and it was pleasantly warm without the need of a fire. St John gestured for his aunt and uncle to be seated and rang a hand bell to order a maid to bring them tea.

'How long will you be away?' Elspeth demanded.

'A few days.' He did not intend this to turn into an interrogation. Neither did he wish for them to suspect that he was journeying to Plymouth. It was not one of his usual haunts. 'Since my time is limited, we will forgo the usual pleasantries.' He paced the white marble floor. 'You both look serious. What is it you have to say?'

'Your manners are appalling, nephew,' Elspeth began.

Joshua held up a hand to silence her. 'We will not delay you long from your business. I am here more as an intermediary and to prevent any further family misunderstandings.'

St John frowned, still suspecting recriminations.

Joshua smiled. 'We are not here to cause trouble. The family wondered what your plans are for Christmas.'

'I have received some invitations from friends.' St John remained guarded.

'So you do not intend to be at Trevowan?' Joshua cleared his throat. 'Elspeth said you were prepared to accept a truce between yourself and Adam, but you have not joined the family at church on a Sunday, or visited your brother.'

'Business has taken me elsewhere.'

'This is a waste of time,' Elspeth cut in. 'He will not mend his wastrel ways.'

Joshua forestalled his nephew's reply. 'In your father's day the family gathered at Trevowan for the festivities. Is that your intent? If not, Adam would have us celebrate at Boscabel. There is much extra work for the servants and that may be an easier solution.'

'So Adam seeks to usurp my place as head of the family?' St John snapped.

'Nothing of the sort! It is important at this time for the family to show solidarity. It is also Hannah's first Christmas as a widow. For her sake, and that of the children, arrangements need to be settled. Mr Deverell will be at Boscabel for a month to spend some time with Tamasine. There is room for us all to stay at Adam's home. Elspeth could then relax and enjoy the hunting. Now you are a widower, the responsibility of the housekeeping and meals at Trevowan would fall to her.'

'Not that I would complain,' Elspeth assured them. 'Tradition is important. Christmas for the whole of the family has always been at Trevowan.'

St John would have preferred to spend the time with his friends, where the entertainment would be more to his liking. Though that would bring the temptation to gamble, and he did not wish to risk further debts. Last night had provided unexpected riches. He had been fortunate. He was unlikely to find another search for valuables so lucrative.

He thrust his antagonism aside. Uncle Joshua was speaking with good intentions. Adam might relish taking over the role of family host, which rankled with St John. But then the cost of such a gathering would be extensive. The money from the sale of Lisette's jewels would not go far if he entertained on the lavish scale of his father.

'We are aware that your fortunes are depleted,' Elspeth said, as if reading his thoughts. 'We would all contribute to the food. Senara will send her cook and maids to help Winnie Fraddon in the kitchen here.'

'I can entertain my relatives without accepting such charity.' St John bristled. 'My father would never—'

'Those days are past.' Joshua spoke quietly. 'Times and circumstances change. The family is much larger. It is the spirit of Christmas to share.'

Elspeth shook her head. 'Hannah is proud too. She would never accept charity and will insist on doing her share of the baking. It is also your first year as a widower. Would it not be easier for Adam and Senara to be our hosts this year?'

St John was angered by their reasonableness. It would stick in his craw to see Adam lording it as host at Boscabel. But he did not want his house overrun with servants. With so many guests, all the bedrooms would be in use. That would mean that Lisette's room must be cleared and her possessions stored in the attic. He certainly did not want the servants in there.

He rubbed his brow. 'I really had not given Christmas much thought.'

'Tradition is tradition,' Elspeth insisted.

'And since you are without a hostess,' Joshua argued, 'common sense decrees Boscabel would be the better choice.'

'So you have all discussed this behind my back and made your decision.' St John bridled. 'Adam as the favourite, with his new-found wealth and house, is now kowtowed to in his elevated status.'

'There is no question of favourites. How could we discuss it with you when you were not here?' Joshua placated. 'We simply wished to resolve the matter so that we are together at this crucial time. Loyalty is what makes us strong.'

St John continued to glower at his relatives, his lips set in a stubborn line.

Joshua spread his hands in supplication. 'Your rivalry with Adam distorts your reason. It could destroy our family. It has been a difficult year for you. If you are honest, you have made mistakes that have had serious repercussions. But that is behind us now. Let us go forward in unity. I thought you and Adam had decided to resolve your differences.'

'It is not easy when Adam continues to undermine me.'

'Adam would be your greatest ally if you allowed him. He did his best for Trevowan after Edward died and you had yet to return from America. He got little thanks, from what I hear.'

The narrowing of St John's eyes made Joshua shake his head. 'You and Adam are both more worthy than this petty rivalry. Adam will leave the choice to you. If you do not intend to spend the holy days with us, then we shall gather at Boscabel. And since your *business* takes you again from our midst, you will have little time to make adequate preparations. Why do you not join us at Boscabel, where you are most welcome?'

St John felt trapped. His anger made him irrational. He read accusation in his aunt's eyes. Then she sighed and with a rare effort conciliated. 'This year at least let us gather at Boscabel. Trevowan has been shut up too long. It would take an army of servants to clean the place properly. And I would prefer not to lose several hunting days supervising them. Next year it will all be different. Then Trevowan can be host with style and proper preparations.'

St John controlled his anger. He was allowing his pride to get in the way of common sense. He did not want the disruption or the expense. It would be a hollow victory for his twin.

Chapter Eleven

There were times when Senara felt overwhelmed by the grand preparations for Christmas. Every bedroom in the house would be occupied, with even the family who lived close staying for at least three nights. Maximillian Deverell was arriving with his mother, who would meet Tamasine for the first time, and Max's sister and her husband were accompanying them. With so many undercurrents of tension within the family, she hoped that everything would pass smoothly. Extra servants had been engaged from among the shipwrights' wives at Trevowan Hard to help with the cleaning and cooking.

Adam was working long hours at the yard. Ben Mumford, the master shipwright and overseer, had moved into their old residence, Mariner's House, with his family, and his two sons, Abel and Paul, both worked as apprentices in the yard. Senara still visited the yard every morning to attend any patients who needed her remedies, and used the room at the back of Mariner's House that Adam had had specially built for her use. It was not only the shipwrights' families who called upon her skills, but also local villagers and farm workers. Charity Mumford had been interested to learn the art of healing from Senara, and now that Adam no longer resided at the yard took her role as the wife of the master shipwright seriously. She helped Senara with the patients and was on hand to assist any of the families as diligently as a parson's wife. There were now fourteen cottages for the workers on Loveday land around the yard, and they formed a tight community.

On her visits to the yard Senara also had the opportunity to spend an hour twice a week with her sister after the children had been dismissed from the school. The other days Bridie rushed back to Polruggan for the lace-making meetings.

Today there had been few patients to attend, and as Senara rode home, her mind was filled with the tasks still to be completed at Boscabel before Maximillian Deverell and his party arrived in three days. When

75

she passed the wood at the rear of the yard she saw that a group of gypsies had set up their camp. Adam had given them permission to use the land, fish in the stream and also catch game in the wood. The dozen brightly coloured caravans brightened the grey starkness of the leafless trees. Smoke spiralled from campfires and the smell of rabbit cooking filled the air. Senara was delighted to recognise her brother Caleph's caravan amongst the group. A score of piebald ponies were tethered in a clearing and grazed on the long grass.

As she entered the camp, several of the women viewed her with suspicion and called to their children to stay close. Senara recognised most of them and greeted them by name and with a smile. Few smiled back. It had been many years since she had lived with them. Even when she had stayed with them for several months before her marriage to Adam, they had kept their distance from her. Those days seemed a lifetime away. She had left Cornwall after a misunderstanding when she thought Adam intended to marry another. Aware of the differences in their birth, she had never expected to be his bride, and although she had been carrying his child, she had fled rather than be the mistress of a married man. Adam had searched for her for months and found her at the gypsy camp the day that Nathan was born.

It would be the winter solstice in a few days – a special time for her people, as well as her elder son's birthday. Maddie, Caleph's wife, sat on the steps of her caravan. Her dark hair hung loose and a yellow shawl covered her shoulders. There were several different-coloured patches sewn into her dark blue skirt. Her unruly black hair was covered by a yellow head square

'I wondered how long it would be before you came.' Once Maddie had been Senara's best friend, but now the woman stared at her with hostility. 'You be a grand lady of the manor now, so I hear.'

Senara ignored her sniping. Life on the road could be grim and uncompromising. Maddie was jealous at her sister-in-law's prosperity, but rather than admit it, she sneered at Senara for wedding outside her race.

'How are you and the children, Maddie?'

'There be only three of them to feed now. Two died last winter and the youngest were born last month.' Her knees were spread wide, and beneath the frayed hem of her long skirt she wore sturdy boots, the leather cracked and scuffed from several years of wear. Her voice became gruff. 'My eldest daughter died trying to save her brother from drowning when he fell in the river. I lost them both.'

Senara closed her eyes against a rush of grief for the two little ones.

She knew Maddie would resent any sign of pity from her. 'Life is fraught with danger on the road. They were lovely children. I am so very sorry they died. I am pleased for you about the baby.'

The gypsy shrugged, but her dark eyes were shadowed with pain. 'I hear you've got four of your own now. Fortune just keeps smiling on you, don't it?'

Inside the caravan the baby began to cry. Maddie rose and gestured for Senara to come inside. The caravan was clean and tidy, with everything stored away. The sleeping quarters would be cramped and the beds served as seats during the day, the children's truckles sliding under the larger bed used by Maddie and Caleph. A child of about three was lying on the bed. The older child would be out laying traps for game or gathering nuts in the woods. The baby was in a battered crib. Maddie picked up the infant and put it to her breast, where it suckled noisily.

'Caleph has gone to the cottage to see Leah,' she said, her head bent over the child.

'Ma no longer lives there. She is at Polruggan now. Bridie married Adam's cousin Peter last year. He is the parson there.'

'Very nice for her. This has been a bad winter for us.'

'You are welcome to stay here for as long as you wish. There is game aplenty. And if there is anything else you need—'

'We don't want your charity,' Maddie cut in.

'When is it charity to help one's brother's family?'

'You bain't one of us no longer. Caleph leads us now but the others don't like you visiting the camp.'

Senara knew how the band disliked strangers in their midst. She was no longer part of their world, and since Maddie had made it obvious that she too regarded her as an outsider, she would in future meet her brother on neutral ground. 'I shall ride to the cottage and may pass Caleph on the way.'

Senara left the camp. She met Caleph a mile along the road. A lump rose in her throat to see him riding his piebald stallion. His black hair curled to his shoulders and his skin was nut brown, though she was concerned to see how drawn he looked, with deep furrows curving from his nose to his mouth. She also noticed that his nose had been broken and had set at a twisted angle and he now sported a gold tooth at the front of his mouth. The horse fairs must have been favourable to him. However, his red shirt beneath his jerkin was ragged around the collar and his spotted neckerchief was frayed at the ends.

'What's happened to Ma? The cottage was deserted.' He leapt to the ground in one easy movement. He had been riding bareback.

'Ma is fine.' Senara dismounted and ran to hug him. She felt him momentarily stiffen, unused to such displays of emotion. Then he laughed and embraced her. 'Same old Senara. Impetuous as ever. I thought you'd be all cool and aloof in your manners by now.'

'In some things I will never change.' She gazed adoringly into his dark eyes. 'I've missed you. Why did you stay away so long? Adam said there was always land here for you to set up camp. You do intend to winter here?'

He grinned, but there was a stiffness and wariness in his stance that had not been present in their past meetings. It saddened her.

'If that welcome still holds,' he said. 'Though do you want a reminder of your gypsy blood now that your husband has done so well for himself? The name of Adam Loveday is never far from people's lips. They speak of him with reverence. He is owner of the shipyard now, and a man of property, so I hear.'

'Adam would never turn away my family.'

'But we would be an embarrassment to him.'

'Not to Adam.'

'It would do him no good in the eyes of his neighbours.'

She sighed in exasperation. 'There is always a place for you here. And you would not feel happy mixing with our more illustrious neighbours, would you? Or have you put your roving ways behind you and wish to settle down yourself with a farm?'

'I could never give up the travelling.' He laughed and held her at arm's length to allow his gaze to travel over her figure. 'You are more beautiful than I remember. And you look like a real high-bred woman. I've no need to ask if your husband treats you well.'

They walked side by side, leading their horses by the reins. Senara said, 'I met Maddie at the camp. I was sorry to hear about your children drowning.'

He nodded but did not comment, and she added, 'Your wife did not seem pleased to see me. I have no place in the camp now.'

'And I would not be welcome at your grand Boscabel, would I, sister?'

She could feel the rift widening between them. She adored Caleph and did not want to lose him from her life. 'There are other places we can meet. But let us not put barriers between us. It is such a joy to see you.'

'And you, sweet sister. Is Ma living with you? Though I cannot see her happy in your fine house.'

Senara explained the changes in Leah and Bridie's lives.

'Little Bridie has wed a parson?' Caleph's shock was obvious. He shook his head, his weathered features set in resigned lines. 'How you both have changed. Life has been good to you. And Bridie is also a schoolteacher, while I can do no more than make a mark for my name. Who would have thought it?'

'I am very proud of her.'

'Aye, both my sisters have achieved much. I still think of Bridie as a child. And Ma lives with her at Polruggan. It bain't far. So Ma sees a lot of you?'

'I will bring her and Bridie to visit you at the old cottage tomorrow.'

He nodded and vaulted on to his stallion's back. His expression was sombre. 'Our worlds are very different – even for Ma and Bridie. I don't fit in with them no more.'

'You will break Ma's heart if she hears you speaking that way.' Senara desperately needed to reassure him. She refused to admit that their worlds did not mix. 'Bridie and I care for you. You are part of us. There is game and fish aplenty in the copse. I do hope you will spend the winter here.'

He shrugged and looked into the distance. 'There are wild ponies on the moor. I will break some of them for the spring fair. We need a safe place to stay through the winter. I'll make sure the others cause you no trouble.'

He had again withdrawn from her and Senara felt a stab of remorse. How could she expect to be part of her brother's life in the same way as she had been before? And she was ashamed to acknowledge that she hoped the gypsies would cause no trouble in the district.

As the day of the arrival of the Deverell party drew near, Tamasine was beset with apprehension. She had been filled with confusion since she had accepted Max's proposal. Why had she rushed into giving him an answer?

With each day she became more nervous at meeting her fiancé and his family. It made her restless. She had not seen Max for two months and had only received one letter from him in that time. In many ways he was still a stranger to her, and her apprehension was not something she felt she could discuss with her family. To keep herself occupied she often rode to Hannah's farm. There, to fill her time, she either exercised Japhet's mares or kept the children out of Hannah's way when her cousin was busy.

This morning she returned from a ride and entered the farmhouse kitchen, where Hannah was sorting through a pile of children's clothes.

The older woman sighed and held up a pair of woollen hose, wiggling her finger through a hole in the knee. 'These are not worth repairing. Florence is accident-prone and is always falling over.'

'Give them to me, I will darn them.'

'They are past mending. Or beyond my skill.' Hannah pulled a face. 'But I suppose I should try. There have been so many expenses of late.'

Tamasine took the hose from her. 'I will mend them. I enjoy sewing and darning, and these are less taxing on the fingers than when I worked in the milliner's shop.' She rummaged through Hannah's sewing box, which was on the sideboard, and found a needle and darning wool. Ten minutes later the task was done and she held them up. 'These should now last through the winter. Providing Florrie does not fall over every single day.'

Hannah laughed and shook her head. 'It is strange to think of you as a sewing woman. I have no patience for it. And you are so full of life. You rarely sit still.'

Tamasine pulled a face. 'Sewing was a penance at school. We had to sit for hours on end at our work, but it was better than scrubbing the floors with cold water on a freezing day. I used to sew and daydream of the life my mother led and whether I would be a part of it.' She grimaced. 'They were terrible days and best forgotten. But I do not mind sewing. There is quite a pile here. Let me help you. I never dreamed I'd have a life with my father's family, or even learn who he was. I have been fortunate. I owe so much to you all.'

'You have brought us pleasure. We are the fortunate ones,' Hannah reassured her. She sensed something was troubling the young woman, but knew that if Tamasine wished to discuss it she would raise the matter in her own time. 'Much as I appreciate your help, are you not needed at Boscabel?'

Tamasine shrugged and selected some wool to darn another child's sock. 'Senara said she did not need me today. She is taking Leah to visit her brother. Have you met the gypsies of Senara's family?'

'No. Caleph is aware of the problems it could cause for Senara if his group settle too often in the area. I have had trouble from some of their bands in the past.' Hannah frowned. 'Much as I have great respect for Senara and Bridie, their brother's presence can do no good for the repu-tation of the family, which has suffered so much in recent years through the wilder exploits of my brother and cousins.'

'Yet Adam would no more deny them access to his land than he would any member of our family,' Tamasine added. 'He would see it as disloyalty to his wife.'

'I agree. But how would your Mr Deverell view our association with gypsies?'

A shudder of fear passed through Tamasine. 'I have no idea if he knows of Senara's gypsy blood. You could never guess on meeting her. She is now every inch a gentlewoman of refinement. Max overlooked my birth when he asked me to be his bride. That is quite remarkable and I revere him for such consideration. But when first we met he seemed to uphold such rigid principles of family and honour.'

In her growing agitation she pricked her finger and put it to her mouth to suck the blood and stop it bleeding. Her heart was beating uncomfortably fast as she continued, 'Max is a complex man. I hardly know him at all. That is daunting when our wedding is so close.'

Hannah saw the uncertainty in the young woman's eyes. 'Max is an exceptional man. He did not strike me as a hypocrite, and unlike Rupert Carlton, who betrayed your love so heartlessly, he would never break his betrothal vows to you. Is that what you fear?'

Tamasine hung her head. Her emotions were in turmoil where Maximillian Deverell was concerned. She knew it was her duty to marry well, and a fateful visit to London last year, when she had been subjected to Margaret Mercer and Amelia's diligent matchmaking, had filled her with panic. None of the men they introduced her to interested her. She had been deeply affected by Rupert's betrayal. It had knocked her confidence. The years of ridicule in the ladies' academy, where all the girls were illegitimate, had shown her how a bastard was regarded with the same disdain as a leper or outcast. Her pride had made her rebel. She could not be responsible for the circumstances of her birth and it incensed her that she should be regarded as a creature of contempt. To the outside world she showed a brave face, for she would allow no one to think her birth made her a victim.

She was aware how fortunate she had been that Edward Loveday had accepted her into his family when he had learned of her existence. To be part of such a family was something she had dreamed of as a child. But even so she could not crush her spirit, and though her pride was deemed false for a woman of her circumstances, she would not deny it and marry a man she did not respect and ultimately could not love.

There was no question that she respected Max and held him in the highest esteem. He was handsome, charming and had proved his bravery by saving her from abduction and rape. Any woman would admire a man for such chivalry and courage. Undoubtedly she was attracted to him. The few times he had kissed her had left her weak-kneed and half swooning with pleasure. But still she held back on accepting that she loved him.

'You do not doubt Max's devotion, do you?' Hannah looked concerned.

'No . . . but . . . Well, I have met his sister Venetia and she is charming, but what of his mother? Venetia hinted that she could be something of a martinet. She is very proud of her ancient lineage. How will she ever accept that her only son is to marry a by-blow?'

'You must never think of yourself that way. You are not responsible for the circumstances of your birth.'

'But it stopped Rupert from marrying me.' Her voice was thick with pain.

'Rupert Carlton was weak. Max loves you. He will never play you false.'

'But what if birth and breeding are so important to his family? His mother will despise me.'

Hannah reached across the table and squeezed Tamasine's hand. 'Then she would be a very foolish woman. Max will never allow her to treat you with anything but the greatest respect.'

'It would cause problems in the marriage, though, would it not?' Briefly the fear of rejection was stark in Tamasine's eyes, and she hung her head, afraid of revealing too much.

Hannah had meet several women who prided their high breeding above all else. She prayed that Clarissa Deverell was not such a one.

Tamasine fell quiet as she continued her sewing, her thoughts troubled. Max's proposal had been a shock. At first she had thought he regarded her as a wayward child. He had been aloof and enigmatic, showing no interest in her as a woman. During the painful months in London when Amelia had been desperate to marry her off to be free of her responsibilities to a stepdaughter she had never accepted, she had been introduced to several possible suitors, but had taken to none of them. Amelia had accused her of expecting too much from a suitor and told her that she should be grateful that they offered her security and respectability. Tamasine was young and idealistic. The courageous and adventurous lives of her half-brother and cousins had coloured her views of men. She had dreamed of a man who would be dashing and bold like Adam or her father Edward, or who had a lively, intelligent wit like cousin Thomas. The eligible men her stepmother and aunt had introduced to her were bank clerks, shopkeepers, widowers who needed a mother for their children, or witless fops. During their first meetings Max had been coolly polite, hardly seeming to notice her at all. On more than one occasion in his company she had shown her wilder side and she had learned that he expected sobriety and decorum in a woman.

She stifled a heartfelt sigh. Max was ten years older than herself and she had found his self-possession and commanding presence rather daunting. She had witnessed his wit and charm, the sharpness of his mind when he had been a family guest, and in his company she had always been strangely tongue-tied. His valour in saving her from abduction had been outstanding, but he had told her in no uncertain terms that she was a wilful, ungrateful creature who had caused her family ill-deserved pain by running away from a match Amelia had planned for her. He had been shocked that she had taken work in a milliner's shop to support herself. Tamasine had thought that he despised her.

When he had arrived unexpectedly at Boscabel, his presence had disturbed her, for she always found his company unsettling. His proposal had been a complete shock. Apparently he had admired her fortitude and his anger had stemmed from the danger she had placed herself in.

Hannah's soft laugh jolted her back to the present.

'You are wool-gathering, Tamasine. And is that a blush? I hope it is for sweet memories of the intriguing Mr Deverell.' She laughed again. 'Methinks your betrothed is not as staid as you protest. Did he steal a kiss or two?'

To her annoyance, Tamasine's blush deepend. 'You are a cruel tease, cousin. He was the perfect gentleman.'

Hannah continued to regard her with amusement. 'Your blush says otherwise. And who would want a perfect gentleman as a lover?'

Tamasine threw the sock she was darning at her cousin. 'I refuse to discuss such matters. It would be unladylike.'

'So he did kiss you and you found it enjoyable? And if I am any judge of men, the experience was more pleasurable than any kiss that young tyke Carlton gave you.'

The heat in Tamasine's cheeks flared like a blazing furnace. 'It was, but I know so little of men. Does that pleasure mean I love him? Or was it the wildness in my blood? I have heard how people view a daughter born out of wedlock . . .' Her stare was overbright and defiant. 'They think that if the mother was a wanton, then the child will be likewise.'

'The Lady Eleanor Keyne was no wanton,' Hannah retorted fiercely. 'She loved your father. Do not allow your experiences with Carlton to cloud the true meaning of love. Passion is but part of it: there must also be respect, feeling alive in that person's company and knowing they are your best friend as well as your lover.'

'Was that how it was for you and Oswald?'

Hannah nodded, the sudden overwhelming pain of her loss bringing a rush of tears to her eyes. She did not attempt to brush them aside.

'I am sorry, Hannah. You must miss him so much.' Tamasine could feel the now-familiar panic tightening her stomach. That was the love she craved in her marriage. Could it be like that for her and Maximillian? If it were not, how would she find lasting happiness with him?

Hannah studied her closely, a frown showing that despite her own pain she was concerned for her cousin. 'I do miss Oswald, but I have so many wonderful memories. Enough to last me a lifetime.'

'But you are young. You will marry again.'

'It would have to be an exceptional man to take the place of Oswald in my heart and my life.'

'And that will happen in time.'

Hannah shrugged. 'If fate wills it.'

Chapter Twelve

Tamasine was more nervous than she had ever been in her life. This was the moment she had been both looking forward to and dreading. Their guests had arrived. She stood in the oak-panelled hall to greet them with Adam and Senara. The square entrance with its flagstone floor was large and a fire burned in the stone fireplace. From its centre a carved staircase rose majestically to the upper floors. On a wooden chest a large blue and white Delft bowl was filled with dried lavender and rose petals which scented the air, and a dozen candles lit the entrance, their flames reflected in the polished wood.

She bit her lip to quell her trepidation and held back as the others swarmed around Max and his mother. Clarissa Deverell was dressed in a russet velvet cloak, its wide hood trimmed with sable. She was as tall as Tamasine, slim and upright. The slender wrist she extended to Adam to kiss was encased in a wide band of diamonds, and the same jewels glittered in her ears and around her throat. She intended no one to be in doubt of her position or her wealth. She stood beside her son, her eyes sharp and critical as they assessed her hosts and her surroundings. Tamasine's heart sank.

Her gaze sought Max for reassurance. Her fiancé was an inch taller than Adam's two yards' height. When he removed the triple-caped greatcoat, his slim figure and broad shoulders presented a commanding figure. Unerringly his stare settled upon Tamasine and he smiled. It was enough for her confidence to return and her pulse beat in expectation for the chance of a moment alone with him. Just as he moved to join her, his mother asked a question that Tamasine could not hear and Max stooped to answer.

Tamasine controlled her impatience. She was also disappointed to see that Max's sister did not appear to be with the party. They had become friends in London and Venetia's companionship would have eased Tamasine's fear at meeting her future mother-in-law. From what she had heard of Clarissa Deverell, she was a formidable woman, and like her only son had a strong sense of the proprieties. Tamasine was anxious that Mrs Deverell would not find her wanting. Would she see her as a child? How could Tamasine face her if she knew of how Max had rescued her in London after she had almost compromised her reputation? And how would Mrs Deverell receive a by-blow into her family?

'And where is the delightful creature who is to be my new daughter?' Clarissa demanded in strident tones that tightened the knot of apprehension in Tamasine's insides.

Her fiancé's mother had been regarded as one of the great beauties of her day. She remained a striking woman, with upswept blonde hair and high cheekbones. Her Roman nose and wide mouth gave her an imperious air, and the hauteur in the grey eyes seemed to look into the depths of one's soul. Tamasine was not easily intimidated, but this woman sent shivers of dread through her.

The family parted around them and Tamasine had a clearer view of the woman who could be her friend or her greatest adversary. This was a woman whose lineage went back to the Norman Conquest – a woman whose blood had mixed with Plantagenet royalty. A woman who could have married the heir to an earldom but had chosen instead to wed Marcus Deverell, a colonel in the King's Hussars.

Tamasine swallowed painfully, her throat dry with apprehension. Then her pride came to her rescue. She was a Loveday, and unashamed of her heritage.

Max came forward to take her arm. His gaze held hers and the tenderness and warmth in its depths was the only reassurance she needed.

'Mama, may I present Miss Tamasine Loveday, the sweetest and most incomparable of women.'

He raised Tamasine's hand to his lips as he spoke, and a flush of pleasure simmered through her body. He was more handsome than she remembered and his smile rendered her breathless.

'Incomparable indeed if she has taken your fancy, my son.' The tone was charming but cool and the penetrating glance that swept over Tamasine was sharper than a hawk. 'She is quite beautiful – as I expected – but sweet . . . I detect a certain feistiness in her eyes. She has spirit. That can be a blessing or a curse.' She bowed her head to Tamasine and favoured her with a tight smile. 'I look forward to furthering our acquaintance, Miss Loveday.'

Clarissa Deverell then turned to Adam and began to bombard him with questions about the history of the house.

Feeling dismissed and of little consequence in the older woman's eyes, Tamasine groaned under her breath, 'Your mama does not like me, Max.'

He squeezed her hand. 'Nonsense. Mama is charmed by you. And despite her words she admires spirit in a woman. Also intelligence and resourcefulness. To test your mettle she can be deliberately provoking, and I suspect she will not find you a disappointment.'

The sparkle in his eyes warmed her blood, but there was also a containment about him. He was a man who guarded his emotions and was not easy to read. That made him more intriguing, and when she had not known him better she had misinterpreted that aloofness as arrogance.

'I do not see Venetia with you.' She could not contain her disappointment.

'She is indisposed with a cold that has settled on her chest. Mama declared it unwise for her to travel. My sister sends you her love.'

'I hope her recovery will be swift and her Christmas is not spoiled.'

'Her husband has a large family who are always visiting.'

The stentorian tones of Clarissa Deverell were now questioning Adam on his family. He laughed. 'My family are ordinary people who I believe have led extraordinary lives, but then most lives have a remarkable quality about them, do you not agree, Mrs Deverell?'

'I certainly do not. You are imprudent, young man. Quality is in the breeding. One must not forget that, for therein lies our greatness.'

Adam spoke with charm, but there was a ring of iron in his reply. 'Then with respect, Mrs Deverell, I would quote our greatest bard – a man of humble origin but one who has left a magnificent legacy to all mankind. "Be not afraid of greatness: some men are born great, some achieve greatness, and some have greatness thrust upon them."'

'You have a clever wit but I do not agree with your sentiments. You cannot deny breeding.' Her voice rang with an authority which would not have her opinion disputed. 'We passed several notable houses in the last stages of our journey. Will we meet your neighbours?'

'Squire Penwithick will join us. And Lord Fetherington has invited us to the hunt and ball on New Year's Day. We will stay at the hall for two days.'

'I do not believe I have met his lordship,' Clarissa declared.

'He prefers life in the country to that in London.'

Clarissa's reply was lost to Tamasine, but her foreboding grew that her future mother-in-law had such concern for breeding and status.

Their guests had retired to their rooms to change their travelling clothes and to refresh themselves. Tamasine also changed, into a blue velvet gown trimmed with silver braid. The slim line of the gown gathered under her bust flattered her trim figure. Her first meeting with Max had made her realise how favourably she had come to regard him. She was now eager to spend as much time as possible in his company.

Her satin slippers were silent on the oak floorboards, and as she passed the bedchamber allotted to Clarissa Deverell the door was ajar. She glimpsed Mrs Deverell seated before her dressing table, her elderly maid attending to her hair.

'This must be a happy occasion for you, mistress, to meet the master's future bride.' The maid spoke with the familiarity of a servant who had been engaged by the family for a great many years.

'It has so far been informative. Happy . . . well, that is too early to say.'

The words made Tamasine stop in her tracks and pull back to conceal herself behind a large Chinese vase on a marble pedestal.

'The girl is pretty enough but younger than I expected,' Mrs Deverell went on. 'And the family is in *trade*; that is not something I approve of. Though Maximillian assures me they are an old and respected family. On the great-grandmother's side it may be. She was a Penhaligan. But the Lovedays have been living at Trevowan a mere four generations.'

Tamasine felt the colour drain from her face. How dare this woman speak so discourteously about her family!

'You have said many times that you despaired the young master would never settle down,' answered the maid.

'I had expected him to be more circumspect in his choice. I thought he would see through the wiles of a fortune-hunter. The Lovedays may own a shipyard, but it is far from large and has seen more prosperous times. Also their reputation is quite scandalous – one of them was convicted of highway robbery. The rogue was sent to Botany Bay but not before he had secured himself an heiress in marriage . . .'

Tamasine could not bear to hear more. It was obvious Mrs Deverell despised both herself and her family. She had never felt so mortified or humiliated. She had not even considered how wealthy Max was when he proposed to her. She had not sought money and position, only happiness with a man she could love and respect. Clearly Max had not enlightened his mother as to the truth of her birth. If he had, the arrogant matriarch would never even receive her, let alone accept her as her son's bride.

And did Max feel the same? The thought flayed her to the core. Had he come to regret his impetuous proposal? He would be too honourable

to break his word. All her fears crowded back. The rejection and humiliation at being born a bastard, that she had never been allowed to live
down as a child, had destroyed her trust in her fellow man. Had not
Rupert Carlton confirmed that she was unworthy of marrying a
gentleman?

She ran down the corridor, needing time on her own to review the
raw emotion that was grinding through her. If she returned to her
bedchamber someone would soon find her there. To her consternation
as she passed a landing window she saw that it was raining heavily. There
would be no sanctuary for her in the garden. The family rooms would
soon be occupied and she was too out of countenance to endure polite
chatter. The nursery would be too noisy, the demands of the children
allowing her no peace to sort out her thoughts. She could feel her rage
increasing against Clarissa Deverell. In such circumstances anger would
be her worst enemy. When she faced their guests she must be calm and
in control of her emotions.

To reach the minstrels' gallery in the old hall where she knew she
could find seclusion she had to climb a narrow spiral staircase. In the
gallery she sat in darkness and dropped her head into her hands. She
could not endure the idea that Clarissa Deverell would make Max
ashamed of her lowly origins. She had sounded no better than Lord
Keyne, Rupert's guardian, who had forced Tamasine's first love to wed
another.

Was that to be her fate again? Her pride rebelled. She would release
Max from their betrothal. Instead of relief, her defiance sent a spear of
pain through her heart and she was unprepared for the depths of
wretchedness that now swamped her. It was a shock to acknowledge
how deeply she loved Max. At the moment of accepting her feelings
for him, was the chance of happiness about to be stripped from her?

Voices drifted to her from the room below. The family were gathering to enjoy a glass of madeira before they dined. She lifted her head
from her hands and stood up. Clarissa Deverell's words still haunted her.
Her chin tilted with stubborn pride and the gleam of battle was in her
eyes.

'Eavesdroppers hear no good of themselves, but forewarned is fore-
armed,' she declared to herself.

She stared down at the assembled group below. The walls of the old
hall were decorated with garlands of holly, ivy and mistletoe. The huge
Yule log, specially selected by Senara and cut by Adam, burned in one
of the hearths and would be kept alight throughout the festivities. A
second fire had also been lit in the fireplace at the far end of the room

for the greater warmth and comfort of their guests. For his first Christmas at Boscabel Adam was determined to spare no expense. Half a hundred candles had been lit in the wall sconces and two central chandeliers.

Her gaze was drawn like a lodestone to Max, who stood at ease talking to Adam. Again she marvelled at how her betrothed cut such a distinguished figure in his burgundy coat and dove-grey breeches. One hand rested on his hip, displaying a cream waistcoat decorated with black and gold thread. Amongst the white ruffles of his cravat gleamed a large ruby pin, and a single gold ring adorned his little finger. His expression was intense but not severe as he listened to Adam, showing his lively intelligence and interest in others. The easy grace with which he carried himself revealed him to be unassuming but self-confident. How could she have doubted that she loved him?

She gripped her hands together over her heart to still its frantic beating. Her emotion overwhelmed her. This was a man worthy of her love. She vowed that nothing and no one would come between them.

Then, as though sensing Tamasine's presence, Max lifted his gaze to the gallery. The faintest of shadows darkened his brow at finding her there. Then he smiled and raised his glass in a silent toast to her. It was a simple gesture but it heartened her that his love had not changed. It confirmed her resolution to have faith in him. He might hold his mother in the highest regard, but Tamasine doubted anything Mrs Deverell said would sway him to turn against his chosen bride.

She returned his smile with such radiance that Max's expression softened with tenderness. At that moment into her vision floated Clarissa Deverell, who placed a possessive hand on her son's arm. Her stare was raised to see what held her son's attention, and she stiffened at recognising Tamasine. The two women's eyes locked, battle igniting in both of them. Clarissa Deverell's features tightened with disapproval. Tamasine combated the older woman's censure with an assured smile. The gauntlet had been thrown down and she was determined to rise to the challenge.

'I love Max. I will not lose him without a fight,' she declared under her breath. She would show the haughty Mrs Deverell that a Loveday was very much the equal of her mouldering old lineage.

Chapter Thirteen

Hannah was attending one of Japhet's colts in the stable. It had still been dark when Mark asked her to inspect the horse. It had injured its forelock in the night and sustained a deep gash. She had cleaned the wound and strapped on a poultice to prevent infection, but was concerned that something must have spooked the colt for it to lash out in such a manner.

A cock crowed and the sky was still pink from the rising sun. The weather would be uncertain today and the outside work must be done before it rained.

'Mrs Rabson, the cart's not in the barn and Dick Caine bain't delivered the milk.' Tilda ambled into the stable, rubbing the sleep from her eyes and yawning. 'And Mab bain't showed her face yet. She were supposed to help us in the buttery this morning. Bain't right she be shirking again.'

'Go to the cottage and tell Mab I want to see her right away.'

A poultice was placed on the colt's leg and a nosebag of bran over his muzzle to help to settle him, and Hannah went to the yard pump to wash her hands. She had assumed the absence of the carthorse meant Dick had left to deliver the milk. If he had taken the cart it meant only one other thing: he had used it for illicit means. She would check with Sam first to ensure that he had not sent the farmhand on another errand. Dick Caine was supposed to be helping Mark and Sam with cutting back a reed bed that had overgrown in one of the ditches and caused it to flood. She could see only two figures working on the edge of the south field.

Davey was by the woodpile filling a wicker basket with logs for the fires. She called to him. 'Please ask Mr Deacon to come up to the house.'

Davey ran off and Hannah saw Tilda returning from the Caines' cottage. She was alone. The dairymaid's face was red and angry. Hannah entered the farmhouse kitchen. The rabbit stew should have been put on to cook an hour ago; the floor was unswept and the breakfast dishes were still in the sink — all work that was supposed to have been done by Mab. Tilda found Hannah in the larder counting out the turnips and onions. Aggie was upstairs dressing Luke and cleaning the bedrooms.

'Mab was snoring in her bed and stank of brandy. I couldna rouse the lazy slut, Mrs Rabson, so I threw a bucket of water over her and got a torrent of abuse for me pains. At least she'll smell a bit sweeter now.'

Sam arrived at the house before Mab. He came into the kitchen where Hannah was peeling vegetables.

'You should not be doing that,' he said. 'Where's Mab?'

'Still in her cottage. But more importantly, where is her husband? The horse and cart have gone but the milk churns are still in the yard. Did you set him other work this morning?'

'The milk delivery has to be done first. I thought he had set out early for once when I saw the cart gone. I am sorry, I should have checked more thoroughly, Mrs Rabson.' He stood awkwardly inside the door, conscious of the thick mud on his boots. He had removed his slouch hat on entering and his dark blond hair was freshly washed, and as always he never started work without shaving.

'There is no need to apologise, Sam. Dick knows his duties. He must have taken the cart last night but I heard nothing. He's been forbidden to use it to carry contraband. And to miss the milk delivery adds to the insult of his disobedience and the lack of respect he shows to my orders.'

Sam's jaw hardened. 'It's time you got rid of them. They are lazy parasites. With respect, Mrs Rabson, I'll send them packing now.'

'But it is coming up to Christmas. How can I throw them out of the cottage in the middle of winter?'

'It is not as though they have not had their warnings. I would have dismissed them months ago. You are too kind-hearted. They are taking advantage of your generous nature.'

Hannah nodded. She disliked making the couple homeless but she had given them too many chances. They would never change their idle ways. She could not afford to pay servants who did not do their work.

'You do not have to be the one to sack them. I'll speak with Mab now. She will be ready to leave by the time Dick returns.'

As she spoke they heard the cart pull into the yard and Dick swearing and cursing at the horse. Hannah went outside. The horse had lost a shoe and was lame and hobbling. She was appalled that Dick had continued to drive him.

Sam pulled Dick off the cart and threw him up against the front wheels. 'You could have ruined that horse. He'll not be fit for work for weeks. You're no use to Mrs Rabson. You and that lazy slut of a wife can get out of the cottage today.'

Dick was pale and shaking. 'You can't turn us out. We'll starve and freeze to death.'

'You should have thought of that before you took the cart last night. You threw in your lot with the smugglers, let them look after you.'

'I don't hold with the likes of smuggling! You got it wrong, Deacon.' Caine squirmed; his eyes darting towards Hannah were round with fear. 'I had no choice, Mrs Rabson. They would have done for me if I didn't obey them.'

'If they had threatened you I would have informed the authorities.' She had lost patience with his lies.

'Your loyalty is to Mrs Rabson,' Sam rapped out. 'Do you wish to place charges against Sawle?'

Caine broke out in a sweat. 'It weren't Sawle. It be more than my life's worth . . .'

'Get your things and go, or I will be pressing charges for theft of a horse and cart. Now get on your way.'

Dick wrung his hands. 'Mrs Rabson, I had no choice. I beg you . . .'

Hannah turned away. She was furious that Sawle had used her servant to transport his contraband. 'You had every choice. You chose greed and loyalty to Sawle and blatantly disregarded my orders.' She walked into the farmhouse as Caine started to swear at Sam. The cussing was cut off short when Sam grabbed hold of Caine's jacket and frogmarched him towards his cottage.

Hannah was shaken by the events. Her conscience troubled her that she had condemned the couple to a winter of hardship. If they found no work at the hiring fair they would have to beg on the streets or go to the workhouse.

The responsibility of running the farm was heavy on her shoulders. She missed Oswald so much. The knife slipped from her fingers as she peeled a carrot. She could at least make up a basket of food and ensure that their wages were paid up to date. She counted out the coins and wrapped a large wedge of cheese, a freshly baked loaf and the remains of yesterday's meat pie into a piece of cloth. They would probably drink the money away at the first kiddley, but that was their choice.

Aggie emerged from the parlour, where she had been setting the fires and dusting. 'I heard what happened. Good riddance to them.'

'Take this food to their cottage,' Hannah said, and then busied herself tackling the pile of dirty dishes.

Sam came into the kitchen as Aggie left. The dishes in the sink had blurred before Hannah's eyes. She straightened her shoulders and turned to Sam but could not meet his gaze.

'They are not worth you upsetting yourself, Mrs Rabson.'

'Sawle used Caine to get back at me because I informed the authorities that he stored his illicit goods on Japhet's land.'

'Caine has been in league with the smugglers for years. That couple were taking advantage of your kind heart. I will hire another labourer and female servant after the holy days. You are to spend the festivities with your family at Boscabel and there is little work to be done on the farm. Mark can deliver the milk.'

'Thank you, Sam.'

'I am just doing my job.' He shrugged and his expression became grave. Since his return to the farm he had been preoccupied and kept his own company.

'Is aught troubling you, Sam? I have seen little of you since you returned. Were there problems at the funeral? You did not say who had died, but they must have been close to you.'

He did not hold her gaze, which was uncharacteristic of Sam. Obviously he did not wish to discuss the matter. In another she would have found such conduct disrespectful, but Sam was no ordinary field hand.

'I'm sorry. I had no wish to pry,' she amended hastily. 'This day has unsettled me.'

His gaze now regarded her with an intensity that she found disconcerting. His voice was gruff when he replied. 'It was my mother's funeral.'

'My condolences, Sam. I am sorry.'

He turned away but she could sense his pain. She lifted a hand to comfort him, and then let it drop, as the gesture would be inappropriate. She realised with a start that she did not regard Sam merely as a hired servant. She relied on his wisdom and his uncompromising support in the way she would a friend.

The sound of angry voices carried to them from across the field. Through the window Hannah saw Mab repeatedly striking the shoulders of her husband with the bundle of clothes she carried as they left the cottage. She was screaming abuse at him.

'I'll escort the Caines from the farm,' Sam said. 'Dick can be vindictive and I'll give him no chance to cause damage.'

He strode out purposefully to confront the couple. It was a task

Hannah would not have enjoyed, and again she realised how much she relied on her overseer in times of need.

She picked up a list of jobs to be done with Christmas approaching. She wanted to make it special for the children, for they, like her, would be missing Oswald. Her eyes misted as her grief for her husband struck without warning. It was at special family times like this that she missed him the most. And he was not the only one who would not be here to celebrate the festivities. It would be so wonderful to look up and see the tall figure of her elder brother duck his head to enter the room. His laughter would ring out as he swept her into his arms for an unceremonious hug. Where was he now? Surely Gwen had been reunited with him and he had received news of his pardon. They should be on the high seas now, returning to England. Japhet's return was indeed something joyful to look forward to.

She shivered at an icy blast from the door of the kitchen as Davey ran in and left the door open. Hannah closed it and gazed out at the sky. There was a sharpness in the air that had not been present for the last few winters. This year there could be snow at Christmas.

Chapter Fourteen

Japhet sweated in the hot sun. He had never known temperatures like it, even on the hottest days in Cornwall. He had rolled up the sleeves of his shirt and his arms were brown as polished oak from his labours on the land. His long black hair was tied back with a strip of leather, and though in England it was fashionable for men to be clean-shaven, he had grown a goatee beard. He was smoothing the lines of the front door of his house with a plane to ensure a weatherproof fit. Tonight they would move out of the single-room building he had hastily erected to protect them from the worst of the weather, to sleep in this four-room structure with its front veranda that looked towards the river half a mile away.

The heat made it hard to breathe, and by midday work was impossible unless there was shade. He realised with a start that in a few days it would be Christmas. A Christmas unlike any other he had experienced before. He would celebrate it in the house he had built with his own hands. He had called his new land Trewenna Place in memory of his home and had worked from first light to dark to get it finished in time for Gwen and his son to spend Christmas in a proper home. He wiped the sweat from his brow. It would be a proud moment when he carried his wife over the threshold. He stared around at the trees that had been cleared. The two convicts he had been assigned by the government were working in the fields. Two other men he now employed who had worked their sentence were in the sawpit. To cut down on the cost of buying planks from the sawmill in Sydney, he had dug the pit for his own use, modelling it after the one at Trevowan Hard. To his surprise it had turned into a profitable venture as more settlers took up land grants in this district and were prepared to pay Japhet for cut wood. He had built an outhouse to shelter his workers from the heat and a pile of wood was growing that would be suitably seasoned.

The carpentry skills he had seen and learned as a youth helping in his uncle's shipyard were invaluable here. Uncle Edward had offered him an apprenticeship as a shipwright and he had refused it. He had not intended to spend his life in such hard toil. Ironically, the knowledge he had gained in his youth had made him a man of influence as other settlers came to him for advice. Many like his friend Silas Hope had no experience of life outside a town, but had seen the new colony as a way of improving their lives and status.

Japhet drew on skills he had taken for granted and discarded. How wrong he had been. So much of his former life he had believed was unimportant now ensured his survival and the success of new friends and neighbours. He had often helped Hannah on the farm; usually when his creditors in London were clamouring for payment and he needed to escape their vigilance until success at the card tables enabled him to settle his debts. Yet now these carpentry and farming skills gave him a far greater sense of fulfilment than ever he had felt gaming and whoring. Even the store in Parramatta had benefited from his easy charm, and he had the gift of convincing money-strapped settlers to purchase goods from him rather than from the government stores. He had expected further repercussions from the New South Wales Corp, but there had been several incidents of convicts escaping to the bush and the military were involved in tracking them down, so Japhet had been left alone.

'No experience is ever wasted,' he remembered Senara once saying. She was a wise woman indeed. Even his wilder days when he had lived by his wits had made him a sharp observer of men and situations, something that was an asset here. It was as though every event from his past had come together in perfect symmetry: each circumstance had been a stepping-stone that had moulded the path of his present and his future.

Japhet shook his head and chuckled at dwelling upon so deep a philosophy. He had spent too long in the sun. He rolled his shoulders to ease the ache in his muscles. He might not take his achievements seriously, but he was proud of what he had accomplished in this new land. Apart from the government land grant, he had purchased another adjoining plot from a ticket-of-leave convict who had farmed his land for a year until the floods had wiped out his crop. It was on this land that Japhet had located the sawpit. His reputation as a fighter and a leader earned on the voyage here had won the respect of the old lags who worked in the sawpit, and they knew he would not be a master to cross. Even so he did not entirely trust them. These men had been transported for larceny and forgery. That Japhet had been arrested for highway robbery had put him above them in the hierarchy of the criminal world. Though he may have been innocent of the crime for which he had been tried and found guilty, on an earlier occasion he had slipped from grace and robbed a coach to settle his gaming debts. For years previous to that he had lived on his wits and walked a tightrope perilously close to the wrong side of the law. But that was all behind him now. The life of a rakehell no longer appealed. He had vowed on his betrothal to Gwendolyn to reform, and it had been a bitter irony to be arrested on their wedding day for a robbery he had not committed. A year in Newgate awaiting trial and transportation had shown him the foolhardiness of his old way of life.

On receiving his pardon he had been free to return to England an innocent man. But pride held him back. Gwen had shown her love and devotion by risking her life to bring his pardon in person. He had married her for love, but many had mocked her, saying that she had been duped by a fortune-hunter. He was resolved to prove those tattle-tongues wrong. He would make his own fortune here using only his hands and honest labour. The store and the sawpit were just the start of any means to make his wealth.

Even so, these first months here had not been easy. It had been hard for him to witness the deprivation Gwen had had to face. Acres of land had to be cleared of trees and a well dug to avoid a half-mile walk to the river. With the land grant for settlers the government also provided them with a tent until a wooden shelter could be built, and basic monthly rations of dried meat and dried peas, flour and rice. The rations were meagre and they needed to produce their own food to supplement them or starve. Japhet's natural instincts for survival had told him that the natives knew the secrets of living off this land. He had set about befriending them and learning a few words of their language. With only one tent supplied by the government he had been unwilling for the convicts and servants to share it with his family. The natives had shown him how to build bark huts for the others, and these had been surprisingly waterproof during the heavy rains. He had also traded coloured beads and small metal implements for the fish, wild fruit and meat the natives brought to the farm. Japhet had hunted for game with a musket to stock the larder, but it was the natives who had shown him how to cook the sweet-fleshed guana.

He had been eager to provide better shelter than the cramped confines of the tent for his wife, and on a natural clearing on the land he had erected a single-roomed dwelling. This would later be used for the animals when a proper house had been constructed.

It would take an idealistic romantic to describe life in the new colony as paradise. For most of the inhabitants brought out from England it remained a living hell. The convicts who arrived might not be facing the utter deprivation and near starvation of the first and second fleets, but food remained scarce. The first transportees had served their term, but they were far from grateful for the land grants given to them. Work on the land was as unremitting for the master as for the convict, and to succeed you had to work harder than any slave. Luxuries even for the established landowner were few and far between. Stories abounded of escaped convicts on the rampage. Also the natives, who had endured a decade of invasion by people who understood neither their language nor their customs, had realised that the settlers were here to stay and that with each month more land was being claimed and cleared by them. Land the natives had been free to roam and keep sacred for their rituals, with no concept of ownership other than tribal territories. They had begun killing settlers who disturbed their ceremonial grounds.

Japhet lifted the finished door on to its hinges and was about to call Gwendolyn when she came out of the old building carrying garlands of greenery she had woven to decorate their new home for Christmas. Watching her brought a rush of love that caught his breath. Even dressed in her cotton work gown and with her hair simply tied back she was elegant, and though not a great beauty she was a strikingly attractive woman. She carried herself with a graceful confidence that had been present ever since their betrothal. The timid girl he had once known had matured into a woman who would brave any danger with poise and equanimity. She met life with a proud tilt of her chin, straight back and squared shoulders and a ready generous smile.

'Welcome to your new home, my love.' His hazel eyes flashed with green lights of tenderness, and with a laugh he scooped her into his arms and carried her over the threshold. 'It is no stately mansion, or even as fine as Tor Farm, but one day you will have the elegant home you deserve.' He kissed her before setting her down.

'But how could any other house be as beautiful? Every line, every piece of wood has been fashioned with your hands and from your love.'

He held her tight. 'This will be a memorable Christmas. Silas and Eliza Hope arrive for a few days tomorrow. And you have made garlands for the walls. For the first time since I arrived here I feel I am back amongst a more civilised nation.'

'It will certainly be like no other Christmas before,' she laughed. 'We have roast kangaroo and guana pie instead of beef and capon. Japhet Edward helped me gather enough wild fruit to make an exotic pudding and cake.'

His expression sobered. 'Will you miss your family?'

'You and our son are my family. The most important people in my life. I do not miss Mama's constant machinations or my sister's complaints. And we will drink a toast to your family, who have been so loyal to us. They will hear soon of our decision to stay here. My thoughts will be with Cecily and Hannah. They will miss you dreadfully.'

Japhet held her against his chest. Memories of his mother and sister speared him. He thought of them constantly. The idea of a Christmas without his father's sermon and the entire Loveday family gathered around the dining table made him close his eyes against the pain of missing them.

Gwendolyn cupped his face in her hands. 'You made the right decision to remain here, my love. I have no regrets and neither must you. You have achieved so much already. This is one of the finest houses along the river apart from one or two built in stone. But such a house will be ours in time. The sawmill and store will prosper beyond even your expectations. Our fortune is assured. Japhet Edward thrives, and so too will our next little one. I waited to tell you until the house was finished: I am again with child. A child that would never have been conceived had I stayed in England and waited for your return, for we would still be apart. The child is the blessing of our new life.'

'And you are my redemption from the old Japhet who deserved to end his days dancing at the end of a rope. I love you, Gwen. I will not fail you.'

Chapter Fifteen

'I fear this Yuletide will not go entirely as we planned,' Senara said with a yawn as she climbed back into bed. She had been woken in the early hours of Christmas morning by Joel crying and then he had refused to settle. He had become overexcited by so many guests in the house and by knowing that his young cousins would be staying for the next few days. It had taken Senara an hour to get him back to sleep.

Her body was chilled and Adam held her in his arms to warm her, his voice thick with sleep. 'I hope this is not another of your prophesies warning that fate is conspiring against us.'

She laughed softly. 'No. Not fate, my love, just the weather. It is snowing hard and lying deep on the ground. The children will love it, they have never seen it like that before. The last winters have been wet but mild. However, if the roads are blocked few guests will be able to travel.'

'The snow could yet turn to rain and be gone by morning. But you are freezing. Let me warm you.'

He kissed her hair and she turned in his arms. Her hands were bold as she caressed him. 'Make love to me, Adam. We will have little time for privacy with so many guests. Do you remember when first we met how we made love under the standing stone on the moor? They were simple times – no demanding children, no ties.'

'Would you return to that life?' He paused in caressing her, his tone sombre.

'I would change nothing because I have you and your love.' She kissed him ardently, unwilling to spoil this special moment. Her desire matched Adam's, the chill of the night chased away by their passion.

When they finally rolled apart Adam leaned up on one elbow and stared down at her, his hair casting shadows over his handsome face in the first glimmer of dawn's light. 'Is it because your brother is camped nearby? Are you restless for your travels?'

She thought he would have forgotten her words but should have known that her husband was not a man to allow anything of consequence to be overlooked. 'It was not a life I enjoyed. And I am no longer part of that band now that Grandmother is dead. I have had some years to accept my new life. It will not be so for Tamasine – her life will soon change drastically. Have you noticed how quiet your sister has become in company?'

'I heard her laughing with Max in the long gallery yesterday, and she teased me mercilessly when I tripped over Scamp, who ran through my legs.'

'It is Mrs Deverell who is the problem. She watches Tamasine as though waiting for her to disgrace herself in some way. I have seen her look at me the same way when she learned I came from a family without property. Heaven knows what she would think if she learned of my gypsy blood. And I do not think that Max has been honest with his mother about Tamasine's circumstances.'

'Max is not a man to deceive his family.'

'I do not dispute that. But he knows his mother better than any. Perhaps he has omitted telling her the truth because he fears that Clarissa Deverell will despise his fiancée's birth.'

'Max would never have asked her to marry him without having considered all this. He will protect Tamasine from any spite. His mother seldom resides with him. She has her own property in Surrey and a house in London.' He kissed her before lying on his back and propping his head in the fold of his elbow. 'I am sure you are worrying without cause. Tamasine is no doubt missing Bridie and Hannah. She has spent a great deal of time at the farm recently, which Hannah appreciates. With her friends around her, her spirits will rally.'

Senara did not think the solution was so simple. She had overheard several cutting remarks from Clarissa Deverell about position and status in polite society, and the woman rarely lost an opportunity to remind her or Tamasine of the ancient lineage of her own family.

She drifted off to a final hour's sleep before she must rise to ensure everything ran without hitch over the next twelve days. When she awoke and drew back the window hangings, she could not stifle a groan of frustration. 'The snow has settled. We could be cut off from Trewenna and Polruggan.'

Adam joined her by the window and put his arms around her waist. The grounds of the house were pristine, with snow lying several inches thick. He paused a moment to take in the beauty of the scene, but the consequences of the snowfall were too vexing for the transient virgin whiteness to be enjoyed.

'Few guests will risk travelling with the snow so thick.' There was disappointment in his voice. 'I'll send Billy Brown to see if the roads are passable to Trewenna, or we will have to forgo the morning service. Eli Rudge will check the road to Trevowan. Elspeth, Amelia and St John were to join us here after the service and then to stay.'

'It will be hard for Hannah if the roads from the farm are blocked.' As Senara spoke it began to snow again. She leaned back against her husband's chest with a sigh. 'All our plans for Christmas will be ruined. And this was important to you.'

She felt him shrug. 'It was more important that the family were united in peace and harmony. Let us hope that will still be so.' He walked to the door. 'I'll give Brown and Rudge their orders now. We need to know how bad the roads are. Also, if Hannah cannot travel she may need help on the farm with the livestock.'

Senara pulled on a thick morning gown. Her mind was running ahead with the changes that might be needed. She spent a long time studying the sky. The clouds were low and laden with snow. The signs were not good that it would clear within a day or so. That would mean that the hunting would be cancelled and therefore everyone would be confined in the house. That did not bode well with the tensions still running high within the family. And poor Tamasine would be thrown into even closer proximity with her future mother-in-law. Senara made a mental note to ensure that she was not cornered by Clarissa Deverell and subjected to an interrogation that she guessed Max's mother would be capable of instigating.

As Senara had suspected, the numbers attending the Christmas feast were greatly reduced. The roads from Trewenna and Polruggan were blocked. Both these villages were further inland and set in steep valleys. It took Rudge all morning to get to the Rabson farm and return. Hannah had decided not to risk the journey to Boscabel in case she was needed for some emergency at the farm. Fortunately the road to Trevowan was close to the coast and the snow there was only an inch thick. It was decided that they would all attend the service at Penruan church, the old family place of worship before Joshua had become the incumbent vicar of Trewenna.

The Reverend Mr Snell was flustered at the unexpected arrival of the Lovedays and their guests in three carriages. Their appearance also caused a stir amongst the villagers. The ornate family pew built by Adam's great-grandfather had been designed to seat a dozen people in two rows, and since Adam had decided it was best for his young children to remain at home there was adequate room. Elspeth, Rowena and Amelia joined Adam, Senara, Tamasine, Max and his mother. St John was already seated at the end of the aisle in the seat always used by Edward. Adam hesitated as he approached, tactfully deciding to take his place in the second row. To his surprise St John rose and stepped into the aisle so that Adam could sit beside him.

This caused a spate of murmurings amongst the congregation and Adam was aware that his family was being closely scrutinised. He could feel his twin's tension and knew this public meeting was as difficult for St John as it was for him. As they waited for the service to begin, he spoke to his brother of the weather and other inconsequential matters. He also took time to gauge the mood of the villagers.

Opposite the Loveday pew was an edifice built by Thadeous Lanyon that was today occupied by Goldie and Hester. Goldie, with her loud voice used to ordering sailors in the boarding house she had run in Bristol, drew a great deal of attention to herself as she waved and called to her neighbours. Hester smiled shyly at Adam and Senara, then sat quietly with her head bowed. She did not look up when her sister and her brother-in-law, Dr Chegwidden, took their places, and they ignored her presence. That was another family feud instigated by Sawle.

Hester held her daughter in her arms, and though only a toddler, the girl had the same piercing stare and features as Harry Sawle, the father who refused to acknowledge her.

The Fraddons, the Nance family and other estate workers were present, and Adam saw the wicker basket full of oranges at the back of the church. This was a tradition started by his grandmother where each of the children from the village and estate was given the gift of an orange and a shiny new penny at Christmas. This had also been extended to Trewenna church, and Adam had paid for a similar basket to be given out by Bridie to the children of Polruggan and Polmasryn.

The first verse of the opening carol was being sung when there was a commotion by the door and Mordecai and Ella Nance arrived. They were gaudy as peacocks in second-hand finery with tarnished gold braid and torn lace purchased from a travelling pedlar. They ran the Dolphin Inn for Harry Sawle, and Adam had heard that Ella had installed two women and the place had become a bawdy house. Ella created a further distraction by commenting sarcastically, 'Lordy be, we are honoured by such high-ranking guests.'

Her husband shot St John a malevolent stare. Adam sensed that there was something more than Nance's dismissal from Trevowan behind the innkeeper's hostility. He stifled his irritation. Mordecai Nance was a bully and rumoured now to be Harry Sawle's right-hand man. He could make trouble for his twin.

The sermon was lengthy and Adam could feel Senara's impatience mounting, but when he glanced over his shoulder at her, she sat calm and serene. He winked and she smiled. Senara had her own way of worshipping, preferring an ancient sacred grove to the hidebound ritual of a church.

Clarissa Deverell was also growing impatient and fidgeted with her prayer book, her voice uncomfortably loud as she complained to her son. 'These country parsons forget their place. They are too fond of the sound of their own voice and forget decent folk have other duties to attend.'

The Reverend Mr Snell flushed darkly and stumbled over his words.

'This is the most holy of days, Mama,' Max replied in a low voice that Adam strained to hear. 'A sermon of an hour on the virtues of peace and goodwill is not inappropriate.'

Adam remembered Senara's early misgivings about Clarissa Deverell and was pleased to hear that Max did not allow his mother to exhibit any untoward sentiments of grandeur.

Anxious to please the Lovedays, who were patrons of his church, and their guests, Snell ended his sermon abruptly and announced the final hymn. Adam found his own attention wandering and he studied the congregation. He was shocked at some of the changes he saw in the people he had grown up with. They looked older, more careworn, many of their features hardened by adversity and poverty. In recent years, his voyages and then his involvement with the shipyard had detached him from the local community in Penruan. Several of the fishermen were fidgeting in their seats, their glances shifty and often fearful as they watched Mordecai Nance.

Adam frowned. Reuban and Harry Sawle had always had a hold over the villagers, ruling the smugglers by fear, though Reuban had mellowed in his later years. Clearly not so Harry. There was something far more sinister in the way the men now regarded Mordecai Nance.

The service over, it was customary for the Lovedays to file out behind the rector. As the family processed to the back of the church, Adam noticed the curious stares upon Max and Tamasine. Max had tucked Tamasine's arm through his and was paying her a great deal of attention. His mother's lips were taut with displeasure.

When the family passed Mordecai Nance, the hostility in the man's eyes as he glared at St John troubled Adam. That look had been murderous.

'Is there a problem with Mordecai Nance?' he said to his brother.

St John shrugged. 'Why should there be?'

Adam stood back to allow the women to pass out of the church first and drew his brother to one side. 'He looks like he could kill you.'

St John shrugged. 'There was an incident. His wife offered herself to me for money. I refused her. I dismissed Nance. A woman who plays the whore like that would cause trouble on the estate.'

'I fear you have made an enemy.'

St John did not seem concerned. 'He can do nothing to me. He is unimportant.'

'Do not underestimate him. Sawle hates us. Nance is not to be trusted.'

Adam paid his respects to Snell, congratulating him on the sermon. Clem Sawle had emerged from the church with his wife Keziah and son Zach. His mother, Sal, was with them. St John ignored the family of his dead wife but Adam was pleased to see Sal looking so well. She kept glancing at Rowena, who was holding Elspeth's hand. Clem had given up smuggling when he married Keziah and could be relied upon to keep a semblance of peace in the community. The family were dressed in their best clothes. Clem was unusually smart in a greatcoat and a beaver hat with a narrow brim, and Keziah wore a hooded cloak.

Adam approached Clem and his family. He smiled at Sal. 'Life looks to be treating you well, Sal.'

Rowena had sidled up to them and held out a package to Sal. She had wrapped four oranges in a large white-spotted red handkerchief. 'Happy Christmas, Grandmama.'

'Oh, my lovely, you be the sweetest child.' Sal brushed a tear from her eye. 'Seeing you be gift enough. But I've nothing for you.'

'Perhaps you could invite me to tea in your new cottage. Papa did not like me visiting you when you lived in the tavern, but I am sure he will not mind now, will he, Uncle Adam?'

'You must ask your papa.'

'I'll do it now.' She ran off.

Sal shook her head, visibly upset. 'There bain't no place for me in Rowena's life. I accept that, Cap'n Loveday.'

'Rowena seems to think differently.'

Behind them they could hear Rowena crying. Sal continued to shake her head. 'I would not make life harder for the lass.'

'I will talk to my Aunt Elspeth. She has the best interests of your granddaughter at heart. She would not stop her seeing you under the right circumstances. I am sure that something can be arranged.'

To his embarrassment, Sal grabbed his hand and kissed it. 'Thank you, Cap'n. I did my best to raise all my children right. I be proud of Clem and Mark. They be hardworking and have made something of their lives. The other two – Meriel and Harry . . .' She dropped her gaze. 'They inherited their father's blood – mean, vindictive and grasping.'

Adam studied Clem, who had stayed silent throughout the conversation. There was only two years' difference in their ages, with Clem the older. In their youth they had fought many times and had been evenly matched. Clem had been as bullying and hard-nosed as Harry in those days. Then he had wed Keziah and had changed. He was now respected in Penruan.

'How do the new innkeeper and his wife fit into life in the village?' Adam asked Clem.

'There bain't many who would try and run them out,' Clem replied, clearly unwilling to discuss the subject.

'I've my little cottage now.' Sal clumsily attempted to change the subject. 'It be such a joy. Running an inn is hard work.' A snowball fight had broken out amongst the children and Zach screamed when one hit him on the side of the face. 'Oh my poor lovely. You bain't hurt. Good day to you, Cap'n Loveday.'

Carrying Zach in her arms she hurried away to join Keziah, who was talking to a group of women.

When Clem made to follow his mother, Adam asked, 'You'd let me know if there is trouble in the village? If I can help . . .'

'The trouble could be landing on your brother's doorstep. Tell him to steer clear of Nance and my brother. He made it clear what he thought of the Sawles when he had his wife's body removed from your family vault.'

'That was wrong. He was angry. But Meriel did lead him a pretty dance.'

'It weren't right of her to run off the way she did. She always were headstrong.' Clem was usually a man of few words and it was rare for him to say so much.

Another commotion had broken out in the churchyard. Adam saw Mrs Deverell leaning against the stone cross of a headstone. Max had left Tamasine's side to assist her. She fussed and held tightly to his arm. 'Take me to the carriage. The ground is treacherous. I could have fallen. My ankle twisted.'

Max escorted his mother to the carriage. To Adam's sharp eye Clarissa

Deverell showed no sign of harm and was not limping. Tamasine held back, looking puzzled at the fuss her future mother-in-law had created.

Senara was with his sister when he joined them. His wife commented to Tamasine, 'Mrs Deverell is jealous of the attention her son is paying you. You must ignore her pettiness.'

Tamasine nodded, but out of loyalty to her fiancé did not reply. The carriages were ready for them to depart and it had begun to snow again. Adam waited for the women to be settled with their feet on foot-warmers. St John was returning from the direction of the family vault, holding Amelia's arm. They had laid flowers on Edward's grave.

Mordecai Nance had been lolling against the lychgate. Suddenly he propelled himself forward at such a pace that he skidded into St John and knocked him sideways. Amelia screamed but was close enough to the carriage to avoid being hurt. St John rounded on Nance.

'Watch where the devil you are going!'

'What you gonna do about it?' The words were slurred and the man's breath reeked of brandy.

'I could have you clapped in irons for disturbing the peace if you do not get on your way,' St John flared.

When Nance bunched his fist, Adam stepped between the two men.

'Be on your way, Nance. Do you want to spend Christmas in the lock-up for an unprovoked attack?' Adam cautioned.

'You forget yourself, innkeeper.' St John shoved the man aside with his hand.

Nance would have hit him but Adam was faster and blocked the punch. He grabbed Nance's wrist and bent it up between his shoulder blades. 'Back off or I'll break your arm.'

Nance scowled.

Adam wanted to avoid a scene, especially with Mrs Deverell watching. 'You slipped in the snow. It was an accident. Apologise to my brother and we will forget the incident.'

'I apologise to no one – specially him.'

Adam increased the pressure on the innkeeper's wrist. Nance's face contorted with pain. 'All right. Don't break my arm. I apologise.'

'The man should be clapped in irons for such conduct.' St John was still angry.

'Accept his apology. It is Christmas Day,' Adam warned. 'We do not brawl in public or in front of our womenfolk and guests.'

St John glared at him and then at the carriages. He was ready for a fight. Some demon was driving him where Nance was concerned. He suspected that Nance, as Harry Sawle's henchman, was behind the firing of the haystacks at Boscabel. The injustice of the family blaming him still rankled with St John. Someone had attacked him from behind and left him unconscious that night. He was tempted to give Nance the thrashing the knave deserved. Then common sense took precedence over thoughts of revenge. This was not the place.

'I accept your apology. It was an accident. Now be on your way.'

Adam released Nance, who stumbled away rubbing his wrist.

'This bain't the last you'll hear of this, Loveday.'

Cut off from her family on Christmas Day, Hannah was determined to make it a happy one for her children. Fortunately there were several pheasants that Sam had shot hanging in the stables and she ordered Aggie to pluck and cook these to provide a meal for all the servants. Apart from the milking and the animals being cared for, no other work would be done on the farm and everyone had been invited to the farmhouse for a meal. Hannah had made two large plum puddings and mince pies that she would have taken to Boscabel, and these were now added to the feast that had been prepared for the farm hands.

Mark and Sam had taken out shovels to clear the snow from in front of the milking shed and a path from there to the house. The cows had been brought in and would be kept in the barn and fed with hay until the snow thawed. After the milking the children were given their presents from Hannah, and the servants, now wearing their best clothes, had gathered in the parlour, where each received a gift from their mistress. The milkmaids and Aggie had been given lace collars purchased from the women at Polruggan. Mark had a woollen muffler, and for Sam Hannah had chosen a briar pipe and a pouch of tobacco.

As they were unable to attend a church service Hannah sat at the harpsichord that had been Oswald's mother's and accompanied them as they sang several carols. The parlour had been decorated with holly, ivy and pine branches. Pine cones had been put on the log fire to sweeten the air. While the women finished preparing the meal to be eaten at the large kitchen table, Sam took the children outside to play in the snow. It was not long before Hannah joined them. They were rolling a huge ball of snow along the ground to form the base of a snowman. A second ball was put on top of this, and a smaller ball formed its head. It was as high as a man, with two stones for eyes, a row of red berries for its mouth and a carrot for its nose. Davey had run indoors and brought out an old hat and scarf that been his father's to complete the image.

The children danced around the figure, their faces red from the cold as they laughed and began a snowball fight with each other. Luke and Charlie kept falling over, and seven-year-old Florence tried valiantly to duck the barrage of snowballs hurled at her by Abigail and Davey. Hannah joined in. Sam had gone into the stable to root out a sledge that had been Oswald's and returned to pull the children in groups of two through the snow.

A solitary rider appeared on the track leading to the house. The horse was struggling in the snowdrifts, that were past its knees. On recognising her brother Peter, Hannah gave a cheer of joy and the children, overexcited from their fight, ran towards him and pelted him with snow.

Hannah called for them to stop. She did not want the children's fun spoilt by Peter giving them a sermon. To her surprise Peter dismounted and scooped up a ball of snow and threw it at Davey. It made the children even more excited, and his black greatcoat and hat were soon covered with the white powder.

'Children, is that any way to treat a parson, even if he is your uncle?' Hannah said, though she had trouble keeping the laughter from her voice.

'They take their role from their mother,' Peter proclaimed, then suddenly grinned and scooped up a great mound of snow and threw it at his sister. It landed on her neck and its icy chill ran down inside her collar.

'Right, that is war,' she cried, hurling snowballs at him as fast as she could form them. She was transported back to the days of her childhood, when she and Peter had ganged up on Japhet and somehow their elder brother still managed to get the better of them.

She stumbled and sank into the snow and was laughing so hard she could not rise. Peter was looming over her holding a huge ball of snow that made her shriek in protest: 'Don't you dare!'

He grinned and dropped it on the back of her neck. Her hat had fallen off and again the icy water trickled down her neck as it melted.

'Fiend!' She gasped with laughter and grabbed his leg, and yanked it so that he toppled over and lay in the snow beside her. They were both laughing so hard, their breath steamed from their mouths.

Peter clambered to his feet and held out his hand for his sister to rise. She was panting heavily from her exertion and clung to him for support. 'Oh, Peter, I needed that so much. I was missing everyone and we used to have such fun in the snow as children.'

'Not a very dignified way for a parson to behave, was it?' Even he seemed surprised by his momentary lack of decorum. 'But Japhet would have taken you on in such a fight.'

110

She held his stare, a rush of love welling up for him. It was so many years since she had seen this once carefree side of Peter. 'It is the perfect way for my brother to behave. Thank you for showing me the old Peter. It is the best Christmas present I could have had. You do not always have to take life so seriously.'

He coughed in embarrassment. 'Bridie said this could be a difficult day for you as we could not get to Boscabel. I brought the presents for the children.'

'And you came all this way in the snow. The journey could not have been easy.' She threw her arms around him and hugged him. 'Thank you. Come into the house and have some mulled wine to warm yourself.'

She paused to watch the children swarming round Sam and demanding more rides on the sledge. Then her stare fell upon the snowman and her heart tightened with pain to see the hat and scarf. The snowman stood like a sentinel guarding their home.

Her sadness lifted. Oswald's spirit was here watching over them and had broken down the barriers Peter had erected around himself, if even only for a brief while. She saw the wistfulness in her brother's eyes as he also watched the children at play.

'You will have children of your own, Peter. And you will make a wonderful father.'

The austere lines settled back around his mouth. 'I will stay just for a glass of wine, then I must return to the parsonage. Do you wish me to lead your servants in a simple prayer on this holiest of days?'

She nodded. Her brother had not really changed, but she had seen that the old Peter still lurked behind the cloak of his religion and his parson's clothes. She prayed that he would reveal that side more often in the future.

Chapter Sixteen

Five days after Christmas the snow thawed and the family were reunited to celebrate the New Year. Confinement had never been easy for those of the Loveday blood, and being trapped in the house by the weather had tested their patience to the limit. It had also strained the truce between St John and Adam, causing an undercurrent of tension whenever a sharp comment provoked an even sharper retort. If it had not been for the arrival of Hannah, Joshua and Peter after the thaw, St John would have left Boscabel to spend time with his friends. He was also disgruntled that any card games were played for shillings and not pounds. Yet their reconciliation had held, any outbreaks of ill temper taken out on each other only when they were alone.

Tamasine found little solace in Maximillian's presence as his mother guarded his company closely. This was done in the most artful manner. Clarissa contrived to sit close to him when they dined and ensured that the conversation centred upon the accomplishments of her family. Whenever he gave more attention to Tamasine than herself she would play upon her health. Max, being an attentive son, would excuse himself and ensure that his mother was comfortable and had everything she required.

'Mama's health has never been robust since Papa died,' he explained, clearly unable to see how she used it to manipulate him.

When Max was present Clarissa was witty and solicitous towards her hosts, but when the women were alone, a more caustic side to her nature became apparent. She was critical of many of the domestic arrangements and freely offered advice without noticing that she had often given offence. The curiosity of the woman was endless. Sometimes it became no less than inquisition if she found Tamasine alone. Clearly, Max had told her nothing of Tamasine's background and she was growing suspicious.

'You have said that you are an orphan. But who was your father?'

'He was the kindest, most honourable man I have ever known.'

'But what did he do, child?' Clarissa Deverell voiced her exasperation.

'He was a gentleman.'

'Well, that is something. But what of your mama? Who were her family?'

'Mama never spoke of her family. I was sent away to school very young.'

'Sent away. You did not have a governess!'

'Apparently not,' Tamasine evaded. 'I understand my parents travelled a great deal.' She hoped that would silence the questions.

'Was he then a diplomat?'

'Would it have mattered if he was?' She stood up and placed a hand over her mouth. 'I find it hard to talk about them. Their death was too dreadful . . .'

'You must forgive Tamasine.' Hannah had realised that Tamasine had not joined her in the nursery as they had arranged and had come to find her. 'She has always been reluctant to talk about her parents. Their death was a great shock to her.'

'How did they die?' Clarissa continued with tactless disregard for Tamasine's feelings.

'It was a tragedy,' Hannah said sharply, and received a relieved look from the younger woman. Tamasine had lost all the colour from her cheeks.

'Max did not mention where they lived. Indeed, he has told me so little of them. Did they own an estate?'

'I believe her father did. It was entailed, of course.'

'Does the girl come to us unendowered?'

Her look of horror enraged Tamasine, and Clarissa proceeded to ride roughshod over any sensibilities as she proclaimed, 'No decent family would not provide for their own. Not that we have need of any financial settlement, you understand. It is a matter of principle.'

Tamasine stood up, unable to control her anger at this final insult. 'My father provided a very adequate dowry. And as you say, that is not why Max is marrying me.'

'Oh, the impudence.' Clarissa put a hand to her brow. 'You overstep yourself, Miss Loveday.'

There was a spate of furious barking from Scamp and Hannah announced, 'The men have returned. Forgive us, Mrs Deverell, I need Tamasine to assist me.' She gestured for Tamasine to follow her from the solar.

In the hallway they bumped into Adam, who had entered ahead of the others. Max and Joshua were discussing the finer points of sword-play. 'Of course it has all changed since my grandfather's day,' Joshua was saying, 'and that is not a bad thing. There were too many duels by far.'

Tamasine had disappeared into an anteroom to regain her composure before meeting Max. Hannah accosted Adam and whispered in a fierce undertone, 'Mrs Deverell is like a hound on a scent. She knows there is something suspicious about Tamasine. She will not rest until she learns the truth. Max must deal with her. Clearly he has been selective in how much he has revealed to his mother. Tam is dealing with it remarkably well, but it is upsetting her.'

Adam frowned. 'The woman is something of a martinet. I used to think that Aunt Elspeth was bad, but she is a kitten compared to that woman. Just make sure that Tam is not alone with her. You are more than capable of changing the conversation if it veers on to dangerous ground.'

'We have turned the conversation from Tamasine's family so many times, it can only make her more suspicious.' Hannah shook her head. 'The woman is tenacious and will not let the matter rest.'

Adam grinned. 'I will put my money on you emerging the winner.'

Before Adam could speak with Max, Clarissa summoned her son to her room. She was reclining on a day bed, pressing her hand to her head.

'Are you unwell, Mama?'

'I am a slave to my megrims. It will pass.'

'Senara will prepare you a tisane, I am sure. Her remedies are most efficacious.'

Clarissa shuddered. 'Country potions are of no use to me. If it persists I will have a physician call upon me. Do please be seated. I cannot peer up at you. It is too uncomfortable.'

Max sat opposite her. 'I shall ask the physician to call. Your health has been poor since our arrival.'

'Is it any wonder? This family is not what I expected – not what I expected at all!'

'I have great respect for Adam.'

'But his wife . . . !' Clarissa waved her smelling salts under her nose, close to swooning. 'She is a nobody. Worse than that, there are gypsies camping on the estate, and from a snatch of conversation my maid over-heard, one of them is her brother.'

'I have no knowledge of that.'

'Yet you do not seem shocked.'

'I never listen to gossip, Mama.' Max was deliberately evasive. 'Senara Loveday is a charming and accomplished woman.'

'You used to be more discerning, Maximillian.'

When he did not answer she continued in a more energetic tone, 'And I can learn nothing of your betrothed's background. Is that not most odd? The family are avoiding answering my questions.'

Max stood up. 'I know all there is to know about Tamasine. I do not wish her family interrogated.'

Clarissa sucked in her lips in a show of displeasure. 'You are besotted by the minx. There is something not right here. I thought you had more pride in your lineage.'

'You have never allowed me to forget my heritage, Mama,' he answered tersely. 'We are here as guests of the Lovedays. Miss Loveday is of impeccable character and family: that is all you need to know.'

Her son had never spoken to her in such a fashion. It alarmed Clarissa. She forced a smile. 'I am being overfanciful. I worry about you and your future happiness, that is all. I know how condemning society can be to those they consider their inferiors.'

'But if you receive her, as I know you will because I ask you to, Tamasine will be accepted. Now, I must change before we dine. Your servant, Mama.'

Her eyes narrowed, Clarissa stared at the door after it had closed behind her son. If Tamasine Loveday was not all she ought to be, she, Clarissa Deverell, would not tolerate it.

Even though they managed to divert the conversation from family matters, Mrs Deverell was a difficult guest to keep amused. She dominated every conversation; she had an opinion on every subject and clearly disliked having any judgement she made contradicted.

As each day passed she grew ever more suspicious of Tamasine. She had been incensed to learn of her son's betrothal to a family with no connections. She despaired when she learned that they were in trade. She had set her heart on Max marrying well. He had been unconscionably stubborn and refused to be guided in the matter. For a decade she had paraded suitable women before him. There had been a time when she thought she had succeeded and he had become engaged to the Lady Catherine. She shuddered at the memory. Who would have thought the girl would play him false and run off with a soldier? Max had followed them and called the blackguard out. Honour had been satisfied, but Max had thenceforth been harsh in his judgement of women. Then this minx Tamasine Loveday, a nobody, had appeared on the scene. It really had been extremely vexing. And now that she had met the family, Clarissa found them wanting . . . found them very wanting indeed. It was enough to send her into a fit of the vapours, and she took to her bed, unable to bear more of their company. Her heartfelt prayer was that Max would yet see sense about the unsuitability of such a marriage.

The absence of Clarissa brought no respite to Tamasine's fears. Max's mother was showing her disapproval in the most blatant way possible.

Adam was aware of the chill atmosphere whenever Clarissa was present. He tried to divert it with musical entertainments. Hannah was an accomplished pianist and Tamasine had a lovely singing voice. Indoor skittles were set up in the long gallery and of an evening there was cards or charades. Clarissa Deverell would spend over half of each day in her room, complaining that a houseful of children was too noisy for her delicate nerves. However, Adam was concerned that Hannah was quieter than usual and looked pale. He hoped the next few days would bring the colour back into her cheeks and lift her spirits. Her first Christmas as a widow could not be easy.

Today Squire Penwithick and his wife had called and were also to stay the night. His son and daughter-in-law had sailed with his regiment to India in the summer. The arrival of the squire enticed Clarissa Deverell from her room.

'How delightful to meet you,' she gushed. 'You have duties at court, I believe.'

'I have that honour.'

'This dreadful weather has isolated us. I have met so few of my hosts' neighbours in polite society.'

'And I regret that I bring news that will further curtail your pleasure.' Squire Penwithick addressed the room. 'Word has come from Fetherington Hall that his lordship has suffered a seizure. The hunt and ball has been cancelled.'

While the family extended their good wishes for Lord Fetherington's speedy recovery, Clarissa Deverell fell silent, the downward turn of her mouth showing her displeasure. After they had dined, she again complained of a headache and retired to her room. The rest of the women gathered in the solar and the men retired to the long gallery, where the conversation soon turned to politics.

'Squire Penwithick, do you think the war with France will end next year?' Max asked.

'Mr Pitt is optimistic since the fall of Robespierre. France is on the brink of bankruptcy. Her soldiers are in rags. The people are starving.'

'But her armies remain undefeated on the Rhine,' Adam observed. 'And in Italy the young Corsican General Bonaparte has achieved unprecedented success.'

'Even if the armies are not paid, they have to be fed,' the squire cut in, his eyes bright with fervour. 'The French treasury is depleted. For seven years the country has been torn apart by anarchy. Throughout that time she has been fighting upon all her frontiers. No country can sustain that for long. The people have revolted once, driven by destitution. Little has changed under the new government.'

'But France refuses to draw back. They have shown superb resilience and fought on to win many battles over our allies in Europe,' Adam returned. 'This summer Spain joined forces with France and declared war on us in October. That added another fifty ships of the line against us.'

'I think France has come too far to consider negotiations for peace.' Max regarded each of the men with an impatient stare. 'Invasion of Italy is a means to refill their coffers.'

'And we have to consider our own resources. This war is not popular with everyone. For over a year there has been unrest. There were the riots in the Mall last year when the King opened Parliament. His coach was stoned. The masses booed him. He has never been so unpopular. And the Prince of Wales with his extravagant spending is lampooned and reviled by the pamphleteers of the day.'

'And what of our Austrian allies, sir?' Max persisted.

'They fight on but are equally finding the cost of the war hard to bear.'

'But would not the cost of defeat be even more?' Adam conjectured. 'Our navy is undefeated. Do we not rule the seas?'

The squire did not immediately answer. 'The British fleet is our pride, but there have been losses. We need more ships, but our treasury is over-stretched.'

Adam nodded. He had been hoping for an order from the Admiralty for more cutters for the revenue office. To attract the order he had offered them a cheap price, but so far he had been unsuccessful. Few small shipyards had won orders for ships of the line.

'This war has cost our government millions.' Peter voiced his condemnation. 'It is the poor who suffer. They are starving. Few farmers have had good harvests this year. The price of bread will rise and that will cause more suffering.'

'Poor harvests bring hardship to us all. I should know.' St John glowered at his cousin. 'And taxes are high.'

'Few prosper in times of war.' Maximillian shrugged. 'But the alternative would be more dire. Would you have us invaded by the troops of this new upstart Corsican General Bonaparte?'

'Could it come to that?' St John helped himself to another brandy from the decanter and passed it to the squire. 'Our navy is invincible.'

'No fleet or army is ever entirely that,' Penwithick returned. 'The new coalition in France have much to prove. The country is desperate to recoup its losses from the Revolution.'

'Then God save us all!' St John downed his drink.

Adam rose. 'This is supposed to be a time of rejoicing. I have faith in our ability to trounce the French. Let us rejoin the ladies.'

Chapter Seventeen

'So this is where you hide yourself away.' Max had discovered Tamasine in the minstrels' gallery, her favourite place to escape the interrogation of his mother. 'I had not thought you a woman who liked seclusion. I have neglected you today. Adam and I were discussing business longer than I intended.'

'I am pleased you and Adam have so much in common. And at school I came to prize time to myself. I do not fear my own company.' She did not wish to mention her true reason for being here. She had drawn her legs up on a wooden bench and had been reading. She set her book aside.

'And I have disturbed your peace. I shall leave you to your contemplations.' Max bowed.

She reached out to stop him. 'I welcome the chance for us to be alone.' She blushed. 'Now you will think me forward.'

He took her hand and raised her to her feet. His smile was tender and beguiling. 'Your company is far more enjoyable than Adam's. We have had too little time alone.'

'I have been occupied with the children. They fret at being so long confined in the house.' She laughed. 'They can be so amusing. Joel is demanding that the snow comes back. They loved playing in it. It was a shame the thaw came so fast. If the river had frozen we could have skated on it. It is something I have always wanted to do.'

'In Dorset the lake on my estate freezes most winters. I shall teach you to skate. But is that the only reason you regret the thaw? Tomorrow I must take my leave of you. Mama has not been herself these last days. She frets to return to her own home and recover her health.'

'She is not happy here. Our family is a disappointment to her.'

'Mama has exacting standards and grand expectations of too many things. But it is her ill health that has cast her low. Adam has charmed her, and of course your sweet self. She finds you delightful.'

Tamasine did not answer. His nearness sent her heart skittering. With each day that passed she fell more deeply in love with him. Even his devotion to his mother, though it stopped him seeing the manipulative side of her nature, proved his loyalty to his family. She admired that, but would it also be her downfall? Rupert had forsaken her when his family took against her. Clarissa Deverell would never accept her if she learned the truth of her birth, and how could Max keep that truth from his mother?

'Your mama does not approve of me. Should she learn of my parentage . . .'

He stopped her words with a kiss. 'You must not torment yourself. Nothing will stop our marriage.' His voice deepened to a husky timbre as he drew her closer.

A shiver of expectancy rippled down her spine. She held his loving gaze, her hand lifted to caress his clean-shaven cheek, and her lips parted breathlessly, inviting a second kiss. Its ardour robbed her of breath. There had been too few moments when they had been able to steal time alone. And with so full a house there had been no privacy for him to speak of love.

'I shall be counting the weeks until our wedding, my love,' he whispered against her cheek.

There was an urgency to his kiss which carried her along on a surging tide of passion.

'Max. Are you there? Maximillian!'

The sound of Clarissa Deverell's voice shattered the stolen moment of joy. There was a shocked gasp and Tamasine turned in her lover's arms to see his mother staring up at the minstrels' gallery from the old hall. Her face was deadly white at witnessing their kiss.

'You must go to your mama. She appears upset.'

To her surprise Max grinned. 'Her sensibilities will of course be outraged.'

Tamasine's cheeks stung with embarrassment and she covered them with her hands. 'Your mother will think I am a wanton.'

'A kiss is permitted between a betrothed couple. I should have been more circumspect, but you entice me . . . and I am lost.'

She could feel the steady rhythm of his heartbeat beneath her hand; its strength was absurdly intoxicating. He stepped back from her, his gaze adoring, and offered her his arm. 'You will never regret your decision to marry me. I will protect your honour and reputation with my life.'

If any doubts lingered as to the worthiness of Max's devotion, they now dispersed. Bathed in that love, Tamasine knew she could slay dragons or walk through fire without fear.

When they emerged from the steps leading to the minstrels' gallery, Clarissa Deverell stood with her hands clasped and her manner imperious.

'I would have speech with this young woman on my own. You will leave us, Maximillian.'

'Nothing you have to say to Tamasine cannot be said before me, Mama.'

Tamasine felt her heart lurch. This was the confrontation she had dreaded. She breathed slowly and evenly and painted a smile on her lips. 'Mrs Deverell is most kind to take the trouble to further our acquaintance. We have been but two weeks in each other's company and now there is less than a day before you leave.'

'I do not tolerate insolence.'

'Then you misinterpret my intention.' Tamasine raised a brow, questioning the outburst. Her voice was sweet and courteous but there was a warning in the tilt of her chin that any who knew her well would recognise and be wary against. 'I am pleased that with so little time left we have this opportunity to talk.'

The older woman's eyes were cold. 'I will not be trifled with. And I will not have the reputation of my family sullied by allowing this charade to continue further.'

'Mama, you do yourself no service by your remarks,' Max cautioned his mother.

'I would hear her out, my love,' Tamasine stated as she dipped a respectful curtsey to her future mother-in-law. She was determined that her manners would be impeccable in the face of such rudeness and arrogance.

'What do you truly know of this woman, my son? Her family has been tight-lipped about her parentage, her home and her background. The young woman herself has evaded my questions.'

'I chose not to answer certain questions but I have no shame about my background,' Tamasine countered. 'My family is an honourable one.'

'I doubt it or there would be no need for this secrecy.'

'There has been no secrecy on my part. Max knows everything about me. If he sees no dishonour in my family connections, then you gravely insult his integrity by questioning his choice of bride.'

The aggression would not be halted. Clarissa sneered, 'Even now the minx evades the truth. What are you hiding? You speak of honour, but where is the honour in aspiring to raise yourself above your station by marrying my son and bringing his good name into disrepute among his peers?'

Beneath her fingers Tamasine felt the muscles in Max's arm tense. Before he could defend her, she spoke out. 'My father was a gentleman; my mother's lineage was the equal of your own. They are not the reason I have been favoured by your son's high regard. He is the most remarkable of men. I owe him my life. He has my respect, my devotion and my loyalty.'

Clarissa Deverell glared at her son. 'I thought better of you, truly I did. How can you so forget your name and your heritage? This is a tawdry—'

'Mama, you will say no more or face the consequences of your unworthy discourse.' Max cut curtly across his mother's tirade. 'Miss Loveday has honoured me by agreeing to become my wife. Her background is a matter of concern only between ourselves.'

'I have never been so poorly served by my own son. Where is the respect that is my due?'

'You have my undying devotion, Mama. Respect can be lost or won. Do not allow this moment of ill judgement to destroy the high regard in which I hold you.' There was steel in Max's voice. 'I will brook no discord between my wife and my mother.'

He raised Tamasine's fingers to his lips. 'This is the woman I choose to marry. I have deemed no other worthy to carry on our name and bear my children. And for your own peace of mind, you may rest assured that Tamasine's mother's family fought with Henry V at Agincourt.'

Clarissa closed her eyes and took several moments to compose herself. When she opened them the hostility had been tempered. 'I cannot understand why you found it necessary to keep this knowledge from me.'

'I did not feel it was of import,' Max parried.

'Not important!' She gasped in disbelief. 'It is of the highest importance.'

'And I hope you are now satisfied, Mama.'

Clarissa took another deep breath and turned her assessing stare upon Tamasine. 'Are you not proud of your heritage that you would hide it?'

'My mother never spoke of her family connections.' Tamasine's stare was unwavering upon the older woman and she could not halt the put-down the arrogant woman deserved. 'And with the greatest respect, Mrs Deverell, my mother considered it pretentious and not a little vulgar to boast of one's forebears.'

'How very singular of her,' Clarissa snapped.

'Your approval pleases me, Mama.' Max checked his mother's retort.

Clarissa flushed, then sighed dramatically. 'This is not helping my megrims.' She stared long and hard at her son before she capitulated to say, 'Tamasine, my dear, you have won my son's heart and have shown yourself to be a woman of mettle. Few have stood up to me in the past. Courage is to be prized. Family pride is not to be derided and loyalty is a rare gift to be treasured. You may do very well, Miss Loveday. You may do very well indeed.'

Max squeezed Tamasine's hand. 'Did I not say that you would charm Mama? You have quite won her over.'

Tamasine curtseyed to Clarissa. 'I believe Mrs Deverell and I understand each other very well. We wish only for your happiness.'

Max's mother inclined her head. They had reached an understanding. Clarissa Deverell might be a martinet, but she loved her son too dearly to risk losing him by contesting his marriage.

Chapter Eighteen

With the departure of their guests life returned to normal at Boscabel, or as normal as any household could be with a wedding to be planned. The women spoke of nothing else but Tamasine's trousseau in the following months. Aunt Margaret had sent the latest fashion plates from London and two seamstresses were engaged to work on the garments. Max had insisted that the account was to be sent to him. Adam did not argue. Tamasine's dowry was provided by his father's estate and he would spend lavishly on the wedding celebrations to be held at Boscabel.

When the family heard how Tamasine had stood up to Clarissa they applauded her actions. Tamasine was transformed. She could speak barely five sentences without Max's name being mentioned and praised. Her laughter and excitement about her forthcoming nuptials filled the house.

The family settled into their usual routines and the truce held between Adam and St John, though the brothers led separate lives and St John only joined his family for the sermon at Trewenna and lunch at Boscabel once a month. Hannah had no further trouble on the farm and had learned that the Caines had found work in St Austell. There were no sightings of Harry Sawle either to cause trouble or rekindle old grievances.

Then came the shock that no one had predicted.

In April a letter was delivered from a government ship returning from Botany Bay. Japhet's decision to stay in Australia and make his fortune as a settler in the new land was a blow to everyone. The family had gathered together at Trewenna to discuss the news. Cecily could not hide her sorrow.

'But Japhet has his home here. He has Tor Farm.' Tears streamed down her cheeks.

'And he will keep that,' Joshua tried to console his wife. 'He says he will return in a year or so.'

'But he lives in a penal colony. What life is that for Gwen and that dear sweet child of theirs? Japhet Edward will grow up a savage. It is a barbarous land, is it not?'

Adam was quick to reassure her. 'Before Sir Gregory Kilmarthen left he had found out much about the colony for the benefit of our investors. There is a township growing up around Parramatta as well as Sydney. Many genteel settlers have taken up land grants. Not all are emancipated convicts.'

Joshua added, 'Japhet can be hardworking when he sets his mind to a venture. He is clearly determined to return to England with a fortune that was not carved from his wife's inheritance.'

'But Gwen is such a gentle creature.' Cecily was not appeased. 'How will she fare? This is too bad of him. Too bad . . .' She dabbed at her eyes and glanced at her daughter. 'Oh Hannah, what new madness is this that he has been driven to undertake?'

Hannah took her mother's hands in hers and put her own shock aside to voice her confidence in her brother. 'Gwen has a backbone of steel or she would not have travelled halfway round the world to be with her husband. You should be proud of Japhet.'

Joshua put a hand on his wife's shoulder. 'It is what Japhet needs to curb his wildness. It will be the making of him. And he asks that Tor Farm be rented to a tenant on a yearly basis, his mares all but Sheba sold and the money invested. Hannah is to keep Sheba for when he returns.'

Hannah had also wept at the news but now her spirits rallied. 'If anyone can make a success in this new land it is my brother. I wish him well, but will miss him dreadfully. I shall write and send them our good wishes for their future. There must be no recriminations. Japhet for all his wildness would not have made this decision lightly. He will return in a year or so as he has said. He has never broken his word to us. We must pray that when he does return, the restlessness that fed the devil which always rode on his back is finally at peace and he will stay in Cornwall.'

Her words had been brave but Adam had heard the pain behind them. Concerned for his cousin, he visited her the following week. He found her in the stable grooming Japhet's mare. The other beasts were to be sold at the next horse fair.

'How are you, Hannah? Japhet's decision must have hit you hard. We all miss him.'

'We should have expected something of the kind. Japhet was never predictable. The unknown was always a challenge to him.' She ran her hand down the shiny coat of the Arab mare. 'Nothing stays the same, does it? No matter how much we would like it to.'

She did not look at him, and feeling her pain Adam took her into his arms. She leaned her head on his shoulder and he heard her sniff back her tears. 'I adore Japhet. He is a rogue but so irresistibly charming. I hope he has found happiness now.'

'I know how much you were looking forward to his return. This has been a difficult winter for you.'

Her head tipped back and there was firm resolve in her hazel eyes. 'He'll be back. And I am so lucky to have you, Adam. You must not concern yourself over me. The crops are sown, my children are healthy and I have a wonderful family nearby.'

'*Pegasus* will return in another two months. Sir Gregory will have more news of Japhet for us. And you are welcome to stay at Boscabel whenever you wish. None of us likes to think of you alone out here.'

She laughed and stepped away from him. 'I appreciate your offer, but I am far from alone. I have the milkmaids, the servants and Mark and Sam.'

'But you have not replaced the Caines. Another man here would be greater protection.'

She waved aside his concern. 'Mark has taken on Dick Caine's work as well as his own. He is a hard worker.'

'Can you trust Mark Sawle in a showdown with his brother?'

'I trust him implicitly.'

'I would still prefer you take on another man.'

Hannah shook her head. 'I cannot afford the wages. And I will not leave the farm at this time. The cows must be bulled soon and the fields sown. Would you have me become as negligent in my duties as St John? Or has your brother mended his ways in recent weeks? Elspeth says he rarely leaves Trevowan.'

'His finances do not permit him to leave the estate. I have not heard from him for a month. He is licking his wounds in private.'

'He needs the love of a good wife to curb his wild ways.'

'He needs a rich one to save Trevowan.' Adam vented his derision.

'We have all been very hard on him. Life with Meriel could not have been easy.' She patted Sheba on the rump and walked with Adam into the yard. She sensed that Adam was becoming restless to leave. 'I am keeping you from your work.'

He paused. 'Have you had any further trouble from Sawle? He has not been seen in these parts for some weeks.'

'There has been no sign of him. And for that I thank God. But he knows he is no match for you. He was all bluster with his threats.'

'It is best to stay on your guard.'

She pointed to a dagger in a sheath attached to a belt around her waist. 'I also carry a pistol when I leave the farm.'

'You are more than a match for him.' Adam's eyes glittered with mirth. 'But he is a sly one. If there is any hint of trouble you must tell me.'

'I will.' She smiled brightly and waved as he rode away. Once he was out of sight her smile faded. It had been many weeks since her last confrontation with Harry Sawle, but she did not fool herself that the smuggler had forgotten his threats.

Another fortnight passed. The leaves were opening on the trees; the birds were gathering worms and insects for their first brood of chicks and the air was filled with their song as they proclaimed their territory. The warmth of the sun grew stronger with every day and the winter-sown crops marched in green rows like miniature armies across the fields. Hannah was returning from taking the children to school and Mark Sawle sat beside her driving the farm cart and humming softly. He had already delivered the milk and he completed his round an hour faster than Dick Caine had ever done.

'You are in good spirits, Mark,' she observed.

When he blushed, she laughed. 'Has it anything to do with Jeannie?' The new housemaid, Jeannie, was also a diligent worker. She knew from the way the maid giggled in Mark's company that she was attracted to the shy groom. 'Are you courting her?'

'I wouldn't know about courting, Mrs Rabson.' His blush deepened. 'Jeannie be sweet and kind.'

'And she is pretty, is she not?' Hannah could not resist teasing.

'Aye, she be fetching.'

'She likes you,' Hannah prompted. She was not usually so indiscreet, but she had always had a romantic streak and the spring air brought the matchmaker out in her. The two servants could not take their eyes off each other and their characters were perfectly suited. 'She would make some lucky man a good wife.'

Mark swallowed and his cheeks were afire with colour. 'Would you have any objection if I was to court her, Mrs Rabson? I know she has only been at the farm a month, but I've never met anyone quite like her.'

'Why should I object? I do not rule the private lives of my servants. But I would have you treat her with respect and your intentions must be honourable. I say this only because I wish for no ill feeling amongst my workers, which might occur if you were trifling with her affections.'

'I would not do that, Mrs Rabson.' He sounded genuinely shocked.

'I did not think you would. If you wish to court Jeannie, you have my blessing.'

Hannah smiled and tipped back her head to enjoy the warmth of the sun on her face. It was rare for her to have a peaceful moment to herself, and she was enjoying the birdsong that accompanied the steady clop of the horse's hoofs. A muttered curse from Mark broke her moment of reverie. She opened her eyes and the euphoria was dashed, replaced by a sick feeling of apprehension. Ahead of them on the road was a lone rider, who had drawn to a halt, his horse blocking the road.

'Well, if this bain't a pleasant surprise. Good day to you, Mrs Rabson.' Harry Sawle ignored his younger brother and bowed over his saddle to Hannah. The brim of his hat shadowed his face but she could feel his gaze undressing her. The man made her flesh crawl.

'Good day, Mr Sawle,' Hannah replied crisply. 'You are blocking the road. Be so kind as to move aside.'

'I expected a warmer greeting after so long.' His lips stretched into a mocking smile.

'Out of the way, Harry. You be stopping Mrs Rabson from her business,' Mark said, his knuckles whitening on the reins.

Harry did not move, and unable to manoeuvre the wagon around him, they had no choice but to halt.

'So, my little brother thinks he be man enough to give me orders.' Harry spoke in a cold and aggressive tone. 'Happen you be forgetting who you be addressing.'

Wishing to avoid a confrontation, Hannah intervened. 'Have you something you wish to say to me, Mr Sawle?'

He studied her without speaking for several moments. Hannah held his gaze, her features devoid of any emotion although her heart was thumping uncomfortably fast. Sawle was as unpredictable as a smouldering fuse on a powder keg.

'Happen you know my intentions, Hannah.'

His smirk chilled her to the core but she did not drop her gaze from the smuggler. She would not let him see that she was nervous.

'It is you who forget your place and to whom you are speaking, Sawle,' she reminded him.

'Just what do you mean, Harry?' Mark challenged. 'Mrs Rabson don't want nothing to do with the likes of you. You stay away from her.'

'Keep out of this, brother,' the smuggler rapped out.

Hannah touched the younger man's arm. 'I am in no danger, Mark.'

'I know him.' Mark used his cuff to wipe away the sweat that had formed on his upper lip. 'He be a devil. He does nothing without some sinister purpose.'

Harry sneered. 'What you gonna do about anything, little brother?'

'I am not impressed by your threats, Sawle.' Hannah lost patience. 'And I do not take kindly to my employees being threatened either.'

'You gonna hide behind her skirts, Mark?' Sawle's gelding edged closer. 'Mrs Rabson and I have some business to discuss.'

Mark secured the reins on the dashboard and crouched, ready to spring to the ground.

'Stay where you are, Mark,' Hannah ordered. 'He is spoiling for a fight.' She snatched the whip from the holder at the side of the wagon and cracked it in the air. 'Move out of my way, Sawle. I have nothing to say to you, and certainly no business to discuss. I made that clear on the last occasion.'

His disfigured cheek puckered as his manner turned malevolent. 'You stepped out of line then, but I was prepared to forgive you. A bit of fire in a woman's blood is something I appreciate.' He tipped back his head and his eyes glittered with a devilish light. 'But no woman threatens me.'

'Then kindly allow us to pass,' she replied.

When he did not move she cracked the whip again, flicking it so that its tip landed on the rump of Harry Sawle's bay gelding. The horse reared, almost unseating its rider. Sawle was no accomplished horseman. He sawed on the reins to keep control, which caused the horse to land on all fours with a jolt that shook his body. The gelding snorted and sidestepped in an erratic fashion. Sawle clung on as it lunged into the stile, slamming its rider's leg against the wooden post.

The air was thick with the sound of Sawle's cursing. Hannah had the reins in her hands, and with the smuggler out of the way, clicked her tongue and urged her mare into a brisk trot.

Mark laughed as they passed his brother. 'You bain't no horseman, Hal. You'll never make a gentleman, though you like to think yourself one.'

Harry Sawle grunted as his knee collided with the stile a second time before he brought his horse under control. The cart was disappearing round the bend in the road ahead. His anger channelled towards his brother. Mark needed teaching a lesson in respect, and that would also show Hannah Rabson that Harry Sawle did not make idle threats.

Chapter Nineteen

St John was restless and disgruntled. He had been tied to Trevowan too long. Life was too quiet, too restricted. The money he had realised from Lisette's jewellery was spent. His gaming debts had been honoured, the servants' wages paid and the rest had gone on seed to put two fields under the plough and the purchase of two horses to work in the fields. He needed to escape. The Bracewaites had invited a dozen guests for a weekend of dancing and gaming. He had no money for the gaming tables and common sense told him that it would be unwise to attend.

Resentment stirred in him. He was tired of the restraints placed on his social life. Trevowan was not free from debt. There was still the loan from Cousin Thomas to repay. Not that his cousin was putting any pressure on him, but he did not want to be beholden to him. The loan was a reminder of his failure. The ghost of his father haunted his dreams with reprimands upon his wastrel habits and reminders that Adam would never have endangered the future of Trevowan if he had been its master. St John was ashamed of how close he had come to losing the estate through his negligence. Yet an inner battle raged in him continually, the profligate warring with the side of him that wanted to prove his family wrong and succeed in making Trevowan as great as it had been in his father's day. And he would do it without the income from the shipyard.

Yet despite this new-found conscience and acknowledgement of responsibility, he still craved his old life. He had no intention of becoming a slave to the land. The only solution was to marry a woman with a considerable fortune.

He paced the family rooms of his home, the sound of his footsteps and the ticking of the many clocks his only companions. The orangery, once the centre of morning gatherings, was stark and unwelcoming in the grey morning light. The portraits of his grandfather and grandmother in the dining room mocked him for its emptiness. The silver candlesticks and tureen covers on the oak coffer gleamed brightly and the room smelt of beeswax from the recently polished table and chairs. Too often he dined alone at a table that could seat a score of people. Even Rowena took her meals in the Dower House with Elspeth. His daughter rose an hour earlier than himself to ride her pony, then, accompanied by a groom, attended the school at Trevowan Hard. She was abed before St John partook of his evening meal.

He glanced around the room, acknowledging that with Amelia spending half the year in London, Elspeth ran the house with military precision, although his aunt spent little time in his company.

He wandered into the winter parlour with its faded yellow and blue peacock wallpaper. The blue brocade on the padded chairs was grey with wear and the Venetian mirror above the fireplace was speckled with patches of black and in need of resilvering. His father had resisted Amelia's requests to pay for new upholstery, hangings and wallpaper. It was a cosy room, despite its declining elegance. A breeze from an open window caused the crystal droplets on the central chandelier to tinkle briefly and then fall still. The silence was unnerving and St John shivered. Where was the sound of animated conversation, laughter, or even heated discussion? His home had become a mausoleum.

His wild parties were to blame for that. He had driven his aunt and stepmother to take up residence in the Dower House. Hannah, Peter, Uncle Joshua and Cecily no longer visited, his long absences disrupting the routine of Sunday family meals. And as for Adam . . .

St John was surprised by the intensity with which he missed the sparring with his twin. Adam now had Boscabel – the house that had become the new focus for family gatherings.

He could hear the muffled voices of Winnie Fraddon and a maid in the kitchen. Outside Isaac Nance shouted an order to a farm hand. It accentuated his feeling of isolation. His reflective mood sobered his resentment towards his family, especially Adam. His brother's energy had brought vitality to Trevowan. Elspeth's strident fortitude had been its stability. The visits by Hannah, Japhet and Peter had given it purpose and a sense of continuity. Loneliness smote him with cruel force. He had been a fool to alienate his family and until now had not realised how deeply he missed them.

He reached for the comfort of the brandy decanter and his hand froze before lifting the stopper. Drink was no substitute for companionship. Regret was a waste of time and solved nothing. He turned abruptly on his heel and was startled to see Elspeth standing in the doorway. He had been so lost in thought he had not heard her approach.

'The house has lost its spirit.' The admission burst unexpectedly from him.

'So you are coming to your senses at last.'

At his scowl her expression softened. 'It is not lost. It is but slumbering. But it should not be neglected too long, or decay will set in.'

Surprised by the lack of condemnation in her voice, St John nodded agreement. 'It is time to resurrect all that Trevowan once was. But without money . . .' He shrugged. 'I have no wish to drag the estate deeper into debt.'

'Trevowan needs new blood – a new generation, a new young mistress.'

'That is not so easy when my reputation is not all it should be,' he said with rare honesty. 'Local families are suspicious that I have led a wild life in recent years.'

Elspeth regarded him over the top of her pince-nez and her tone was unexpectedly without censure. 'You judge yourself too harshly. Trevowan is no small prize to bring to a bride. It is often the way in our family that the young men sow their wild oats before settling down to a respectable life. You have responsibilities now and are no longer so young. Take heart from Japhet. He was the black sheep of this irrepressible family. His life fell apart when he was sent to Botany Bay. He must have thought he had lost everything: his freedom, his wife, his son, his home. Yet when his pardon came through he chose the new colony to make his fortune and change his ways. Marriage and fatherhood have been his salvation. It can be the same for you.'

St John thrust his thumbs into the pockets of his waistcoat and shrugged. 'Japhet loves Gwen and was blessed that she brought him a fortune. I have little faith in love.'

'You must put the past behind you. Meriel was an adventuress and you fell for her seductive charms. As for the other episode with that cold-hearted Virginian wench – well, the less said about that the better. What possessed you to ask her to wed you while Meriel still lived, even though your wife was on her deathbed?'

St John's mouth clamped shut and he glared at his aunt. He should have known her compassion for his plight would be but momentary.

Again she surprised him. 'But that regrettable escapade aside . . . There are good women of fortune aplenty, though men too often fall for beauty when they should pay more heed to character, position and fortune. Tamasine's wedding will be a grand affair. Many eligible women will be present. What better opportunity for you to impress society with your sobriety. You are a handsome landowner. Trevowan is a home any woman would wish to possess and be proud of.'

She left him to ponder her words. He mentally listed the women of fortune of his acquaintance. Elspeth was clearly more optimistic than himself. Last year he had paid court to a wealthy widow, Felicity Barrett, who years ago as an unmarried woman had set her cap at him before his marriage to Meriel. He had thought Felicity easy to win. She had proved surprisingly difficult.

His blood ran hot with humiliation as he remembered how she had turned down his proposal, condemning him for his gaming and drinking. She told him that if he was serious in his intentions he must prove his worthiness to win her hand by changing his libertine ways. Furious at her rejection, he had walked out of her house in Truro and not been in contact with her since.

In the last six months he had rarely gambled and never been in his cups in public. Not through any intention to reform, but because resources and circumstances had kept him tied to Trevowan.

Perhaps those months had not been without purpose. Felicity was a rich woman. He had been overhasty. But had his neglect jeopardised his chance to win her hand? He had thought at the time that their attraction had been mutual. But had another suitor appeared in the intervening months? He could afford to lose no more time if he intended to win her.

Last night had been a full moon. A time that could bring madness to the fore and when emotions became volatile. Senara slept badly, her dreams vivid and violent. The images faded when she awoke and she could not recall their content, but a feeling of tension and nervous unease remained.

The feeling remained throughout the morning. It was her day to take her mother to the old cottage for Caleph's visit. Usually Bridie accompanied them if she was free of parish duties, but today she had gone to St Austell with Maura Keppel to sell the lace made by the village women. Bridie was excited, for it was only the second time that the women had produced enough lace in their homes for sale. She had spoken of nothing else all week, and how she hoped to repay a small instalment of the loan she had taken from Sir Henry Traherne to get the women started with thread, spinning wheels and bobbins.

The old cottage in the clearing in the wood where Hannah and Bridie had once lived with their mother was deserted; it increased Senara's sense that all was not well. Caleph was always here before them. The minutes of waiting stretched into an hour, and while Senara paced the cottage, Leah kept herself occupied by sweeping the floor with a besom.

'What is keeping him?' Senara said for the fourth time.

'Patience, my lovely. He will have forgotten the time.'

An owl hooted. Senara's heart jolted. 'Did you hear that, Ma? An ill omen to be sure. An owl hooting during the day could mean a death.'

Leah swept more vigorously. 'You and your superstitions.' But she paused and made a surreptitious sign of the cross over her heart.

'Ma, there is no need to sweep the floor.' Senara was exasperated by her mother's work. 'Caleph will not notice.'

'This be my home. Even though I don't live here any more, I don't like to see it neglected.'

Senara did not comment. Leah must find it hard to visit here now that the house was empty. The clearing itself was becoming overgrown without the farmyard animals to crop the grass. The vegetable patch beside the cottage was already overrun with brambles.

'Where be Caleph?' Leah voiced her own impatience. 'He is never late. We've been here at least an hour.'

Senara went to the door and looked out. There was no sound of her brother approaching. She frowned, suppressing her worry that some-thing untoward had happened. The gypsies were still camped in the wood at Boscabel, for she had seen the caravan roofs at a distance that morning.

The empty cottage also unsettled her. Most of the furniture had been taken to Polruggan parsonage when Leah had left, and Senara had brought three stools from Boscabel for their use during these visits. Caleph still refused to visit his family at Boscabel or the parsonage. A wicker basket of food and a jug of cider stood on the floor. These Caleph would take back to the campsite. Senara never came to her brother empty-handed even though he argued that he did not like accepting what he consid-ered to be charity.

'You are family,' she would protest. 'The food is for my nieces and nephews if you and Maddie are too proud to eat from my larder.'

As the weeks progressed Caleph had stopped objecting. The basket was laid on the floor and he would collect it without acknowledge-ment when he left. She had been surprised her brother had stayed in the district for so long; usually the gypsies moved on within a week or so. But it was obvious that the death of two of his children had affected him deeply. There was an anger in him that had not been present before. She would sometimes catch him looking at her as though he despised her for her new life of comfort and wealth.

She could understand his jealousy. Life on the road was hard and unremitting, and wherever the gypsies went they were viewed with suspicion and often hatred. Yet in his gruff way she knew Caleph cared for her and Bridie and Leah.

In the distance she heard the clock of Penruan church strike one.

'Something has happened to Caleph.' Leah came to her daughter's side. 'He has never been late.'

'Aunt Senara!' called a breathless voice.

Senara hurried outside. Caleph's son, Ty, was running towards the cottage. 'Come quickly,' he shouted and bent double to relieve a stitch in his side. 'It be me da. He's got a fever.'

Leah put a hand on Senara's arm to stop her darting forward. 'I'll tend him. You cannot risk taking a fever – not with your young ones.'

Ty straightened. 'Da were stabbed in a fight last week. Now he got the fever. Ma can't do nothin' more. Ma says for you to get the doctor. Says you'd pay for him.'

'I'll ride to Fowey and bring Dr Yeo.' Senara knew Maddie's healing knowledge was as skilful as her own. Both had been taught by her grandmother. She controlled her fear that an internal organ had been damaged in the stabbing. Even Dr Yeo would not be able to save Caleph if that had occurred. 'Hop in the wagon, Ty, you can drive with us.'

The lad shook his head. 'Ma said for me to get back.' He ran off.

Leah hobbled out of the cottage with the wicker basket of food and Senara helped her climb into the wagon. When she set her mother down in the campsite before riding on to Fowey, Leah asked anxiously, 'Will Dr Yeo come to the camp? No decent doctor would help the likes of Caleph.'

'Dr Yeo will tend my brother and will be paid well for his services.' Senara was confident that the doctor would come with her. He would not wish to lose the patronage of her family by refusing. She drove the horse hard, sick with dread that Maddie had allowed the infection to take hold for too long before asking for help. She cursed her sister-in-law's stubborn pride.

An hour later Senara returned to the gypsy camp with Dr Yeo riding his mare beside her pony trap. She was shocked to see the families gathered around Maddie's campfire. Inside the wagon Caleph's voice was high-pitched with delirium. Maddie appeared at the doorway and stood aside for Dr Yeo to enter. She barred Senara. 'No point in us all crowding the doc. Best you wait by the fire.'

'How bad is Caleph?' Senara demanded.

The slump to Maddie's shoulders and the fear in her eyes told her the worst.

135

'He be in good hands now,' Leah comforted, emerging from the caravan. 'I know you did your best, Maddie.'

The gypsy woman did not answer and stepped back into the dark interior.

'She should have come to us before this,' Senara seethed under her breath. She itched to enter the caravan and help Dr Yeo, but Maddie would resent her intrusion, so she bit back her impatience.

'But she did swallow her pride and ask for help. That would have cost her dear. She be a wise woman.' Leah wrung her hands. 'What life is this that I brought Caleph into?'

'Caleph is all Romany,' Senara consoled her. 'He took after Pa. He would never have settled away from this life.'

Two of the gypsies moved away from the fire to allow them room on a felled tree trunk. No one spoke to them. Leah gripped her daughter's hand as they waited for Dr Yeo to reappear. An hour passed and Senara's nerves were strained to their limits. She knew too well the dangers facing her brother.

'How did he get in a knife fight?' She could no longer contain her anguish.

Leah shrugged. 'From the shifty looks of the men, it was one of their own. You know their hot tempers.'

'They don't like it that we are staying here,' Maddie said, coming silently up to them. 'His leadership was challenged.'

'How is he?' Leah rose stiffly, her stare on the caravan.

'That doctor do reckon he will live as he be so strong. He purged him and cut him to burst a pustule that ran green when it were opened. He reckoned there were some cloth in the wound – deep inside. He said Caleph be lucky he operated in time. Now he's sewing him up.'

'Praise the Lord for that,' Leah declared and wiped a tear from her eye.

Dr Yeo stepped from the caravan and addressed Maddie. 'Put a fresh poultice on the wound twice a day to draw out any residual ill humours. I've left the wound partly open to drain. If a secondary infection does not set in then he has a chance. He needs lots of nourishing broth; even a little brandy will strengthen the blood.'

He tipped his hat to Senara. 'The fever is abating. If it persists past tomorrow I will attend again.'

'Thank you for your courtesy and time, Dr Yeo,' Senara replied as he looked with relief towards his mare as though he half expected to find the animal missing. He left the camp with a nervous glance at the gypsies who had gathered round to hear his words.

'May I see him, Maddie?' Leah asked.

It annoyed Senara to hear her mother asking permission. Maddie nodded and gestured for both women to follow her. Caleph lay under a patchwork quilt and did not stir as they approached. Senara touched his brow and found it not unduly hot.

'He is sleeping, Ma. That is the best healer.'

She left Leah to spend some moments alone with Caleph and sought out Maddie, who was stirring a pot of gruel over the campfire.

'I will send a bottle of brandy, and two chickens for the broth for Caleph.'

'We don't want your charity. We manage well enough. There weren't no money for a doctor or I would not have sent for you.' The woman's resentment was fiercer than a roaring fire blasting Senara.

'Surely we both want what is best for Caleph. I know you think Ma and I betrayed you all by leaving, but that does not mean we have stopped loving you. You were my dearest friend, Maddie.'

'There bain't no place for me in your world. We were only here because—' She bit her words off short and turned her back on Senara to stir the cauldron.

'Is Caleph in trouble with the law?' Senara probed. 'Though you are welcome here, you usually stay only a few weeks.'

'It was to protect Jojo. My brother fell foul of the Mowat brothers at the goose fair. They want his hide but they spend their summers in Wales. We can move on soon.'

'And how did Caleph get stabbed? Was that to do with Jojo?'

'Happen that be our affair.' Maddie clamped her mouth shut.

Jojo was a hothead and Caleph had got into several fights through his brother-in-law. Caleph was loyal to every man, woman and child under his leadership. She noticed one caravan was missing from the clearing and guessed it had left after the stabbing. But Caleph's blood would be avenged. It was the gypsy way.

'Billy Brown will bring the chickens and brandy. Ma will not rest easy until she knows that Caleph is out of danger. I will bring her again tomorrow.'

Maddie nodded. It was a truce of some sorts between them. Senara did not want Caleph to leave Boscabel until he was completely recovered. As she left the campsite she noticed the pale sphere of the moon large and sinister against the blue sky. It rarely showed its power and force to the earth during the day, and again she saw it as an omen of ill fortune. She could not shake the feeling that further violence would be afoot before the dawn rose tomorrow.

Chapter Twenty

Harry Sawle was burning for revenge. He had been drinking heavily all day. He would not allow his brother to think he had got the better of him. With the approach of dusk Harry, Mordecai Nance and three other men were hidden behind the stone wall of the meadow where the Rabson cattle grazed. Harry could hear his brother whistling as he came to bring the herd into the barn to be milked for the evening.

They leapt over the wall and knocked Mark to the ground before he could even cry out.

Mark was slightly built and all his attackers were heavily muscled. The first blow to his jaw felled him. Another to his gut had him gagging on a rush of vomit. His fists swung feebly against hands slamming into his body. Even his kicks were futile.

'Thought you could laugh at me, did you?' Harry grunted as he kicked his brother viciously in the ribs. 'There be no woman here now for you to hide behind.'

Several more kicks to his back and head followed as Harry warned, 'And if that uppity bitch says one word to the authorities of this, she'll regret it.' His violent attack made him pant from exertion.

There was a shout from Sam and the sound of a blunderbuss being discharged.

'Run for it!' Harry ordered.

They had horses hidden in a copse on the other side of the wall. Harry Sawle did not expect his brother to regain consciousness, neither did he care.

The assailants had gone by the time Sam knelt at the side of Mark's bloodied figure. 'Who did this to you?' he demanded. The men had all had mufflers over their lower faces and he had been too far away to see them clearly. He thought he had recognised Harry Sawle, but in the fading light he could not be sure. Mark was barely conscious.

'Was it your brother?' Sam demanded.

'No!' Mark croaked, spitting out a broken tooth. Blood was running from his mouth and ears. 'No.' The effort needed to speak made him pass out.

Sam did not believe him. There had been fear in the young man's eyes. Sam swallowed a rush of bile to his throat at the savageness of the attack and struggled to calm his anger. He despised bullies and mindless violence. He picked up the broken body and carried it back to the house.

Hannah had heard the shot and had run outside. She cried out in alarm as her overseer approached and ran back into the house to sweep aside the remnants of the supper laid out on the kitchen table where the children had just finished eating. At seeing the bloodied and beaten figure she ordered Davey to take the younger children up to their room. Horror gripped her at the extent of Mark's injuries. His face was a bloodied mess, his eyes and mouth cut. His shirt and jerkin were torn and blood seeped through the rough material. He looked more dead than alive.

'Is he dead, Sam?' she demanded.

Jeannie wailed at the sight of Mark's figure. 'He can't be dead.' The maid wrung her hands and started to scream.

'He lives – just,' Sam informed the women, laying Mark gently on the table. He rounded on Jeannie with uncharacteristic temper. 'Quit wailing. It will not help him. Your mistress needs you to help her.'

The maid was too locked in her misery to heed him and her screams rose in intensity. Hannah placed a towel under Mark's head. 'Fetch Dr Chegwidden, Sam. These injuries are too bad for Senara to deal with. And then ride for the authorities. This is Harry Sawle's doing.'

Mark stirred. His eyes, swollen from his beating, were narrow bloodshot slits. 'Not Harry.'

'Then who was it?' Hannah pressed. 'They must be brought to justice for this outrage.'

'It weren't Harry.' The words slurred and Mark slipped back into unconsciousness.

Hannah was frightened by the violence of the beating. It had all the hallmarks of an attack by Sawle.

'Don't let him die!' Jeannie clawed at her face. 'Please, God, don't let him die!'

The continued wailing jarred Hannah's already raw nerves. She lost patience and slapped the woman's cheek. The maid fell on a chair, her eyes wide with shock, her mouth open but no sound now coming from it.

'Hysteria will not help Mark,' she explained. 'Boil up some water, Jeannie. I will clean his wounds until Dr Chegwidden arrives.'

Jeannie continued to sob as she worked. Hannah cut Mark's shirt from his battered torso. Bruises were already forming across his ribcage and clumps of mud stuck to his lacerated flesh from the heavy boots that had slammed into him.

'Did you see who it was, Sam?' Hannah asked. 'I think Mark is covering for his brother.'

The older man shrugged. 'It could have been Sawle. There were five of them. But if he says not . . . Would he lie to save his brother if Sawle did this?'

Hannah shook her head, her eyes misted with tears as Mark groaned at a light touch to a bruise. She prayed that he had no internal bleeding, for that would kill him.

Jeannie carried a bowl of heated water to the table, 'Let me tend him, mistress. I know how.'

Hannah stepped aside as the maid tenderly bathed Mark's wounds. Her expression was tight with worry as she addressed Sam. 'Why then was he beaten?' She was shocked to think that the incident on the road could have led to such brutality. 'Take Sheba to summon the doctor. She is the fastest. Whoever did this must pay.'

Chegwidden arrived an hour later. Hannah left the room while the doctor stripped off Mark's remaining clothes to examine him. She was called in when he had finished.

'He has a nasty wound to his head. Get Deacon to tie him to his bed tonight. He could become violent. Head wounds do that to a man. Three ribs are broken and I've strapped them up. There could be damage to his kidneys and liver. If he lives through the night he could survive. You may wish to send for his mother.'

He placed two phials on the table. 'Give him six drops of this if he starts to stir. He must lie still or he will cause further internal damage. I shall call again on the morrow. He will also get a fever and for this he needs the physic in the second bottle. Your servant should stay with him through the night.'

'I will not leave his side.' Jeannie, ashen with fear, had returned to the kitchen after the doctor's inspection and was now clasping Mark's hand.

Hannah nodded. 'Aggie will make up a truckle bed in the parlour for Mark and another for you, Jeannie.'

The older maid sniffed her disapproval. 'Jeannie be too young. Her reputation . . .'

'Nothing untoward will happen. Mark needs the tender care Jeannie can give him.' Hannah was irritated by the petty foolishness of her complaints. Jeannie, who was clearing away the bloodied rags from the table, smiled her gratitude at her mistress.

Chegwidden shrugged on his greatcoat and picked up his gloves. 'Who did this?'

Before Sam could speak, Hannah said, 'We do not know. But they were men up to no good.'

'There have been reports of cattle rustlers.' Chegwidden sniffed his disapproval. 'And the free-traders are a law unto themselves. There was the murder of your brother's bailiff not long ago.'

'I intend that the culprits will be found and brought to justice.' Hannah placed a cooling cloth on Mark's brow. She remembered Harry's threats when he had come across her in the barn. This was a warning of what would happen to anyone who crossed the smuggler. Did he intend for Sam to be next? Or Adam? Or herself? Or worst of all, as he had once threatened, if she did not comply with his demands, would an accident befall one of her children? From the way Sawle had waylaid her on the road, she sensed a sinister motive behind his actions. Somehow he had to be stopped.

After Chegwidden had left and Mark was settled in the parlour, Hannah sat at the kitchen table with Sam, talking in low voices.

'We must have proof that Harry Sawle did this,' she said. 'We cannot act against him without it.'

'Sawle covers his tracks well.'

Hannah's eyes blazed with fury. 'Whatever the cost, he must be stopped. Adam will agree with me. Sawle has escaped justice for too long.'

The next morning she called on Sir Henry Traherne and he ordered Sawle to be arrested on suspicion of the attack. But Sawle had left the district, and no one when questioned knew of his whereabouts, or if they did, they were too frightened to talk.

Chapter Twenty-one

Senara could never witness a wedding ceremony and remain dry-eyed. Today was no exception. Tamasine looked beautiful in a slim-fitting dress of white silk with a band of gold embroidery under the high waist and on its hem. Her hair was piled high on her crown in a Grecian style threaded through with a rope of pearls, and she wore the ruby necklace and earrings that had been her father's gift to her mother.

Trewenna church was filled with the scent of flowers, and as the couple emerged a chorus of cheers from the villagers greeted them. The hot June sun shone in a cloudless sky but its brightness was eclipsed by the radiance of Tamasine's smile.

'It is a perfect match,' Senara said to Adam. 'Tamasine has found the happiness she deserves.'

The service over, Max and Tamasine rode back to Boscabel in an open carriage decorated with roses and pulled by four matching grey horses. A minstrel rode behind the bridal couple strumming a be-ribboned guitar. The family and guests processed in their own carriages and coaches behind them. As the couple rode under the gatehouse arch at Boscabel a shower of wild flower petals floated over them and they were cheered by the shipwright families and Loveday servants who had not attended the service.

The dancing and feasting continued throughout the day. Boscabel had been transformed for the occasion. The old hall had been garlanded with lilies and honeysuckle and a wedding feast of seven courses had been prepared for the guests. Outside two pigs had been roasted on spits, casks of cider opened and a fiddler engaged for the shipwrights' and estate workers' entertainment. While family and friends enjoyed a sumptuous wedding feast in the old hall to the music of a string quartet in the minstrels' gallery, outside a troupe of tumblers entertained the children.

Adam surveyed the scene with pride as seventy guests sat down to dine. Several members of Max's family were present, including his mother, sister Venetia and her husband Leo, six cousins and two aunts and uncles. After the criticisms of Clarissa Deverell at Christmas it had been a relief to witness Venetia greet Tamasine with genuine pleasure and the warmth of an old friend. The Deverell cousins, although more reserved, soon fell under the young bride's charms and after the meal crowded around her to vie for her attention. The last of Adam's reservations that trouble lay ahead from Tamasine's in-laws was dispelled when Clarissa Deverell acted as though she had introduced Max and Tamasine herself. She was often heard pronouncing to any who would listen that Tamasine's fore-bears had fought at Agincourt and that her mother was a famed beauty of her day.

Both Boscabel and Trevowan were full of guests. Aunt Margaret lodged at the Dower House with Elspeth and Amelia. St John, who had distanced himself from the family since Christmas, had insisted that Max's cousins stay at Trevowan together with several friends of their own family who had travelled from all over Cornwall. The truce had held between the twins and St John had been remarkably accommo-dating and helpful. Adam was surprised at how much deference his brother showed to one of his guests in particular. He studied St John, interested that he chatted animatedly with Felicity Barrett and drank only sparingly from his goblet.

St John knew his family and neighbours were judging his conduct. His pride still smarted from their condemnation in recent years. He was determined to show them that he took his responsibilities to Trevowan seriously. He was no longer under the influence of his libertine friends Basil Bracewaite and the Honourable Percy Fetherington. It had been a shock when both of them had married in the last three months after whirlwind romances. Percy had been devastated by the sudden seizure and slow recovery of his father. His mother had browbeaten him into marriage to the daughter of a childhood friend to ensure an heir for the title and estate. After a heavy gaming session when Basil had lost a thousand guineas in one night, his father had sent him to relatives in Cheshire, where he had fallen for the charms of a pretty young gentle-woman of frivolous character and the dowry of a church mouse. He had married her within a month and she was now carrying his child. So far marriage had curbed both his friends' wilder ways and they were disinclined to spend time away from their wives gaming in Bodmin or Truro.

Aunt Margaret had travelled down from London with Amelia and Rafe and they were to spend the summer in Cornwall. The edge had been taken off Margaret's happiness over the wedding at having to travel without her son Thomas and his wife Georganna. Ten days before they were to travel, Georganna's uncle, who was joint owner of Mercer and Lascalles Bank, had died. Thomas and his wife had stayed behind to deal with the legal matters arising from Lascalles' death and Thomas had had to take over the running of the bank.

With his home overflowing with guests, St John had been apprehensive at how the family would view his request that Felicity, her daughter Charlotte and her mother Sophia Quinton be included amongst the guests. Adam, eager for a show of family solidarity, had been delighted. Hannah had also expressed her pleasure. Before their marriages she had been friendly with Felicity, whose parents had then lived in a large house on the outskirts of Fowey. Sophia Quinton and Hannah's mother had been friends since childhood, so Cecily was excited to renew an old acquaintanceship.

St John had been uncertain how Felicity would receive the invitation, as they had parted rather stormily when she had turned down his proposal of marriage last autumn. From discreet enquiries he had learned that she remained unattached, although it was rumoured that Bernard Ottershawe continued to pay court to her in the hope of winning her as his bride. Felicity had accepted the invitation by return of messenger providing that her mother accompanied her to preserve her reputation. St John reluctantly agreed.

Felicity was not the only guest to unexpectedly accept the invitation to attend. Sir Henry Traherne, his wife and his mother-in-law the Lady Anne Druce were also present. Lady Anne and her daughter Roslyn had refused to receive the Loveday family after Japhet had been arrested on his wedding day to Gwendolyn Druce. Sir Henry had continued his friendship with Adam at no little expense to his personal peace within his own home. Japhet and Gwen's letters home had not changed the two women's minds about the couple, but Sir Henry had lost patience and threatened to banish Lady Anne from his home if she refused to act civilly towards his friends and attend the wedding. Roslyn and Lady Anne remained dour-faced in their disapproval but they had complied with his wishes.

Adam continued his appraisal of the guests. The only absentees of any consequence were Lord and Lady Fetherington and Squire Penwithick and his wife, who were in London attending to government business. Before he had left Cornwall, Squire Penwithick had shown his approval of Tamasine and had been adamant that his home be placed at the disposal of the newlyweds for the first two days of their honeymoon before they left for Max's estate in Dorset. This was another arrangement that pleased Clarissa Deverell and her reception of Tamasine had been markedly warmer than on her previous visit.

Adam performed his role as the perfect host, moving amongst and talking to everyone to ensure that all their needs were satisfied. It was early evening before he found a moment to himself and enjoyed standing alone to watch the proceedings around him. The old hall and solar buzzed with animated conversation and many of the guests were dancing. He experienced a moment of intense pride that his home was such an apt setting for the occasion. After so many problems in recent years it was uplifting to have such a joyful cause for celebration.

It made him magnanimous and he approached Lady Traherne to ask her to dance. He had seen her signalling across the room to where her husband was dancing with Hannah. Roslyn was sour-faced and intent upon attracting her husband's attention so they could make their departure.

'Lady Traherne, your servant. May I have the honour of this dance?'

Her stare was glacial and he thought she was about to refuse him. He had never liked Roslyn, a woman with little humour and too great a sense of her own importance. He bowed to her. 'I have not thanked you for gracing Boscabel with your presence today. It has saddened us that you have not called before.'

'You know my reasons,' she said coldly. 'Henry was insistent that we attend.'

'Sir Henry has proved himself a loyal friend on many occasions.' Adam checked a rush of anger at her ill grace. 'I hope we can put our differences aside, Lady Traherne.'

He held out his hand for her to take. She bristled with indignation and disapproval and avoided meeting his eye. She had never accepted Senara as his wife and had refused to receive her. To accept Adam's invitation now was tantamount to giving her approval to that marriage and everything that had happened since. Yet to refuse one's host was the grossest breach of manners.

'Lady Traherne is regretfully indisposed, Mr Loveday,' Lady Anne intervened.

At the same moment Sir Henry appeared at Adam's side. 'So you are to dance with my wife, Adam. Good show. I must seek out your own pretty spouse. It will be my pleasure.' He shot Roslyn a fierce look before approaching Senara.

'I suppose you regard this as a victory,' Lady Traherne muttered as Adam led her on to the space cleared for dancing.

'We have always been saddened by the rift between Gwendolyn and yourself and your mother.'

'My sister was wilful and disobedient. Your cousin proved how disastrous the marriage would be.'

'They love each other and to a degree few find in this lifetime,' Adam retaliated in support of the couple. It was obvious that there was little love between Sir Henry and his wife. Sir Henry had married Roslyn for her inheritance and she him for the status he could give her.

'Gwen had no right to put love before duty.'

'I put love before duty. My father was an exceptional man in forgiving me. I could never have found the happiness I now have married to any woman except Senara. My father was wise. Like him I prize family loyalty above everything. Can you not be happy that Gwendolyn is with the man she loves?'

'She is on the other side of the world, living little better than a vagabond.' Roslyn spat her venom. 'Your cousin has proved he cannot provide a decent home for her, or even any home for all we know.'

Adam clenched his jaw to stop a heated reply. His voice held a lethal calmness. 'It takes a rare courage to leave one's family and a comfortable and protected world. Gwendolyn has my admiration. She has the heart of a pioneer. It is women such as her who brought the old colony in America to such greatness.'

'You are entitled to your opinion.' Lady Traherne regarded him sourly. 'I think her a fool.'

'Then long may loyalty, steadfastness, belief in our fellow man and unremitting courage make fools of us all,' Adam countered. 'Gwendolyn has my respect and admiration. It is no wonder that Japhet worships her.'

An outraged hiss through her protruding teeth was Roslyn's only reply. Adam kept his voice even, though her callous disregard for her sister's welfare or happiness appalled him. 'Do you not miss her?' he asked.

'She brought shame to our family. You would not be so critical if you knew the gossip my mother and I have had to endure.'

'I would have thought that you who have so much – a luxurious home, every comfort provided for, healthy children and a devoted husband . . .' He left the sentence unfinished. Sir Henry's many affairs had become less discreet in the last year. Roslyn was a harridan who brought no warmth to their marriage. 'You could not be jealous of your sister, could you, Lady Traherne? Gwendolyn was always such a sweet-natured, caring woman.'

The music ended and he bowed to her. Her glare could have frozen

Hades. Adam pitied his friend at being chained to such a wife. It made him want to seek out Senara, but she was dancing with Leo.

Max waylaid him. 'You have made this day a memorable occasion. For that I thank you. My wife and I shall be leaving shortly. I hope you will take time away from the shipyard to visit us in Dorset.'

Adam grinned. 'It will be a pleasure, but I am loath to leave the yard until the first of the merchantmen is launched. It is the largest ship we have built.'

'And she will be the first of many. Our business partners are pleased with her progress. You will not fail us, my friend.'

'Are you two still talking business?' Tamasine had finished a dance with one of Max's older cousins and her cheeks were flushed with excitement.

'I was saying to Adam that it is almost time for us to leave, my dear.' Max raised her fingers to his lips to kiss them.

'Oh, but I must dance with him before I go.' Tamasine linked her arm through her brother's.

'She's a determined minx.' Adam laughed back over his shoulder at the smiling bridegroom. 'She'll need a firm hand to control her.'

'Max knows how headstrong I am and he loves me for it.' Tamasine was breathless with happiness. 'This is the most wonderful day of my life. But I shall miss you all.'

'And we will miss you. Father would be proud of you this day.'

A shadow clouded the happiness in her eyes. 'I wish he was here. I owe everything to him, and to you, of course, for also accepting me.'

'Our family would not be complete without you.' Adam raised her hand to his lips in salute to her.

She stopped dancing and impetuously kissed his cheek. 'You are the best of brothers and I am the most fortunate of women to have found such happiness. And it seems that my wedding has brought our family together. St John has been extremely pleasant and helpful. I pray your differences with him are at an end.'

Adam hid his reservations, unwilling to spoil her happiness. 'I hope so too. Now your husband grows impatient.' He twirled her under his arm and led her back to Maximillian.

Ten minutes later everyone was gathered outside cheering as the couple rode away.

'The day is still young. There is more dancing,' Adam declared to the remainder of his guests. He placed his arm around Senara's waist and kissed her brow as they paused to watch their guests drifting back inside the house or strolling through the grounds.

Senara smiled adoringly at her husband. 'The day has been a great success. It has been many months since the family have been so joyfully united.'

'And much of its success is because of you, my love,' he praised. 'How does it feel to be the lady of the manor?'

'Daunting,' she answered with a grin. 'I have been fearful all day that I have forgotten some important detail for so grand an affair.'

'You gave Tamasine everything to make the day perfect. Yet so much was denied you at our wedding.'

'You wed me by the old rites at Avebury on the winter solstice and our son was born that evening. How could I wish for any of that day to be changed? The ceremony we had here was a simple one to appease your family, but we were already married in the way that mattered to me.'

'You deserved more than such a humble start to our marriage.'

She sighed. 'How can I convince you that my wedding was perfect because the only thing that was important were the vows we made to each other?'

He grinned and whispered in her ear. 'I can think of many ways you can convince me of your love, but sadly we have too many guests clamouring for our attention. I shall be patient and wait.'

'You will not be disappointed,' she promised. 'But first I must see to those clamouring hordes. Were there not strolling players to perform this evening? I must ensure that they have everything they need.' She hurried away to complete her task.

Adam felt a moment's disquiet at noticing St John's frown as he watched Mrs Barrett conversing with Sir Henry Traherne, who was leaning very close to the pretty widow.

He joined his twin. They had said few words to each other all day. 'You have done much to make this day a success, St John.' He was pleased that his brother showed no signs of inebriation. 'Your guest Mrs Barrett has enjoyed herself. She has spent most of the day chatting to Hannah and Lady Traherne. She spoke very warmly of Trevowan. I remember her from my visits home during my time in the navy, but not that well. Is she an old acquaintance of yours?'

St John's expression became wary. 'She was part of the social circle before I wed Meriel. And she was friends with Hannah. She married Captain Barrett and moved away. He was killed in action at sea. I met her again last year in Truro.'

Felicity had glanced at St John several times during her conversation with Sir Henry. Was romance blossoming between his twin and the widow? Adam wondered. She seemed a very pleasant woman, perhaps a little reserved – not quite the passionate type St John usually favoured. But then his choice had proved disastrous in the past.

Sir Henry whispered in Mrs Barrett's ear and she blushed and looked uncomfortable. 'I think you should rescue Mrs Barrett from Sir Henry,' Adam said. 'And Jerome Bracewaite has also shown an interest in her. She is popular.'

'I have neglected my guest.' St John excused himself and sauntered to her side. Felicity took his arm and was smiling up at him as they walked out into the garden.

Adam noticed Aunt Elspeth, who was seated with Amelia, beckoning urgently to him. Concerned, he hurried to their side. Both women looked shaken.

'This is most unfortunate,' Elspeth began. 'Especially on such a day.'

'The past continues to haunt us,' groaned Amelia.

'Whatever has occurred?' Adam was puzzled at their obvious distress.

'Have you seen the jewellery Maria Traherne is wearing?'

Adam had not noticed. Maria had married a cousin of Sir Henry last year and was here with her husband, a lieutenant in the navy whose ship had recently returned to Plymouth.

At his confused expression Amelia lowered her voice. 'That ruby pendant she is wearing belonged to Lisette. It was one of her favourites. How has Sir Henry's cousin come by it? Lisette must have sold it. She must still be in the district.'

Adam groaned inwardly and rubbed his brow. This was not the time to consider such matters, but the mystery must be solved. 'I shall talk with Maria and her husband.'

Lieutenant Traherne greeted Adam warmly, questioning him about his own time in the navy. As soon as he could politely change the conversation, Adam complimented Maria upon her pendant.

'Is it not just too divine?' Maria touched it lovingly. 'Roger gave it to me on his return as an anniversary gift. He is exceedingly generous, is he not?'

'So it was recently purchased?' Adam pursued.

Roger Traherne frowned. 'Strange thing to ask, Loveday.'

'It is very like one possessed by my cousin Lisette. You may recall that she disappeared some time ago. We have been concerned for her welfare.'

'I bought it from a jeweller's in Plymouth.'

'Could I have his name? It may help with our enquiries if it was sold on Lisette's behalf.' Adam spoke as casually as possible but he was disturbed by this news. The pendant was unmistakably Lisette's. He had seen her wear it many times.

'Is your cousin in any trouble?' Lieutenant Traherne looked concerned. 'I mean, selling off the family jewels is a bit drastic.'

'They were hers to sell, but I would not like to think of her in difficulty and too proud to approach our family for help.'

'Quite right, old chap.' The officer's expression cleared. 'The jeweller's name was Mendoza.'

Adam put the information to the back of his mind. Lisette had caused enough problems to his family whilst she had lived at Trevowan; he was not about to allow her to spoil this special day.

The merriment continued for another two hours before the guests who did not have to travel far began to take their leave. Adam and Senara stood in the hall bidding them farewell. Everyone complimented Adam on the success of the celebrations and of the magnificence of Boscabel. Amongst the last to leave was the party returning to Trevowan.

Adam kissed his aunts and stepmother. Amelia held her sleeping son Rafe in her arms. 'Your father would have been proud of all you have done this day. Tamasine has made a good match.'

'She is happy and that is what is important,' Adam replied. Amelia had been desperate to see her stepdaughter married and no longer her responsibility. He hoped that now Tamasine no longer lived at Boscabel Amelia would visit more often. He took Rafe as she climbed into the carriage and handed his half-brother back to her once she was settled. 'Father would have been happy to know that you have accepted his daughter and attended her wedding. Thank you, Amelia. It meant a lot to us all.'

'I should have come to terms with the girl's existence long before this.'

Aunt Margaret paused by his side as he took her hand to assist her into the carriage. She looked pleased as she watched St John draping a shawl over Mrs Barrett's shoulders. 'Do I see a match in the offing, Adam?'

Senara laughed, knowing Margaret's enthusiasm for matchmaking. 'She is the very bride that St John needs, but I gather from Hannah that Mrs Barrett is not playing easily into his hands. She does not approve of St John's drinking and gaming.'

'Then she is wise as well as pretty. And she is not without a handsome fortune from her late husband, I believe.'

Adam wagged a finger at his aunt. 'No matchmaking. Let the couple decide themselves if they are right for each other.'

'If Margaret does not throw them together, I will,' Elspeth said sharply. 'Felicity is indeed the wife St John needs.'

'My brother has certainly been on his best behaviour today,' Adam observed. 'Everyone has. Even the children have been less noisy and disruptive.'

'Happiness is infectious,' Senara replied. 'Tamasine and Max are very much in love.'

When finally everyone not staying overnight at Boscabel had departed, Adam found Senara in the nursery. She put her finger to her lips as she tiptoed to the door. 'They are all sound asleep. For once they have been angels, even Joel, but they are worn out from all the excitement.'

On the dimly lit landing Adam pulled Senara to him and kissed her. 'It has been a remarkable day. Even Peter refrained from his sermonising.'

'Ah, there is just cause for that.' Senara grinned. 'Bridie is four months with child. She said nothing before this because of her miscarriage last year. I have had a difficult time ensuring that she rested and did not fuss over the needs of our guests.'

'She has your mother at the parsonage to help her this time.'

Senara nodded. She was naturally worried about her sister, but Bridie was stronger than she looked. Senara prayed that she would carry this child full term and be delivered safely of a healthy baby.

Chapter Twenty-two

News of a spate of robberies on the day of the wedding was on everyone's lips. The thieves had struck the houses of the guests attending at Boscabel. Some small pieces of silver, including Joshua's grandfather's snuffbox, had been stolen from Trewenna rectory. Coins and trinkets had disappeared from various cottages at Trewenna, Trevowan and Trevowan Hard. Mark Sawle's quarterly wages had been taken from his cottage on the Rabson farm and two bridles from the farm stable. No one had seen any strangers on the farm. It was the first week Mark had been fit enough to return to his full duties and he had been delivering the milk. Sam, who had been repairing a barn roof, had been in his cottage with Charlie preparing their lunch when the robbery occurred and there had been no warning from the dogs. Traherne Hall had been hit the hardest. Though many of the servants were in residence, two of Sir Henry's horses had been taken from a meadow, and again no one had seen the thieves as they had struck when the servants had been eating their supper.

Suspicion fell upon the gypsy camp. The villagers resented that they had stayed in the district for some months. Caleph had been slow to recover from the stabbing and an outbreak of the bloody flux had hit the group and prevented them from travelling to their summer grounds. An elderly woman and one baby had died and there had been nothing even Dr Yeo could do to save them.

Adam learned of the robberies on his family's property when Elspeth and Hannah brought the children to school at the yard. During the morning several men had reported to him that small items of value were missing from their cottages when they returned from the celebrations. For so many thefts to have taken place they must have been carried out by a gang that also knew who would be attending the wedding.

Adam was busy in the yard office when Caleph's son, Ty, ran in. The boy's eyes were wild with fear.

'You gotta come, Uncle Adam. They've come with pitchforks and knives to get us. One had a rope and kept shouting they'd hang us. Pa don't want no trouble. We bain't done nothing.' He spoke so fast and was so out of breath that Adam had trouble deciphering his words. Tears had streaked clean channels down his grubby cheeks.

'Who has come? And what is this about a hanging?'

'It be men from Trewenna mostly.' Ty dashed the tears from his cheeks. 'My brother Milo has gone to fetch the parson. But it be you they will listen to. You gotta come. They want blood. Bain't no one else can save us.' He darted back outside, his bare feet pounding the earth as he took off back to the gypsy camp.

Adam did not stop to saddle his horse Solomon but rode bareback after his nephew. The angry shouts reached him long before he appeared in the camp clearing. A dozen men from Trewenna were fighting with the gypsy menfolk. Several heads were bloodied and one gypsy lay on the ground seemingly unconscious, his wife crouched at his side screaming curses at the villagers.

Adam regretted that in his haste he had left his saddle holster in the yard. A gunshot would have quickly brought the mob to order. He rode into the middle of the mêlée, shouting, 'Stop this fighting at once!'

Few paid him any heed, though some villagers yelled as they fought.

'We want justice.'

'Thieves!'

'Rogues!'

'Hang 'em.'

'There will be no hanging,' Adam ground out as he swung Solomon round to jostle the fighters into breaking apart. 'Stop at once, or I'll have you all arrested for disturbing the peace, and the men of Trewenna for trespass on my land.'

'They must pay for their thieving. You can't protect them, Cap'n Loveday.' Ned Stone, the innkeeper at Trewenna, was red-faced with outrage. He was short, his close-set eyes and pockmarked face not the features of a man who was easily trusted.

'Where is your proof that these men are the culprits?' Adam demanded.

'They be gypsies, thieving tykes the lot of them.' Virgil Stone, Ned's cousin who worked at the remaining Traherne mine, hurled a stone at a gypsy youth. It struck his shoulder. 'We're gonna search their wagons. We'll find the proof. My wife had a silver locket taken.'

The air was thick with menace. Caleph limped forward leaning on a stick to support his still weak body. His shirt was torn and one eye was swollen shut. 'We bain't stole nothing, Mr Loveday.'

153

'Sir Henry lost two horses.' Virgil pointed to the tethered gypsy animals. 'They be horse thieves – always have been. Reckon some of them mares got coal rubbed into white markings to disguise them.'

'None of those horses have the breeding of Sir Henry's hunters,' Adam snapped. 'They are wild ponies.'

'Then they be hidden on the moor,' another miner snarled.

'Those two were in Trewenna yesterday,' Ned Stone pointed to two of the older men, 'just afore the wedding – snooping round to see what could be taken.'

Until now the gypsies had not defended themselves. Adam turned to the two men Stone had indicated. 'Were you in Trewenna?'

'Aye. We had repaired some pots for two of the women. That's what we do as tinkers – mend pots!' They were surly and insolent, and if they were innocent Adam did not blame them for their attitude.

'It don't mean you didna come back to steal from us later,' Ned Stone persisted.

'That is speculation, not proof,' Adam stated, fighting to keep control of his own temper. 'And since when were you a law-abiding citizen, Ned, or your cousin Virgil? You work as a tubman for Sawle.'

'That be a lie.'

Adam fixed him with a chilling glare. 'I would be very careful who you call a liar, Stone. Unlike you, I do have proof.'

Stone glared at him. Some years ago when St John had been Harry Sawle's partner in free-trading, Adam had been suspicious of his twin's dealings and followed him. He had been caught spying on the gang as they landed a cargo. The Stone cousins were amongst the tubmen that night.

Virgil scowled. 'Your family bain't so innocent, Loveday. You be covering for your kinsfolk now. These be your wife's family.'

'Their leader is my brother-in-law. But as you see, he is walking with a crutch. And he has given his word that whilst on my land his people will be law-abiding. He has never broken his word to me. I will make my own investigations upon this matter and inform Sir Henry of my findings.'

'We have nothing to hide,' Caleph answered. 'Those two men were the only ones who left the campsite, apart from Milo and his cousin Abe, who went out to check the rabbit traps.'

'Went thieving, more like.' Virgil Stone wiped the blood from his cut lip with his cuff.

'From what I hear, there were a number of thefts over several miles, including my cousin's farm and the yard. These people would never rob

154

from my family or the workers on my land. They are welcome here.'

'They'd rob from their own grandmother.' Ned Stone glowered. 'Your wife be one of them, Cap'n Loveday. No disrespect to her, but you can't trust them. We're gonna search their wagons. That will prove them guilty.'

'Not whilst they are on my land, Stone. Touch one piece of their property and it will be you who is in the lockup for theft,' Adam warned. 'This is a matter for the justice of the peace. Sir Henry will deal with it. Since he lost two horses, I am sure he will find the culprits. Now all of you go back to your homes.'

'They'll be long gone afore Sir Henry investigates.' Ned Stone shook his fist at the gypsies.

Adam turned to Caleph. 'I do not believe that you would have allowed any here to betray my trust in your people. It was your intention to camp here until the month's end. If all here are innocent you will stay. If you move on before Sir Henry completes his investigations, you will be judged guilty and hunted down.'

Caleph regarded Adam warily. 'When did our kind ever get justice?'

'I believe you are innocent. This is too good a wintering place for you to risk falling foul of the authorities. And out of respect for your sister, you would not condone such thefts.'

Caleph inclined his head. 'We be innocent. But that will only be proved when the true culprits are caught. We are the easy target. We'd be fools to stay and risk arrest.'

'As I said before, flight will prove your guilt. I give you my word everything will be done to ensure the culprits are caught. These were crimes against my family, workers and friends. I take that as a personal insult.'

He stayed until the villagers had departed, then sat down with Caleph on a log on the outskirts of the camp.

'This is a bad business,' he said. 'I must have your word that your men are innocent. There are many who would make trouble for Senara over this.'

Caleph held his stare. Adam did not know his wife's brother well; the gypsy kept himself very much to himself when they camped here. It was a difficult situation for both men. Adam would never slight Senara's family, but neither was it right for him to mix socially with them. He had nothing in common with Caleph except an interest in horses. He also found him churlish and reluctant to accept any help. The wintering campsite had been a compromise to please Senara. Adam had always had misgivings that something like this incident would flare up. He was determined to settle it within the bounds of the law so that he would not be accused of protecting thieves or of favouritism.

'If any of your men were involved, I do need to know,' he said heavily. 'These thefts are too serious not to be investigated.'

'I will question my men, but most were drunk. Senara had sent over a cask of cider and food to celebrate your sister's wedding. Each family gave me their word that nothing like this would happen while we camped on your land. I would consider it a serious offence in the circumstances. Senara has been a good friend to us. I would not have her shamed in this way.'

Adam accepted Caleph's word. But he was worried about the incident. The robberies had been carried out while his family, friends and workers were enjoying the wedding celebrations. Few men had the manpower or the wit to plan such a venture. Harry Sawle came to mind. And with reason. The thieves had struck at those who had shown their defiance to Sawle. Hannah, Mark Sawle, Sir Henry, Adam himself, St John, even Uncle Joshua, who had regularly preached against the ills of violence and the free-traders.

Sawle had not been seen in these parts since his brother Mark had been attacked and Sir Henry had issued a warrant for his arrest. But Mordecai Nance took Sawle's orders. Adam would ask Sir Henry to ensure the Dolphin Inn at Penruan was searched for the stolen goods and a watch put on Nance to discover where the horses had been hidden. These were hanging offences. Sawle had surely overstepped himself this time.

Adam called at Traherne Hall that afternoon and was closeted with Sir Henry for two hours.

'Caleph gave me his word that his people were not involved with these robberies,' he declared. 'And I believe him. He respects Senara and knows that I would ban them from my land if they broke the law.'

'They are the obvious targets for suspicion, but that makes it less likely that they did it. Especially since they did not immediately flee the district. But Tamasine's wedding was no secret, nor who would be attending. It was the social event of this summer.' Sir Henry rubbed his jaw. 'I agree with you it must be an organised gang – the robberies are too scattered to be one or two men working together. But I am not sure about attaching the blame to Sawle. No one has seen him in weeks.'

'He escaped justice over the attack on his brother at Hannah's farm,' Adam rapped out. 'He will not escape again.'

'Mark could not identify who attacked him. They struck him from behind. Since Harry Sawle had disappeared I brought Mordecai Nance in for questioning about the beating. His insolence earned him two weeks in the lockup, but there was no proof against him or charges made and he was released.'

'Nance is capable of organising the robberies. He has hated our family since St John dismissed him and threw him out of his cottage at Trevowan.'

'It will be difficult to prove unless the thieves were recognised or the goods found. They have probably already been sold.'

Adam persisted. 'Sawle and Nance have to be behind this. Nance would rebel against losing his freedom for two weeks in the lockup. Sawle wanted to show you that he could strike even at you for issuing a warrant for his arrest.'

Sir Henry pondered his friend's words. 'It does make sense. But it also proves that Sawle believes himself above the law. There is much bribery and corruption within our judicial system. But it is time men such as Sawle learned that they cannot mock the law. He will be hunted down and questioned and also all those who work for him.'

'You could start with Mordecai Nance, and the way Ned and Virgil Stone stirred up the villagers of Trewenna. I'd wager they were acting on orders to set a mob on the gypsy camp to cause embarrassment to me.'

'Then I shall make my enquiries.' Sir Henry sighed. 'Lately there has been much that needs investigation. There is also that other matter of Lisette's jewellery found in Plymouth. It is strange that there have been no reports of such a well-known figure hereabouts since she disappeared so mysteriously. Do you think Sawle is behind her disappearance?'

Adam shook his head. 'Somehow her brother is involved. I believe that it was no accident that Uncle William drowned. Lisette had been acting wildly since her brother arrived from France. Etienne had lost everything in the Revolution. He was angry that his sister had married William. He wanted her jewels for himself and would have used Lisette to gain a foothold in society. He had no scruples about marrying her to the lecherous Marquis de Gramont before the Terror in France began. Then to save his own life he abandoned his sister to her fate when her husband's chateau was overrun and the marquis was murdered. Lisette escaped by seducing a guard.' Adam's voice was hard as he proclaimed, 'Etienne was capable of murdering my uncle and fleeing the country with Lisette.'

'Then how do you account for a piece of her jewellery only just coming to light? A pendant like that would never stay long in a shop in Plymouth,' Sir Henry observed.

'Lisette was a reckless gambler. She could have used the jewellery to repay a debt and it has only just been sold. The mystery of her disappearance has been neglected for too long.'

Adam had long been mystified as to the truth behind his uncle's death and the disappearance of Lisette and her brother. 'Even if Etienne did kill Uncle William, he did not prosper from his foul deed. Apart from a few items, the bulk of her jewels remain locked in Uncle William's bank.'

'Then surely if they were innocent of murder, Lisette would have claimed her husband's estate,' Sir Henry said. 'A search was made for them at the time. They must have fled the country.'

'But Lisette left her clothes and possessions behind. She would never do that.'

'Then perhaps her brother killed her and her husband and threw both bodies into the sea, but only William's was washed up. We need to know the truth so that your uncle's estate can be released to his beneficiaries. But St John has made enquiries; surely you have discussed this? He approached a lawyer to contest his uncle's will as Lisette has disappeared. I do not know the outcome.'

'Of course, but that was before this pendant turned up in Plymouth,' Adam hedged. He would not admit to his friend that he knew nothing of his twin's scheming. But in one thing St John was right. The mystery of Lisette's disappearance must be solved. They owed it to William's memory.

Chapter Twenty-three

St John had his own worries and they had nothing to do with the robberies. It was the appearance of Lisette's jewellery that troubled him. What if he was identified as the man who had sold it to the jeweller? It was not his property to sell. Mendoza was supposed to be circumspect about his customers. He was also a pawnbroker, and St John knew that in the past Harry Sawle had used him as a fence for stolen goods. The jeweller would not want his own business investigated.

He tried to control his fears. Mendoza did not know him personally. There was no reason why his name would be given to the authorities. He even tried to look on the bright side of the investigation. He was convinced that Lisette and her brother had fled the country. If no trace was found of them, then under William's will his estate passed to his brothers. Naturally Joshua would be entitled to a half share, but Edward Loveday's share would go to St John as heir to his father's estate. That would take the pressure off his debts.

But what if Lisette was found? She could be languishing in a lunatic asylum somewhere having lost her wits. It would not be the first time his highly strung cousin had spent time in such a place. Often her volatile moods had been irrational and even a danger to others. Her brother was capable of abandoning her; he had done it before. He was not to be trusted. And though Lisette had suffered bouts of madness in the past, she had recovered. She would know that the jewellery purchased in Plymouth had been hidden in her bedchamber. She could denounce St John as a thief.

St John was tortured by his thoughts. Lisette's reappearance could ruin everything. His friends and neighbours would despise him. Felicity would certainly turn against him. And since her arrival at Trevowan he had begun to hope that she still looked favourably upon him. He was relieved that in the months since they had last met she remained unwed.

He heard her laughter as he walked down the staircase. He was dressed for riding. Felicity was to borrow one of Elspeth's mares and they were to visit Hannah. Elspeth was with her now and he groaned inwardly, praying that his aunt had no intention of joining them.

Then he heard Aunt Margaret's voice and her words made him pause. 'The transformation in St John has just been astounding. One does not like to speak ill of the dead, but his life has not been easy in recent years. Meriel was a bad influence. A wife should be a helpmeet to her husband, do you not agree, Felicity?'

'Very much so. Though my dear husband was away at sea for most of our marriage, I hope I gave him comfort and support during his time on land.'

Elspeth joined in the conversation. 'Captain Barrett died a hero. The life of a naval captain's wife is one of sacrifice to her husband's career.'

Margaret interrupted her sister with the eagerness of a dog on the scent of a rabbit. 'You must have been lonely at times, though you are blessed with good friends.'

'My daughter was my consolation,' Felicity replied. 'I never sought a giddy social life. And having chosen a naval captain as my husband I had no right to complain at his absences. The tragedy was that he died so young.'

'Widowhood brings many problems for a woman,' Margaret sympathised. 'I miss my own dear Charles so dreadfully. But we were blessed with thirty-four happy years together. A woman has her reputation to consider, and even at my age I am mindful that there are fortune-hunters seeking to divest a widow of her savings. And you are still young, Felicity. Too young to deprive yourself of a husband's companionship.'

He heard his aunt give a heartfelt sigh before she plunged on with renewed vigour. 'But the love of a good woman maketh a man. St John needs such a wife. Rowena needs a mother's love and guidance and Trevowan needs a mistress. A *worthy* mistress,' she emphasised. 'It is a fine house and estate, is it not, Felicity?'

'The house is beautiful and not so large that it has lost it homeliness,' the younger widow replied.

'St John is proud of his heritage,' Margaret added.

'His father would be impressed at how hard he has worked this winter,' Elspeth praised.

Compliments from her were so rare that St John suspected that his two aunts not only approved of Felicity but also saw her as their wayward nephew's redemption. That suited him. Margaret had never been able to resist matchmaking. He had invited Felicity to the wedding to impress her and get back into her good graces.

He left the aunts in conversation, hoping that they would continue to extol his praises. Half an hour later when he entered the orangery he found Felicity with her daughter Charlotte and Rowena sitting at her feet. She had been reading them a story. The aunts were not in sight. Charlotte was wearing one of Rowena's old riding habits. His daughter was also dressed for riding. St John's heart sank. He had hoped for some time alone with Felicity. She had been at Trevowan for four days and people constantly surrounded them.

He was relieved to discover that Sophia Quinton was absent. Felicity's mother had taken their carriage to visit Cecily at Trewenna. He would find an excuse to send the girls to play elsewhere.

Rowena jumped up at his approach. 'Lottie is to learn to ride. Aunt Elspeth has promised to teach her in the paddock. We need to get her a pony, Papa.'

Again he was pleased at his aunt's goodwill towards his guest. 'That is for her mother to decide, Rowena.' He looked across at Felicity. She was dressed in a burgundy riding habit that looked as if it had never been worn before, with a matching tricorne hat, her blonde hair held neatly in a caul of gold thread. In his invitation St John had suggested that if it met with her pleasure they would go riding.

'Charlotte has never been on a horse.' Felicity looked worried. 'She is nervous of animals usually. It has not been practical for us to ride whilst living in Falmouth and Truro. Rowena's pony seems so large for her.'

'Elspeth will allow her to come to no harm,' he replied. 'Hannah's children have a couple of ponies. She will loan one to us during your stay. Would you not like Charlotte to be able to ride? You have said how much you miss it yourself.'

Bodkin, Rowena's cat, strolled through the open door leading to the garden. She headed for the two girls, brushing her head against their laps, her tail flicking across their faces. Charlotte giggled and reached out to hug the cat.

'Your daughter is not nervous of Bodkin,' St John remarked. 'The pony is very placid. Too quiet for Rowena's taste. She is insisting on one with more spirit.'

Elspeth limped into the orangery. 'Rowena is never satisfied. She wants to ride my mares.' There was affection and pride in her voice. 'I was the same at her age where horses were concerned.'

'Are you sure it will not inconvenience you to give Charlotte lessons, Miss Loveday?' Felicity was rather awed by the older woman's formidable nature. 'It will not overtire you? Is your poor hip paining you?'

161

'Oh, I never allow a discomfort to get in the way of my pleasure with horses. It is important for Charlotte to learn to ride,' Elspeth returned. 'A horse if it has been treated properly is a good friend. But it is important for any child to learn discipline and respect towards them.'

Charlotte turned a wide smile upon her mother. 'I would love to ride like Rowena. You will let me, will you not, Mama?'

'Perhaps I should stay and watch your first lessons.' Felicity looked uncertainly at St John.

He curbed his impatience. 'As you wish, my dear. But my aunt will not permit Charlotte to do more than sit in the saddle and get used to the feel of the horse and reins. If we go to Hannah's we will return with the pony and your daughter's lessons can begin in earnest later.'

'You are so wise, St John.' Felicity ran her hands lovingly over her daughter's curls. 'I fuss too much. But Charlotte is so precious. She is all I have.' She rose and smoothed out the skirt of her habit.

'It is natural for a mother to feel as you do,' St John praised. He felt a twinge of sadness for his own daughter. Meriel had never shown concern over her welfare. Even he had been careless in his affection towards her. Yet for all that Rowena was remarkably resilient. It made him add as they walked from the orangery, 'Your daughter is blessed to have such a caring mother. My wife thought only for herself.'

'But Rowena is such a delightful child.' Felicity gasped in astonishment.

'As is your own dear Charlotte.'

'They have become friends in such a short time. That pleases me.'

It also delighted St John and he saw it as a means to get Felicity to extend her stay. She had spoken of returning to Truro tomorrow. 'Rowena has her cousins for playfellows but they can be boisterous, especially Adam's boys. And though Hannah's children are charming, I fear my daughter spends too long in their company working with the farm animals. I would wish her more gently reared. It was a great sadness to me that she was an only child. She has few friends outside the family, and she does not play with her Traherne cousins. Lady Traherne was incensed at Japhet's arrest and trial and though he was pardoned she cannot forgive us for the disgrace he brought to our families.'

'Yet Lady Traherne was at the wedding. And she danced with Adam.'

'At her husband's insistence, I fear. Sir Henry has remained a loyal friend. Lord and Lady Fetherington were only absent due to Lord Fetherington's recent malaise.'

'You have exalted friends, St John.' Felicity's cheeks were flushed with pleasure and she glanced sideways at him as she confided, 'I confess I was never taken with Roslyn before her marriage. She was always a shrew, though she hid it well when Sir Henry was courting her.'

'Lady Traherne would not be the first woman to dupe a man with her complicity.' The bitterness at his own wife's deception hardened his voice.

Felicity placed a hand on his arm. 'Neither of us married the person we thought them to be. Meriel led you a wicked dance and my husband was abusive and a drunkard.'

'I do not like to think that you suffered so.' He covered her fingers with his palm.

She did not withdraw her hand, but demurely changed the subject. 'Dear Gwendolyn was very different to her sister. So sweet and shy. I would never have thought her brave enough to sail across the world to be with her husband. Botany Bay must be a barbaric place. She has my greatest admiration.'

'Gwendolyn has changed remarkably.' St John made his voice serious. 'Love can do that to a person. I hope I too have changed in your eyes. You made me see the error of my ways.'

She smiled enigmatically but did not answer. In his need to keep her at Trevowan he played on her love for her child. 'Since our daughters are happy together, will you not consider extending your stay? Though I have no entertainments planned, I will invite any of your old friends to dine if you wish to be reacquainted with them.'

'I would enjoy Hannah's company but I did not mind the solitude during my marriage. During the eighteen months of my widowhood friends have been so kind as to include me in their entertainments, but I do not always find them necessary.'

At these words a sliver of unease was hastily brushed from St John's mind. Her liking for a quiet life need not hinder his search for amusement. Meriel with her constant quest for new experiences and excitement had been a burden on his purse and his freedom. His thoughts jerked back to the present as she continued.

'Your invitation is most kind. I am glad to think that we did not part bad friends last autumn.'

They had entered the garden on the approach to the stables and St John was conscious of the young groom sweeping the courtyard ahead of them. He did not want their conversation to be overheard and become gossip. He led Felicity to a stone seat with a view across the paddocks and sat beside her. Words tumbled chaotically through his mind. There was a puritanical streak in Felicity that he had learned about to his cost last year.

'I have had much to occupy me in recent months.' He found it impossible to hold her stare, so his gaze continually slipped away to settle upon the distant hills. He hoped she would see it as embarrassment, not a lack of honesty. 'The estate takes a great deal of my time. I have not always acted wisely since my trial.'

'Any man would be wounded if his wife ran off with a lover. And there was the death of your dear father. That was a shock and a tragedy. I may have judged you too harshly. You have led a sober and exemplary life since last we met.'

'You are very understanding, my dear friend.' His heart lifted. Felicity was thawing. He must not rush his pursuit of her, though it irked him to continue with so salubrious and restrained a lifestyle. He did not perceive that he was playing Felicity false in the same way that Meriel had tricked him. He was not a drunkard by any means and he certainly would never physically abuse a woman. Felicity's first husband had been a blackguard. St John considered himself a gentleman of the first order.

Felicity would make an ideal wife and his family would be delighted with the news when he announced their betrothal, which he hoped would be very soon.

'It is time to ride, or we shall have little time with Hannah.'

Felicity stood up and walked purposefully towards the stables. She had been angry that St John had not visited her throughout the winter. Not that she had pined for his company, she reminded herself sternly. Mr Bernard Ottershawe had been a constant visitor and had twice proposed marriage. Each time she had evaded giving him a definite answer, protesting it was still too soon after her husband's death to consider remarriage. He was a good man, attractive and well bred, and he clearly worshipped her. But he did not stir her heart in the way that a future husband should. She had married Captain Barrett knowing that she was not in love with him but hoping that would happen when they were wed. Had his abuse started when he realised that she could not give him her heart? She had married him to save face. She had been in love with St John, and, young and inexperienced with men, had thought that the attentions he had paid her all through the winter and spring meant that he loved her. Then that strumpet Meriel Sawle had set her cap at the heir to Trevowan, and had caught him by using the oldest and most devious trick known to woman. She had fallen pregnant and decency had made St John wed her.

An unhappy marriage had made Felicity cautious of making the same mistake again. She was no longer young and infatuated with St John, but he did hold a strong and probably unwise fascination for her.

Her friends had warned her against his libertine's reputation, but so much of that was hearsay. She would not judge a man on gossip but neither would she be blinded by good looks or simple attraction. She was sensitive to the wealth that she would bring to a marriage and had to be certain that she was being courted for herself and not her fortune. Yet she was flattered by St John's attention and his aunt's obvious intentions to matchmake between them. The family had welcomed her warmly into its heart.

Chapter Twenty-four

Not everyone in the Loveday family was as enamoured with Felicity's visit. The Reverend Joshua Loveday was finding it irksome in the extreme. The cause of his discomfort was not Felicity but her mother. Sophia Quinton was a disconcerting ghost from his past. It had been a shock to discover that she was a guest at the wedding. Cecily had been delighted to be reunited with her old friend, but then his wife knew nothing of the passionate affair Joshua had conducted with Sophia before his marriage. At the time Sophia had been betrothed to Quinton, who had once boasted in his cups that he had fathered half a dozen bastards before he had reached twenty. It was to be a marriage of convenience, not love. Quinton had made his money from clay mines and wanted the social standing Sophia's lineage could give him. Although from an old family, Sophia's parents lived in genteel poverty, their money lost when investments in the South Seas proved worthless. Bad management of their estate had added to their financial troubles and the property had been sold.

Joshua and Sophia had both attended a ball at the house of mutual friends outside Falmouth. Quinton had abandoned his fiancée and flirted with several women. To hide her embarrassment, Sophia had drunk rather copiously. Joshua had not been averse to being seduced by a pretty woman seeking comfort.

After the ball he had not expected to see Sophia again, but she had other ideas. Their affair had lasted six months until her marriage, when she had moved to Falmouth. Three months later Joshua's wild life caught up with him and the husband of another mistress called him out. The man had died in the duel. Stricken with remorse, Joshua had denounced his old life, joined a seminary and on a visit to a fellow student in St Mawes had met Cecily, the daughter of the local rector. He had fallen in love with her and they had married when he was given the parish of Trewenna. It had been one of those strange quirks of fate that for five years during Cecily's childhood, her father had served the parish where Sophia had also lived, and they had become friends.

Sophia represented a life that Joshua had chosen to forget. Today, while he struggled with a sermon on the sins of the flesh as a means of atonement for his past misdemeanours, memories of his affair with her intruded. He tossed down his quill, hating to be a hypocrite. Out of sorts with himself, he questioned his calling. As a young man he had never heeded the wisdom in sermons. Then he believed that you had to experience life to learn from it. Now he berated himself for the recklessness of his wilder days that had ended in a man's death. He knelt before a wooden cross in his study and prayed for guidance.

A repeated knocking at the rectory door reminded him that Cecily and their maid were out visiting an elderly parishioner who lived on her own. He opened the door, half expecting to see the churchwarden. To his dismay Sophia Quinton stood before him. Her chaise was parked in the shade of the trees by the rectory gate, her liveried driver seated patiently at the reins awaiting the return of his mistress.

'I am afraid Cecily is not here, Mrs Quinton.' Joshua quickly recovered his wits. 'She will be upset to have missed you. I thought you were to call on us this afternoon.'

'Are you not going to ask me in, Joshua? And I will have none of this formality between us. I shall be mortified if you do not call me Sophia.'

He stood aside for her to enter and showed her into the parlour. The two small windows let in little of the bright sunlight but it was pleasantly cool. 'Our maid is with my wife visiting a parishioner. Please be seated and make yourself comfortable. I will summon Cecily myself.'

Sophia remained standing and pulled off her gloves, then removed her pelisse and laid it over the wooden arm of a chair. She wore a poke bonnet decorated with large blue and yellow ostrich feathers that touched the ceiling rafters. A choker of pearls was round her neck and her fingers glittered with jewels. The opulence of her blue and yellow silk gown and her expensive perfume made his home appear dowdy and humble. 'Cecily said you had a meeting in another parish this afternoon. I did not want to miss you.' She eyed him archly. 'We have so much in common, Joshua. Such giddy memories as I recall.'

She made no move to be seated and stood uncomfortably close. Joshua moved aside, his voice polite but firm. 'They were a long time ago.'

'Not so very long. And you are ungentlemanly not to remember.' Her laugh was light and provocative. Her complexion was whitened by

167

powder and her cheeks were lightly rouged. She had retained her handsome looks, with fine almond-shaped eyes that sparkled with mischief. 'Did we not have something special? You are a fine figure of a man, Joshua. But then you always were.' She had moved between him and the door. 'And you always knew how to treat a lady to make her feel special – very special indeed.'

'You *were* special, Sophia – a remarkable woman. But it would be disrespectful to my wife for me to recall other than your friendship with Cecily.'

She was unabashed. 'But those wickedly delicious memories were precious to me.'

Joshua averted his gaze from her figure that maturity had rounded to sensual voluptuousness. His years as a preacher had not diminished his appreciation for beauty or a woman's charms. He was flattered and his natural gallantry responded. 'However enjoyable those memories are, they should not colour the present.'

'That is the preacher talking, not the man I remember. You were so bold and dashing.'

Her flirting, however pleasant, was inappropriate, and Joshua was shocked to find he was not as immune to it as propriety demanded. He cleared his throat, making his tone sterner. 'We were young, reckless and carefree then. This is a rectory and my wife's home. You wrong your friend by such talk.'

'Your piety does not fool me, Joshua.' She moved closer, a light scent of rosewater and the musky perfume of her own flesh on this warm day wafting around him. 'You were not always so reticent in my company. Even after you were wed.'

She brushed his cheek with the tips of her fingers, her touch soft as a feather. Unbidden he recalled how he had once caressed her body with an ostrich feather until she had moaned in unrestrained pleasure. The intensity of the image shook him. She had been predatory in her passion then – as he sensed she could be now.

'I wronged Cecily once and it shames me to this day.'

'You were never meant to be faithful, no more than I.' Her smile was sultry. 'We are two of a kind.' She put a hand on the Geneva bands resting on his chest. 'I have never forgotten my passionate parson.'

'You flatter me, dear lady.'

He took her hand to remove it from his body but her fingers curled like tentacles around his own and she lifted a finely plucked brow and ran the tip of her tongue over her full lower lip.

'You were the most memorable of my lovers, Joshua.'

Visions flashed through his mind of them together. She had been entrancing. She still was. She knew the tricks to captivate and entice a man. When her hip brushed against his thigh, his heartbeat quickened and his blood pulsated hotly through his veins.

'You have not forgotten our nights together, have you?' she taunted.

His body broke into a sweat and he fought the urge to loosen his neckband. Sophia studied him with a boldness that was disconcerting. Her flirting was no longer inconsequential; her eyes had darkened with invitation and promise. The minx was up to her old tricks. He would not succumb.

He slammed the door on a flood of carnal memories. She had brought him to the brink of damnation once. But he was no longer that weak and foolish man. If Cecily had ever learned of his affair after their marriage it would have broken her heart. She was a loyal and loving wife and deserved better than that.

They had been married ten years when Cecily had gone to St Mawes to tend a dying aunt, her last living relative. She was away two months. Margaret was down from London for the summer and his children were being cared for at Trevowan. Joshua had been summoned to Truro by the bishop and he had set out intending to stay there a single night before returning to his parish.

Sophia was visiting the town from Falmouth with her husband. Mr Quinton spent most of the days attending to his business affairs. By a perverse twist of fate they were both lodging in the same coaching inn. Sophia, bored and neglected by her husband, was eager for diversion. From their first encounter in a darkened corridor of the inn she had played an artful game to seduce her former lover.

The wildness of the Loveday blood had never been fully tamed in Joshua despite his calling to the cloth. But Cecily was a loving wife and he had no need to look elsewhere to satisfy his needs. It had been easy for him to remain faithful, but Sophia had other ideas. And this was a woman who knew no shame. She came to his chamber naked beneath a hooded cloak, whispering her husband would not return until nightfall. She had been wickedly persuasive and intent upon seduction. To Joshua's mortification his flesh had weakened. He had tried to resist Sophia but the woman was relentless in her pursuit and her eagerness to rekindle their affair. He had succumbed but briefly to the temptation before coming to his senses and ending their relationship.

He drew a sharp breath and disengaged their entwined fingers. 'You were ever a delightful creature, but such memories are an insult to my

169

beloved wife and your friendship with her.' He put several paces between them.

Her mouth tightened with disappointment. 'Yes, sweet Cecily. The perfect parson's wife. Devoted. Unselfish. Unstinting in her charity work. The perfect helpmeet. I admire her. I always did. And I envied her . . . I envied the happiness in your marriage. I wanted to feel the depths of such a love, but Quinton constantly betrayed me. You were loyal and devoted to Cecily. How I longed for such a partner. You showed me all too briefly the true depths of love.'

Joshua was horrified by her confession. He had never loved her and their moment of passion had been a gross act of betrayal to his marriage vows and the woman he loved.

Sophia saw his eyes become guarded. She had said too much and regretted it. She forced a teasing laugh. 'Oh, pay no heed to me. I am an incorrigible flirt. I would never hurt Cecily. This is such a wonderful chance for us all to be friends.'

He did not move and she tilted back her head. 'It was wicked of me to play the tease. I would do nothing to bring pain to Cecily. She is the most estimable of women. Her kindness shames me. I value her friendship. I will have my little games. Your loyalty impresses me, Joshua.'

He breathed more easily but was not convinced that she was being honest.

'Trewenna is a small village. Such diversions are unwise. A lady must guard her reputation against gossip.'

'As must its parson.' She gave a philosophical shrug. 'Or indeed a mother. Felicity sets great store by reputable conduct. She does not like it if I flirt indecorously. But today was a little light-hearted fun for old times' sake, was it not? And I think my daughter may have set her cap at your nephew. How diverting that we could become family, dear Joshua.'

The arrival of Cecily saved him from any more of Felicity's light-hearted fun. It had been far from that for Joshua. He excused himself to the women and shut himself in his study to write his sermon. The words refused to flow. Guilt played heavily on his conscience. The wildness of the Loveday blood could be a curse. It had wrecked many of their lives. He had been fortunate in his escape. Not so his son Japhet.

He dropped his head into his hands. His eldest son was daily in his prayers. He feared for his life and that of his wife. Now that Japhet had won his pardon, how could he risk everything in such an inhospitable land? Sir Gregory Kilmarthen had visited them briefly when *Pegasus* had returned. He had been optimistic about the future of the colony, but Joshua was a realist. Convicts outnumbered the settlers. They were in danger from attack by savage natives, and from what he had heard, the New South Wales Corps, sent to establish order, were corrupt, rough and brutal opportunists. Japhet could handle himself well in a fight and outwit most men, but what of his son and gentle wife? Joshua feared that Japhet had been irresponsible to be lured by the quest for riches in Botany Bay.

Chapter Twenty-Five

All the goods brought ashore from *Pegasus* had been sold by last month and Japhet had been pleased with the profits. He had used his share to complete the store, which now awaited the next shipment from England. With each voyage taking eight months, *Pegasus* would not return for another year. Japhet occasionally visited Sydney and spent an evening gambling with the officers. He invariably won and had agreed to take part of the government ship's consignment as payment of the officers' debts. At least all was in readiness in Parramatta. He could now concentrate on building the sawmill to house the large saws he had ordered from England. The future merchandise for his store was assured.

He was sitting on the veranda of his home with Silas Hope, who was visiting them with his wife Eliza. They had eaten a large lunch and were now enjoying a pipe of tobacco. Silas's brother, Lieutenant Matthew Hope, and his fellow officer in the New South Wales Corps, Captain Jonas Pyke, had also joined them. Both officers had been on the ship that had brought Japhet to Australia. Whilst Japhet had been looking after the livestock on the voyage he had been given special privileges, and being a natural raconteur he had befriended some of the officers and gambled with them. Hope and Pyke had been heavily in debt to him when they arrived in Port Jackson, and Japhet had diplomatically cancelled their debts, knowing he would need the support of such men to avoid the worst of the conditions of the common convict.

The first months of Japhet's sentence he had worked as overseer to Silas Hope, and when his pardon had arrived he had maintained his friendship with the officers. With so much corruption amongst the New South Wales Corps that friendship had lessened many of the difficulties Japhet would otherwise have encountered.

The women were in the house with their two children. The men had been discussing the progress on the farms and had wandered outside despite the deluge of rain that was falling.

'The storms are more violent than in England,' Silas groaned. 'The fields are flooded. Most of the vegetables I planted are rotting in the ground. You have been more fortunate and your crops have not been affected.'

'Those fields should be put to grazing and crops sown higher in the valley,' Japhet advised. 'I did warn you. The valley flooded in the first years of the colony.'

'But those fields did not flood last year.' Silas was struggling as a farmer and his wife was counselling him to sell up so that they could move to Parramatta, where he could take up his old trade as a cobbler. He had lost his shop in England and had seen himself in this new life as a landowner. 'Is this rain neverending? The road will be a quagmire soon.'

'The weather patterns are unpredictable and this year there has been more rain.' Japhet glanced at the sky darkened by rain clouds. He breathed in the sharp scent of the eucalyptus trees. The downpour had quietened the strident cries of the kookaburras. Abruptly the rain eased, then stopped, and sunlight lanced through the cracks appearing in the clouds. A flock of green parakeets flew across the field in front of them. 'This is a land of sudden changes and contrasts. A land of beauty and brutality.'

Over the distant mountains the mist was lifting, and as the sun gained in heat steam rose from the sodden outbuildings and fences.

Captain Pyke stretched out his legs and blew a cloud of tobacco smoke. 'You see it through the eyes of the privileged few, Loveday. It would be an Eden but for the scum of the English gaols we have emptied on to this land. The last soldiers to arrive were little better than the convicts themselves, having been dragged from the gutters to take the King's shilling. The war with France has taken our best men. I'd give much to be back in Essex with my sweet wife Mary Anne.'

Despite his protestations of devotion to his wife, Pyke lived with a convict woman, Dorcas Smedley, who had borne him two children, the first conceived on the transport ship when he had been her protector. It was a common arrangement amongst the soldiers. Matthew Hope had remained single and helped his brother on his farm when he was off duty.

'Have you had any more trouble from Haughton?' Matthew asked Japhet.

'Nothing that I could not handle. He tried to demand a share of the takings from myself and other tradesmen. Some paid but most of us refused, so he picked on the weakest and gave a beating to a baker who would not pay. We can either give in to their bullying or stand up to them.'

'That is a dangerous move, Japhet,' Silas warned. 'Haughton can declare that you are inciting rebellion and have you arrested.'

'It would rebound on him if he did. It would be the word of respectable citizens against the soldiers. He can only win if he tries to provoke us when there are no other witnesses. The tradesmen have now banded together. If Haughton's men are in town a close eye is kept on them, and if they try and demand money by intimidation, word is sent round to the others and we rally together. So far we have avoided violence.'

'To attack a soldier would mean arrest,' Matthew Hope reminded them. 'The governor has been informed of such persecution but he seems powerless to act against officers like Haughton who blatantly disregard his orders.'

'Haughton picks on the weak, not the strong,' Captain Pyke observed. 'I doubt he will trouble you, Loveday. You have too much influence and too many friends in the colony.'

'Even so, I would not trust him.' Silas glanced worriedly at his friend.

Japhet shrugged with apparent unconcern. 'I did not survive a year in Newgate and months in the hold of the transport ship without knowing how to take the measure of a man. I will tackle Haughton in my own way within the bounds of the law.'

Adam knew that the villagers close to Boscabel remained hostile towards the gypsies. Caleph was now well enough to move with them to their summer grounds, but until they were cleared of suspicion, any flight would be viewed as guilt. He had a hard time persuading Caleph to stay and the gypsy had agreed to one more week. For Senara's peace of mind Adam needed to prove them innocent. That meant finding out who was guilty.

Convinced that Harry Sawle was behind the thefts, he had somehow to find proof. The smuggler had not been in the area for weeks but his henchman Mordecai Nance had gained a reputation for violence if any man crossed him.

So far the enquiries by the authorities had brought no evidence to light on the real robbers. Frustrated by the delay, Adam started his own enquiries. He went first to Penruan. Out of habit he took the road past Trevowan and over the headland, entering the village close to the Dolphin Inn.

Etta Nance posed in the doorway as he passed. Her hands rested on her hips and her stare was bold and challenging as she called out, 'It bain't often we be honoured by one of the Loveday men. I thought Penruan were too lowly a place for them now they have their grand houses.'

The sunlight glinted off her large gold hoop earrings and a gold chain with a pearl drop at her neck. She was a fool to flash her newly acquired wealth. It would help put Nance in gaol for smuggling.

Adam ignored her taunting. Etta was a feisty wench with a grudge against his family ever since St John had dismissed her husband from work at Trevowan.

'We serve the best ale around,' Etta goaded with a laugh. 'And there be more than beers and spirits to set a man's blood afire. Or are you not man enough to enter here, my bold captain?'

Another woman sauntered out to sit on a bench in the sunlight. She was young and had once been pretty but her face was pitted with pock-marks. She flicked her petticoats above her knees and her bodice was loosely fastened, displaying her breasts. Adam had heard that the Dolphin was now a bawdy house. He rode on as the women giggled behind their hands.

The fishing fleet were not in the harbour and the drying and salting sheds were deserted. The quay would come alive once the fleet returned. Four old men retired from the sea sat smoking their clay pipes on a stone wall at the edge of the harbour. They nodded in greeting to Adam. Half a dozen women could be heard laughing as they worked at the washing slab near the village pump. Their sleeves were rolled up and their faces were red from beating the laundry and rubbing the cloth with blocks of soap. A frothy rivulet of water ran over the cobblestones to drain into the sea on the edge of the quayside.

Sal Sawle recognised Adam and raised a hand in nervous greeting. He was pleased to see how well she looked. Life free of the drudgery of work in the Dolphin Inn suited her. Her patched skirt no longer hung loose about her waist and her eyes were brighter than he had seen them in years. It was time life treated Sal more kindly. She had slaved at the inn throughout her marriage and had been ill rewarded by her husband and children.

At the lychgate of the church, Dr Chegwidden and his wife were in conversation with the Reverend Mr Snell. Adam tipped his hat to Mrs Chegwidden, who simpered.

'Good day, Captain Loveday. I trust your wife and children are well. We do not often see you in Penruan.' The daughter of the local chandler, she had always been eager to pander to the Lovedays, but Adam had never trusted her, finding her sly and sulky, unlike her sister Hester.

175

At that moment Hester appeared, returning to her house on the slope of the coombe carrying her infant daughter in her arms. Neither the doctor nor his wife acknowledged the younger woman with her bastard child.

'My family are in good health, Mrs Chegwidden,' Adam replied. 'As I trust are your children.' He then turned his attention to the men. 'Gentlemen, it is fortunate that we meet. I have a matter I would discuss with you both. Would it be convenient for you to meet in the rectory in an hour? I have some other business to attend to first.'

'My dear, are we not due at the Bracewaites' this afternoon?' Annie Chegwidden cut in. She clearly did not like Adam purloining her husband in such a manner and at the same time reminded him that they moved in exalted circles.

'There is time aplenty, my dear,' Simon Chegwidden placated. 'What is this business and how long do you think it will take, Captain Loveday?'

'A half-hour should be time enough if you have an appointment elsewhere,' Adam said. 'I would value your opinion on a matter.' He had no wish to say more in front of Mrs Chegwidden, who would spread the gossip through the village.

'I am at your disposal,' Snell replied.

'Your servant, Captain. An hour's time it is then.' Chegwidden nodded his agreement.

Adam left them to tether his horse in the shade of the drying sheds by the quay and entered the general store.

'Goldie loves a lover,' a parrot on its perch announced. 'How about a shilling, sailor?'

Goldie Lanyon flapped her hand at the bird. 'Enough of your foul talk. How can I be of service to you, Cap'n Loveday?'

Two other women were in the shop and cast curious glances at Adam. 'Continue to serve your customers. I can wait. You have an excellent display of goods. It quite outshines what is sold in the kiddley at the shipyard.'

'So you've come to check out the competition,' Goldie laughed. 'There be some articles of quality out the back which you may find of interest to your dear wife. Mrs Amelia Loveday buys her sewing silks here, as do Mrs Snell and Mrs Chegwidden. It be all honestly bought, our goods. No contraband, if that be what you fear. I'd be put out of business if the excise men discovered anything not having its proper purchase receipts.'

Adam ducked his head under a side of bacon hanging from the rafters. A large cheese covered in muslin sat on the counter. The contents of the shop were diverse. There were dried goods in sacks on the floor, earthen and tin ware stacked on shelves. Calico and worsted cloth was folded into piles on shelves. Everything was neat and orderly and the floor scrubbed clean.

Goldie finished serving her customers and studied Adam from behind the counter. 'You didn't come here to tell me I've a goodly stock of wares, Mr Loveday.'

'You have a sharp eye and an honest tongue, Goldie. I respect that.'

She folded her arms across her chest. There was no subservience in her manner. Nor did he expect it. Goldie worked hard and had won the grudging respect of the villagers in a short space of time. 'You be wanting information of some sort. I don't hold with gossip.'

'Neither do I. But I need facts. I do not like to see my workers at Trevowan Hard or local villagers robbed.'

'No one likes a thief. Most folk be honest round here.'

'And the ones who are not?'

She shrugged. 'There bain't no need to mention names. They be known.'

Goldie was no fool. She knew how to guard her tongue. Her survival in the past had depended upon it.

'But would they rob their own kind?' Adam pressed.

'There's some who would rob their own mother's grave clothes. They think they can come here and rule the roost. I never could abide bullies.' Her stare had drifted through the open door of the shop to settle upon the Dolphin Inn.

'Has Harry Sawle been around?' Adam asked.

'He don't need to be to have his dirty work done.'

'Has anyone been spending more than usual since the robberies on the day of my sister's wedding?'

Her hawk-like stare held his gaze. She raised a brow, her voice harsh. 'Do you think I'd be foolish enough to say? Two fishermen over Polruan had the masts on their fishing sloops smashed after Nance were put in the lockup last time. Folk says they spoke to the authorities. They were lucky worse weren't done to them. Nance has been threatening any who says a word against him or Sawle.'

From her careful words Nance was obviously behind the robberies. Adam reached across and lifted down a roll of white linen. He did not want Goldie suspected of speaking against the smugglers and would be seen leaving her shop with a purchase. 'I'll take this. Senara is making sheets for the children's beds.'

He then went to the cobbler's shop to order some new work boots.

Joseph Roche had always made shoes for his family. He was an accomplished shoemaker and thrived on gossip.

'Cap'n Loveday, this be an honour.' Roche had been sitting at his bench and stopped work to touch his forelock to Adam.

'I need new work boots. When can they be ready?' On hooks around the workbench were wooden lasts shaped to fit Roche's customers' feet and labelled with their names.

'By the end of the week, unless you require them more urgently, Cap'n.'

'The end of the week will be fine.'

The shoemaker had been working on a pair of fine-quality leather knee boots of the type only a gentleman would usually wear. The only hook without a last was labelled with the name of Mordecai Nance. The innkeeper and his wife were spending lavishly on jewellery and these boots. Money in excess of Nance's wages as an innkeeper.

Adam left the shop, certain now that Nance was behind the robberies. The cash could not be traced and Nance would not be foolish enough to keep the trinkets or other valuables stolen. Harry Sawle fenced stolen goods but he would not touch those wares for fear of incriminating himself. Adam would check the pawnbrokers in the area, and on the matter of the suspicious sale of jewels there was Lisette's necklace to be investigated too. He needed to place an order with the ship's chandler in Plymouth and would call on the jeweller when he was in the port. He did not want the trail to go cold on the pendant.

It was time to attend upon Snell and the doctor at the rectory. Snell offered him a class of claret, which he accepted. Simon Chegwidden declined; his wife was known to disapprove of strong drink.

'I will come straight to the point,' Adam said. 'The authorities have not discovered who did the recent robberies.'

''Pon my word, I would have thought that was obvious.' Dr Chegwidden sniffed haughtily. 'With respect, Captain Loveday, it was the gypsies. Why you choose to defend them is beyond me.'

'Because they have given their word that they are innocent.'

'The word of a Romany is worthless,' the doctor sneered.

'They would not lie to my wife.' Adam fixed Simon Chegwidden with a challenging stare.

The doctor flushed and cleared his throat in a self-conscious manner, unable to meet Adam's gaze. 'I still say they cannot be trusted.'

The reverend coughed, embarrassed by the confrontation. 'We must not judge too hastily. I am sure Mr Loveday wants justice. His workers were robbed.'

'Also my cousin. I would not suffer thieves to settle on my land.'

'Indeed not.' Snell nodded vigorously.

'Have either of you noticed anyone who is spending more lavishly? The new landlord of the Dolphin and his wife are dressing in greater finery.'

The preacher and doctor exchanged nervous glances.

'I do not mix with such lowly men who encourage drunkenness and debauchery,' Chegwidden declared.

'But you have eyes and ears. Do they tell you nothing?' Adam found his patience slipping.

'They have never engaged my services but I have noticed that that particular couple dress above their station,' he replied.

'Reverend, have you an opinion?' Adam persisted.

'We all know that there are illicit goings-on. I am not a strong man. I can lambaste the sinful from the pulpit and remind them of the Commandments, but to do more . . .' He faltered and coughed into his hand.

'Our good reverend has a mind to keep his health,' Dr Chegwidden finished for him. 'The inn is an ungodly place. It attracts the most unsavoury customers. The lower orders of the military frequent it. Penruan is not safe on such nights.'

'That has nothing to do with the robberies.' Adam returned to the main subject to be dealt with. 'You must have heard the current opinion.'

'It is easier for the villagers to blame the gypsies. Penruan was not directly affected,' Snell said apologetically.

Adam rose from his chair to round on his two companions. 'But these crimes affect all of us. If the culprit is not found, where will they strike next?'

The Reverend Mr Snell put up a placating hand. 'You have lived here long enough to know how and why certain events take place. Certain people have placed information before the authorities . . . Retaliation against informants is often swift. The informants should be thankful that they were robbed and suffered no more serious mishap.'

'And you are prepared to accept that is how justice should be mocked?' Adam flared.

'We are powerless . . .' Snell began

'No, you are craven!' Adam returned. 'I am not afraid of these scoundrels. I will not see bullies take justice into their own hands.'

'I give you my blessing, Captain Loveday,' the preacher said sooth-ingly. 'But we have to live as best we can. The military presence at the inn does not bode well for the moral welfare of my flock.'

179

Adam accepted the reverend's reasoning. Bribery and corruption were rife in all walks of society. Sawle and Nance knew how to protect themselves.

'If any information comes to your hand, you know where I am, gentlemen.' There was no point in losing his temper. Snell was elderly and Chegwidden was weak. 'I will not take up any more of your time.'

As Adam left the village, several redcoats were lounging on the low boundary wall of the inn, drinking quart tankards of ale. Mordecai Nance was chatting to them. Adam doubted the soldiers had paid for their drink.

'Have you thrown those thieving gypsies off your land, Cap'n Loveday?' Mordecai jeered as Adam passed. 'Happen these good men should pay their camp a call. Folk quake in their beds that they could be killed and robbed.'

'A higher authority than your friends there has investigated the camp and found no evidence as to any crime. It is neighbourly of you, Nance, to show such concern for your fellow man.'

He turned to the officer in charge. 'You are new to the district, are you not, sir? I am Adam Loveday, shipbuilder.'

The officer clicked his heels together. He was younger than Adam, with wide side-whiskers, and his face was reddened by the sun. The silver officer's insignia at his throat and the buttons on his coat were tarnished. It showed Adam that the man had no pride in his career. 'Lieutenant Tregare at your service, Captain Loveday. I have been stationed at Fowey this last month.'

Adam nodded and rode on. The soldiers guffawed at some remark made by the landlord that Adam guessed was at his expense. He ignored it. The time would soon come when Nance would face justice, as would Harry Sawle.

Chapter Twenty-Six

A tenant farmer, Uriah Bradstock, had been found for Tor Farm. He and his family had moved in six weeks ago. Anxious that her brother's property should be properly maintained by the new tenants, Hannah decided to pay them a neighbourly call and asked Sam to accompany her. She rode Sheba, her brother's favourite mare. Hannah did not believe that Japhet would stay in Australia indefinitely or he would have instructed her to sell Tor Farm and have the money sent out to him. The mare was spirited, but that suited Hannah, who was an accomplished horse-woman, and riding Sheba kept a part of her beloved brother with her always.

As they approached the farm, Hannah was pleased to see sheep grazing the meadows and a late crop sprouting in a field.

'Bradstock has wasted no time in utilising the land, Sam.' She also felt reassured at discovering that the barn door that had needed repair had been mended and the overgrown weeds and brambles had been cut back from around the house.

At the sound of their approach, the short, stocky figure of Bradstock appeared out of the barn. Shock registered briefly on his broad features before his ruddy face twisted into a smile. He snatched his battered felt hat from his thinning hair and ducked his head in salute.

'Good day to thee, Mrs Rabson. This be an unexpected pleasure, to be sure.' He fidgeted with his hat, leaving sweat stains from his hands on the brim.

Hannah returned his greeting and studied him closely. Why was he so nervous? Bradstock was in his mid thirties, with heavy arms and thick fingers encrusted with mud, testimony to his morning work in the fields. 'I came to enquire if you have settled comfortably here and am impressed to see a crop already sprouting. You have wasted no time, Mr Bradstock.'

He cuffed pearls of sweat from his upper lip and did not meet her gaze as he nodded towards the sown field. 'That crop will help get us through the first winter, until my sheep flock be established. It be prime land. But thee stipulated the meadows were to be kept for grazing and it will be just the one field I'll put to the plough.'

Hannah dismounted and tied the reins to a post at the front of the house. 'You will get the wool from the sheep this year and lambs next year. That is a good start. There are two large fields, which will produce two hay crops, and you can sell the surplus. And I see you have repaired the barn door.'

Did she imagine it or did his eyes suddenly take on a furtive look? He rubbed his hooked nose before replying. 'I've taken on a shepherd for the flock and will move them on to the moor. Thought I'd get a few calves from the market and start a small beef herd.'

'That will improve your profit,' Sam agreed. 'Will you be adding stalls in the barn for the cattle?'

Again Bradstock shifted uncomfortably. 'Aye. That won't be a problem, will it?'

'Certainly not.' Hannah suppressed a growing sense of unease at his manner. 'Could we see the improvements?'

Bradstock slammed his hat on his head and pulled the brim down over his eyes. 'Hadn't thought I'd have everything I do inspected.' There was no mistaking the aggression now in his voice.

'You are impertinent, Bradstock,' Sam warned. 'Take care how you speak to Mrs Rabson.'

'Are you hiding something from us?' Hannah regarded the farmyard with greater interest, sensing that all was not as it should be.

'I bain't hiding nothing, Mrs Rabson.' He kept his head lowered, avoiding her stare, and a tic twitched the corner of his mouth. 'I thought by renting this farm I'd be my own master.'

'As indeed you are, but your lease is short term. It is only courteous to show us any alterations to buildings.' Hannah was now very suspicious of his conduct. She glanced at Sam, whose face was flushed with anger. He also guessed the tenant was not being honest with them. She felt a sickly dread and hoped that she would be proved wrong.

Bradstock looked trapped, and wiped his sweating face with his sleeve. Sam dismounted and moved closer to him. 'I must insist we look inside the barn.'

'There bain't nothing to see. I bain't done no work inside yet,' the farmer blustered, his voice rising and the convulsive twitching of the side of his mouth out of control.

182

'Then what are you afraid of, man?' Sam marched towards the outbuilding.

Bradstock hurried after him. 'Thee can't go in there. It bain't right to come here and throw thy weight around. I know my rights.'

Sam spun on his heel and grabbed the farmer by his shirt front. 'Is there contraband in there? Is that what you are hiding?'

'I bain't done nothing . . .' Bradstock trembled and held up his arm as though to ward off a blow.

Sam shoved the shorter man aside and wrenched open the barn door. Hannah gasped, her worst fears realised. Dozens of brandy kegs were piled in rows. She rounded on the farmer. 'You know the conditions of rent. There is to be no contraband stored on the land. The authorities will be immediately informed.'

'But they'll arrest me,' Bradstock wailed. 'I couldn't stop them. I tried. Truly, I tried.'

'Then you should have reported it,' Sam blasted at him.

'They said they'd harm my family. It were only meant to be there a night or two. It should be gone by tomorrow.' He wrung his hands together. 'It bain't doing no harm, Mrs Rabson. Just another night . . .'

'Pack your bags and get off my brother's land, Bradstock.' Hannah bore down on him in her fury. 'I made the conditions quite clear. I will not have smugglers using this land. I will repay your first quarter's rent. I want you gone within the hour. Sam will remain here while I send word to the revenue men. The goods will be confiscated.'

'They'll kill us if the goods be taken,' Bradstock's eyes bulged in terror. 'Do thee want our deaths on thy conscience?'

Hannah hardened her heart. 'Then you should not have allowed the contraband to be stored here.'

'I had no choice.' He shook his head, now weeping freely. 'They came at night and unloaded their carts and horses without a by-your-leave. The noise woke me. When I came out to confront them I had a pistol put to my head. They threatened to murder my wife and children in their beds. They said it would be gone in two nights. Thee have children, Mrs Rabson. I couldn't risk their lives. I didn't want to help them, but what can one man do against so many?'

'The authorities will act against them. Who were the men who came here?' Sam demanded.

'I don't know. I recognised no one. I've met few people since we moved here from t'other side of Bodmin.' He turned to Hannah, pleading. 'Thee can't turn me off the land, Mrs Rabson. I had no choice. My wife were terrified enough afore this. Thee didn't tell us when we took the tenancy that the smugglers had murdered a man here. The rumours put the fear of God into my dear Sarah. She fears we'll be murdered in our beds.'

A young boy and girl ran out of the house calling for their father. The sight of them tugged at Hannah's conscience. They were the same age as Florrie and Luke. They watched her warily, their thumbs stuck in their mouths. Their clothes were clean and their hair recently brushed, the girl's neatly plaited. Sarah Bradstock cared for her children well. Hannah also noted the curtains that had been hung at the bedroom windows and the beginning of a flower garden by the front door to the farmhouse. They were a hardworking couple, but Uriah Bradstock was weak. If the smugglers got away once with hiding their goods here, they would continue to bully him into allowing it to happen again.

'I have stood up to the smugglers before,' Hannah declared. 'If Sawle is behind this, he strikes at my family as well as your own. I warned him that the authorities would be told if our land was so used. I cannot allow my wishes to be flouted.'

Bradstock was frantic in his desperation. 'I've invested my life savings in the sheep and seed. Would thee see us in the workhouse? Or arrested by the authorities? Who will provide for my family then?'

The stout figure of Sarah Bradstock leaned against the doorframe, her arms folded. 'I told thee, Uriah, that no good would come of this. We be good law-abiding Methodists but we be simple farmers. My husband is not a man of violence.'

'I have no choice in this matter, Mrs Bradstock.' Hannah could not take her gaze from the children. The girl ran to her father and hugged his legs with one arm. Hannah's conscience warred with her and she could not risk the children being harmed.

Sarah Bradstock took the hand of her son. 'I reckon this farm be cursed. It brings ruin to any who work it. We've heard tell of our land-lord who was packed off to Botany Bay, and then his bailiff were murdered here. It be cursed and we should have been told.'

'This place is not cursed.' Hannah lost patience but she could appreciate that they found themselves in a frightening situation and felt threatened by it. 'Sawle or his men murdered Mr Black the bailiff. For that I vowed to bring the smuggler to justice. He has stayed away from the district and escaped arrest. This farm will provide you with a good income but not if you turn a blind eye to the smugglers.'

She addressed Uriah. 'Report the smugglers to save yourself from imprisonment. Do that and I will allow you to continue your tenancy.'

'And how do I survive the violence of those godless men?'

'The revenue officers will lie in wait for the smugglers to return and they will be arrested,' Hannah assured him.

Sarah Bradstock picked up her son and hugged him close, her face drawn with misery. 'We will all be murdered in our beds. Everything we had went into this farm.'

'I will help you protect your family, Mr Bradstock,' Sam offered.

The children caught their parents' fear and began to cry. It tore at Hannah's heart but she could not back down. There had been no need for Sam to offer his services and risk his life, but it was typical of him. His bravery and consideration touched her profoundly.

'Mr Deacon will allow no harm to come to your family, I promise,' she reassured the couple.

'I pray thee be right, Mrs Rabson.' Sarah Bradstock turned her back on Hannah and went into the house.

Sam turned to Bradstock. 'Do you wish me to ride to the authorities with you? They will need to be hidden before the smugglers arrive after dark. And their presence will prevent any harm to your family.'

'They can't protect us once they've gone,' Bradstock groaned. 'If I go free, the smugglers will know I informed on them.'

'Then stay here,' Sam ordered in a gentler tone. 'I will explain that you came to me about the hidden goods and to protect you I said I would inform the authorities. I'll make sure they understand that you were an innocent party.'

The farmer did not look entirely convinced that he would escape harm or imprisonment. Hannah felt sorry for the Bradstocks, but she could not allow Sawle to think he could triumph over her family. Only by his incarceration would his reign of terror upon innocent people such as this be ended.

She could not leave without giving some words of comfort to Sarah Bradstock. She found the farmer's wife weeping in the kitchen. 'I know how worrying this is for you. But if you give in to the smugglers now, they will come back time and again. They are dangerous men and have no respect for the lives of those they bully into submission to their orders. At any time the militia could search the farm for contraband and your husband would be arrested as an accomplice.'

'I thought it was a trade even the magistrates ignored. It has been going on for centuries.' Sarah wiped her eyes on her apron.

'Sawle's gang has got out of hand with their vicious attacks and flouting of the law. He must be brought to justice.'

Sarah stared at her despondently. 'This farm was to be our hope for the future. What future do we have now if we go against them?'

185

'You have no choice,' Hannah replied heavily. 'But you will not face them alone. Sir Henry Traherne wants Sawle convicted. He will put men he trusts here to work your farm and safeguard you until Sawle is caught.'

'When will the men come?' Sarah put her arms around her children, who stood silently at her side. 'Mrs Rabson, will you swear on your own children's lives that my little ones will be safe?'

'As safe as any child can be. Do not let them wander far from the house. Sir Henry's men will come after the contraband has been removed. If he does not agree to this, then my family will provide men for your protection. This is Loveday land. We are loyal to those who support us.'

Troubled by what lay ahead for the Bradstocks, Hannah returned to her farm to see Mark and Jeannie sharing their lunch of bread and cheese on a low wall by the farmhouse. Her heart lightened to witness them so carefree and enjoying each other's company. She had been aware in the last weeks of the blossoming romance between the couple. They were clearly good for each other. Mark had suffered so much at his brother's hands; it was time he found happiness.

Mark had been washing out the milk churns by the farmyard pump and they lay drying in the sun. Unaware of Hannah's approach, the couple's heads were close together and Jeannie giggled. Mark caught her to him and kissed her. Sheba neighed, announcing Hannah's presence, and Jeannie jumped up and bobbed a nervous curtsey. Hannah dismounted, smiling at the young woman. Mark also stood up to unsaddle Sheba and turn her in to the paddock.

'Please, finish your food. I will tend to Sheba.' Hannah waved them aside.

Jeannie nudged Mark in the ribs, then ran inside the house. Mark blushed crimson and shifted uncomfortably from one foot to the other. 'I'll tend to Sheba, Mrs Rabson, but could I have a word with you?'

Hannah continued to walk the mare to the stable and loosened her girth. She remained worried about what could happen at Tor Farm. If any harm came to the Bradstock children she would never forgive herself.

Mark lifted the saddle from Sheba's back and hesitated before addressing Hannah. 'It be like this, Mrs Rabson. Jeannie has agreed to be my bride. Would you give us your blessing?'

Hannah smiled at him. 'It is good to have happy news for a change. Of course I give my blessing. I hope you do not intend to leave my service.'

'I would not do that.' Mark took up some straw and rubbed Sheba's back. 'Not after all you've done for me. Jeannie too would want to continue to work here. I wondered if it be too forward to ask if we could have the Caines' old cottage.'

Hannah had not replaced the slovenly couple, and once Mark had recovered from his beating he had taken on much of Dick Caine's work as well as his own, while Jeannie did twice as much in the house as Mab had ever done. She was quick to reassure him. 'I should have offered it to you before. But I was concerned you would take on too much too soon after your beating.'

'I be perfectly well now, Mrs Rabson,' Mark replied.

'The cottage needs work done to it. A thorough cleaning to start with, and the roof leaks. I asked Dick all last winter to mend it. He could not be bothered. I should burn the old mattress bedding and rag rugs. They will be alive with fleas and lice. I will get a new mattress for you and I've a bag of rags Jeannie can use to make new rugs. When do you intend to wed?'

'I will call on your father to read the banns on Sunday and we will wed in three weeks.' He rubbed a hand over his blond hair, making it stand up in spikes. 'I'll have the roof mended by then. I'll do it in my own time and so will Jeannie when she cleans the cottage. She will be so joyful to have her own home.'

After the bad news she had given to the Bradstocks, Mark's happiness eased the weight of Hannah's burdens. It was hard being responsible for so many lives. For a moment she wondered if she had acted too hastily at Tor Farm. Then, seeing the barely healed scars on this young man's face where he had suffered at the hands of his own brother's bullies, she knew her decision was the right one. She patted Sheba on the rump as Mark led the mare towards the paddock, and called after him.

'It will be good to have a wedding on the farm. I shall provide the feast, and your family — all except Harry, that is — are welcome.'

Mark removed Sheba's bridle and she ran across the meadow whinnying to her companions, her mane and tail lifted by the breeze. He shut the gate and when he turned to Hannah his face was dark with anger. 'I would not have that devil's spawn anywhere near you or my Jeannie, Mrs Rabson. And we never expected you to do so much for us. Just a quiet wedding would have done us.'

If she needed confirmation of his loyalty it was in those words. She would reward that allegiance. 'You cannot have a wedding and not a feast. It is what we all need before the hard work of the next month.'

Chapter Twenty-seven

Law and order occupied Adam's thoughts. He had been unable to find any evidence to indicate who had undertaken the robberies on the day of Tamasine's wedding. The villagers still remained suspicious of the gypsies. Also nothing further had come to light concerning Lisette's jewellery. On his return from Plymouth he called at Trevowan to inform St John of his findings.

He was surprised to see Felicity Barrett and Sophia Quinton seated in the grounds of the Dower House with his stepmother. They had now been St John's guests for almost a month. Rowena and Charlotte Barrett were playing skittles and young Rafe was laughing every time a wooden skittle was knocked over.

He paused to talk a few minutes to the ladies before excusing himself to find his twin.

'St John has ridden to the top field. Nance was concerned that some blight had caused the corn to rot,' Amelia informed him.

'I hope that is not the case,' Adam returned. A crop failure would ruin St John's chances of getting the estate out of debt. 'And if there is a blight it could spread to other fields.'

Adam walked to the top field. He found his brother striding through the furrows of the ripening corn with Isaac Nance. St John left the bailiff to join him.

'Is there blight?' Adam asked, climbing over the gate into the field. 'Amelia said there could be a problem.'

'What do you think?' St John waited while Adam examined several rows. The corn had strange-coloured speckles on some of the leaves.

'I've not seen anything quite like it.' Adam was puzzled.

'There were something similar a dozen years past,' Nance informed him. 'There bain't no bugs on the stalks to cause it. We did not lose the crop last time. Only this small patch has been affected so far. Your father had the affected plants pulled up and burned as a precaution.'

'Then that is what we will do,' St John confirmed. 'I do not want to risk the rest of the crop.'

'I shall check my crop at Boscabel as a precaution,' Adam stated. His own finances were precarious, with so much of his money tied up in the yard.

'It don't look to be any of the usual blights that kill a crop,' Isaac Nance reassured him.

They left the field and Nance walked rapidly ahead of the brothers. When the bailiff was out of earshot, Adam said, 'I have just returned from Plymouth. Mendoza could tell me nothing about the person who sold him Lisette's jewellery, other than it was a man – and he definitely did not have a French accent.'

St John felt the tension leave his body. He had been on edge ever since he had learned that his twin had gone to Plymouth.

'Lisette must have used it to honour a gaming debt,' he replied, watching Adam for his reaction.

'Mendoza was not honest with me,' Adam continued. 'But he probably thought the jewellery had come into the man's possession as the result of a robbery and he feared being accused of fencing stolen property.'

'So we have no leads as to Lisette's whereabouts, or even if she is still alive?'

'Nothing.'

'She must have drowned with Uncle William,' St John announced. 'Otherwise her clothes would have gone from the house. Do you not agree?'

'It seems most likely, but I do not like mysteries, especially when it concerns the death of members of our family.'

St John hoped that this did not mean that Adam would prove difficult. 'It has been nearly two years since Uncle William's body washed up on the beach. The sea may never give up her body. It is time to have her officially declared dead and her property released by the bank and paid out to William's beneficiaries.'

Adam walked for some yards before replying. 'William left everything to his brothers and Elspeth, I believe.'

St John faced him with a triumphant glitter in his eyes. 'And Father's share would come to me as his heir.'

Adam ignored the taunt. He was not surprised that his twin wanted the matter resolved so that he could profit. 'Uncle Joshua will find the money most welcome. Elspeth deserves to live without the constraints of her allowance from the estate. But Lisette could have left her own will. She would have made Etienne her heir.'

189

'There is no such will in Uncle William's lawyer's possession. Or at Trevowan. Etienne has also disappeared. If he showed his face here I would have him arrested on suspicion of murdering Uncle William and Lisette. Etienne was with them the day of the disappearance and was probably the last one to see them alive. Uncle William often quarrelled with him over the way he would manipulate Lisette. He could have murdered them. He will not show his face even if he lives.'

'Then you must get legal advice on the matter, and as trustee to Father's will, Uncle Joshua should accompany you.' Adam shrugged off any resentment he felt that this money would benefit his twin and not him. At least it would free Trevowan of debt. 'I trust you will use the money wisely, brother.'

'Lisette's jewels will be a fine wedding present for a wife,' St John smirked. 'Mrs Barrett is covetous of her own fortune. They may persuade her that I have no need of it.'

'So you have a mind to marry Mrs Barrett?' It explained to Adam the lady's continued stay here. 'She will be a worthy mistress of Trevowan. Her reputation is beyond reproach.'

'I am confident that she will accept me this summer,' St John confided.

Adam hid a smile. Mrs Barrett disapproved of heavy drinking and gaming. If St John loved her, she could end his wastrel habits and bring Trevowan to a greater glory. Though if he had reasons other than love for choosing her as his bride, their future would bring them both more misery than happiness.

When Adam returned to Boscabel, he was greeted by Senara, who waved a parchment excitedly at him.

'This was delivered by a messenger from Plymouth. It has the Admiralty seal.'

Whilst in Plymouth visiting the jeweller Mendoza, Adam had also wandered around the port. He was interested in the ships and it was rare now he had the opportunity to study foreign vessels and their design. There was no ship that warranted his interest, but he had by chance met Lieutenant Shaver, an officer who had patrolled the English coast during his last years at sea and who despised the lawless trade of the smugglers. Shaver had surprised Adam by inviting him to dine that evening. Last year the lieutenant had accompanied Admiral Thorpe when he had come aboard *Sea Mist* while Adam was docked in Plymouth during her sea trials, and the two officers had shown an interest in her speed. It was some years since the revenue office had taken possession of the cutter *Challenger* from Adam's yard which had proved successful against the smugglers. Adam had tendered a price to build three more such cutters for the revenue but had received no commission. The cost of the war with France had meant only ships of the line had been purchased.

It had made the smugglers more audacious, and Adam knew Harry Sawle had successfully landed dozens of cargoes since he purchased *Sea Mist*.

Lieutenant Shaver had suffered a seizure some years ago, which had contorted one side of his face, and he dragged one leg when he walked. The candle on the table of the dimly lit chophouse flickered, turning his face into a macabre mask. The seats were like high-backed settles, giving them some privacy from curious stares.

'The cutter built in your yard last year was sold to a smuggler,' Shaver accused. His speech was slow and slurred but his wits remained sharp and his hatred for the free-traders had not abated. 'These men rob our country of its rightful taxes. Taxes needed if we are to win the war with France.'

'I am not responsible for how the vessels I build are used.' Adam defended his yard. 'The contract stated the owner to be a merchant. He would hardly put on paper that he was a free-trader. And I have heard that *Challenger* has had much success in curbing the trade.'

'But her success could be undermined by similar craft.' A white-knuckled fist slammed down on to the table as Shaver's outrage mounted. 'A second such cutter was recently delivered to Guernsey. The island is known to supply contraband to English smugglers.'

Adam had leaned back in his seat in a relaxed manner. If Shaver was trying to goad him, there was no point in rising to the bait. He needed the commission for more cutters. 'I am in the business of building ships, not casting moral judgements on my customers who tell me they are merchants.'

The officer would normally have been retired from the navy after his seizure prevented him from serving on board ship, but with the continuing war with France, the government needed his experience to perform duties on land. Adam had met many officers like Shaver during his time in the navy. Men who had never married and whose mistress was the sea. Men who would follow orders without question and show no compassion to those who transgressed against their patriotic duty.

'I know your game, Loveday. You sell these fast ships to free-traders to outwit us. Where is your loyalty to your country?'

'I tendered a good price to build three more cutters for the revenue. It was not accepted. There is no law against building fast ships.'

Lieutenant Shaver had brought the conversation to an abrupt end and left their meeting. Now, as Adam broke open the red seal, he held his breath expectantly. It was a curt note asking him to resubmit a tender for a single cutter to be built at a patriotic cost to the government.

It would have been more cost-effective to build two ships at a cheaper price, but Adam needed this order to continue the success of the yard. And what better justice upon Harry Sawle to have the *Sea Mist* overrun and confiscated by her sister ship. It would mean another trip to Plymouth to discuss some internal changes to the vessel that would help keep the cost to a minimum.

Knowing he would be away for some days, Adam visited the gypsy camp before returning to Plymouth. Caleph was training a wild pony to run on a leading rein. He threw the reins to his son and walked towards Adam. He showed no sign now of the wound that had kept him here for so long.

'Unfortunately I have found no evidence to link anyone with the robberies on the day of my sister's wedding. Neither has Sir Henry Traherne. But no blame has been placed on your people. If you now wish to move on to your summer grounds you are free to leave with no suspicion cast upon you. I appreciate your cooperation in this. It meant a great deal to Senara.'

'We are innocent. I would not break my word to my sister.' Caleph remained antagonistic. He trusted no one outside his own blood. 'Tell Senara I'll send word if we be at the local fairs. We won't use this land again. It will only cause trouble for her.'

'Senara will be upset by your decision. I hold no grudge against you and I trust your word that you would do nothing to bring dishonour to your sister's name while you are camped here. The ground will always be yours to use if you change your mind.' He held out his hand in friendship and after a brief hesitation Caleph shook it.

'You've always done right by us. But the villagers have took against us. That bain't nothing we bain't used to, but I'll not bring shame to Senara. The villagers don't need reminding your wife were one of us. They'd use it against her given the chance.'

Adam looked across to where seven wild ponies from the moor had been broken to the saddle and were tethered under the trees. 'At least your stay here has provided you with horses to sell. I wish you well, Caleph. You will not leave without saying farewell to your sisters and mother, I trust. I'll send word to them to visit within the hour. I expect you are now eager to return to your travels.'

Chapter Twenty-eight

An hour before dark, a dozen armed excise men arrived at Tor Farm. Their horses had been left in a wood on the far side of the farm. The men lay in wait in the barn and other outbuildings. Lieutenant Tregare was in the kitchen with Sam and Uriah Bradstock. His wife had gone to the children's bedroom as they slept. She stood by the window holding a pistol that Sam had shown her how to fire. Although her teeth were rattling with fear, she would kill any smuggler who came through the door intent on harming her children.

Tregare had been antagonistic towards Bradstock since his arrival. The officer was middle-aged and thickset, with a bullish jut to his jaw. 'You say you gave the smugglers no permission to store their goods on this land, but why would they then think you would allow them to use your barn?'

'They put a pistol to my head. That would make most men agree to their demands, would it not?' Bradstock was nervous under the interrogation. 'The farm has been untenanted for some years. They could have used the outbuildings afore. Was not the owner's bailiff found murdered last year?'

'The owner of this farm is no better than a thief himself.' Lieutenant Tregare had removed his hat and scratched his head beneath his powdered military wig. 'He's serving time at His Majesty's pleasure in Botany Bay.'

'There you are mistaken, Lieutenant,' Sam curtly informed the pompous officer. 'Mr Loveday received a full pardon. He was wrongly accused. He has settled upriver from Sydney Cove with his wife and son and acts as agent for Adam Loveday and his fellow investors, who import essential goods to the new colony.'

'There is no smoke without fire,' the officer sneered. He stretched his bandy legs out in front of the kitchen range, hogging the heat given off by the fire.

Sam bit back an angry retort. Tregare had the air of a man who used his officer status to his own advantage. He had close-set eyes and Sam did not entirely trust him. Hannah had learned from Adam that the militia frequented the Dolphin Inn. Any association with Mordecai Nance could mean that they were in Sawle's pay.

Sam decided that he would keep a sharp eye on Tregare when the smugglers came. If the officer showed any neglect in his duty it would be reported to his superiors. Hannah had risked her own safety by insisting Bradstock report the hidden contraband. He admired her courage. She was the most resilient of women. In that she was a true Loveday, and having come to know the rest of her family that bravery no longer surprised him. Though born a gentlewoman, Hannah was not afraid to help with the birthing of a foal or calf, or pitch in with the milking when necessary. That he did find remarkable, for in his experience most women of her class would never deign to do such menial work.

His respect for her grew with every week. Her encounters with Sawle had shown bravery and integrity. No red-blooded male could fail to be struck by her beauty, but that alone would not have moved him. He had known many beautiful women who were shallow and feckless. He had stayed at Rabson Farm longer than any previous employment in the last four years. He preferred seasonal work amongst people who did not know him, moving on with Charlie so that no awkward questions were asked about his previous life.

Rabson Farm had been different. Hannah worked longer hours than any of her servants and still found the time to play with her children and tend to a husband who had become an invalid. He had never heard her complain, and where such a workload would have made many women bitter, she laughed frequently and dismissed her cares.

Sam often found it hard to settle of a night and would spend hours wandering around the farmyard to conquer his own troubled thoughts of his past. There had been many occasions after Oswald died that he had seen Hannah through the illuminated windows of the farmhouse. Believing herself alone and unobserved, she would lower her head into her arms and weep until he thought her heart would break. A love and loyalty like that was humbling to behold.

When Oswald Rabson became bedridden, Sam had taken the position of overseer instead of moving on. It had enabled the lawyer in Bodmin to track him down but he did not regret having been able to attend his mother's funeral. Though that had brought further confrontations with his father and uncle, men who could make life difficult for Charlie if they chose. Fortunately the boy was as yet too young to be important to them.

He was uneasy that the family knew his whereabouts and usually he would have moved on. Yet his loyalty to Hannah had kept him here. Since Oswald had died he had witnessed Hannah's strength of character, and he had been drawn to protect her in any way that might be necessary. Tonight that included ensuring that Tregare did not fail in his duty to capture the smugglers and any leader present.

There was a new moon, and outside the farm was in almost total darkness. So far there had been no sounds of packhorses or carts from without. Tonight must appear as any other, and at his usual bedtime Uriah took the single candle that had been burning downstairs up to his bedchamber and a few moments later doused its light. He then returned to the kitchen to join Sam and the officer.

'Rake out the fire so that only a few embers are burning,' Sam ordered Bradstock.

'The light from a fire will not stop them coming to claim their goods.' Tregare leaned back on his wooden chair and put his dirty boots on the scrubbed table.

Sam swiped them away. 'Have you no respect for these people? In any flames from the fire the red of your uniform will be visible from outside. Would you warn them off?'

'Are you telling me how to do my duty?' Tregare stood up, his manner belligerent.

'I am beginning to question how many times you have been successful in catching the free-traders. Now your voice will carry to them. Your military training would have taught you how important silence and invisibility are in an ambush.'

Tregare scowled. 'I've had my successes. I want no interference from you, or I'll have you clapped in irons for impeding my duty. How do I know you aren't here to warn them? An overseer can be bribed to turn a blind eye when need be. Did your mistress uncover your scheming to make a profit from these goods? Mayhap it was you who murdered Mr Black. Did he discover your dealings?'

Sam realised he was being deliberately provoked and did not respond.

Bradstock groaned. 'My family could be murdered in their beds.'

'Get a grip on yourself, man.' Tregare snapped, but he remembered to lower his voice.

Sam did not like the way the evening was developing. If the officer was not in the smugglers' pay, he was clearly incompetent. He should be reassuring Bradstock, not making him more nervous.

Tregare continued to taunt the farmer. 'Are you worried that your smuggling cronies will make you pay when they lose their cargo, Bradstock?'

'They should all be in gaol, if thee do your duty,' Bradstock whispered, wringing his hands in growing anguish.

'No one likes informers,' the officer goaded. 'Have you got any brandy or cider? I'm parched.'

'Mr Bradstock has acted as a law-abiding citizen,' Sam defended. The farmer looked at breaking point. 'And you need to be sober, Lieutenant.'

The officer chuckled maliciously. 'Are you a brave man, Bradstock? Do you know what the free-traders do to informers? They cut out their tongues and stuff them down their throats until they choke. Or tie them to a stake on the shore so that the high tide drowns them.'

Sam leapt to his feet. 'For the love of God, man! Stop tormenting him.'

'Do you think yourself impervious to their vengeance?' Tregare sniggered. 'Mayhap you are their ringleader. You talk mighty fine for a servant.'

'And you talk as though you are scared of their power.' Sam rounded on him. 'We will see who puts duty and honour first this night.'

'Please, keep thy voices down,' Bradstock pleaded. 'If they are alerted to danger, the free-traders will flee. Then who will protect me from their vengeance?'

'Huh! I knew he was a coward,' Tregare spat.

'Hush. I hear something,' Sam hissed. 'It better not be your men making that commotion.'

Voices and the sound of stamping boots grew louder by the moment. Sam snatched up his primed pistol from the table and stuck it into his belt. He held a cudgel in his left hand.

Lieutenant Tregare went to the window and peered out. 'It's them. Once they enter the barn my men will have them.'

Sam stood by the door. Tregare shoved him aside. 'This is military business. You can protect the house if you must, but I want no interference out there. My men will as likely crack your head open as that of a smuggler in the dark.'

'Don't thee leave us to their mercy, Mr Deacon.' Bradstock held a shotgun in trembling hands.

Sam nodded agreement. As long as the soldiers did their duty, he had no need to interfere. He watched through the window. He could make out the shape of a score of pack ponies and two carts. The smugglers entered the barn and there was a roar of angry shouts. Two shots were fired before the smugglers ran back into the farmyard, their figures dark silhouettes in the pale moonlight. The white of the soldiers' leggings and waistcoats appeared as silvery spectres as the two groups fought. A horse whinnied and Sam saw the outline of a rider watching the proceedings. It was obvious that the smugglers were being overpowered, but no one had tackled their leader. When the rider wheeled his horse to make his escape, Sam wrenched open the door to run across the yard and grab the horse's bridle. He struck the rider several times with his cudgel, shouting, 'This is the leader! This is the man we want.'

The rider's foot came out of the stirrup and too late Sam saw it aimed at his head. He ducked but it struck his temple. Pain exploded through his skull and he was knocked sideways by the force of the blow, the bridle torn from his fingers. The sound of the fleeing horse was a mocking tattoo to his failure. He drew his pistol to fire, but in his dazed state the shot went wide. As he struggled to his knees, the scene swirled chaotically around him. Two other figures broke away from the mêlée and ran into the darkness.

The sound of the fighting was violent. The soldiers gained control and tied a dozen prisoners to their own carts; even then the smugglers kicked out and shouted curses and abuse. Many of the men's faces were streaked with blood and several of the soldiers were limping or holding their sides from their injuries. Sam wiped his own blood from his eyes. Tregare was standing in the farmhouse doorway, holding a lantern high to inspect the night's work. Its glow also showed that the officer was unarmed and his uniform not even dirtied or dishevelled. To Sam's disgust Tregare had taken no part in the fighting.

'Well done, men! This will fill the lockup and show the smugglers we mean business,' the officer bragged.

'The leader got away,' Sam raged, the ripped sleeve on his jacket hanging loose.

'One of these will talk. To save their lives they will inform against him,' Tregare declared.

'Not if they want to save their families from harm.' Still groggy from the blow to his head, Sam put a supporting hand to the wall of the house.

The prisoners were rounded up and the soldiers began to load the contraband on to the carts and ponies, to be taken to the customs house.

Uriah Bradstock confronted Tregare. 'If the leader is free, what will happen to my family?'

The officer shrugged. His work was done and he was impatient to leave. 'You'd do well to pray one of them speaks out. Count yourself lucky you aren't being arrested as an accomplice.'

The farmer staggered back into the farmhouse, his expression haggard as he groaned, 'Then my family is doomed.'

Sam followed. Bradstock picked up his shotgun and held the barrel to his mouth. Sam grabbed it from his hands before he could sit down and pull the trigger.

'That will solve nothing.'

'It may spare my loved ones.'

'For what? Life in the workhouse?' Sam put a hand on his shoulder. 'You are a good man, Bradstock. You just had a bad break.'

The farmer wept, his hands covering his face. 'There bain't no point in staying here. I've lost my life savings but I've still got me family. I'll get work. But not in these parts.'

'I'm sorry, Bradstock.' Sam's head was pounding and he had trouble focusing, but he was determined to give the farmer some hope and reassurance for the future. 'Mrs Rabson will reimburse your rent and the savings you spent on planting and repairs. I could meet you in Launceston market next week with the money.'

'I can't risk being recognised.' Bradstock sighed and wiped away his tears.

A soft gasp drew their attention to his wife standing by the stairs. 'This place never felt like home to me. Not with a man murdered. There be little enough to put on our wagon. Once it is packed I'll rouse the children. In a few weeks it will be harvest time. There'll be work aplenty. We won't starve, Uriah.'

'The leader will be brought to justice,' Sam promised. He admired the woman's fortitude. 'Then you will be safe. I shall be at Launceston market with the money. Grow a beard and keep your hat over your eyes and no one will recognise you. I wish it had not come to this.'

The room was beginning to spin, and somehow Sam gathered his senses together enough to mount his mare, which had been hidden in the barn. He gave the animal its head and it found its own way home. Sam drooped in the saddle, every jolt from the horse sending arrows of pain through his skull.

He was dimly aware that lights still burned in Hannah's kitchen as his mare clopped into the farmyard. He swayed in the saddle and suddenly found his body slamming into the ground. A woman's voice cried out.

'Sam! You're hurt.'

He could smell the lavender scent of her perfume as she bent over him. He struggled to rise and her arm went round his waist to support him.

'You are covered in blood. Come into the kitchen.'

Even half conscious, he was aware that blood was dripping on to her cream shawl. 'I will ruin your shawl.'

'It will wash. Your welfare is more important than any garment.'

His step was unsteady and she staggered under his weight but managed to get him to a bench by the kitchen table. His eyes closed against his pain as he slumped on to the seat. Hannah brought the candlestick closer to inspect his wound. She poured water from a pitcher into a bowl and bathed the bloody flesh with a clean cloth.

Despite her tender touch, Sam winced.

'I'm sorry. I am being as gentle as I can. You have a livid bruise but the bleeding has stopped. You are clearly dazed and you have lost a great deal of blood. Your jacket and shirt are covered in it.'

'It's not all mine.'

Her face was hazy before his gaze. He could feel his senses fading and battled to find his voice. It was hoarse and weak. 'We failed to capture the leader. Several smugglers were taken but Bradstock is terrified. He and his family are leaving Tor Farm tonight. I failed him. I failed you.'

'You failed no one, Sam. How can any of us fight the smugglers and win? My uncle lost his life when he took them on.'

Her voice sounded strange and he struggled to keep his eyes focused. She was bending close to him, her face wet with tears. Her hazel eyes were large and luminous in the candlelight.

'My stubbornness is the cause of all this,' she said. 'First Mark is savagely beaten, now you.'

He caught her hand and held it. 'You would uphold the freedom of people to say no to these bullies and villains.'

'But Bradstock has lost so much.' Her control on her emotions slipped and she sobbed in her distress. 'Had I not been so pig-headed, he could have made a success of Tor Farm. He had done so much. I have destroyed his livelihood.'

'Someone has to stand up to the smugglers. Sawle chose his farm to get back at your family. You had no choice.'

She sank down on the bench beside him, shocking him with the violence of her tears. 'I had no right to involve Bradstock or you in my fight.'

Forgetting the boundaries of propriety, Sam gathered her into his arms. Even in his pain he needed to comfort her. 'You did what was right. I chose to support your wishes; you did not order me. I would give my life to protect you.' He stroked the silken softness of her hair to calm her.

Hannah sniffed back her tears and drew back. For a long moment she stared into his eyes, then gently touched his cheek. Then his lips were on hers and Hannah, caught in the vulnerability of the moment, responded. The kiss was intoxicating. She could drown in its strength and passion. Desire turned her blood to fire and she clung to him, momentarily enslaved by its potency. A whinny from Sam's horse left unattended in the yard returned her to her senses. She was shocked by the intensity of the emotions the kiss had aroused, and with a gasp pulled away.

She cleared her throat and made her manner brisk and efficient. 'We must get you back to your cottage, Sam. Your horse must be bedded down. I will brew a tisane to ease your pain and send Aggie over with it.'

His gaze remained on her face as he rose. She noticed that he no longer stumbled. He did not apologise for the kiss and without further comment walked out of the kitchen. Hannah put his actions down to his injury and dazed state. As to her own reaction – it was disloyal to her love for Oswald. Sam would not remember the kiss tomorrow and she was also determined to put it from her mind.

Chapter Twenty-nine

The news of the contraband being seized at Tor Farm was not the only outrage the villagers gossiped about the next morning. Widow Tenkin, who lived in an isolated cottage a mile from Trevowan Hard, had been terrorised in the night. The middle-aged widow had lived alone for three years, preferring the company of a score of cats and two horses to other people. The villagers thought her eccentric ways bordered on the insane and kept away from her. Her husband had been a farrier and had provided well for her. He had been killed along with her only child when their dinghy capsized as they rowed home one evening from Fowey.

Widow Tenkin had dismissed her two servants after the funeral. She dressed in widow's weeds and a black veil always covered her face. She rode to the kiddley at Trevowan Hard once a month to stock up on provisions but never spoke more than the curtest greeting to her neighbours. She had been discovered dazed and confused on the road outside her home by a farm labourer on his way to work that morning. She had been beaten until she told the robbers where she kept her life savings, in a pot buried in the garden, and her two horses had also been stolen.

'We know who be responsible,' Ned Stone raged. The innkeeper at Trewenna resented the way Adam had interfered over the last robberies. 'It be time the gypsies learned they can't hide behind Loveday's protection.'

'Loveday bain't at Boscabel. He left for Plymouth, so I hear.' Hal Wibbley, who was a shiftless farm labourer, was spoiling for a fight. He was one of several Wibbley brothers and cousins.

Ned hawked in his throat and spat on the ground. 'Then now is the time to strike and run them off. We'll make sure they don't show their ugly faces in these parts again. This time we go armed.'

Emotions ran high on the march to the Romany encampment, the men and women who had joined it dragging up any incident to blame upon the gypsies. A bottle of illicit brandy was also handed around to bolster their courage and it further charged their anger.

They halted by the open gate. The field was empty and their prey had gone.

'They've run off!' Hal Wibbley shrieked. 'That proves they robbed Widow Tenkin. They took their chance while their protector were away.'

'They can't have got far. Let's be after them,' his cousin Spike goaded.

'They have too long a start.' Mrs Newton from Trewenna did not like the violence in the men's manner. She was a thin, nervous woman and had come along against her better judgement when she had heard the news while talking to her friend Gertrude Wibbley.

Gertrude was not so reticent. Big, blowsy and a harridan, she liked a fight as much as did her kinfolk. 'They should never have been allowed to camp here. It be that uppity bitch Senara that got Cap'n Loveday to let them stay. Not that she be no better. Gypsy-bred she be herself.'

'None of us be safe in our beds,' Mrs Newton found the courage to state.

'Gertie is,' Hal sniggered. 'Her old man bain't touched her in years.'

'But they be gone and good riddance,' Mrs Newton added.

'The Loveday woman bain't got no right to inflict such as them on decent folk.' Gertrude waved a meaty fist in the air.

'Happen we should think on this,' Mrs Newton cautioned. 'Senara Loveday has cured many of our ills. We've all worked on Loveday land at the harvest and we got a lot to thank Bridie Loveday for what with teaching us how to make lace.'

'We bain't gonna stand it.' Virgil Stone, Ned's brother, shook his cudgel with threatening intent, overruling the words of warning.

'What has the Loveday woman got to say about Widow Tenkin?' Ned Stone also brandished his cudgel, his small eyes glittering with malice. 'She be as guilty as them she brought here.'

The heat of the midday sun and the quantity of brandy that had been drunk incensed the men further. Gertrude Wibbley puffed out her ample chest, her face reddened by the drink. She had always been jealous of Senara and Bridie Loveday for marrying so well. They had never had to work like she did; her life one long drudge to keep her children fed, and receiving abuse from her drunken, useless husband for her pains. Spite made her urge the men on. 'She takes too much on herself, do that Senara Loveday. A gypsy brat born and bred, but she thinks she now be better than us.'

'Aye, remember when she lived with her mother in a hovel and sold her pottery at market,' Virgil sneered. 'No man from round here was good enough for her.'

Senara had rebuffed Virgil before she took up with Adam Loveday and he had never forgotten the insult. He was a womaniser and had thought the gypsy wench easy game. Time and again she had avoided his advances. She had seemed to know when he was lying in wait to waylay her. The fact that she had thought he wasn't good enough for her had wounded his pride.

'She played the whore fast enough when Adam Loveday took an interest in her,' Ruth Nance spat. She was married to Mordecai's brother Josh, and Mordecai's wife Etta had been spilling venom about the Lovedays since her husband had been dismissed from Trevowan. Ruth played up to her attentive audience. 'And her sister weren't much better. She got her claws in young Parson Loveday. Who'd've thought he'd take such a strumpet to wife.'

'Happen he had no choice. Happen she used dark powers,' Gert pronounced grimly.

Three of the women hastily held up their fingers in the sign to ward off evil.

Lily Mawes, who had held her tongue until now, lost patience with the women. She had come along to see the gypsies run off Loveday land. The drunken villagers were going too far. 'You wrong a good woman. Like Lizzy Newton says, Senara Loveday has cured many in your families when you had no money to pay for a physician or apothecary.' She glared at Gertrude Wibbley, 'Neither is Bridie Loveday what you say. She can read and write, which is more than you can, Gert. She be the schoolmarm. My Tich and Bobby can write because of her.'

'So they can use their dark forces on us. 'Tis how the devil catches unwary souls.' Gert continued to spread her mischief. She snatched the brandy bottle from her cousin and drank from it. She then swung out with her fist at Lily and missed. Off balance, she crumpled to the ground and giggled inanely as she struggled to get up. No one bothered to help her.

'You be drunk, Gert,' Lizzie Newton said. 'And you've a viper's tongue.'

'When did gentry such as the Lovedays marry commoners?' Ruth Nance saw the men were losing interest with the women's bickering and wanted to stir them up.

'St John did,' said a pretty young woman who had had a bold eye upon the Loveday men, her youthful dreams filled with one of the twins paying court to her.

'That don't count,' Ruth sneered. She was a homely woman with large-boned features and a figure gaunt from discontent. Her husband worked for Mordecai as a tubman, and Ruth drank more than her fair share of the brandy taken as his nightly payment. She had been drinking all night, waiting for her husband to return from a run. He'd got in an hour before dawn saying that revenue men at Japhet Loveday's farm had overrun the gang. Half the men had been taken prisoner. That was reason enough for Ruth to cause trouble for the Lovedays. Her voice rose higher. 'St John Loveday's wife were a whore. He were arrogant enough to fool around with Sawle's sister and get her in the family way. That were a shotgun wedding. Edward Loveday knew nothing of it until the deed were done.'

'The Polglase sisters weren't no whores,' Lily Mawes defended. 'Senara cured my two children of the morbid fever. If it weren't for her they'd be dead. And young Bridie did a fine thing to set up the lace-making. How many of us ate better last winter from the money we earned when the lace were sold at market?'

'That were their way of tricking us,' persisted Ruth Nance, and Gert Wibbley nodded in agreement.

Lily Mawes edged backwards, disgusted by the way the crowd were now baying for anyone's blood. They would turn on her if she said more. She was a short, timid woman. She had enough violence from her heavy-handed husband and was unwilling to attract more. Shouting abuse at gypsies was one thing; turning on a Loveday was another matter. 'I got me little ones to see to. Ma can't keep an eye on them all morning.' She shuffled away.

Mrs Newton also turned to go. 'We all got work to do. Bain't Mrs Helland hiring today for the hay to be cut on her farm?' Three of the men followed her.

'What about Widow Tenkin?' Ruth was not about to lose her audience. She had come here to witness the gypsies stoned out of the parish. Her blood lust was up. 'Weren't Widow Tenkin innocent and near murdered in her bed? I say it be time Senara Loveday answered to us. We won't put up with her brother's kind round here.'

Several men shifted uncomfortably. Ruth rounded on them. 'Turned yellow, have you now? Not got the balls to face a woman – a jumped-up whore?'

'We bain't afeared of no one – least of all a woman,' Ned Stone roared. He raised his cudgel like a banner. 'Who's with me to go to Boscabel?'

'No point in going all that way.' Virgil sat down on the ground. 'Both

Loveday women be at Trevowan Hard. Senara be tending her patients and Bridie be teaching. Might as well wait for them here.'

Ruth lowered herself next to him and handed him the brandy bottle to drink from. 'Virgil be right. We bain't gonna get nowhere near them at the yard. There be too many men to defend them. Best we wait here until they pass this way.'

'Then hand over the brandy,' Ned demanded. 'We might as well enjoy our wait.'

Lily shuddered as she heard the roar of agreement. Most of the men worked for Nance and Sawle. They wanted vengeance for their lost wages last night. But this action was foolhardy. She did not want Senara or her sister harmed. They had saved her babies and helped feed her family through the winter. She knew where her loyalty lay. Thank God her man Joe had not been with the smugglers last night. He had injured his shoulder falling from a ladder when he had been repairing the thatch.

Lily prayed the villagers would be too drunk to act. It would be an hour or more before the Loveday women journeyed home. Time enough to warn their family. Lily ran across the fields to Trewenna. It was closer than Boscabel, and with Adam Loveday away she needed to alert his uncle, the Reverend Mr Loveday, to protect the young women of his family.

Her heavy work boots were awkward on the rough ground and her long skirts contrived to wrap around her legs and trip her. She fell several times, grazing her knee and cheek, but picked herself up and pressed forward, the spire of Trewenna church like a homing beacon in the distance. She hauled herself over a stile and bent double to ease a stitch building in her side. She was not usually given to such strenuous exertion. Her lungs were bursting and her throat burned from gasping for breath.

Near to swooning, she stumbled up the rectory path and banged on the door. The sound echoed dully through the interior but no one answered. She was sobbing as she banged louder.

'Reverend! Sir! You be needed most urgent.'

A woman paused in walking by. She carried a wicker basket of laundry she had been washing by the stream. A baby was tied to a shawl on her back and two young children tugged on her skirts.

She called out to Lily, 'Reverend bain't home. He be in Bodmin with his nephew. Mrs Loveday be calling on her daughter at the farm.'

Lily sank against the oak door, fighting to regain her breath. She did not know who else to turn to. It was four miles to Polruggan and young

Parson Loveday's parish. Defeated, and her energy gone, she groaned, 'What do I do now?'

The other woman had paused and placed her heavy washing basket on the ground. 'Be there trouble with your family? Happen young Parson Loveday can help. He be in the church. His horse be tethered outside.'

Lily stumbled to the church. She burst in to find Peter kneeling in prayer by the altar. He turned and frowned at her indecorous entrance.

'Madam, this is God's house. Enter with reverence and respect,' he said, rising to his feet.

'Parson, you gotta get to Trevowan Hard. There be trouble for your wife and Mrs Loveday.' She blurted out her story and Peter listened without interruption. His face had grown extremely pale. She wished it had been anyone but him. Parson Loveday did not hold with violence and she had never known him to be involved in a fight, unlike his brother and cousins. His father might preach peace and be a man of God, but the Reverend Mr Loveday had been known to knock two skulls together if young men needed teaching a lesson in manners. He was also reputed to be adept with a sword.

Peter put a hand on her shoulder. 'Thank you, Mrs Mawes. You did well this day. The gypsies left yesterday with my cousin's permission. They could not have robbed Widow Tenkin. I shall ride to Trevowan Hard.'

'But you bain't armed, Parson.' Lily was appalled. If the men were drunk, they would set upon the preacher as well as the women.

Unaware of the danger to her brother, Hannah was concerned about the events of last night at Tor Farm. Sam had recovered from the attack, though his temple bore a large gash and a blackened bruise that partially closed his left eye.

'I should ride to Tor Farm,' he informed her. 'If Uriah Bradstock has fled the district, something must be done with the sheep. The shepherd will need reassurance that his wages will be paid.'

'I hope Bradstock has slept on his decision and changed his mind,' Hannah replied. 'How are you this morning, Sam?'

'My head feels like Old Nick is playing ninepins inside it.'

He appeared to have forgotten that he had kissed her last night. Perhaps that was just as well. She did not want to dismiss him for over-familiarity. Yet it was disconcerting that the incident was so insignificant that he remembered nothing about it. She had tossed and turned all night, her blood stirred by the passion of her own emotions. Emotions she did not wish to consider.

'I will also visit Tor Farm.' She walked to the stable with him and they saddled the horses.

There was no smoke rising from the farmhouse chimney at Tor Farm and Hannah's heart sank. It brought back memories of Black's murder, and she shuddered.

'Should the sheep not be in the near field, Sam?' She frowned at discovering the meadow empty and the gate swinging open.

'The shepherd could have taken them to the moor to graze.'

She surveyed the farmyard, and as her gaze travelled to the sprouting crop, Sam muttered a curse. The field had been trampled, the green stalks broken and beaten into the ground. Investigation showed them that the earth had been trodden flat by the sheep. But there was no sign of the flock, or the shepherd.

'The shepherd must have left after Bradstock,' Sam groaned. 'I cannot say I blame him in the circumstances. The sheep could have scattered, or someone knew Bradstock fled last night and they were driven through the crop then stolen. The leader of the smugglers escaped last night. He'd see the sheep as repayment for the lost cargo and the destroyed crop punishment for your interference.'

Hannah was flushed with anger. 'Of all the petty, vengeful, mindless destruction . . .'

'And may it be the only vengeance they take for last night.' Sam shook his head. 'If so, you got off lightly.'

'Their spite goes deeper than that. This farm is now marked as a place to be wary of. First Black's murder. Now this. Sarah Bradstock was right. It is cursed. What tenant will risk farming here? Damn Sawle.' Hannah was shaking with rage. 'We could have harvested that crop and compensated Bradstock.'

She kicked Sheba into a canter. 'I am going to search the moor. There is a chance the sheep are there.'

Sam did not try and stop her, knowing Hannah needed to do something to overcome her anger. Two hours later they were forced to admit that the sheep had been stolen, for there was no sign of them on the moor.

'Yet again Sawle strikes at us.' Hannah stared across the rugged landscape, patchworked with purple heather and yellow gorse. Other sheep grazed but none had the distinctive black faces and curling horns of the Bradstocks' flock. 'Do you think any of the smugglers taken last night will speak out and name Sawle for hiding the goods at the farm? I shall pay a reward of fifty pounds. The magistrate may even let the informer go free. Those found guilty will be transported.'

Sam shrugged. 'Sawle rules by terror. He'd kill any informer.'

Hannah's knuckles whitened over the reins. 'This cannot be allowed to continue. I will not let Sawle beat us. If he thought I'd be frightened by his bullying and violence, he gravely underestimated me.'

Sam felt powerless against her determination. Hannah was the most courageous woman he had ever encountered. Yet how could he as a humble farmhand properly protect her?

His own past must be laid to rest. For too long anger and pride had clouded his family commitments and loyalty. He could no longer dismiss the issues. The lion had to be bearded in its den and the consequences met.

Chapter Thirty

Peter had long ago thought himself master of the wild nature of his Loveday blood. For years he had prayed and fasted to overcome his hot temper. He suppressed an irrational need for adventure and channelled his energy into his preaching. He had witnessed the downfall of his cousins and brother as they took life by the horns and scorned propriety. St John, with his disastrous marriage and his smuggling exploits with Sawle that had led to his trial for murder; Japhet, whose thirst for adventure had led him to highway robbery, incarceration in Newgate and eventual transportation. Even Adam, who was considered the most loyal and steadfast, had fallen from grace when he had married Senara against his father's wishes and had almost lost his inheritance. And Uncle Edward himself had led a secret life as the lover of Lady Eleanor Keyne. He had shocked his family by introducing Tamasine as his illegitimate child. It had caused further rifts in the family before Tamasine was fully accepted. And had revenue men not shot Edward when contraband had been found on Loveday land?

Peter prided himself that he had led a moral and decent life. But now as he rode to confront the villagers lying in wait for his wife and her sister, his body burned with outrage. He had never felt such hatred, yet these were the villagers he had grown up with and who were his own and his father's parishioners. The intensity of his emotions shocked him. The words of compassion and love for his fellow man, taught by his Saviour, now mocked him. He was too incensed to heed them. He had suffered abuse and aggression since his youth for his beliefs, but now that Bridie and Senara were in danger, there was murder in his heart.

He did not spare his horse. The mare galloped along the lanes at such a pace that clods of earth flew up from her hoofs over the top of the hedgerows on either side of the track. He paid no attention to the danger of meeting a rider or cart travelling in the opposite direction that might be hidden from his view by the steep curves of the lane. The sound of his pounding heart echoed the thunder of his mare's hoofs, and the force of the breeze that whipped his wide-brimmed hat from his head to beat upon his shoulders as it hung by a cord did not cool the heat of fury that darkened his cheeks.

The sound of the horse's approach on the hard ground must have alerted the villagers as he rounded the final bend. They were swaying to their feet after being sprawled on the grass banks where the track opened out into a green triangle at the crossroads that led to Trevowan Hard. Several women screamed as Peter appeared like a vengeful demon into their midst. Many of the men were weaving uncertainly and red-faced from intoxication.

To Peter's relief there was no sign of Bridie or Senara. He had reached the villagers in time. That did not diminish his rage.

'Get back to your work!' he fumed.

'This bain't nothing to do with you, preacher.' Ned Stone was obviously drunk as he blinked several times to focus his vision. When he recognised Peter, his expression hardened with malice.

'How dare you lie in wait to threaten my family!'

'What you gonna do about it.' Virgil Stone swayed towards his cousin, having taken some moments to recover from the shock of Peter's abrupt descent upon them.

'We bain't gonna stand for them gypsies robbing us and getting away with it,' shouted Spike Wibbley, a bow-legged swineherd who reeked of the pigsties he cleaned.

'No evidence could be found against them.' Peter battled to cool his anger and reason with them. All he could think of was the danger to his wife. 'Now get back to your work. You are drunk and disgusting.'

'You gonna make us?' Virgil raised his cudgel. He lived in Polmasryn and supposedly made his living as a carter. But he was drunk most of the time and Peter suspected his cart was used to haul contraband, not legal goods. He was often seen in Penruan and drank at the Dolphin Inn.

Two of Stone's cousins closed ranks and came nearer to Peter, cudgels in hand and their expressions menacing. Peter regarded them sourly. He was sweating from the exertion of his hard ride but he felt no fear.

'I know each of your names. Use your weapons at your peril. You will spend the rest of the summer in Launceston gaol.'

One woman lost her nerve and whined, 'What we be doing here? The gypsies have gone. You can't fight him. He be a preacher.'

Ruth Nance shook her fist and mocked, 'He be a Loveday first and a preacher man second. It be time the Lovedays learned not to interfere in our business. We gotta right to tell Mrs High and Mighty Senara Loveday that her gypsy kind bain't welcome here.'

'They have gone. So where is your grudge?' Peter glared contemptuously at the throng. His horse snorted and shook its head, uneasy at the mood of the people. 'You should be more concerned at the evils that lurk within your own communities. Repent your own sins before you denounce another. The revenue men confiscated a vast quantity of contraband last night. How many of you were safe in your beds at the time?'

The men's mood changed abruptly. They had allowed Ned to be speaker but now they all roared in angry unison.

'That bain't your concern, preacher.'

'Who you calling a free-trader?'

'If you know what be good for you, lock your doors of a night, parson. Hear and see nothing.' Virgil Stone shook his fist. 'We bain't doing nothing that bain't been going on for generations.'

Peter raised a hand to point an accusing finger at the Wibbley and Stone cousins. 'Your leader made it my business when he took up against our family. Sawle leads the innocent to the brink of the abyss. The devil lies in wait for the ungodly.'

Hal Wibbley thrust out his bull neck and squared up, ready to fight. 'We know nothing about those goings-on. Are you gonna make something of it, parson?'

'What about Widow Tenkin being attacked?' Ruth feared the men were drunk enough to be incautious and condemn themselves if the subject turned to the raid by the excise men last night. Most of them had been present and they resented that their associates had been arrested. 'Decent folks bain't safe in their beds with gypsies waiting to rob us.' She raised her voice. 'Don't the widow deserve to be protected from thieves and ruffians?'

'That robbery will be investigated,' Peter declared, and added ominously, 'And the gypsies were not involved. They left yesterday with my cousin Adam's permission. The robbers lurk within your own community, and I suspect they are the same people who carried out the robberies on my cousin's wedding day. Be assured that they will be hunted down. Now go back to your homes. Enough harm has been caused.'

Peter moved his horse forward so that he towered over Ned and Virgil Stone. 'All of you are drunk. Go home now and I shall forget this incident.'

Ned grabbed Virgil's shoulder and pulled him back. The brandy was making his cousin careless. His own head was reeling. He had roused the villagers to attack the Lovedays through the gypsies. Things were getting out of hand. He did not want gossip reaching Mordecai that he could not hold his liquor. He had been given his instructions last night after the revenue men had confiscated the cargo. As much trouble as possible had to be made for the Lovedays. He and Virgil had been behind the original robberies on the day the young Loveday woman had been married. It had been a lucrative venture for both of them. Virgil had suggested that they rob Widow Tenkin. He had broken some goods of hers when carrying them from Bodmin and she had refused to pay him. Virgil never forgot a grudge. It was rumoured that she had a fortune stashed away in her cottage.

Ned had believed she would make an easy target. Wearing flour sacks over their faces with holes cut out for their eyes, they had entered her cottage through a downstairs window with a broken latch. He had not thought she would be so stubborn and hold out so long against his questioning. Virgil had got impatient and had almost beaten her senseless until Ned had stopped him. The robbery was to be blamed on the gypsies. The story that they had left this morning had helped convince the villagers of their guilt. And that had made it easy for him to blame the Lovedays. Yet if the parson was right and the gypsies had left yesterday, suspicion for the robbery would fall on any who had more than a few pence in their pocket to spend in the local kiddley. He would have to keep an eye on Virgil; a rush of spending could get them both arrested.

Guilt made Ned defensive and his mood turned uglier. He did not like the pious man who now presumed to teach them their place. The Lovedays had a reputation for valour, but this one was weak. He was easy game. If Ned put the haughty preacher in his place, it would please Harry Sawle. It might even earn him a reward from the smuggler.

'What you gonna do about it, parson? We bain't your parishioners. You bain't got your strong cousin here to defend you.'

Half a dozen of the men sniggered.

Peter's anger blazed. He was sick of being unfavourably compared to Adam or Japhet. Unfortunately, he was armed only with his riding crop. He was raising his hand to strike the nearest man when a horse and the dogcart appeared at the crossroads behind them. Senara and Bridie's faces were white with shock against the shadow of the overhanging trees.

'What is all this ado?' Senara demanded.

Then Ruth Nance cried out, 'There she be. There be the gypsy whore.'

A hail of stones left the women's hands and clattered around the sisters. Three hit the dogcart, and one struck Senara's horse, Hera, who reared in terror. The village women scattered from the flailing hoofs, and when Senara had the mare under control, Peter was appalled to see that her cheek was bleeding.

'Where be the thieving bastards?' Ruth Nance yelled. She did not believe Peter's tale that the gypsies had left yesterday. 'What you got to say about your folk beating up a feeble old woman and stealing her savings, then running away to escape justice?'

'I heard the Widow Tenkin had been beaten and robbed.' Senara faced them calmly. 'But if you are accusing my brother of such atrocities, then first get your facts straight. My brother's people left just after noon yesterday.'

'Then they must have slunk back to do their evil work.' Ned Stone took control. He flashed Ruth a warning glare. He was in charge of this, not her.

Senara sat straight and defiant in her saddle and stared piercingly at the ringleader. 'You know the culprit was not my brother or any of his people. You should look closer to your own community to bring the thief to justice.'

Ned Stone shuddered at her look. It went right through him. He'd swear she could see into his mind. In which case she'd know he was guilty. Didn't she have unnatural powers with her healing remedies? That was witchcraft. What evil spell would she put on him?

Senara saw the fear darkening Ned Stone's eyes and the sweat speckling his florid face. His guilt was obvious and she said in accusation, 'You will answer to the authorities, Ned Stone. Those who shout loudest in blaming another often have the most to hide.'

In a panic he raised his cudgel to strike her. 'Devil spawn! You'll not bewitch me!'

Peter kicked out and his boot caught Ned on the shoulder. Before Ned knew what was happening, the parson had leapt to the ground and was wrestling him.

'Bridie, there is rope in the cart. Give it to me,' Peter ordered. 'He knows who is behind the robberies. Justice will be served.'

His words acted as a catalyst to the villagers. The women screamed abuse at the Lovedays. Virgil Stone feared he and Ned would both hang if they were put on trial. He drew a dagger and jumped on to the dogcart and pressed the blade to Bridie's throat.

'Let him go, preacher, or she dies.' His attention was fixed on Peter, who was staring at his wife with horror.

Senara was behind Stone. She took a pistol from her saddle holster and with every ounce of her strength slammed the butt down on to the smuggler's head with a force that knocked him sideways. She held her breath, terrified that she had miscalculated how Stone would fall and that Bridie would be harmed. To her relief he toppled over the side of the dogcart and was out cold when he crashed into the ground. Bridie clutched at the back of the seat to save herself from falling from the cart. She was panting heavily but appeared unharmed.

Whilst this was happening Ned Stone fought wildly to throw off his lighter opponent, but the parson was tougher than he thought. Blows hammered down on his head and chest and his arm was caught and a rope looped over it. He saw Senara staring at him, a pistol in her hand. His blood chilled. Suddenly he found his arms were heavy and would not move. He was convinced she'd put a hex on him, forgetting that he had been drinking all day and had been almost too drunk to stand.

Virgil staggered to his feet, and as he raised his cudgel to attack, Bridie screamed a warning to her husband. Agile as a cat, Peter leapt to his feet, drew the rope around Ned's neck and yanked it tight.

'Back off or he chokes to death.' Peter hauled the smuggler to his feet.

'You bain't gonna kill no one, preacher,' Virgil sneered.

'Are you going to risk his life on that!' Peter held his stare.

Virgil saw murder in the usually meek parson's eyes. He'd be a fool to chance that a Loveday would back down. He'd underestimated the preacher. Holding up his hands, he backed away. He cast around him, searching for support. Most of his companions had disappeared. Ruth Nance stood with her arms folded across her chest, hatred glittering in her eyes. She lowered her hands and one fist was closed around a clod of hard earth.

'What be the matter with you, Virgil? Fight him! It bain't but the parson,' she challenged.

'I believe you owe my wife and her sister an apology, Ned Stone,' Peter demanded, giving the rope another yank.

Ned choked, his eyes starting to bulge as the air was cut off from his lungs. Hoarsely he gasped, 'Your pardon, Mrs Loveday, Mrs Loveday.' He could not look either of the women in the eye. His limbs still refused to move properly and he disregarded the fact that on countless occasions when he had been drinking he had woken in the morning on

214

the taproom floor where he had passed out. He'd been hexed. How else could the parson have overpowered him?

'You lily-livered bastard, Virgil,' Ruth Nance yelled. She flung the clod at Senara but rage spoiled her aim and it went wide. She then picked up her skirts and fled.

Peter unwound the rope from Ned's neck and tied both his hands together behind his back. Senara pressed Hera closer to Virgil and kept her pistol aimed at his head. The smuggler was trapped between the horse and the stone wall. Peter tied his hands, then with another piece of rope from the dogcart secured it around both men's waists. 'You will be wasting your time trying to escape.'

The rest of the villagers had disappeared. Ruth Nance was running across the fields in the direction of Penruan, no doubt to inform Mordecai of the men's arrest.

Peter looked drawn and haggard as he stared across at Bridie. 'Are you hurt?'

Bridie shook her head, shaken by the incident. 'You were so brave, Peter.'

Senara tied Hera's reins to the back of the dogcart and climbed in beside her sister. 'I will drive her home to the parsonage, Peter. You must take the men to the lockup. You did well. Thank you. Take my pistol in case they cause trouble.' She handed him the weapon.

'You may need it to protect yourselves,' he protested.

'You have the violent ones under control. We will be safe.'

Peter rode away, and the two men attached by rope to his saddle pommel were forced to walk behind him or be dragged along the ground.

'That could have been an unpleasant incident.' Senara sighed and turned to her sister. She was shocked to see Bridie hunched over, her hands on her stomach and tears rolling down her cheeks.

'Get me home quickly, sister. I fear some harm has come to the baby. My stomach is cramping.'

The track was rough and Senara did not want to risk jolting her sister more than could be helped, so their journey was slower than she would have liked. Guiding the pony with one hand on the reins, she squeezed Bridie's hand. 'You will be fine,' she encouraged as she swallowed down her own fears that Bridie might miscarry. 'You've had a big upset. Once you are in bed and resting, the pains will stop.'

Bridie shook her head in silent answer, her face now grey with pain. When they reached the parsonage and Leah saw Senara helping Bridie inside, she put her hand to her mouth. 'Dear Lord, not again.'

'Ma, heat some water while I take her upstairs and examine her.'

Bridie groaned as she stretched out on the bed. Senara gently pressed her stomach and lifted her skirts to inspect her petticoats. 'There is no blood; that is a good sign. I'll prepare you a sleeping draught and I shall stay here for a few hours as a precaution while you sleep.'

'You will not tell Peter? He has set such store by this child and he worries too much about me.'

'I shall stay and help Ma prepare your meal and pretend I have lost track of time if Peter returns before I leave.'

When Senara came back to the bedroom, Bridie was staring at the wooden cross on the wall at the foot of the bed, her mouth moving in prayer and her cheeks wet with tears. 'Help me, Senara, do not let me lose this child.'

'You are worrying too much. You must relax and rest.' Senara supported her sister's head and held the sleeping draught to her lips. 'Drink it all up. A sleep will restore your strength.' She sat on the bed until Bridie fell asleep, then went downstairs to talk with her mother.

'Will the child be all right?' Leah asked.

'The next few hours will tell, but there have been no contractions whilst I was with her.'

They both kept busy with small household tasks, their gazes straying to the ceiling at any groan of the ancient wood. After three hours Senara heard the bed creak and ran up the stairs to stop Bridie from coming down.

'The pains have stopped,' Bridie said.

'But you will stay in bed. I'll help you undress and you must close the school for the remainder of the week.'

She helped Bridie back into bed and again felt her stomach. The baby kicked beneath her hand and she grinned at her sister. 'The child seems settled enough where he is. But you must rest more. This has been a warning for you.'

'I will rest, but promise me you will not tell Peter. He will worry too much.'

Reluctantly Senara agreed. With Leah in the parsonage, their mother would ensure that Bridie did not overtire herself.

Chapter Thirty-one

Japhet and Gwendolyn were in Parramatta. Japhet had driven their newly acquired wagon to deliver some wood cut into floorboards at the mill to a house being built by two ex-convict couples. The women had set up business as seamstresses in the town and their men hired themselves for labour wherever they could find work. Whilst Japhet was delivering the wood, Gwendolyn called on a family who had recently settled in the town after arriving on a ship from England. The governor had asked her to keep an eye on the female settlers and to give them advice if any problems arose. Gwendolyn enjoyed meeting new neighbours. Some of the women were anxious that they would not be able to survive and she did her best to reassure them.

The woman she called on today was wary of her visit. She lived in a tent on the edge of the expanding town and her husband had started building a wooden house in a fenced-off area of ground. She had come out of the tent when Gwendolyn called a greeting but had not invited her inside. The heat was intense and in the last weeks of her pregnancy Gwendolyn's back and legs were aching. Japhet had not wanted her to accompany him, but they so rarely visited the town and she had been eager for feminine company. Calling on this woman had been a mistake. She could sense her hostility at any interference. Some of the settlers had decided to make a new life in the colony to get away from a dark secret in their past and took on new names.

Gwendolyn smiled and rallied her flagging energy. The loose gown she wore concealed her pregnancy and her daily chores had kept her figure slim. 'The convicts vastly outnumber the settlers and the climate here is very different. I came to introduce myself and welcome you to Parramatta. Once a month a group of women settlers meet to share our experiences and offer help to each other if needed.'

'I keep myself mostly to myself, thank you kindly, Mrs Loveday.'

'Just as long as you know you are welcome to join us if you wish.'

The sullenness of the woman was not uncommon; many had come here with high expectations and found themselves living in hovels with little food to feed their families. Gwendolyn decided to visit a friend with five children who would be the midwife she called on when her labour started. She was deep in thought, and started as a figure stepped in front of her.

'Oh, Captain Haughton, you startled me.' She was disconcerted to encounter the officer.

He did not move aside, and when she sidestepped to pass him, he also moved and continued to block her passage. 'Do I not warrant a good day, Mrs Loveday?' His tone was derisive.

'Your pardon, my mind was on my business here. How are you, Captain?' She made an effort to be polite, though she had no liking for the man.

'I am well and my day is the brighter for seeing you, Mrs Loveday. It is not often you are in Parramatta these days.'

'We no longer need to open the store as my husband's cousin's goods were all sold.'

'That was a reckless venture on your husband's part. He would do well to heed who holds the real balance of power here. To try such an enterprise again when his cousin's ship brings merchandise may be met with less tolerance.'

'I fear that will not sit well with Adam Loveday's fellow investors in England. Squire Penwithick in particular is interested in the progress of the colony. He has worked for many years with the government, advising them of events in France through a network of spies. Adam Loveday, who owns *Pegasus* worked for him for some time. And of course Sir Gregory will be reinvesting and he has the ear of Mr Pitt.'

'Your connections have no jurisdiction here,' he said tersely.

'Your words sound like a threat, Captain Haughton. I hope I am mistaken. My husband is a free man and will not be intimidated by bullies.'

'Those are harsh words, Mrs Loveday.'

'As were yours, sir. You hold a position of responsibility and trust from the British government. You are unworthy of your gentleman's status if you abuse it.'

'We are a long way from England, Mrs Loveday.' Menace edged his voice.

Gwendolyn felt herself grow hot, but it had nothing to do with the heat of the sun. If Japhet learned of the officer's threats he would act against them. She wanted to avoid that. No one could doubt her husband's bravery, but sometimes his hot temper got the better of his diplomacy.

'Yes, we are a long way from England. But our friends and relatives have a keen interest in how the colony thrives and progresses. That is why my godfather, the Earl of Craigsmoor, was most insistent that I keep a journal of all my experiences and my opinions of what is happening here. He also expects a letter detailing such events to be carried on each vessel that returns to England. My godfather has the ear of many at court, including the King.'

Haughton was now frowning and she pressed her point more emphatically, 'And if I am not mistaken, my mother came out in the same season as your own mother. They correspond regularly. Your mother is Lady Blanche Haughton, I believe, or is she an aunt?'

'An aunt.' His expression stiffened with annoyance.

Gwendolyn nodded. 'Mama will be so delighted that we have made your acquaintance. And my husband's cousin Colonel Penhaligan was most interested to learn that many of the troops here go on to a tour of duty in India. He served there for many years.'

She smiled sweetly to soften her words as she continued. 'Yes, we are a long way from England, Captain. But is it not remarkable how small the world really is and how we know so many of the same people? I do miss the genteel life in England. To fill the time I find I write copiously to my friends and family.'

He regarded her through narrowed eyes. Gwendolyn did not believe in making enemies out of people unnecessarily. 'It would not be a bad thing to put behind us any misunderstandings between yourself and my husband. Do you not agree? It will be some months before another Loveday ship brings merchandise to our shores. There is room for such enterprise for both of us, is there not?'

Haughton did not answer, but tipped his black bicorne hat to her as he stepped aside to allow her to pass. Japhet was marching down the road towards them, but the officer had disappeared into a building.

'What did Haughton want?' Japhet looked angry. 'Did he hurt or threaten you?'

'We had a most informative conversation. I do not believe in making enemies if it can be avoided.'

'Your heart is too generous. Haughton is a rogue. I can smell them. Do not trust him.'

'And I ask that you reserve judgement on his past actions. I did inform him that Lord Craigsmoor is interested in our experiences here. And that Squire Penwithick is one of Adam's investors.'

'That will not impress such as he.'

219

'Perhaps not, but his aunt is acquainted with my mother. Haughton is not to know that I have little correspondence with my family.' She grinned impishly. 'I thought it would do no harm to let him believe that I was an avid letter-writer to friends in England.'

'Then we can but wait and see if your devious ploy works.' Japhet linked her arm through his. 'I shall remain on my guard against him. I will concentrate on the farm and sawmill and will have no trouble from the militia until Adam's next ship arrives. Before then, there are ways to win such men over. I shall work on it.'

He saw her frown, and grinned. 'It will be nothing dishonest, I promise. I am a reformed man, am I not?'

'Elspeth and I are beneficiaries under my brother William's will, and I am trustee for your father's will,' Joshua reminded St John. He had insisted on accompanying his nephew to the lawyer in Bodmin. 'I want the mystery surrounding William's death cleared up. If Lisette is alive she could need protecting from her brother, or even from herself. She has been mentally unstable in recent years.'

To protest could make his uncle suspicious of his motives, so St John reluctantly accepted Joshua's company. Felicity and her mother had left Trevowan to visit her late father's sister. The woman had been recently widowed and lived in St Austell.

The lawyer saw them late in the afternoon. The office smelt musty and the floor was piled high with legal documents rolled into scrolls.

'Good afternoon to you, Mr Loveday, Reverend Mr Loveday.' Mr Dawkins, the senior partner of Dawkins, Dawkins and Son, illustrious lawyers, bowed to them. He wore a freshly powdered wig with two rolls of curls over his large red ears, and horn-rimmed spectacles were perched on the end of his bony nose. 'How may I be of service?'

Joshua cleared his throat. 'As you may recall, my brother drowned two years ago and his wife disappeared.'

The lawyer nodded and Joshua plunged on. 'In the intervening time no word has been received from her. And despite extensive investigations by our family in London and locally, no one has seen her. Some months ago a pendant that once belonged to her was purchased in a jeweller's in Plymouth. The jeweller could not remember who had sold the piece to him. I regret to say that my brother's wife in her lifetime incurred debts at the gaming tables and that several pieces of her jewellery were used by her to pay off those debts.'

'That is not unusual.' Mr Dawkins spread his hands in acceptance.

'What we need to know . . .' St John interrupted impatiently. 'Since

220

it has now been over two years since Mrs William Loveday went missing, can her property now be released to her late husband's estate?'

Mr Dawkins rubbed his chin. 'If I recall correctly, Mrs William Loveday was French. She could have returned to her own country.'

'Not without her jewels and clothes. And though more stable than once it was, France is still a hotbed of unrest,' St John snapped. He did not like Dawkins. The man had been supercilious and proved of no support when he had been on trial. Left to the lawyer's incompetence, St John would have been convicted.

'We fear that she also drowned with her husband.' Joshua did not wish to complicate the matter by mentioning that Lisette's brother could have been involved in one or both of the deaths.

'It is certainly perplexing that Mrs Loveday did not claim her rights to her husband's estate.' Dawkins straightened the inkwell, which was already perfectly aligned on his desk. 'Her jewellery is worth many hundreds of pounds.'

'Surely that proves that she is dead?' St John urged. 'She would need to sell her jewels to live, and although not wealthy my uncle had saved most of his naval pay for over twenty years. She would have been well provided for. How is she living without these funds?'

'If the pendant had not come to light, then it may have been judged that she was deceased. However, its appearance changes everything. No magistrate will declare her dead. They will see the necklace as evidence that she could be alive.'

'That is absurd.' St John leapt to his feet. 'I shall write to a lawyer in London for his opinion.' He marched from the room, furious with himself that desperation to settle his own gaming debts had led to him selling the jewellery.

Joshua stood up. 'I apologise for my nephew's rudeness, Mr Dawkins.'

'He has a reputation for rash action.' The lawyer sniffed his disapproval. 'No doubt the responsibilities of Trevowan weigh heavily on his shoulders.'

Joshua barely concealed his own dislike for the lawyer. 'Thank you for your time, Mr Dawkins. I fear you are right over a judge's ruling upon the necklace. But my brother's wife would not have departed without her jewels if she had left Cornwall.'

The lawyer regarded him sourly. 'Some would take the view that they were left out of guilt or fear. Your brother may not have drowned accidentally but been murdered. His wife had spent some months in an asylum.'

'I will not countenance that. No evidence of murder was found at the time,' Joshua curtly informed the lawyer. His brother's body had been in the sea for some weeks before it was washed up. But on the day he and his wife disappeared, Edward had found one of Lisette's shoes in Trevowan Cove. For reasons of his own Edward had not informed the authorities of that discovery. Too many scandals had circulated about the family following Japhet's arrest for highway robbery. Joshua too did not want William to become the subject of further gossip. There had been enough speculation about the unsuitability of his marriage to Lisette. Let his memory now rest in peace.

St John was furious that he had been thwarted in getting his hands on his uncle's estate and Lisette's jewellery. To win Felicity he needed to court her in style. From their conversations he knew she was wary of marrying anyone who was interested in her because of her fortune. The gift of an expensive bracelet or necklace would delight her, but it would have to be one his family would not recognise as Lisette's. For that he needed to get his hands on his uncle's money.

He returned to the inn where they were lodging for the night and began to drink heavily. On leaving the lawyer's office Joshua had called upon his cousin Colonel Penhaligan. He had been invited to dine and spend the evening. St John wanted nothing to do with his irascible relative. The colonel had scorned him last year when Garfield Penhaligan had come to England from Virginia and St John's betrothal to Garfield's niece had been discovered. St John had spent over a year in Virginia living on Garfield's tobacco plantation after his trial. That was a time of his life he wanted to forget, and the colonel was bound to dwell upon the past.

He remained in a bad mood all evening and continued to drink heavily. When a group of three gentlemen started a game of hazard in the taproom of the inn, he was drawn to join them. Gambling had always been his passion and for the first part of the evening the dice were generous to him. At one time he had a hundred pounds in winnings piled in front of him. He laughed at his success, buying drinks for the crowd who had gathered around their table. The glass at his side was continually filled. Then, as his wits became befuddled with brandy, he started to lose. The alcohol made him reckless and boosted his euphoria. He felt invincible, convinced that luck was with him. He wagered recklessly, and when the pile of money was gone, he used his stock pin and a ring to fund his game. When these were lost he wrote IOUs.

By the time Joshua returned to the inn St John had passed out unconscious from his drinking and lay sprawled across the gaming table. His companions had gone to their beds. Joshua was appalled to find him in a drunken stupor. When he called the landlord to have his nephew carried to his chamber, St John vomited over the floor. The landlord stepped back from him in disgust.

'He can stay in his own filth. He'll be throwing up all night in his room.'

Joshua tossed a silver coin on the table. 'That should recompense you for your trouble. I will not have my nephew the cause of ridicule for his indiscretion.'

'He'll have his new-found friends banging on his door come morning expecting their gaming wagers to be paid.'

Joshua was angered at St John's stupidity. His nephew was carried to his room and left spread-eagled on his bed.

When St John woke in the morning his skull felt like it was about to split open. He swung his legs to the ground and doubled over in agony to hold his head in his hands. The thudding of fists on his door sent further arrows of pain through his skull.

'Be off with you! Leave a man to sleep in peace.'

When the banging continued, he staggered to the portal and wrenched it open. Two effeminate fops greeted him and pressed lace-edged hand-kerchiefs to their noses.

'Egad, man! You reek of the cesspit,' one whined.

'We've come for our money,' his taller companion demanded. 'The post chaise leaves for London in an hour and we've seats upon it.'

'Who the devil are you?' St John had little recollection of last night.

'The man to whom you owe two hundred guineas.' The taller of the two discarded his mincing manners and thrust a threatening finger into St John's face. 'Don't play the innocent. Pay up or I'll call the constable and have you thrown in gaol for debt.'

The other fop brandished St John's IOUs. 'Here's the evidence of what you owe. Two hundred guineas to my friend and one hundred and twenty to me.'

The amount sobered him but brought another rush of nausea to his mouth. He stumbled to the washbasin and emptied the contests of his stomach. When he straightened, the two men were standing inside the room. The taller man scowled. 'You ain't about to cry off what you owe. That would be a mistake.'

'I have never reneged on a gaming debt,' St John informed him with as much dignity as he could muster. He was aware of the smell of vomit on his shirt and breeches. 'You will have your money. I must freshen myself and go to the bank.'

He cut his jaw twice whilst shaving in his haste to leave the inn without his uncle seeing him. Three hundred and twenty guineas was a great deal of money. How could he have been so stupid to risk so much at the tables? The banks in Bodmin had refused him loans last year. They would not give him one now. He had already raised a mortgage on Trevowan. He would have to apply to a moneylender, who would charge extortionate rates.

The man he sought lived in a gloomy side alley, and St John glanced up and down the street with its overhanging houses before entering, not wanting to be observed. Harold Foxe, the moneylender, sat behind a large desk covered in official-looking parchments. His face was fleshless as a skull and grey as a cadaver in the single candlelight. Tufts of ginger hair sprouted from a worn black velvet skullcap. He was as wily and cunning as his name. Behind him stood a heavily muscled black slave in a faded red velvet jacket and black breeches.

'You want the loan for three months, you say, Mr Loveday,' Foxe wheezed through several missing teeth.

'To be repaid after the harvest,' St John answered, also hoping that by then he would be married to Felicity.

'That will be a repayment of five hundred pounds in three months, sir. If you extend it to six months, the repayment fee is eight hundred pounds.'

He had not thought the rate would be that extortionate. But he had no option but to agree to it and sign the document. The moneylender sanded the page and patted it affectionately. 'Full repayment in six months or your beef herd will be taken in exchange. That or you face prison, and we would not want it to come to that, Mr Loveday, would we?'

'The loan will be repaid.' St John felt nausea again churning his stomach and he swallowed it down. Men like Foxe were a boil on the backside of humanity. He despised them and was filled with self-loathing that he had placed himself at Foxe's mercy. It was more expedient than ever that he wed Felicity. She must not hear of his catastrophic fall from grace last night or she would never marry him.

He was about to enter the inn when his blood froze at hearing his name called. The nightmare continued. He turned slowly, praying his ears had deceived him. In the street outside the inn, stepping down from their carriage, were Felicity and her mother.

'Dear ladies, this is unexpected. And such a pleasure.' He rallied his drooping spirits, determined to overcome this new disaster.

'Mama was set on a visit to Bodmin,' Felicity explained, her stare devouring St John. 'My aunt can be disagreeable at times.'

'Loveday, there you are!' The shrill voice of the fop who was waiting for St John set his nerves jangling. The man stood in the doorway tapping his foot with impatience. 'Just in time. The poste chaise is about to leave.'

St John bowed to Felicity. 'Your pardon, dear lady. I have urgent business with this gentleman before he takes the coach to London.'

St John hurried to the fop and grabbed his arm to pull him back into the inn out of sight of Felicity and her mother. He pressed the pouch of three hundred and twenty guineas into his hand. 'It is all there. Settle with your friend on the coach. I would rather the lady I was with were not aware that I have been gambling.'

As he finished speaking, Felicity entered the inn. Her lovely face was pinched with anger. She clearly did not like the way he had abandoned her. 'Will you not introduce me to your business associate?'

The fop minced and with an extravagant flourish of his hand bowed to her. 'Charles Fortesque, at your service.'

'Mr Fortesque wanted an introduction to a playhouse manager in London. I have given him the address of Lucien Greene, my cousin Thomas's friend.'

The horn sounded for the post chaise to be boarded. Fortesque raised Felicity's hand to his lips. 'How regrettably short our acquaintance has been, fair lady. Mayhap if the fates are kind to us we will meet again.'

He waved to his companion, who was signalling for him to join him in the inn yard, and disappeared amongst the press of people jostling to board the chaise.

'What a singular man,' Sophia remarked. 'Why would he want an introduction to a playhouse manager?'

'He has aspirations to be a playwright,' St John improvised. 'He also has money to invest which my cousin Thomas could advise him upon. His bank has a reputation for sound investments and it is my duty to my family to guide customers there.'

His heart rate was returning to normal now that the fops were out of sight. He smiled at Felicity. 'My profoundest apologies for rushing off in such a manner, my dear. You were speaking of your aunt. Was your visit then unpleasant?'

'That would be too strong a word. Family duty can be onerous.' Felicity sighed. 'Aunt Mary Jane has always been melancholy. It was a difficult visit.'

'And you must put it behind you now.' St John smiled in his most charming manner. 'You must permit me to show you the sights of Bodmin.'

'Oh, and there is Joshua,' Sophia cut across their conversation. 'Our shopping can wait. He must join us in a tour of the town.'

'We had planned to return to Trevowan today.' Joshua spread his hands in apology as he joined them and heard her remark. 'I have my flock to tend and Cecily expects me.'

'You must not disappoint your dear wife,' Sophia trilled.

Felicity pouted and fluttered her lashes at St John. 'I promised Hannah I would enquire of the dressmaker about a dress pattern for the girls. Would you be so kind as to take it to her, St John?'

'I am sure Hannah would welcome more of your company,' he replied. 'Can I not persuade you to return with us to Trevowan for another few days. It will lift your spirits after your visit to your aunt. Though if you prefer to stay in Bodmin to shop . . .'

'Trevowan is conveniently close to several of my old friends,' Sophia cut in and touched Joshua's arm. 'It was so wonderful to be with Cecily.'

'I would not like to think we overstay our welcome,' Felicity simpered. 'We have already taken up so much of your time, St John.'

'Every minute was my pleasure.' He wanted Felicity to leave Bodmin before any knowledge of his gaming reached her.

A blush coloured Felicity's cheeks and Sophia exchanged a long, meaningful glance with her daughter.

'Your offer is most generous,' Felicity said, 'but there are several articles I should purchase now we are here. It will take longer than one afternoon. And I have a friend living in Bodmin who I have not seen for three years. I had written to her to say I would call.'

'Then you must not disappoint her.' St John bowed stiffly, annoyed she had not been more enthusiastic about his invitation. Just as he thought she was growing compliant to his attentions, she became difficult.

'My dear, Catherine will understand. You were never that close as I remember,' her mother claimed, her stare watchful upon Joshua. 'Besides, she has a clutch of seven children. Do you really prefer to subject yourself to their boisterous ways? I am sure St John has something far more diverting for your entertainment.'

'I do not break my word once it is given, Mama. How can you consider that I would?' The silk flowers decorating Felicity's peaked bonnet danced in her agitation. The smile she turned upon St John was tight and her voice rose unnaturally high. 'Your invitation is welcome, but I would not delay your departure. We could travel to Trevowan on Friday, if that would not inconvenience any plans of yours?'

He hid his annoyance. Her manner was disconcerting. Was her irritation directed at her mother or himself? Felicity had shown on several occasions that she could be stubborn in following her own principles. She certainly was not the compliant woman he remembered from the summer before his marriage.

Since Joshua had travelled with him in the Trevowan coach, St John could not stay when his uncle needed to attend to his parish duties.

Aware of his nephew's dilemma, Joshua said, 'I can hire a hack to return to Trewenna. You need not leave on my account, nephew.'

'I have my own duties at Trevowan.' St John needed to show Felicity that he took his role as master of his estate seriously. He raised her hand to his lips and bowed to her. 'I shall count the hours until you join us on Friday.'

She looked startled that he would not remain in Bodmin as her escort. But she replied graciously, 'As shall I.'

Sophia simpered at his uncle. 'It will be wonderful to spend more time with Cecily. We have so many memories of old friends to share, do we not, Joshua?'

She then startled St John by kissing his uncle on the cheek. Joshua looked furious and was barely able to keep his voice polite as he extricated himself from her proximity. 'I shall summon the ostler to have the coach made ready for us.'

Undeterred by Joshua's uncharacteristic behaviour, Sophia smiled coyly. 'You must not mind my forwardness, St John. Joshua has been a dear, dear friend to me for forty years. Long before he met Cecily. Now I will leave you two alone to say your goodbyes.' Her manner was both flirtatious and conspiratorial.

There were undercurrents of tension in the inn St John did not understand. But he was not given to analysing other people's reactions. He needed to reassure Felicity of his devotion and spent the short time they had together praising and complimenting her until her mood lightened. He was relieved that she and her mother were staying at another inn, and his earlier misgivings were discarded as she responded to his charm. He felt he had redeemed himself in her eyes, but as his coach left the town he was nervous that gossip about his recent gaming might reach her. It would ruin everything.

Chapter Thirty-two

Hannah refused to allow the incident at Tor Farm to spoil Mark and Jeannie's wedding. Work on the farm had begun two hours earlier than normal so that the servants and dairymaids could attend the ceremony at Trewenna church. She hoped there would be no problems from Mark's eldest brother Clem. Since his marriage Clem had led a sober and respectable life, earning his living by fishing, but he had an uncertain temper, and might take it as an insult that his brother's smuggling gang had been apprehended on Loveday land.

The gathering in Trewenna church was small and Hannah and Sam sat at the back of the congregation. This was to be Mark and Jeannie's day and she did not want their families to feel uncomfortable at her presence. Mark had sleeked down his spiky hair with oil but tufts of it had refused to be tamed and stuck out. Jeannie at sixteen looked loving and trusting as she gazed into her lover's face. She was slender as a waif but her figure belied her resilience and strength to work long hours. The milkmaids giggled incessantly throughout the service.

After the ceremony Hannah paused to speak with her father. Friends and family surrounded Mark and Jeannie and were joking and making ribald comments as the couple mounted the farm cart that had been decorated with wild flowers to return them to the farm.

'I pray this heralds a change in events in our community.' Joshua watched the couple drive away. 'There is an uneasy atmosphere in the villages since the incident at Tor Farm. The men arrested were after all local. Harry Sawle will stir up trouble. Our family is not as popular as once it was with many villagers. The robberies did not help and some have taken against Adam for encouraging the gypsies to camp on his land.'

'We have no quarrel with the free-traders providing they keep off our land,' Hannah replied.

Joshua continued to frown. 'Adam and St John make no secret of their hatred for Sawle and blame him for Edward's death. And Peter has taken it into his head to preach hell and damnation for any use of violence or intimidation or the mocking of God's laws.'

'Where in the Bible does it say "Thou shall not smuggle illicit goods"?' Hannah shook her head in despair over her zealous younger brother.

'Peter equates free-trading with stealing the rightful taxes from our government when we need every penny to pay for this war with France.' Joshua spread his hands in resignation 'And there is violence when rival gangs clash. Men get killed and goods get stolen. There is about it the work of the devil.'

'It is human nature to evade taxes, especially when they seem so unjust to people who have so little,' Hannah replied.

Joshua glanced at Sam, who stood a few feet away waiting to accompany Hannah home. The overseer held his hat in his hands and his hair, the colour of ripened corn, glinted in the sunlight. In his Sunday-best clothes he cut an impressive figure. There was a military bearing to his stance. Clearly he was no ordinary farmhand but was well educated and from a good family. Sam Deacon had been a godsend to Hannah this last year and his presence had stopped Joshua worrying about his daughter's safety alone on an isolated farm.

'We must leave.' Hannah kissed her father's cheek. 'Pray for us that the day goes well and Harry Sawle does not turn up to ruin his brother's celebrations.'

'I heard in Fowey that *Sea Mist* was seen recently in Bristol taking on a cargo to deliver in Ireland. Sawle is covering his tracks. If he has any sense he'll be on board her.'

When Hannah and Sam arrived at the farm the wedding party were already seated on benches each side of two long trestle tables laden with food set outside. A pig had been roasted over a spit yesterday and this had been carved and laid on large wooden platters with a ham and potted pilchards. Potatoes had been cooked and mashed and carrots served with butter. A cask of cider provided the drink.

Hannah was pleased that Mark's mother Sal was present and that Clem and Keziah were laughing with the milkmaids. She stayed long enough to toast the couple. The fiddler from Penruan had arrived and when the food was finished he would play for the dancing.

Sal Sawle approached her. Hannah rarely travelled to Penruan and she had not seen Sal since Meriel's funeral. Since Reuban's death Sal was no longer a slave to her husband's tyranny at the Dolphin Inn, but she was stooped and her face etched with wrinkles from the hard life she had lived.

'You be an angel to do so much for my Mark,' Sal praised. 'I know there's been trouble because of you giving him work, and I don't need to say who be behind it.'

'Mark is a good worker.' Hannah knew that Sal Sawle had been ashamed of her second son and also of her daughter when Meriel ran off with a lover.

'He be a good lad. You've given him the chance to make something of his life. An honest life,' she emphasised with a nod of her head. 'Jeannie seems a nice girl. She won't lead him astray. Mark says you've given them a cottage. That be a fine thing for you to do.'

'I reward my servants for their loyalty.' Hannah dismissed her praise. 'He paid the price for it when he was beaten so savagely. Those responsible for that should be locked up.'

The old woman's rheumy eyes filled with tears. 'Aye, they say a mother should stand by her children no matter what. But we must take the blame for bearing them with devil's blood.'

Hannah felt her pain. This was her youngest son's wedding day and Sal deserved what happiness came her way. 'Enjoy today, Mrs Sawle. You have two sons to be proud of. Clem is a hard-working fisherman and dotes on Keziah and his son.'

'Bless you for that. You see the good in people. Not many do.' As Sal walked stiffly back to her place at the table, Clem lifted his tankard to salute Hannah. It was a strange feeling to have so many Sawles dining at her farm, especially as the one who was not present was her sworn enemy. And thank God he was not here to cause havoc. Even so, Hannah cast a nervous stare over the wedding party and the surrounding fields. Harry was eaten up with the need to rule or destroy. He would ruin his brother's wedding just for the hell of it.

The fiddler played a country reel and there was a burst of laughter as a circle was formed for the dancing. It brought a rush of memories for Hannah. She pushed aside her anger towards Harry Sawle. There had been many happy gatherings on the farm when the rest of her family had joined them. In those days Oswald had been hardworking and healthy. He would be up at dawn to milk the cows and would still be dancing with her at sundown, before milking the cows again in the evening. They had been so in love and so full of fun and life that the work had seemed no hardship. She felt the tightness of grief in her chest and left the merriment to take refuge in the farmhouse. She would change out of her good gown in time for the milking that evening.

There was a pile of dishes needing washing in the kitchen. A kettle steamed on the range and she emptied it into the sink and rolled up her sleeves to work through her pain. There was a mound of clean pans and plates by the sink when Sam found her.

'The servants should be doing this.' He sounded exasperated. 'There is dancing. I thought you might like to join in a reel.'

'They will feel self-conscious with me there.' Hannah shook her head. 'And I have given Mark and Jeannie the evening off, while Tilda and Bessie will be tired from all their junketing. I was about to change and begin the milking. I can hear the children enjoying themselves outside. They will not go to bed for another hour.'

'Mark's family have left. Tilda and Bessie are paid to milk the cows,' Sam said firmly. 'The fiddler is on the point of passing out. He has been drinking all afternoon.' He saw the dark shadows under her eyes. 'You have been up since dawn. Rest for a while before you call the children in. I will start the milking and order the milkmaids to join me.'

Suddenly she turned away and Sam saw her shoulders shaking. He could not bear to see her weep. She was driving herself too hard. 'What ails you?'

'Memories.' She sniffed and wiped frantically at her tears with her hands.

'It cannot be easy for you with Mark's brother here.'

'Clem had nothing to do with the trouble between our families, neither did his mother. Weddings are a good time for families to be reunited and past disagreements healed.'

'You have a romantic ideal of families,' he teased.

The strain of the past days caught up with her. To her mortification she burst into tears again and turned away from Sam to wipe them away.

'What is wrong, Hannah? This is unlike you.' His concern stripped her still further of her usual resilience.

'Weddings always make me cry.' She sniffed and blew her nose on her handkerchief.

He stood behind her and lightly placed his hands on her shoulders. 'You have been talking a lot about Japhet lately. You clearly miss him.'

She nodded. The farmhouse suddenly seemed to echo with the voices of her loved ones. Japhet, Uncle Edward, and most of all Oswald. In that moment loneliness hit her and she missed the touch of a man's comforting embrace. As though sensing her need, Sam enfolded her in his arms and gently pressed her head into his shoulder.

'Do not hold back, Hannah, if you need to cry. You cannot always be expected to be strong.'

His hand stroked her hair and she felt calm again. 'This is so foolish. It is a joyous day. Oswald would have done so much for them. He loved such occasions.'

'You cannot grieve for him for ever, Hannah.' Sam sounded sharp.

'I miss him every day.' Her pain was wrenched from her. 'It is so hard without him.'

'It has been over a year.' He let out a harsh breath and held her tight.

The warmth of his body was a solace, the strength of his arms a haven in her loneliness. The pounding of his heartbeat against her cheek was a deep primeval pulse that echoed the rhythm of life itself. He smelt pleasantly of soap and the outdoors. She knew she should pull away, for there was danger in the pleasure of his touch. But she wanted to savour it for a moment longer.

The pressure of his fingers increased and they slid along her spine. 'Hannah, my sweet, lovely woman. You were made for fun and laughter. Not this constant drudgery.' His lips were against her hair. 'You should be fêted and live in comfort. These pretty hands . . .' He took one reddened hand to inspect it. 'They should lift nothing more onerous than a beautiful jewel.'

He bowed his head and kissed her palm, the tenderness of his gesture opening the floodgates of her emotions. It had been so long since she had received love and tenderness except from her close family. And this was different. It was a tenderness that awakened her dormant passion. It was from a handsome man who was not a brother or cousin – a man capable of setting her pulse racing.

'Sam, you must not say such things,' she said in a hoarse whisper, but she found it impossible to pull away.

'You are the strongest, most admirable woman I know.' His breath fanned her ear in a sweet caress. 'And you should be cherished.'

His lips claimed hers with a warmth and sweetness that turned her bones to fluid and she clung to him, her passionate nature reawakened, the sweetness of the kiss a solace in her loneliness.

Outside, Bessie, Tilda and Aggie were calling out to the bridal couple as they made their way back to their cottage now that the wedding guests had left. The sunset was turning the limewashed walls of the kitchen crimson. The clatter of dishes being stacked outside and the sound of Bessie complaining of the night's work ahead of them made Hannah come to her senses. The servants could walk in at any moment and it was a wonder that one of the children had not come in already.

'This is wrong, Sam.' She pushed against his chest and his arms dropped to his sides. She covered her cheeks with her hands. She was shocked that she had responded to the wanton fire in her blood. She did not love Sam – how could she when Oswald had filled her thoughts all day? 'What if the children had seen us?'

'You are denying your womanhood if you deny there is attraction between us.' He did not attempt to touch her and his voice was thick with exasperation.

Her fingers touched her mouth, which throbbed from the passion of his kiss. 'But I still love Oswald. I cannot betray him.'

'He would not want you to mourn him for ever.'

His stare impaled her. 'I know. But it is too soon. My grief is too raw.' She lowered her head and rubbed her temples with her fingers. 'Sam, this is a midsummer madness. What I feel is so wrong – so disloyal. It is too soon.'

'Then I must give you time.' He picked up his hat, which he had placed on the table, and walked out without another word.

She stared after him, uncertain whether she was relieved or disappointed at his reaction. His touch had made her feel alive for the first time in months.

Two days later Lieutenant Tregare visited Rabson Farm. His troop remained in the yard, and when she saw the seriousness of his expression, Hannah was relieved that Sam was approaching from the field. She waited for him to reach the house and led them both into the parlour.

'Have the arrested smugglers given evidence against their leader?' Hannah asked.

The officer shook his head, his manner grave. 'Two of them were found dead this morning in their cell. Ale had been sent in to them last night. It had been poisoned. It was a warning to them all that if they talk, they will be killed.'

Hannah gasped at the horror of these events.

'At least you have the cargo.' Sam rubbed his brow, which still pained him from the attack.

'So you have not heard that the customs house was broken into last night. The goods were stolen and one of the guards was killed.'

It was too much for Hannah. She sank down into a chair and dropped her head into her hands. 'Another death! Is there no end to their evil? So many have suffered. It is my fault. I must have been mad to think I could strike at Sawle. What have I done? I thought Bradstock would be safe – that the militia would protect him. He has lost everything and three men have been murdered.'

She glared at Lieutenant Tregare. 'What are you going to do about it?'

'I need evidence to act.' He remained haughty and showed no remorse that the raid on the farm had been a failure. 'You may rest assured that Tor Farm will be kept under surveillance. It will not be used again by those villains.' He bowed and left.

'You must end this feud with Sawle,' Sam advised. 'It is too dangerous. He may still strike at this farm. We must be extra vigilant.'

'I will not give up the fight. He hates the Lovedays. He wants to see all of us broken.'

'But you do not need to be involved. And Adam would be the first to agree with me. He would be horrified that you take such risks. It is too dangerous.'

Her throat seized with fear and she could only nod in acknowledgement.

'You are worn out from trying to cope with this alone. Let Adam deal with it. That knave believes he is a law unto himself. And so does his henchman Nance.'

Hannah shuddered, but she had regained her composure and her defiance had returned. Sam's anger and concern undermined her defences. It would have been all too easy to find comfort in his arms, but she would not give in to her momentary weakness.

His voice roughened. 'You must let Adam deal with Sawle. I will help him in any way I can. Sawle will be brought to justice.' He spoke with confidence and authority.

Sam was a complex man, and something of a mystery. Hannah had long suspected that he was the son of a gentleman and well educated. 'Promise me you will not antagonise Sawle further, Hannah,' he now insisted.

She gave a shaky laugh. 'If he steps foot on this farm, I have told him I will shoot him.'

'That is brave, but what has caused this?' He frowned. 'Has he pressed his attentions upon you? If he has touched you . . .' His anger exploded.

Her head shot up at his tone. 'Your concern is appreciated but you forget your place, Sam. What happened the other night gives you no rights over me.'

He studied her for a long moment. There was a slight twitch to his lips. 'As a gentleman I have put what happened between us that night from my mind. I am, as always, your humble servant.'

Again he had managed to disconcert her. 'Then I thank you for your concern and apologise for judging you falsely. This has been an upsetting day.'

She felt Sam had put her in her place, not the other way round as she had intended. She was being oversensitive. The last thing she wanted was to antagonise her overseer. Apart from her family he was the only man she trusted.

She shrugged, trying to lighten the moment. 'I think of you as a friend, not a servant. And in answer to your question, Sawle did not harm me. He wanted to hide contraband on the farm. I refused to let him.' She did not want to speak of how Sawle had waylaid her in her own barn late one night.

'You are remarkably brave, but it is foolhardy to continue this vendetta against Sawle.' Sam did not move and his expression was tight with tension. 'Hannah, you have dared to challenge him in a way that is a threat to his manhood. Sawle does not play games. He is a womaniser and completely without principles. I am going to talk to Adam.' He strode towards the door.

'Adam is in Plymouth again. He will not be back for some days.'

He put a hand on the doorpost and looked back at her. His frame filled the doorway. 'Then you must allow me to protect you. Promise me that you will go nowhere unless I accompany you.'

'I appreciate your intentions, but that will not always be practical. You have many duties here. And I will not allow Sawle to curtail my freedom.'

'Then if you will not think of your own safety, think of your children. They have lost one parent; would you make them orphans?'

At her horrified expression, his voice softened. 'Sawle has had a valuable cargo confiscated. The stakes have changed. He has lost face and he will want someone to pay. I ask you to reconsider my offer, at least for the next weeks. I can juggle any job on the farm to escort you to your family or to school with the children. I would take them myself but that would leave you unprotected here.'

She weighed his words. Common sense prevailed. 'I seldom leave the farm and I appreciate your offer. I shall carry a dagger at all times.'

Chapter Thirty-three

The spirit of adventure had driven Japhet all his life. But until his arrest and imprisonment he had never suffered hardship, his lack of money buffered by the generosity of his family. They were always there to welcome him in times of crisis, yet he had never thought he would miss them so much in this new life he had chosen. He did not mind the deprivations and hard work, for he still held his vision for the future, but he often wondered if he had been fair on Gwendolyn by insisting that they stay here. It was a volatile continent.

He glanced anxiously towards the house, where his wife had been in labour since early light. The midwife from Parramatta and Eliza Hope were tending to her. He hoped Gwendolyn's ordeal would soon be over. A woman giving birth was always vulnerable, and today not only was his wife risking her life in childbirth, but other dangers were perilously close that could destroy them.

Work was the only way for Japhet to cope with his fears. He swung the axe and his body juddered as the steel bit deep into the trunk of a tree. The eucalyptus trees with their strange peeling bark were of hard wood and the axe constantly needed sharpening. He set up a rhythm until his torso was slick with sweat. If insurrection from escaped or rebellious convicts was not a problem serious enough to threaten their existence, in the last months they had suffered terrifying bush fires that swallowed up entire homesteads. Flames spread through the tinder-dry trees and across the parched meadows painstakingly cleared by their countrymen. The conflagrations were terrifying to behold. The roar of the flames was like some demented beast on the rampage, the heat so intense the skin would blister on anyone reckless enough to try and combat it. Whole trees were consumed in seconds. When the fires laid waste to a farm, livestock and buildings were devoured and nothing survived their onslaught. The destruction of whole crops of wheat and Indian corn had jeopardised the colony's self-sufficiency.

Japhet had never expected life here to be easy, but as he paused to lean on his long-handled axe, having just felled another tree, he stared at the line of smoke forming a semicircle a few miles from the farm. So far the wind had kept the bush fires away from his home, but that could change at any minute. He held off on the decision to evacuate. He had vowed this land would never defeat him. To save his farm he had followed the advice of one of the natives to make a fire break around its perimeter. It was taking days to cut down the trees so that he could burn a controlled fire to scorch the land.

Japhet still believed in the wealth this land could offer but he was beginning to wonder whether he had not been selfish in his need to prove his independence from Gwendolyn's inheritance. He did not miss his wild life in London but he was increasingly homesick for his family. Was it stubborn pride that kept him here when they could take the next passage home to Cornwall?

When he had broached the matter to his wife, Gwen had shown surprising mettle. He had thought she would instantly agree. Instead she had stared at him with battle in her lovely eyes.

'How can you even suggest it for a moment? I want to show people back at home how much we can achieve. I was not blind to the sly looks at our wedding from those who thought you had wed me for my money. I want them proved wrong. For years my mother and sister browbeat me and I was too timid to act against them. Loving you changed all that. Loving you showed me I have the strength to fight for what I want.'

'And was ever a man more unworthy of such trust and devotion?' Japhet had shaken his head. 'I was a selfish knave. I cared only for the pursuit of pleasure.'

She had thrown a cushion she was stuffing with old rags at him. 'You were the most exciting man I'd met. And perhaps it was the kindness you showed to me then that proved to me that you were never as black as you paint yourself. I know you were not attracted to me in those days, but you took the time and trouble to compliment small changes I had made in myself and were courteous enough to laugh at my attempt at wit.'

Japhet launched the cushion back at her with a grin. 'But you had the sharpest wit. Your dullard of a sister and mother never appreciated it. And you are a top-class horsewoman. I never saw you falter at a fence during the hunt. That won my admiration. I was an idiot not to have seen your true beauty then.'

'I will not dispute that.' She laughed and the cushion struck the side of his head with extra force. 'But most importantly I know you were never the fortune-hunter my mother proclaimed. It was me you fell in love with, not my money.'

He made a grab for her and tickled her until she begged for mercy.

'I would have proper subservience from my wench,' he teased, his mouth nuzzling her neck. The baby in her stomach kicked in protest and Japhet let out a mock yell. 'My child doth protest that I show no due respect to its mama.'

Gwendolyn giggled. 'Let us never grow old or staid.'

He kissed her. 'That is why you are the only woman who has stolen my heart. But in truth we both have bees in our heads to work like slaves when a life of comfort would be ours in Cornwall.'

'Would you not find Cornwall dull after all your recent adventures, my love?' she had shocked him by asking.

'I have had more than my share of adventures after a year in Newgate, eight months at sea and over a year facing daily challenges here. I think my wild days are far behind me and I have no hunger for them to return. It is time your rogue of a husband became respectable.'

He grinned at the memory, his teeth flashing whitely against his swarthy skin. He had never thought he would say such words, but it was true. Soon he would have not one but two children to provide for.

He squinted against the bright sun and stared at the line of smoke, then reluctantly returned to his task. His entire body ached from his exertions but another dozen trees needed to be cut and dragged away, then the last of the undergrowth forming the circle around his crops and house could be cut down and the controlled fire lit to scorch the earth in a wide band that no bush fire could cross. His assigned convicts and ticket-of-leave men should complete the task before nightfall. Thankfully the fires were no closer and it looked as though they had turned east. The burned forest would provide a natural fire break and it seemed as though they had been spared.

Even so, Japhet kept his men working. There were only two more trees to cut when Eliza Hope rang the warning bell on the veranda. Japhet dropped his axe and ran to the house.

'Has the child arrived? Is Gwen safe?'

Eliza nodded. 'Go to your wife, Japhet, and see for yourself.'

Gwendolyn was propped up on the pillows holding the baby in her arms. Her hair was loose about her shoulders and her eyes were bright with pride and happiness. She had never looked more radiant. The sight took Japhet's breath away. He had missed all this when Japhet Edward was born whilst he was in prison.

'We have another son, my love.' Gwendolyn held the baby out to him.

He stared down at his dirty hands and shook his head. Eliza appeared with a bowl of water and a towel. 'It will not take a moment for you to wash and be able to hold him. He is a fine boy.'

Japhet dried his hands on the towel and was unprepared for the rush of joy that holding the tiny baby roused. 'Are they always this small?'

Gwendolyn laughed. 'He is a good ten pounds. Japhet Edward was only seven.'

'We did not decide on a name for him.' Japhet frowned. 'What is your preference, my love?'

'There could be no other name but Japhet Edward for our first-born. With so many family names to choose, I am at a loss.'

'Family names are important. Especially when we are so cut off from them. I never intended that my name be notorious but there are many who may view our children as tainted by my reputation. I would not wish that for them. They have two proud heritages and sometimes it is no bad thing to remind others that though I may have failed in their eyes, their mother is the most worthy of women. I would call him Druce Loveday. And it can do us no harm that his name reminds others here of your noble connections with Rannulph Druce, Earl of Craigsmoor.'

'Druce Loveday has a distinguished ring to it.' Gwendolyn smiled, then giggled. 'And my mother will be furious.'

Japhet stroked his son's cheek. 'I do not name him to spite her. The Lady Anne will be proud of her grandsons. And I will make her proud of all we have achieved.'

'The righteous shall inherit God's kingdom. Close the door to your thoughts where evil dwells. And be not corrupted by fear when brutality would be forced upon you.' Peter Loveday gripped the sides of his lectern. The sweat was pouring from his brow. He had been delivering his Sunday morning sermon for over an hour. 'The perpetration of evil against your fellow man will condemn you to eternal damnation.'

His voice rose with the force of his fervour. He prided himself that guiding the ungodly back to the fold was his duty if not his destiny. He knew the temptations of the flesh and the power of the demons of lust that had tormented him before his marriage. He had overcome them by prayer and fasting. His piety had been his salvation from the wildness of his Loveday blood. He had seen from an early age the pain that his older brother's escapades had brought to his parents. Yet people had been enchanted by Japhet's quick wit and easy charm. Beside him Peter had appeared dull as pewter. Yet Peter had always wanted to shine, to be the most popular, the most beloved. He had emulated his father by turning to the Church. In his teenage years he had been fanatical in his devotions. But instead of approval, he had too often seen sadness in his father's eyes. Even his gentle mother had urged him to be more forgiving instead of condemning his brother, sister and cousin for their love of life and fun.

He knew his cousins had mocked him for his piety, but he had remained true to his calling. And his duty remained clear. The devil must be cast out of Cornwall in the shape of the smugglers and their bullying. Men like Harry Sawle and Mordecai Nance must be shown for the demons they were and driven from their community.

For the last month he had been caustic in preaching against the brutality of the smugglers.

A loud snore from the churchwarden won a snigger from the parishioners and a glare from Peter. The congregation were restless and uneasy. Bridie, who was seated in the front pew, signalled to her husband to end his sermon. He ignored her. The word of God was pounding through his brain. He would not be silenced. His tirade continued until his voice cracked and began to lose its power and the shuffling of feet and whine of children no longer silenced by bored parents drowned his words.

No one was listening to him. Again he felt he had failed in his zest to guide them to give up the lawlessness of their lives. Bridie was now frantically signalling him to draw the service to a close. She was biting her lip, her fingers locked together in tension. She was too sensitive to the mood of the villagers. Peter would have to remonstrate with her yet again. Nevertheless he ended the service. As he walked down the aisle to the door for the congregation to file past him, he heard their discontented mutterings.

His fingers clenched around his Bible, which he pressed to his chest. Too many of the villagers worked of a night for Harry Sawle. Three times in as many weeks they had smashed a window in the parsonage. The women who attended the lace-making afternoons had dropped in number, sending excuses that now they were proficient it fitted around their daily labours better if they made the lace in their own homes.

Bridie led the congregation from the church, her step slow as she smiled at each woman and child, silently pleading with them to understand that her husband's fervour was a tribute to his love for them and his fear of their damnation. Few women met her eye. Only Maura

240

Keppel smiled encouragingly. Despite teaching the women their lace-making skills, Maura was still regarded as an outsider to the village and had made few friends amongst the women. Bridie had confided to her her anguish that her husband was unpopular with his parishioners.

In the church porch Peter stood ramrod straight and spoke a pleasant word to each man, woman and child who filed past him. Few replied with more than a grunt. Leah paused by her daughter's side before continuing to the parsonage. 'Was so much preachifying necessary? Our meal will be burnt to a cinder in the oven.'

'Ma, please don't criticise Peter. He wants to save their souls. There is much ungodliness in the world.'

Leah shook her head. 'Not in you, my lovely. There be not an unkind bone in your body. But he be turning the women against you. Turn the other cheek, that's what the good book says. The men be as they are. It bain't for the preacher to tell them how to bring bread to their table. Free-trading was their fathers' way and their grandfathers' afore them.'

Bridie hung her head, her face pale beneath the starched whiteness of her Dutch cap. Leah was right, but Peter would not listen to such reasoning. It took courage to face the censure of the villagers. Peter was no coward. As a man of God he abhorred violence, and although he was proficient with a sword he refused to carry one. Neither did he use a pistol, though he was a good shot. He had even refused to strap a dagger to his waist though Bridie had pleaded with him to carry some form of protection. Bridie admired his bravery to speak his mind and preach as he felt guided by the Lord his God.

But it was the way of men not to heed what they did not wish to hear. The villagers resented his sermons. Peter also took family loyalty seriously. He held the smugglers responsible for the wounding and death of Edward Loveday and was outraged that Harry Sawle had stepped above himself to play a cat-and-mouse game with his sister Hannah. It was no secret that Peter had sided with his cousin Adam and was determined to see Harry Sawle brought to justice. What worried Bridie most was that if Sawle was caught it could mean dozens of local men also ending their days in gaol and their families facing starvation.

Bridie also was no craven; she had faced persecution in some form or other all her life. First for her bastard blood and then for her twisted spine and hobbling gait. She had overcome ridicule to attend the school at Trevowan Hard and had excelled above all other pupils until she had become schoolmistress there.

241

Her heart sank as she stood to one side of her husband and saw the hostility that sparked in the men's eyes after Peter's sermon.

'Who do 'e think 'e be, telling us we bain't worthy to meet our maker?' one farmhand growled to his companion. 'Who be the Lovedays in times past? Old Arthur Loveday weren't no better than a pirate until he wed a Penhaligan who brought him Trevowan as her dowry. Parson should remember his own blood bain't so innocent.'

His companion was equally incensed. 'Parson Loveday be the pot calling the kettle black, if you ask me. Even young Adam has been a privateer in recent years. What be the difference between stealing a ship and taking the cargo as plunder, and bringing a bit of comfort to the shores of our land with cheap tea and brandy?'

The first man sneered. 'And St John were once Sawle's partner. Him and Sawle had a share in the barque *Merry Maid*, which were taken by the revenue for carrying brandy from France.'

They passed out of Bridie's hearing. Her stomach was tight with worry. There had been real hatred in their voices.

'Peter can take care of himself.' Leah linked her arm through her daughter's. 'The men will always grumble to defend themselves when they be in the wrong. But Peter is a Loveday. No one would dare strike at him.'

'Sawle would!' Bridie groaned.

'Sawle is all hot air and bluster. He knows he'd be the first accused of any foul action taken against your man or his family.'

Bridie could not be pacified. The feud between Harry Sawle and the Lovedays had been going on too long. As they entered the kitchen of the parsonage they could smell the burnt meat in the oven. A thin haze of acrid-smelling smoke escaped from the Cornish range. Leah tutted and hurried forward to open the oven door. More smoke poured out and Bridie put a hand over her mouth and pushed open the window and door to allow the air to clear.

'There bain't no saving that chicken.' Leah scowled. 'It be charred to cinders. A wicked waste of good food.'

The smoke stung Bridie's eyes and throat. She felt suddenly bone weary and a wave of dizziness made her clutch at the stout oak table for support.

Leah cried out in alarm. 'Sit yourself down and rest, child.' She fussed around her daughter. 'I'll cook something for your husband. Dr Yeo told you to rest.'

'You fuss too much, Ma. I miscarried before because I pushed myself too hard. I won't let anything happen to this one. It is too precious.'

242

'Then take yourself to your bed for an hour,' Leah pulled the blackened chicken carcass from the oven and banged the copper roasting pan down on the table in disgust. 'Peter can make do with yesterday's pottage and bread.'

'He needs more than that. The evening service is at Polmasryn,' Bridie protested.

'Then I shall cook him some pilchards.' Leah waved her daughter away. 'You rest.'

Bridie was too tired to protest. This pregnancy had stripped her of energy from the first month. Her legs felt leaden and her head ached. 'I will lie down for an hour. I would see Peter before he leaves.'

Leah cooked for her son-in-law and gave him a tongue-lashing when she served it. 'Chicken were burnt. You'll have to make do with pilchards. And I've sent Bridie to her bed. She were dead on her feet. Near two hours you were preaching. Did you give no thought to her delicate health?'

Peter looked startled. 'The sermon may have been a little overlong, but what was said needed saying.'

'Could you not see how upset Bridie was?' Leah persisted.

Peter glared at her. 'My wife knows her duty—'

Leah cut him short. 'Bridie be fearful for you. The villagers are angry at the way you condemn them. Does your father lecture them about the evils of free-trading? He does not. He be a wise man.'

'I am not my father.' Peter pushed aside his half-eaten fish and stood up. 'I have work to attend at Polmasryn before evensong. If Bridie is tired, let her sleep on.'

Bridie woke to the sound of their raised voices and dragged her legs over the side of the bed. Momentarily the room spun around her and she dropped her head into her hands. The arguments between her mother and her husband were more frequent of late. Leah had never been much of a churchgoer. When she had come to live at the parsonage she had promised Bridie that she would attend one church service a week so that Peter did not lose face with his parishioners. Peter had agreed not to sermonise to Leah or insist that she attend the prayers morning and evening in the house. They were both strong-willed and opinionated in their beliefs and inevitably they clashed. Bridie hated dissent of any kind within her family. She entered the kitchen to find that Peter had already left and ran outside to the stable, where he was saddling his mare.

'Were you going to leave without saying goodbye?'

He turned and smiled. 'I thought to let you sleep.' He brushed her cheek with his hand, his dark eyes softening with love. 'I am a poor husband. I allow my zeal to overcome my duty to protect you. Another meal was ruined because I preached for too long.' It was the closest he would get to an apology for his religious fervour.

'The villagers will return to their cottages to discover their cooking pots burned dry. They cannot afford to have a meal ruined.' She kissed his hand to take the sting from her words. 'You promised me the sermons would be shorter. Would you see the church empty of a Sunday, for they will stop attending or go elsewhere?'

'I have my duty as the Lord guides me.' Peter remained stubborn.

'Then concentrate on the scriptures. I beg you, my love, do not castigate your flock about their involvement with Sawle and his ways.'

'Sawle has to be stopped. He did not baulk at poisoning his own men in prison so that they could not speak against him.'

'He will be brought to justice in time.'

Peter led his mare out of the stable and, once mounted, gazed down at his wife. Bridie looked so young and vulnerable and so very beautiful in the evening light. Her body was heavy with her pregnancy. She was so delicate and he loved her dearly. He must not upset her; the forthcoming child meant so much to them both. He leaned over in the saddle to kiss her.

'I can only do the Lord's work as I am guided. But I will take care and I will keep the sermons shorter, I promise. So you can stop worrying. Your health and that of our child is what is important.'

She pressed a dagger and its belt into his hand. 'At least carry this for protection. I will not rest easy if you go unarmed.'

He stared at the dagger for a long moment and she feared he would not accept it. Then he buckled the belt over his black waistcoat and tipped his broad-brimmed hat to her. She watched him ride away until he was out of sight. She still felt uneasy but made herself believe that her mother was right. Peter was a Loveday. No one would harm him.

She ate with Leah and remained on edge waiting for Peter to return. At each noise outside she went to the door to listen for the sound of his mare. A score of bats darted and dived in the sky above her head. The yew trees outside the kitchen door loomed dark and oppressive. A vixen and three cubs skirted the edge of the chicken coop, the chooks locked safely in their wooden hutch. There was no sign of her husband and Bridie's fear for him grew as darkness fell.

'Will you sit and rest, daughter. Peter is often delayed. He'll be sermonising again,' Leah consoled.

'He has never been this late before.' Bridie fingered the gold cross on her breast. It was only a mile to Polmasryn church.

'Have faith in him,' Leah warned.

Bridie reluctantly returned to the kitchen. She had baked a gooseberry and honey pie, which was one of Peter's favourites, and it was cooling on the table. A jug of cream was beside it with a cloth cover protecting it from dust. To keep busy she took up a besom and vigorously swept the floor, which was already spotless. The clop of hoofs had her running to the door. Peter's mare was trotting towards its stable.

It was riderless.

Chapter Thirty-four

Bridie was thrown into panic. She ran to the stable to harness the pony to the dogcart. Leah's voice was harsh as she followed her with a lantern.

'Child, you cannot go out this time of night. Send word to Sam Deacon. It is too bad that Adam and Joshua and St John are all away at the moment.' Leah wrung her hands.

'There is no time. Peter could be hurt. What if he is unconscious in a ditch?' She cursed the darkness. Thick clouds shielded the moon. A glance at the sky showed few stars in the heavens. There was also a sharp tang of dampness in the air. Senara had taught her that was a sign that usually heralded rain.

'You cannot go alone,' Leah insisted. 'Wait for me to get my shawl and come with you.'

Bridie's hands were shaking so violently, she had trouble getting the bridle over the pony's head. The mare sensed her fear and shied, refusing to back into the shafts of the dogcart. Bridie was thrown aside and pushed against the wall of the stable. Her hand covered her swollen stomach, protecting her unborn child from the pressure of the pony crushed against her.

'That animal will do you harm.' Leah slapped its rump to move it aside. She was carrying a second lantern and spoke soothingly to the mare, who did not like the darkness. The pony calmed and Bridie managed to get her hitched to the dogcart. The two lanterns were fixed on poles each side of the cart to give them some light on the pitch-black track.

It was too dangerous to travel at more than a trot. Though impatient to find her husband, Bridie feared that if Peter had been thrown, he could have fallen in the road and they might trample on him. There was also the chance that he was lying in a ditch, his body hidden from them if they passed it too quickly.

Both women shouted Peter's name and peered into the hedgerows and ditches. Their only reply was a hoot from a barn owl, its ghostly white body skimming over the hedges in front of them. The tall tower of Polmasryn church ahead of them was barely visible in the dark. Bridie had never liked this church. It had been abandoned and had fallen into ruin for many years before Peter became parson to the village. The diocese had repaired its roof, but the church always smelt of decay and Bridie felt its sanctity had been abused when for years its crypt had been a storehouse for the smugglers.

Her alarm increased when she could see no candles illuminating the windows of the church. At the lychgate she leapt from the cart and holding one of the lanterns stumbled along the rough path, banging her hip against a tilted tombstone. The door was never locked and it swung open with a creak of rusty hinges.

'Peter! Peter, where are you?' Her voice echoed chillingly around her.

Leah had followed more slowly with the second lantern and found her daughter kneeling by the altar.

'Sweet Jesu, keep your loving servant safe!' Bridie prayed. The words tumbled forth and were repeated like a litany.

Leah put a hand on her shoulder. 'He bain't here, my lovely. You'll take a chill. If his mare threw him, he could have walked across the fields to the parsonage. It be shorter that way.'

Hope returned to Bridie as she clutched her mother's hand for support. 'The good Lord would not let any harm come to Peter. He is too loyal a servant, is he not, Ma?'

'Best we return home.' Leah put an arm around her daughter's waist and was shocked at how violently the young woman was shaking. 'The good Lord looks after his own. He won't let no harm come to your man, my lovely. Happen he were called to a parishioner, perhaps to say the last rites. Are any sick to death that you know?'

Bridie shook her head. 'Oh Ma, I'm so afeared for him.'

'You take a hold on yourself.' Leah spoke sharply. 'Has he not often been home late? Sickness and death can claim a life suddenly. A seizure or apoplexy can strike without warning and a person can die within hours. He could have been called to any of the parish villages. We must go home and wait.'

'But his horse would never have returned without him unless it had been frightened,' Bridie forced through a throat tight with fear.

'Anything can startle a dumb animal.' Leah snorted. 'Peter may not have tethered her properly in his haste to attend a parishioner. Come now, my lovely. Let us get ourselves to the parsonage. Your husband will be cold and hungry and wanting his supper.'

Bridie was not convinced. She was certain something terrible had happened to Peter, even that he was dead. Short of knocking on the door of every cottage in the three villages of the parish there was nothing they could do but wait and pray that he was safe.

Leah carefully guided Bridie back down the aisle. She held the lantern in such a way that it threw no light on the small puddle of blood she had seen by the door. Bridie was sobbing. She had been through so much strain in the last few days since the attack by the villagers. She had dealt with that with fortitude and courage, but a woman in her condition could only take so much and Bridie was not physically strong.

Leah's hand was gripped in a bone-crunching hold and she clenched her jaw not to cry out in pain. Bridie had doubled over clutching her side. They halted in the porch of the church.

'Ma, the pain, it must be the child!' Her voice rose in torment and she wrung her hands. 'Dear God, don't let me lose Peter and my child. That would be too cruel. Dear Lord, hear my prayers.'

'Sit awhile and calm yourself.' Leah's voice was gruff with her concern for her daughter. 'I'll get this door shut properly.'

She paused with her gnarled hands on the iron ring of the latch and glanced along the nave to the altar. Her voice was too low for her sobbing daughter to hear. 'I don't ask you for much, Lord. And I know I be a sinner, all my brood born out of proper wedlock like they were, and I don't come to your house as much as I should, but Bridie believes you be a compassionate God. She's suffered enough for the way she were conceived when I were attacked and raped. She bain't got a harsh word or act in her body, never complained when she were spat on or jeered at for her twisted back. I ask you now to show her compassion. Don't let her lose her precious child. Watch over the baby and her husband, Lord. Keep them safe and I will be a better Christian. I will never rebuke Peter for his fervour and will say my prayers with him twice a day.'

The moon came out from behind a cloud and its light fell briefly on an angel on a gravestone. Living with the gypsies so long, Leah saw it as an omen that all would be well.

Chapter Thirty-five

The excruciating pain throbbing through his skull and attacking cramped muscles in his legs and arms penetrated Peter's returning senses. His head felt as though it had been split asunder and his first conscious thought was that he had been blinded. He blinked several times but nothing was visible. A complete and stifling darkness enshrouded him. The air was rank, warning him he was in an enclosed space, but as he hauled great mouthfuls into his lungs it was at least breathable. Though for how long . . .

And where was he?

White-hot shafts of agony obliterated his attempt at reasoning. He was lying on his side, his arms tied behind his back and his legs bound. Every bone in his body ached. The ground felt solid beneath his cheek. It was cold, moist and unyieldingly hard.

He struggled to sit up, the pain now like axes slicing into his temple and torso. His arms were numb and would not hold his weight and with a groan he crashed back to the ground. He took several moments to test what limbs he could move and discern whether or not they were broken. As far as he could tell his legs and arms were intact but the agony of any movement sent his head reeling and he battled to stay conscious. He lay panting and gathering his wits before he attempted to move again. His tongue stuck to the roof of his mouth and thirst rasped his throat. The musty air and the coldness against his cheek was more than dampness. His senses sharpened to his surroundings and he became aware that water was trickling beneath him. He was lying in a channel of wet that had soaked his clothes. He licked the ground, scooping water into his mouth with his tongue. It was fresh and helped to restore his dazed wits.

He wriggled his fingers, biting his lip to still the discomfort as the stabbing tingling brought a return to his circulation. There was the slightest give in his bonds and he worked his hands more feverishly.

The rough hemp lacerated his wrists and within minutes his skin was rubbed raw and bleeding. Still he continued. He had to be free of his bonds to escape this dark pit. By the time his arms were losing their strength there appeared to be more give in the rope. He had no idea how long he had been conscious. It seemed like hours.

He worked through his agony, willing his tired arms to continue their task; at the same time he strained to listen for sounds. At first the silence was complete. Then he heard the slightest rustle and realised it was water running down a wall of some kind. That made him suspect that he was in a cave or a disused mine. But how had he got there? The fresh water he was lying in at least proved it was not a cave on the seashore that would flood with the next tide. It would be a convenient way for the smugglers to murder him. No one else but those villains would dare to attack him and serve him in this manner. And he feared they wanted him dead.

The last thing he remembered was dousing the candles after the evening service at Polmasryn. He had thought himself alone in the church. He must have been struck from behind. The free-traders would want retribution after his recent sermons. But how dare they attack him in this manner? His anger refuelled his energy and his efforts to be free became more vigorous.

The suffocating darkness pressed like weights around him, intensifying his fear. If the smugglers returned he would be at their mercy. A scurrying and scampering from rats crawling over his face and legs chilled his blood even further. He hated rats for the unclean, disease-carrying creatures they were. His flesh crawled at their touch and with a violent shudder he shook them off, but they were relentless and he felt teeth bite his neck.

It goaded him to work more frantically, and after what felt like an eternity the knots began to loosen. With sharp jerks of his hands he managed to slide one palm along the other and free of the rope. He tore off the remaining bond and sat up to reach for his dagger. It was missing from his belt, which did not surprise him. He fumbled with the cords around his ankles and released himself from his tethers. His knees buckled as he rose shakily to his feet and he flung out an arm to encounter a sharp edge of rock.

He steadied himself against a wave of dizziness and pressed a hand to his temple. His face was distorted and swollen and he felt cuts on his mouth, nose and eyes. He stared upwards and to the right and left, but the darkness was complete. Remembering his tinderbox, he struck the flint a score of times before it finally sparked on to the dry lint and a flame briefly flared. He held it high but it illuminated little of the gloom and his puffy eyelids further obliterated his vision. He could make out rough-hewn rock and guessed he was standing in a narrow tunnel. The roof of the cave was only a few inches above his head. It was impossible to see how far the tunnel ran, though the floor appeared to slope upwards to his left. Then he detected a light breath of air on his face. That must be the way out.

The flame flickered and died. The darkness wrapped itself once more like a blindfold around his eyes. He blinked to adjust his sight but it made no difference; again the dark was impenetrable, like stepping forth into an abyss. He thrust a hand in front of him and with the other guided himself along the wall of rock. Each step was tortuously slow and his hands bled as they scraped over the rough surface. Then he was attacked without warning by several strikes to his temple and shoulders and an involuntary cry of alarm was forced from him. Instinctively he flung up his arms to protect his head. There was a high-pitched squeaking and a thrumming sound buzzing through his ears. Gripped by this new terror, he flailed his arms until he realised that his assailants were bats returning to their roost.

He drew a fragmented breath to calm his beleaguered nerves and continued to edge forwards. Deprived of sight, it was a frightening ordeal and he had to endure continual attacks from the flying bats. Eventually, the floor of the cave rose more steeply and he thought he could make out a pinpoint of greyish light. Dawn was brightening the sky and the mouth of the cave was ahead of him. He offered a prayer of gratitude and stumbled on. The tunnel widened, and despite colliding with an occasional boulder on its floor he made it to the entrance and pushed aside the final barrier to his freedom – the prickly branches of a gorse bush. He found himself standing on a ridge halfway up a steep tor on the moor. It was pouring with rain. It was that rain which had formed the water in the cave and revived his wits.

He tilted his face to the heavens and allowed the rain to splash over his face and cool his wounds. Then he cupped his hands and drank the life-sustaining water.

At first he could discern no familiar landmarks, but as the sun rose above the horizon in the east he recognised two church spires. He was a dozen or so miles from home. His relief was overwhelming; however, the effort to come this far proved too much and he sank down on to a boulder to recover his breath. It would be a long, painful walk.

Mordecai Nance was in a wood three miles from Penruan, waiting for Harry Sawle. He was hunched against the rain, the collar of his greatcoat pulled up around his ears and his hat sheltering his face. A trickle of rain flowed from its brim on to his chin. He sat on a fallen tree trunk, digging at the rotten bark with his dagger, his mood sullen. Sawle was using him like a dogsbody, putting his life in danger whilst staying away from trouble himself. Mordecai had thought that taking over the Dolphin Inn would provide him with more power in the area and a greater income, but his wages were meagre and his share in the profits from the contraband minimal. Sawle had taken him for a fool and it rankled.

'What do you have to report?' Sawle's voice grated in his ear.

Nance started violently; he had not heard the smuggler approach. 'I've dealt with the men taken at Tor Farm. They won't betray us.'

'I heard.' Sawle stayed behind him in the shadows of an oak tree.

An arm circled Nance's neck and a dagger was pressed to his throat. 'Those men were loyal,' Sawle growled. 'They would not have betrayed us. Poison is a woman's weapon.'

'It was the only way. The guards would not be bribed to arrange an escape. We could not risk them talking.'

'I thought you had the military in our pay. They were supposed to bungle any arrests.'

'Their commanding officer wants promotion, not riches,' Nance gasped. His face was slick with sweat and fear was turning his insides to water. 'What else could I do? But I sorted the preacher. He won't cause no more trouble.'

The dagger pricked his flesh and a warm trickle of blood ran down his neck.

'What preacher?' Sawle demanded.

'Loveday. He were stirring up unrest. He had to learn his place.'

'I said nothing about him!' A pistol butt slammed against his cheek and Nance fell to the ground, coloured lights flashing before his eyes. Sawle dragged him to his feet by his neckerchief. The smuggler's scarred face, twisted with anger, was inches from Nance's own.

'You be the one getting above himself. The preacher be harmless. Hot air never stopped us afore.'

'You wanted the Lovedays dealt with,' Nance whined, his eyes now bulging with terror at what the smuggler would do next. 'You said to scare the Rabson woman. She don't frighten easily. She informed the authorities about the contraband. Did you want her to get away with that? The preacher is her brother. That will make her think.'

'Fool! It will make them more determined to see me hang. What did you do with his body?'

'He were beaten and trussed up and left in that old cave back of Long Tor,' Nance declared with a blustering bravado. He did not like the way the conversation was going. He had thought Sawle would be pleased at his initiative.

'You telling me he bain't dead?'

Nance's mouth worked in silent panic, trying to judge the smuggler's wishes. Did he want the parson to be dead or not? He thought Sawle had wanted him to show the Lovedays who ruled here. The preacher had been barely breathing when they dumped him in the cave. His beating had been severe and he would die of thirst and starvation if he survived the night. No one would find him.

'He be dead!' Nance choked out.

He was flung to the ground and a vicious kick landed on his ribs. 'I gave you no orders to kill him. The death of a smuggler won't raise too many eyebrows, but not a preacher.'

'No one will find the body.'

Sawle kicked him again. 'There'll be a bloody good search made for him. There still be a cache of goods hidden in an old mine and on two farms. How we gonna get that safely away now? The militia will be out combing the countryside for a Loveday. And if any of those goods are confiscated then it will be down to you, Nance. You'll repay me every penny I lose. And you'd better make sure my name be kept out of this.'

Mordecai scowled. He had allowed his own hatred for the Lovedays to govern his judgement. He had acted in the heat of temper against the preacher.

'You bain't been seen round here for weeks. No one will blame you.'

'Just make sure they don't, or it will be the worse for you.'

Nance did not like to be threatened. But only a madman acted against Sawle. He would take his revenge on the Lovedays. The preacher was just the beginning.

Farmer Jethro Helland was still drowsy with sleep as his horse clopped along the lane. He was going to market to sell his cheese and eggs. The earlier downpour had stopped but the sky remained overcast and there would be more rain later. It added to his misery. He'd been up all night nursing a sore head after his mother had caught him in the hayloft with a dairymaid. She had struck them both with a besom, screaming abuse at them. The agile girl had scampered away, leaving him to bear the brunt of his mother's fury.

'You bain't nothing but a worthless fornicator,' his mother had railed. 'When I think of the pain I suffered bringing such a useless lump into

the world, only to suffer the humiliation of your rutting with the servants.'
She laid about him ruthlessly with her broom.

Helland was four and thirty, a big man but slow-witted. He was slack-jawed and covered in a down of ginger hair all over his body that sprouted into wiry bristles on his head and cheeks. His face was in constant motion with an eye tic, a frequent sniffing and an uncontrollable shaking of his head. He reckoned his mother had hit him with her broom too often when he was a child and that had stopped him thinking right. He was a grown man and wanted a woman in his bed. He'd take a wife – any wife if someone would have him. But what woman would want to live with Hellmaid Helland, as he knew his ma was called because of her evil temper. All any wife of his would face would be a life of abuse from his ma and drudgery. They did not own the farm, only rented it from his ma's cousin, old Jethro Helland whom he had been named after. The old bugger would turn them out of the farm, kinfolk or not, if they were late paying the rent. But Ma idolised old Jethro. She would not move from the farm.

Usually young Jethro, as he was mostly known, enjoyed market day. It was a day of peace away from his mother's scathing tongue and he could spend an hour in a tavern supping ale – another forbidden pleasure at home – before he left the town. Today that simple joy was denied him. The whore of a dairymaid had insisted on his last pennies before lifting her skirts for him. He did not consider taking a few pence from the price for his cheese and eggs. His ma knew exactly what was paid for the produce he delivered to a woman to sell on one of the stalls.

He let the horse travel at a leisurely pace. If he were braver he'd pocket the day's takings from the market and run away. But he had tried that once and Ma had found him working as a potman in a tavern for the price of two quarts of ale a day. She had beaten him black and blue and now he was too scared of her to fight back or run away again.

His head fell forward in a doze and he was startled awake by a neigh from his horse. The horse shied and the cart tilted precariously in a ditch, throwing him to the ground.

He yelled out in alarm. He must have died and gone to hell. A ghost loomed over him, its face distorted and bloodied.

'I did not mean to startle you,' the spectre declared.

'You be a ghost come to take me to hell?' Jethro whimpered, his head shaking vigorously from side to side.

'I am no ghost. And if you are an honest man about your daily work, then heaven will be your reward, not hell.' The tall figure had quietened the horse and clung to the rail of the cart. 'I was abducted from my church. I need a ride to Polruggan parsonage. It is not far out of your way.'

Helland dragged himself to his feet, his face contorting as he sniffed several times and blinked rapidly. He could see now that the man, despite looking like he had taken on a dozen ruffians in a tavern fight, was dressed in a preacher's black suit and torn Geneva bands.

'I gotta get to market.' His slow mind fixed on the task ahead of him.

Then, to his dismay, the figure before him crumpled to the ground and he could not rouse him. At a loss as to what to do for the best, Helland hauled the clergyman over his shoulder and laid him in the back of the cart beside the cheeses. To protect him from another shower of rain, he covered him with an oiled canvas, then continued on to market. Ma would be cross if he arrived late and the woman might not pay him the full cost of his provisions. He would deliver the preacher to his church on his way home.

The farmer promptly forgot about his passenger, his mind returning to his own problems. He was deep in melancholy thought when a rider pelted along the track, forcing him to pull over sharply. He was about to shout out a protest when he recognised the newcomer in his sodden greatcoat. Jethro kept his twitching head bowed and tried to still the fear that made his body shake. He had suffered the brunt of Mordecai Nance's bullying many times since childhood. Nance had mocked his slow wits and had once stripped him naked and tied him to the horse trough in Penruan when he had gone there for supplies.

The horse halted and Helland flinched as the smuggler demanded, 'How many people you passed on the road this day?'

Helland shook his head, blinking rapidly.

'You dumb idiot! What answer is that? Lost your tongue!'

Helland cowered on the seat of the cart. He hurt all over from his mother's beating. He didn't want another. But Nance's insults made him stubborn.

'I mind me own business, I do. You be the first rider I've seen.'

Nance lashed him across the shoulders with his horsewhip. 'Did I say rider, idiot? What about a man walking?'

The farmer held up his hands to protect his head. 'I mind me own business, I do.' He sniffed and blinked so violently he had trouble forming his words. Finally he stuttered, 'I b-b-bain't s-seen no one w-w-walking.'

'What about through the fields? You seen anyone walking through the fields?'

'V–Valley F–F–Farm had m–m–men in the f–f–field, I remember.'

'I may as well talk to that stone wall for all the sense I get out of you.' Nance glowered.

Jethro shook all over, terrified he would be beaten. He wondered if he should mention the clergyman he had found. His mind was like wet clay refusing to take form. He was no good at making decisions. Nance had not mentioned a preacher. And he wasn't the sort of man to be seeking out a parson even if his own wife were dying. Better not to say anything. He really didn't want another beating.

Nance swore profanely. Jethro Helland hoped the preacher could not hear him.

'You be worse than useless.' Nance brought his horsewhip down on the farmer's shoulders before digging his spurs into his horse's sides, which were already flecked with blood, and galloping off.

Helland clicked his tongue for his horse to walk on. At this rate he'd be late for market.

Nance was frantic with fear as he sped along the lane back to Polruggan. Loveday could not have got far. Not in the state he had left him. After his confrontation with Sawle, Mordecai had gone to the cave to check that the preacher was dead and had been shocked to find him gone.

A body if it had ever been found might have given rise to an investigation, but with Loveday alive and the story of his abduction come out, all hell would break lose. Nance had thought Peter Loveday the easiest of prey. The parson had proved more wily and resilient than he had thought.

At least the men last night had all been masked and Loveday had been unconscious throughout. He would not be able to identify his attackers.

Chapter Thirty-six

When Peter had not returned home by the next morning, Bridie was frenzied with worry. The rain had stopped, so he was not taking shelter anywhere.

'What am I to do, Ma?' She wrung her hands. She was so upset she could not think straight. 'Who do I go to to raise a search for him? Sir Henry? Why are so many of our men away at this time?'

'Joshua and St John are away on business,' Leah soothed. 'Peter can take care of himself. I'm sure he be with a dying parishioner.' She did not speak her thoughts that Peter had been attacked because his cousins were absent and his assailants believed they would get away with it.

'But I've not heard of anyone who is dying. Certainly not in our parishes. I know something bad has happened to him. I just know it, Ma.'

Leah was at her spinning wheel in the parlour. Bridie had been unable to settle to any work to keep her mind occupied, and her mother advised, 'Why not talk to Senara? She will know what to do. Or Hannah – Peter is her brother. Perhaps it will be better to discuss this with her. Miss Elspeth may even be at the farm. She has a level head on her shoulders.'

'I should go to Hannah. You are right, he is her brother. She needs to know Peter is missing.'

As she rode out of the village she saw Mordecai Nance coming out of a miner's cottage. The miner had been one of the troublemakers who made her husband's work here difficult.

Nance glared at her. Then, remembering his manners, he tipped the brim of his felt hat. 'You look worried. Is Parson around?'

'Why would you be wanting him?' She was instantly suspicious that he knew Peter was missing. 'The Reverend Mr Snell is your preacher at Penruan.'

Nance leered at her in a suggestive manner, then sneered, 'I've business with Loveday.'

'If ever a man was in need of his soul saving, it is you, Mordecai Nance,' she retorted. 'But my husband is not in Polruggan this morning.'

She had never seen Nance in the village before. His stare was unnerving. Did he truly not know where Peter was? In that case the smugglers could not be involved in some kind of attack upon him. Or was this a cruel way of taunting her? She tilted her chin, refusing to let him see that she was worried or frightened.

'Where be the parson?' There was a menacing edge to his voice.

'He is attending to parish duties,' she lied, but it took all her courage to hold his chilling glare.

Something sinister had happened between Nance and Peter, Bridie could feel it in her bones. His stare was assessing her reaction with a cold-blooded intensity. She bit her lip to stop herself demanding what had happened last night and insisting that he tell her that Peter was unharmed. Her natural caution kept her silent, and strangely his stare became uncertain and he broke the contact of their gazes and walked away grinding out, 'Happen my business can wait for another day.'

She could not stop her body trembling after the encounter. The journey to the Rabson farm seemed to take for ever and a persistent drizzle accompanied it so that her hooded cloak was sodden by the time she reached the farmhouse. The rain added to her anxiety. If Peter was lying injured somewhere, he could take a mortal chill.

'Bridie, what brings you out in this weather?' Hannah's welcoming smile faded at seeing her sister-in-law's distraught expression. 'Come inside and warm yourself. You are wet through.'

Hannah fussed around her, taking her cloak and placing it by the kitchen range to dry.

'Now, how would you like a warming drink of chocolate, as a special treat on this cold day?'

Bridie had stayed silent because she feared that if she spoke she would burst into tears. She shook her head, declining the drink, and said in a rush, 'Peter did not return from Polmasryn last night. His horse came home without him. Something dreadful has happened. I don't know which way to turn.'

'My poor dear, you must be worried sick,' Hannah gasped. Her own mind was in turmoil. Bridie would not exaggerate the seriousness of the matter.

'Peter has been preaching against the smugglers.' Bridie twisted her fingers together. 'They would not like that.'

'They would be fools to act against him.' Hannah proceeded to make the chocolate; its sweetness would help calm Bridie, who was ashen. She glanced at the grandfather clock in the narrow hallway. It was almost eleven. Her own fears for her brother clenched her stomach. She needed to reassure herself that he was safe as much as Bridie did. 'His horse could have thrown him. A parishioner could have taken him in for the night. It has been pouring on and off for hours.'

Bridie shook her head. 'Someone would have sent word. A search should be made for him. I wish Adam was here.' She hugged her arms around her swollen stomach. 'I'm sorry to be so weak. I did not know who to turn to.'

'Any woman would be distraught in the circumstances,' Hannah consoled. All the colour had drained from her sister-in-law's face and it was pinched with pain. 'Drink the chocolate. It will sustain you. You did the right thing by coming here. Sam will deal with it. You must not fret yourself. You will harm your child.'

A chair scraped on the floor behind Bridie and she was surprised to see Sam Deacon. He must have been discussing the farm work with Hannah.

'Good day to you, Mr Deacon. I did not see you there.' Embarrassed, Bridie dabbed at her eyes, which were bright with tears.

'I shall organise a search, Mrs Loveday. Was your husband preaching at Polmasryn church last night?'

She nodded. 'I have not sent word to his mother. I did not want to upset her with Joshua still away.'

Hannah chewed her lip. 'We will wait until Sam has searched the lanes and fields between here and Polmasryn.'

By the end of the day, with no sign of Peter, the family had gathered at Polruggan parsonage. Joshua had returned and Cecily was with him. St John, who had heard the news of his cousin's disappearance when he visited Trewenna, was shaken by the events. On their arrival at Polruggan, Leah had confided in Joshua and St John that there was blood on the floor of Polmasryn church.

Cecily sat with her arms around a weeping Bridie. 'We must pray that if Peter has been hurt, a kindly goodwife has taken him in to nurse him. Perhaps they were unable to send word. They may live alone.'

'We have done all we can for now.' Joshua was haggard. 'Sam and the men are still searching. Why do we not go into the church and pray for him?'

Cecily rose wearily and her expression was stricken. 'What good will prayers do? I've prayed on my knees until they were swollen for Japhet to be freed. He still ended up on the far side of the world. I prayed for Oswald to be spared. A more kindly man I never met, and he was taken so young. Now Peter. Peter who has served the Lord so diligently – so piously. I truly do not think I have any prayers left.'

Joshua was shocked by his wife's outburst. 'You must keep your faith, my dear. You are distraught or you would not doubt the Lord's benevolence. Japhet was spared. He could have been hanged for his crimes. And being sent to Australia could yet be the making of him. As for Oswald, we miss him dearly but he had suffered for years, never complaining of his pain. He is at peace now. Peter is the most complex of my children and in many ways the most resilient. His faith has sustained him through many emotional and moral battles. It has never failed him. It will not fail him now. Our Lord is with him, protecting him. I do not doubt that.'

'It is almost time for evensong.' Hannah supported her father. 'Peter would want you to take the service, Papa. Or do you wish to attend to your own flock?'

'My prayers are needed here. My curate will take the service at Trewenna if I do not return.'

St John also agreed to stay and offered Hannah his arm to escort her to the church. He could feel his cousin trembling. She was putting on a brave face, but it had been a terrible year for her. She had lost too many who were dear to her.

The family walked in silence to the church. The churchwarden was seated by the door and on their entrance rose and began to ring the bell to summon the villagers. Usually only a half-dozen attended during the week, but as the family sat with their heads bowed, waiting for the service to begin, the church began to fill behind them. It was not just the villagers of Polruggan; many had walked from Polmasryn and Trewenna, having learned of Peter's disappearance.

The church was packed. Mark Sawle was also there with Sam Deacon. St John recognised many of the men as tubmen who had worked for Sawle when he was in partnership with the smuggler. The tubmen were decent, hardworking men by day and supplemented their poor wages by working for Sawle at night. They were appalled that the preacher had been attacked and was missing, and were here to show their loyalty to the family who had given them work, help and sustenance for so many years.

At the end of the service the family stayed to receive the good wishes of the villagers. Bridie was deeply moved. She had not realised how much her husband was respected. She had thought the congregation resented his sermons, especially when he denounced the evils of smuggling.

She was still inside the church when from outside a cheer went up. Hannah was closer to the door and she put a hand to her mouth, joy lighting her face. 'Our prayers have been answered.'

Bridie ran outside to discover Peter surrounded by the villagers. He was standing by the side of a cart with its driver shaking his head and looking bemused. Joshua pushed his way to his son's side and Peter leaned heavily upon his father's arm. Then he lifted his face and Bridie shuddered at how badly he had been beaten. He was barely recognisable. But he was standing and still alive. Their prayers had indeed been answered.

She ran to her husband and, uncaring of the proprieties, flung her arm around his neck and kissed him. 'I thought they had killed you.'

He held her tightly, then, with an embarrassed blush brightening his bruised cheeks, pulled away, but he tucked her arm through his. Several of the women around them were mumbling amongst themselves.

'Poor Parson. He don't deserve that.'

'It bain't right. It be an affront to what be decent.'

'Bain't no one safe, if you ask me.'

'Aye, it be time this were stopped.'

They noticed Bridie close to them and looked away shamefaced.

'They have gone too far this time,' St John proclaimed loudly.

Cecily, Bridie and Hannah were fussing around Peter, who was protesting that he was not badly hurt. St John saw the farmer who had brought Peter home shaking his head and looking confused, even anxious. He went over to him.

'Where did you find my cousin?'

'He found Jethro.' The farmer was nervous and his head shook from side to side. 'I bain't never seen such a crowd in a taking. They bain't cross with Jethro, are they?'

The slow speech showed St John the farmer was a halfwit.

'Ma gonna be cross with Jethro. I be late home.'

'Your mother should be very proud,' St John reassured him. 'When Peter found you, was he close by?'

Helland flinched and belatedly remembered to touch his forelock to the well-dressed gentleman. He did not like the gentry; they made him nervous. And this one also looked angry.

'He were about a m–mile from our farm this m–morning. But I had to go to m–market or M–M–M–Ma would've s–skinned m–me.'

St John controlled his impatience. The man's face was twitching alarmingly as his agitation grew.

'She'll skin m-me anyways. I g-got there late and didn't g-g-get b-best price for our cheese.'

'Where is your farm?'

'Near the m-moor. Helland Farm it be. I had t-to g-go to m-market.'

St John realised he would get little sense from the farmer and suspected that Peter had been with the man all day whilst his family had been at their wits' end with worry. There was no point in getting angry. Peter was safe and that was all that was important. He drew some silver coins from his pocket and handed them to the farmer, who stared at them with disbelief. 'That will pay for your trouble. You saved my cousin's life today. We have been looking for him.'

'Thankee, sir.' Helland beamed a toothless smile. 'Thankee m-most k-kindly.'

He turned the cart around, and St John had begun to walk to the parsonage when the farmer called out, 'That m-man were looking for him afore market then.'

At the fear in his voice, St John retraced his steps and grabbed the horse's bridle to stop the farmer leaving. 'What man was this?'

'The b-bad one. N-n-nance.' His face broke out in such a mêlée of tics, blinks and shakes that St John did not have the heart to question him further.

He marched to the rectory. Hannah and Cecily were in the parlour eating cake and tea served by Leah. Bridie's mother scurried out to bring a cup for St John.

'Papa is helping Bridie get Peter into his bed,' Hannah explained. 'We sent for Dr Yeo. Peter is rambling but does not seem physically at risk, though he had a terrible beating.'

'The farmer said Mordecai Nance was on the road this morning searching for someone. It must have been Peter. I'll have a warrant sworn for Nance's arrest.'

'What good will that do?' Joshua had come downstairs. He lit a small clay pipe to dispel his own anger. He needed to appear calm. St John was too excitable and could jeopardise bringing Nance to justice.

'It will show him he cannot take the law into his own hands,' St John raged. 'He's guilty.'

'Who will condemn him on Farmer Helland's word?' Joshua placated. 'You've seen the man. He's not right in the head.'

'The fool took Peter all the way to market.' Hannah shook her head in despair. 'Any right-thinking man would have brought him straight to his home. Peter could have died. And clearly the farmer is terrified of Nance. He will not testify.'

She stood up. 'I must get back to the farm for the children. Peter is safe. I thank God for that.'

'You cannot ride the lanes alone,' Joshua warned her.

'Sam is still in the church. He will accompany me.'

Her father lifted a grey brow. 'That overseer of yours takes a lot upon himself. But he is a good man. Though should you let him do so much? You must take care of gossip.'

Hannah shrugged. 'There is nothing to gossip about. He is my servant.'

'Deacon is no one's servant.' Joshua puffed on his pipe and a cloud of blue smoke circled his head. 'He is the least likely farmhand I have ever come across. He's hiding from something.'

'Papa, you worry too much,' Hannah objected. 'He is the most honest man I have met in years.'

'There is something not quite right about him.' Joshua would not be silenced. 'He is not all he says he is.'

Hannah agreed with her father but she would not be drawn on the subject. They were interrupted by the arrival of the doctor. He left after a short examination, pronouncing to the family that they were not to worry.

'Mr Loveday has a concussion. He should be over the worst of it by tomorrow. Keep him in bed and give him these drops to sedate him and dull the pain. He will be fit to give his sermon as usual on Sunday.'

Joshua walked with his daughter to her horse. Sam cupped his hands to assist Hannah to mount. Joshua was frowning when he returned to the others and remarked to St John, 'Deacon is in love with Hannah. Do you think something should be said to him?'

St John did not believe his uncle. 'Hannah is still in love with Oswald. She would not thank you for interfering on so personal a matter. Deacon is a man of honour. At least we know he will protect her.'

He picked up his hat from the table. 'I will give you and Aunt Cecily a lift back to Trewenna. Aunt Elspeth will be worried if she has heard anything of Peter's escapade.'

'Hardly an escapade,' Joshua grunted.

'It has been a long and gruelling day, Uncle. Tomorrow I will confront Nance. This is the second time he has struck at our family. He caused the fire at Boscabel for which I was unjustly blamed last year, I am sure of it.'

'Do not let old antagonisms and imagined wrongs cloud your

judgement. We were wrong to blame you for the fire, but if it was Nance he covered his tracks well.'

'He is laughing at us behind our backs,' St John returned, his face flushed and a dangerous glitter in his eyes. 'I will not stand by and allow that to happen.'

'Then wait until Adam returns.'

'Adam! Why does everyone think Adam has the answers? I will not play second fiddle to my brother.' St John stamped out of the room. 'Use the coach and Fraddon will drive it back. I'll ride Peter's mare to Trevowan.'

Joshua realised he had gravely erred. St John would not listen to reason. He hated Nance and Sawle with a vengeance. And by mentioning Adam, Joshua had lit an incendiary on an unstable bomb. He prayed St John would do nothing rash.

Chapter Thirty-seven

Three days later Hannah took some butter and cheese made on the farm to her parents at Trewenna rectory. She had called earlier at the parsonage, but Peter and Bridie were not at home. Leah had been very concerned about the couple.

'The parson should be taking it easy. That were a bad ordeal he suffered. And Bridie be no better. She be off tending to her duties and won't let her precious husband out of her sight. It be madness. She bain't strong, and in her condition . . .' She let the words drift. 'You must speak to them, Mrs Rabson. They don't listen to an old woman like me.'

Leah was not given to exaggeration and Hannah was worried. Peter had ever been selfless in his religious fervour, but he must take more care of Bridie.

On entering the rectory she was met in the hall by her father. 'My dear, it is good to see you. Your mother is out. She has gone to visit Elspeth.' He eyed the cheese in her hands with appreciation. 'And you have brought one of your fine cheeses. Thank you. But should you be riding round the countryside unattended after what happened to Peter?'

'Sam accompanied me. He has gone to the inn for a drink of ale.'

Her father eyed her quizzically. 'You should have asked him in. He is no ordinary servant, is he?'

Hannah ducked her head to remove her straw bonnet and to hide her expression from her father. Little passed his sharp observation.

'It was Sam who insisted on going to the inn. I think he wanted some time to himself. We start the harvest tomorrow. I called at the parsonage. Peter and Bridie were not there. How is he?'

'He is back preaching against the smugglers. He is more passionate than ever. I have cautioned him to show more reason. But you know Peter.' He sounded resigned, but Hannah was not fooled by his manner.

'Are you worried about him?'

'No more than any of my family.'

'It is Peter's way to use words as a weapon.' Hannah shrugged. 'I spoke to Leah at the parsonage. She seemed concerned for Bridie's health. I have neglected her. It has been busy at the farm. Is she well?'

'She is a courageous woman. Like you, my dear.' Joshua smiled fondly at his daughter. 'Do not worry yourself over your brother and his wife. It is St John who has bats in his belfry now. He wants justice for the attack on Peter and will not wait for Adam to return from Plymouth. I've told him to let the authorities deal with it. He thinks Nance is to blame, as there has been no sign of Harry Sawle for weeks.'

'To triumph over Sawle, our family must be united. St John would be foolish to try and bring him to justice alone, and so would Adam.'

'That is what I told St John. But he wants to prove that he is a better man than his twin. I fear he will do something reckless while Adam is away.'

St John wanted Mordecai Nance arrested before Felicity and her mother came to Trevowan. If the innkeeper had burned the haystacks at Boscabel to promote the rift between Adam and himself, and now had dared to strike at Peter, his family were not safe from further attack. St John wanted him behind bars before the innkeeper turned his aggression in his direction.

The previous night, Elspeth and Amelia had been appalled when he had related the story of Peter's abduction and escape.

'I thought by leaving London and coming to Cornwall I would give my children a safe environment in which to live,' Amelia complained. 'It is as dangerous as London with its footpads, highwaymen, and villains of every kind. What ungodly community abducts a preacher? And last week the poor Widow Tenkin was beaten and robbed in her own home.'

'Cornwall is not as bad as London!' Elspeth was outraged at her sister-in-law's condemnation. 'It is true the smugglers take the law into their own hands, but they do not harm those who do not trouble them.'

She regarded St John over the rim of her pince-nez. 'Our family has become embroiled in a feud with the free-traders. It is foolhardy and must end. It cost your dear father his life. And I do not forget the trouble your involvement with Sawle brought to you, nephew. Sawle would have let you hang for the death of Thadeous Lanyon when, as most of us suspect, it was he who killed him. Now Peter could have been murdered. Your grandfather never had dealings or interfered with the smugglers.'

'It was different in his day. There was no reason for us to be involved. But this is personal between Sawle, myself and Adam.'

'Then end it.' Elspeth rapped her walking cane on the floor, her lips thinned with censure. 'Concentrate on Trevowan. That is your duty.'

'It will end when Harry Sawle swings at the end of a rope.'

'Or we lose everything,' Elspeth challenged with anxious insight.

'I will not let Father's death go unavenged.' St John had thought his doughty aunt would support him. No one had condemned Adam when he had begun this feud with Harry Sawle.

He slept badly that night and rose earlier than usual to ride to inform the authorities at Fowey of Peter's ordeal and to instigate a warrant for the arrest of Mordecai Nance. It took longer than expected, with an official clerk wanting to know every minute detail before summoning a justice of the peace. St John fumed at the delay. It was unfortunate that Sir Henry Traherne was away in Truro and not expected back until next week. Nance was wily and to ensure his arrest St John needed the backing of the militia. The justice of the peace, Roland Pallant Esquire, was surly at having been dragged from his bed when he was suffering from gout. He was a man who had done little in the past to stop the outrages committed by Sawle and his gang and St John suspected that he was in the smugglers' pay. But with the evidence St John had presented about Peter's abduction, Pallant had no choice but to issue the warrant.

St John spent another hour cooling his heels in the port before the militia were ready to ride to Penruan. The officer in charge frowned at seeing that St John expected to ride with them.

'Lieutenant Tregare at your service, Mr Loveday. This is military business. It is better if we carry out our duties without civilian assistance.'

St John did not like the officer's haughty manner. 'I have no intention of assisting you. I wish to ensure that Nance is arrested and brought to trial for his crimes.'

'If he is guilty,' Lieutenant Tregare snapped. 'I am surprised your cousin did not apply for the warrant as he was the victim of this grievous attack.'

'My cousin still suffers from the ill effects of his beating and abduction. I trust you will not object if I ride with you. I can of course follow you to Penruan, but that would be absurd, would it not? We both want the guilty to be brought to trial.'

A muscle pulsated along the lieutenant's jaw, showing his annoyance. He nodded curtly to St John to join them. St John did not trust the officer. His arrogance bordered on rudeness. He was not the best judge of character, but Tregare's insolence could well cover the man's deceit. Adam had said that the militia frequently drank at the Dolphin Inn.

Were they also in Sawle's pay? Was that why Nance had been reckless enough to abduct Peter?

His suspicions increased as he noted the leisurely pace at which the troop climbed the steep road out of Fowey. They kept their horses at a trot through the country lanes. The officer was delaying his arrival in Penruan. Had he sent word to warn Nance? St John cursed Sir Henry's absence; his friend would have ensured Nance was arrested without delay.

There was an unnatural quiet to the fishing village. The fleet was not in the harbour and the salting and gutting sheds were deserted of workers. Four elderly fishermen sat on stools outside their houses smoking their pipes, their eyes hard and condemning as they settled upon St John. They did not acknowledge his presence, although two of them lived in cottages owned by him. A group of women had gathered outside Goldie's general store, their stares curious as the troop rode up to the Dolphin Inn.

At the sound of their approach, Etta strolled outside with two of her tavern wenches. The women were slatternly, in coarse brown skirts, their breasts half exposed in their open bodices and their hair matted and unrestrained.

'Well now, my lovers, if this be not a treat for us.' Etta smiled up at Lieutenant Tregare and ran her hand over one generous breast. 'A hand-some officer has come a-visiting. What can my lovely ladies be doing for you brave soldiers?' She sashayed forward and placed a hand sugges-tively upon the lieutenant's thigh. In contrast to her servants, Etta wore a high-waisted muslin dress in dark red that had been dampened to cling seductively to her ample curves.

'Where's your damned husband?' St John flared.

'What you be wanting with him?' Etta tossed back her sandy hair. 'He bain't at your beck and call no more. He be his own master.'

'Is your husband at home, Mrs Nance?' Tregare said, dismounting from his horse.

'Don't I wish he were,' she pouted. 'He's been away these last three days on business. And me left all alone to run a busy inn.' Her smile offered a bold invitation to the officer.

'I must search the inn,' Tregare clipped out. 'I have a warrant for your husband's arrest. Where is this business he is undertaking?'

Etta widened her eyes in feigned innocence. 'It could be anywhere, my handsome. A man like my Mordecai don't tell no one his comings and goings. But you be welcome to search the inn. We bain't got nothing to hide.'

'Would his business be with Harry Sawle?' St John took over the questioning.

Etta ignored him and continued to smile at Tregare. 'It could be. Sawle do own the inn.'

'Then Nance is not his own master, is he?' St John's temper got the better of him. 'The woman is lying. She is covering for him.'

'If Nance is not here, I cannot arrest him.' Lieutenant Tregare turned a chilling glare upon St John before ordering his men to search the inn.

'Won't you come inside and take a sup of ale, Lieutenant,' Etta invited, smoothing her hands over her hips.

'I'm sure the lieutenant would enjoy a glass of your fine French brandy,' St John suggested.

Etta flung back her head, her eyes narrowing as she regarded St John. 'We may have a bottle left. But what with the war with France and the high taxes on such a luxury, a humble inn like ourselves don't get much call for brandy.'

St John was furious that Nance had escaped them, and from the smug expression on the officer's face it was he who had warned the innkeeper of their arrival. Etta was also smirking, thinking she had outwitted him.

St John smiled at her, saying casually, 'Lieutenant Tregare, if your men go into the cellar, the hatch of which is behind the bar, they will discover a false wall at the far end. There you will find your brandy.'

Etta paled. 'I don't know what he be talking of. There bain't no false wall.'

'Then the soldiers will find out.'

The officer darted a glance at Etta before saying tersely to two soldiers who had remained outside whilst the others searched, 'Go to the cellar.'

Etta twirled a finger through a lock of her hair, betraying her nervousness. St John guessed there was something else she was hiding. 'Your men had better inspect the secret chamber closely; they may find more than brandy.'

A few minutes later a sergeant came out grinning. 'There be a dozen kegs full of brandy, Lieutenant.'

'I know nothing about them.' Etta pressed her hands together, her stare pleading as she regarded the officer.

He sighed. 'The contraband will be confiscated by my men.'

'Did you search the room thoroughly, Sergeant?' St John persisted.

The soldier shrugged. 'The brandy be condemning. There bain't been no duty paid on it.'

'I would like to know that the chamber has been thoroughly searched in case there is other incriminating evidence.' St John had been watching

Etta closely and she had begun to cast around her in panic as though looking for a way to escape. He reached down and tweaked a gold chain around her neck. A cross with a garnet at its centre flipped out from inside her bodice. Etta gasped and closed her hand over it.

'Such a cross was reported missing during the robberies that were blamed on the gypsies. It belonged to the blacksmith's wife at Trewenna.'

'I've had it for years. It be a common design.' Etta backed away from him.

'Not so common. And where would an innkeeper's wife get such a valuable piece of jewellery?'

'From an admirer who knows how to treat a woman right,' she blustered.

The sergeant returned from his further inspection of the inn carrying a small sack. 'There are trinkets and some valuable household items in here.' He handed the sack to Lieutenant Tregare, who opened it.

'These are not objects you would keep so carelessly. There is a snuffbox, several trinkets, a small silver dish and some brassware.' He glared at Etta. 'I shall have to take you in for questioning.'

'No!' Etta screamed. 'I'm just a chivvy here. I have no dealings with Sawle. I've done nothing wrong.'

'You run a house of ill repute and have goods in your home that have been brought illicitly to our shores. You are guilty by association if nothing else,' St John crowed in triumph.

'Get your cloak, Mrs Nance,' Lieutenant Tregare ordered. 'I have no choice but to take you to Fowey to answer to the authorities.'

St John was satisfied with the turn of events. But he had no intention of allowing the justice of the peace who had served the warrant for Nance's arrest to be involved in Etta's questioning. With Sir Henry Traherne away, he rode to Squire Penwithick to insist that he interrogate her. Penwithick had recently retired from court, where for many years he had organised a band of spies in the early days of the French Revolution. Sir Gregory Kilmarthen had been one such man, and before his marriage so had Adam. The squire would ensure that the woman was locked up and put under close guard so that there was no chance of her escape. That would show Nance that he could not mess with the Lovedays.

Squire Penwithick looked more appalled than delighted when St John informed him of the morning's events. They were in the stables of the manor house where the squire had been inspecting a two-month-old foal that was sick. The attendant grooms had been dismissed when

Penwithick saw St John's high colour and agitation. He cautioned him to speak in a low voice.

When he had finished telling his tale, Penwithick shook his head. 'Were your actions wise, St John? We have all turned a blind eye to the free-traders, to the extent that many of us ignored your own involvement with Sawle. I was once given evidence that you were involved but out of respect for your father naturally did not follow it up. Now questions will be asked as to how you knew of the secret room at the Dolphin Inn.'

St John did not meet the older man's eye. He was ashamed now of his hunger for money that had driven him into partnership with his wife's brother. He had blamed Meriel and her greed for his fall from grace, but he had wanted the profits from the trade to support his gambling when his father had refused to pay any more of his debts. The accusation made him defiant.

'Meriel told me of the room. I kept quiet in the past because her father's arrest would dredge up the old scandal of my unsuitable marriage.'

'It is a dangerous card you have played. The Dolphin will be closed. Sawle of course will deny any knowledge of Nance's dealings in contraband. Since Sawle no longer lives at the inn, there is no evidence against him. And Nance has yet to be found.'

'Was I supposed to let him get away with what he did to Peter?'

'Sometimes caution is the better part of valour.' Penwithick's wide brow creased with concern and he rubbed his grey side-whiskers. 'We could have gathered more evidence. I doubt this woman knows much. Even Nance is small fry, but he knows Sawle's whereabouts and could have been followed. It is too late for that now. He'll not go near the Dolphin now that his wife has been arrested. Sawle will not let this go unavenged. And he is capable of striking without warning.'

'I suppose you think I should have left it to Adam?' St John was bristling with indignation. 'They attacked a member of my family and those robberies were meant to stir up trouble for us.'

'You must be extra vigilant now. I will do what I can. And how will your bailiff feel now that you have had his nephew's wife arrested?'

'Isaac Nance is loyal to me.'

'Most men put family before their employer.'

'Not Isaac. He knows Mordecai is a troublemaker.'

'And that is what I fear.' Squire Penwithick regarded him gravely. 'If Mordecai Nance goes to ground, we have no idea where to look for him. At least at the Dolphin he could be discreetly watched.'

'He will not abandon his wife. Have a watch put on her and Nance will be caught.'

'I hope you are right, my friend. Mordecai Nance is as dangerous as Sawle. I would not want him as my enemy.'

Chapter Thirty-eight

When St John returned to Trevowan, the maid, Jenna Biddick, informed him that Mrs Barrett and Mrs Quinton had arrived two hours ago and were with Mrs Loveday at the Dower House. St John took the steps of the curving staircase two at a time and hurriedly changed his coat and riding breeches, cursing as he struggled to remove his tight-fitting boots. He really needed a valet to attend upon his needs, but the servants had been cut to the minimum to save on the running expenses of Trevowan.

He surveyed his image in his dressing mirror. His emerald and gold waistcoat flattered his slightly thickened figure and the moleskin trousers and tan cutaway coat were the latest fashion. He ran a brush through his short hair and prided himself that he dressed and acted every inch a gentleman, unlike his twin, who could pass for a pirate with his long hair. He nodded in satisfaction to his reflection. Felicity would be impressed.

He left the house and strode towards the Dower House in a jubilant mood. That Felicity had returned could only mean that she was interested in him as a suitor. In the paddock he heard girlish laughter and smiled at seeing Rowena and Charlotte on their ponies with Aunt Elspeth leaning on her walking cane giving them instruction. Elspeth clapped when Rowena successfully jumped a low fence. His aunt was at her happiest with horses and she took pride in encouraging others. She had been the same with Adam and himself when they were children.

As he crossed the lawn he saw Felicity walking alone, a silk parasol protecting her fair complexion from the sun. She turned into the walled garden without noticing him. Following her, he found her standing in the centre of the path gazing up at the statue of the huntress Diana. St John paused to pick a white rose from a bush that trailed across the wall and presented it to her.

'A perfect rose for a perfect woman.'

'St John, you startled me.' She took the flower and laughed. 'I was lost in thought.'

'A pleasant one, I trust.' He raised the hand holding the rose to his lips. 'Your beauty brightens my home. Did you enjoy your visit to Bodmin and your reunion with your friend?'

'Bodmin was informative.' Her lovely face was shadowed with concern and her eyes regarded him with a wariness he found disconcerting.

Uncomfortable that she might have learned of his gaming and the money he had lost, he stretched his smile wider. 'Bodmin is always a hive of activity. The post chaise from London brings gossip from afar. You must have had much news to catch up on with your friends.'

Felicity moved away from him to sit on a stone bench. 'Trevowan is very peaceful after the noise of a busy town. This rose garden is beautiful. Mama can be tiring at times with her incessant chatter. I came here to gather my thoughts.' She held the rose to her nose to smell, but her mood seemed preoccupied.

It was rare to find time alone at Trevowan, and usually Felicity was followed everywhere by her mother.

'It pleases me that you have made this second visit to my home.' St John sat beside her, but she kept her head bowed and twirled her parasol in an abstracted manner. 'Dare I hope that it is because I have found some favour in your eyes?'

'I thought you had changed since last we met. In Bodmin I was proved wrong. Is it true you lost a great deal of money at the gaming tables?'

'I spent a night at cards to pass the time, but my losses were inconsequential.' The lie rolled easily off his tongue.

'So you did not have to visit a moneylender to pay your gaming debts?'

'Where did you get such a notion?' He was indignant.

'You know I deplore gambling. I thought you cared enough for me to change. Clearly not.' Her voice was cold and her fingers were holding the parasol in a tight grip.

'But my dear, you know that I adore you.'

'Pray do not dissemble. It only contributes to your further detriment. A friend saw you coming out of Harold Foxe's establishment. The man is notorious for his high interest rates. The talk of the town was of a gaming session at your inn where you lost three hundred and twenty pounds. An amount I would not consider inconsequential.'

St John flinched at her scathing tone. He resented being judged so arbitrarily, and it made him defensive. 'I am pained that you take the word of common gossip against my own. I had thought you more worthy, Felicity.'

She had the grace to blush and he continued in an injured tone. 'Yes, I gambled. Yes, I visited the objectionable Foxe, but that was to repay a final instalment on a previous loan that had been taken out by my father.' He whipped up his indignation at having been spied upon and again twisted the truth. 'Papa needed to raise ransom money when Adam was captured by the French, and took a mortgage on the estate. Last year the harvest failed and I had to extend the loan.'

'Amelia said there were no outstanding loans on the estate.' Felicity snapped shut her parasol and regarded him with tight-lipped displeasure.

'The year before my father's death was a difficult time for the family. Amelia spent some time in London and my father would not have wished to distress her further with financial worries. But I see I have been judged and condemned in your eyes.' He stood up. 'I shall leave you to your contemplation and trust your mood is more conducive when we dine this evening.'

He bowed curtly and turned to leave.

'St John, I ask your pardon. The gossip upset me.'

'Are my financial dealings of concern to you, madam?' He allowed his resentment at her censure to sharpen his voice.

Her colour deepened to poppy-red as it spread from her cheeks down her neck. It had nothing to do with the August heat. She hung her head. 'I have presumed too much upon our acquaintance after my visit here. Especially when you invited me to return. I thought it meant we had a special understanding . . .'

She broke off, clearly flustered. Her lower lip was trembling and she looked very beautiful and vulnerable. Her voice shook and she did not meet his eye as she continued in little more than a whisper, 'You know the unhappiness my marriage to Captain Barrett brought me. He was often drunk and abusive. My father gambled to excess and we had lost three-quarters of our property before he died. It caused Mama and me much heartache and no little suffering. That is why I abhor gambling.'

'I would never risk Trevowan or the comfort of my loved ones.'

'Mayhap not, but gambling and drinking are the bane of decent society. It is all too common to hear of a young blood losing everything in the madness that possesses him upon the turn of a card or the throw of the dice.'

'Do you think me capable of that?' St John was shocked. He had never considered his wastrel ways as lunacy. They were but pastimes. He could give them up when he wanted.

'You are a good man, St John.' Her eyes remained veiled by her lashes. 'Your family is much revered. But there is a wildness in your blood.'

They were dancing around the real reason for her concern. Felicity suspected that she had been invited here for him to propose and was trying to be truthful without appearing too forward. St John went down on one knee and took her hand. He was convinced that she was attracted to him and just needed reassurance. 'Only a blackguard would put the happiness of his loved ones at risk. I have lived recklessly in the past. My first wife encouraged it. I was young then and had no real responsibilities. I am master of Trevowan now. My home and family have my first loyalty.'

'Your family is drawn to adventure.' She lifted her head to study him and there was uncertainty in her eyes. 'Japhet was not entirely innocent or he would not have been arrested. Adam almost lost his life at sea when the French captured his ship. And now there is this new talk of Peter being assaulted and abducted. That would not be without cause, yet Peter is a parson and the most restrained of all your generation.'

'Then I will not insult you by repeating my proposal of marriage.' He withdrew his hand from hers, his manner stiff with affront.

She looked stricken and her eyes glistened with tears. He did not understand her. Surely if she cared that much, she would marry him? He swallowed his wounded pride, and the gambler in him took his chance. If he walked away now, he might lose her for good.

'My dearest Felicity, you cannot doubt my love and undying devotion. You will be a worthy mistress of Trevowan. I have put the recklessness of my past behind me. I will do everything in my power to be worthy of you and your love. Make me the happiest of men, fairest of women. Will you marry me?'

A long pause stretched between them before she replied, 'May I give you my answer tomorrow?'

He could not believe her hesitation. He had humbled himself to her. He rose and bowed with dignified grace. 'We may have wildness in our blood, but we are not afraid to live, Felicity.'

St John briefly visited the Dower House to greet Sophia Quinton, then excused himself to attend upon estate business. He was angry at Felicity and felt she was playing him for a fool, but her wealth was still important to him. To cool down he walked across the fields to where Isaac Nance had set some men to mend the roof of a cow byre. Paul Tonkin and Ned Holman helped them. Both the Tonkin and Holman families lived in tied cottages. The men nodded curtly to him and St John sensed frostiness in their manner. They would have heard by now that Etta had been arrested, perhaps even that he had been with the militia at Penruan.

He did not like dissension amongst his servants. 'Isaac, I am sorry that your nephew has become so embroiled with Sawle.'

'He be his own man,' Nance replied with a shrug. 'He were lucky to get work at the inn.'

Dick Nance was less phlegmatic than his father. 'They found not only contraband there, but many items that were stolen on the day of Miss Loveday's marriage.'

St John felt obliged to explain. 'People were quick to point a finger at the gypsies. It seems they were innocent. Etta was brazenly wearing a gold cross that had been stolen.'

'We were not told that,' Dick said, less sullenly. 'I don't hold with no stealing from our own kind. That wife of his is a bad 'un.'

'She was clearly implicated,' St John said. 'A sorry business. The posses-sion of stolen goods is a hanging offence whether she stole them herself or not. Mordecai has much to answer for. There is a warrant out for his arrest. It is your duty to inform the authorities if you hear from him. I will not have him on my land.'

Isaac did not answer. He was a decent man and must feel the shame of his nephew's crimes. St John studied the men's work. 'You have made a good job of that roof. Well done.'

As Felicity watched St John stride across the fields, she felt the need to confide in someone. Her mother was no help; she was too eager for the match. She found her coachman chatting in the stables to Jasper Fraddon.

'Gibson, I need the coach as soon as it is ready. I shall be visiting Rabson Farm.'

Half an hour later she was seated in Hannah's parlour, pouring out her feelings to her.

'It is of course an honour that St John has asked for my hand, but I am in such turmoil. Do you think I can trust your cousin to stand by his word that he will give up his gaming and drinking?'

'Why should you doubt him? A gentleman keeps his word.' Hannah thought her friend was being unnecessarily pedantic. 'Do you love him?'

Felicity fiddled with the lace on her cuff. 'Does not love blind us? He has a certain reputation that I am not sure I approve of.'

'Then I am not the right person for you to discuss this matter with, Felicity.'

'But you know St John better than most.'

'I am first and foremost loyal to my family. St John is master of Trevowan. He has many responsibilities, all of which he takes seriously.'

'But it is rumoured that there is a rift between him and Adam.'

'It is nothing more than sibling rivalry. There is nothing either St John or Adam would not do for the other if they were in trouble.'

Felicity did not look convinced. 'I am not brave like you, Hannah. I fear to let my heart rule my head. Captain Barrett was a womaniser and a drunkard. I was miserable in my marriage. I would not risk making the same mistake again.'

'Then you will marry the man you deserve.' Hannah lost patience. 'My Loveday kin are no saints. I cannot say that St John will be true to you or never gamble again, but he will honour you above all women. Each member of our family will take you into their hearts and cherish you. You are the perfect wife for him.'

'But is he the right husband for me?' Felicity rubbed her brow as though it pained her. 'I always admired your courage and your love of life. Nothing lowers your spirit. You have run this farm as well as any man. Your children are carefree, happy and well provided for.'

'You see the mask I present to the world. I mourn Oswald with every breath I take. My life is empty without him. But the children do not need a mother who mopes. Their lives must be as normal as possible.'

Felicity took her hand and squeezed it. 'I am sorry. I did not mean to sound callous. It is just that you cope so well. I need security – a marriage to someone I can trust. And to be certain he is marrying me for love and not for my money.'

'A disposable fortune can be a curse as well as a blessing for a woman,' Hannah commiserated. Felicity had always been rather too prim and proper for her to be truly close to her as a friend in the past. Hannah had been frivolous before her marriage and perhaps too trusting. Felicity had worn her heart on her sleeve, showing her preference for St John in the months before he had fallen disastrously in love with Meriel. His hasty wedding must have hurt her deeply, and if her own marriage had not been happy, Hannah could understand why she was now cautious. Felicity would be a good influence on her cousin; she was the bride he needed. She did her best to reassure her friend. 'St John married his first wife for love. She certainly brought nothing of wealth to the marriage. Does that not say much of him?'

'There were rumours that it was a shotgun wedding. It was very sudden. And Rowena was born eight months after they wed.'

'You listen to too much gossip, Felicity. A gentleman does not marry his doxy if she is with child. St John loved Meriel.'

Felicity hung her head and took some moments to collect her thoughts before answering. 'Meriel Sawle was beautiful and vivacious. And despite her lowly station she was not reputed to be a woman of easy virtue before her marriage. She had no time for the men of her village. Though perhaps she aimed higher than them. There was a time when I thought her eye was upon Adam before he returned to his naval duties.' She sighed. 'Many men would have desired her. I am so different from her. I prefer a homely life, not the constant attendance at balls and enter-tainments.'

'St John came to hate Meriel for her greed. She betrayed him callously. You are the wife he needs. The wife who can make him happy.'

Felicity nodded. 'I wrong an honourable man. St John was with the militia when they searched the inn at Penruan. They found the trin-kets taken on the day Tamasine married. The woman at the inn was arrested, but there was no sign of her husband.'

'I have heard nothing of this.' Hannah was concerned that St John had somehow stirred up a hornets' nest by accompanying the militia to the Dolphin.

'They found a quantity of brandy in a secret room as well as the stolen property. It was so brave of St John to help to bring those villains to justice.'

Brave or foolhardy? Hannah wondered, but she kept her opinion to herself.

Felicity stood up. 'I have taken so much of your time and I came uninvited.'

'You are always welcome.' Hannah walked with her to the coach. 'St John is no worse than many of his friends. He was never unfaithful to Meriel until she betrayed him. She led him a merry dance. I think drink helped him to forget.'

'Thank you, Hannah.' Felicity waved out of the window as the coach sped away. Her mind was still undecided. She wanted to follow her heart, but would it bring her happiness or sorrow?

Hannah hoped that Felicity would accept St John's proposal. She was about to return to the farmhouse when a well-dressed man talking to Sam outside his cottage caught her attention. Their exchange looked heated. Worried that it was some repercussion that had occurred after St John's intervention and the arrest of Etta Nance, she walked towards them. Sam's back was to her. After a further angry exchange of words he walked away from his companion. There was something disturbing about the meeting and Hannah drew back behind the farm cart to conceal herself as Sam strode towards the field where he had been working.

The man he had been arguing with walked to the farm drive, where he had tied his horse to a hitching post. Hannah stepped out to waylay him.

'I am Mrs Rabson. This is my farm. Can I be of assistance to you?'

The stranger was well dressed and his thin face was pinched with anger. 'You can tell Samuel Deighton to come to his senses.'

'You mean Sam Deacon. That is the name of my overseer.'

'He's Deighton. I should know, I worked for his family long enough.' He touched the brim of his hat in the briefest of salutations and hoisted himself into the saddle. 'He can't hide from his responsibilities for ever. His uncle is not a man to be kept waiting.'

With those ominous words he cantered away, leaving Hannah stunned.

Senara had hoped that Adam would return from Plymouth before the workers arrived to cut the hay and harvest the field of wheat. Before he had left they had spoken of the work to be done if he was delayed, which Adam had feared could be the case. He had been away two weeks and the workers had arrived a day earlier than expected. They were bedded down in the barn and would start cutting the wheat tomorrow. Eli Rudge took charge of the migrant workers and Billy Brown concentrated on the livestock and spent what spare time he could working with his wife in the fields. Senara had faith in her servants and that there would be no problems with the harvest.

The next morning she was delighted when Bridie, Leah and Peter arrived. Her sister and mother were determined to help her prepare the midday meal for the workers and Peter announced that he intended to work in the fields. She had been surprised to see him dressed in old leather breeches and a shirt instead of his black parson's attire. He had allowed his dark hair to grow longer and it had a natural curl that softened the lines of his face. He had also not shaved his side-whiskers since his abduction and he looked much more like his dashing brother now.

'Are you recovered enough from your ordeal?' Senara was concerned for her brother-in-law.

'I am well enough. The swelling from the bruising has gone down, and apart from some stiffness I will show those who would seek to bring us down that the Lovedays are tougher than they think. My recovery is a tribute to your healing skills, cousin-cum-sister-in-law,' he teased. 'Adam would do as much for me.'

This was a side of Peter she had not met before, and she now understood that Bridie had seen beyond his zealous preaching to the humane man beneath. Before the beating there had been an offputting arrogance about Peter that was now replaced by self-assurance. He had after all survived death by his own wits and resilience. She knew Peter had felt overshadowed by the courage and aptitude of his brother and of Adam and had even resented that as the youngest male of his generation he was considered the weakest of the family. His ordeal with the smugglers had proved them all wrong.

'This harvest is important to Adam. Your help is much appreciated, Peter.'

'It is my pleasure. I have also promised Hannah I shall help her when they begin harvesting in four days.' He strode out of the kitchen and there was a swagger to his step.

'My, my.' Senara winked at her sister. 'How your man has changed.'

Bridie grinned. She was standing over the infant Sara, who had fallen asleep on the wooden settle, her cheeks red with two bright spots of colour from teething. 'He is less reserved and more compassionate toward his parishioners. He was genuinely touched by how many of them called at the parsonage with good wishes for his recovery.'

Leah sniffed. 'I always thought that for a Loveday he had too much starch in his undergarments.'

'Ma!' Bridie blushed.

'And how are you keeping, dear sister?' Senara asked. Bridie looked pale and there were dark rings under her eyes. 'You have suffered no spasms, and does the child move regularly?'

'The baby is so active, it will not let me sleep of a night. And Peter insists that I rest for an hour in the morning and again in the afternoon as you advised.'

'Though it takes quite a bit of persuading to make her take her rest,' Leah intervened. She had taken off her straw bonnet ready to begin work in the kitchen. 'She will not spend less time with the lace-making or cut down on her parish duties. She was in Launceston with Maura Keppel yesterday selling some of the lesser-quality lace in the market. Even though the patterns were not perfect, it still fetched a good price. Even Gert Wibbley did not complain.'

'Then you will sit by the range and rest now, Bridie, and if you must do something you can shell peas. Ma and I will prepare the food for the workers. The servants are tending to the livestock and the older children have been taken to play in the orchard out of the way of the workers.'

'And how have you been, daughter?' Leah had filled a kettle from the water bucket by the sink and placed it on the range to boil for tea. 'I see Adam has not returned.'

'The commission for the new revenue cutter is important for the yard. He must stay in Plymouth for as long as it takes to get an answer from them.'

'And what will he make of all that has passed this last week?' Leah continued. 'His brother has put the cat amongst the pigeons by charging down to the Dolphin as he did and getting Etta arrested. There's been no sign of her no-good husband since then. Sawle won't be best pleased. It were bad enough what his men did to Peter, but it won't stop there, you mark my words. You make sure you lock your door of a night, daughter.'

'I am surrounded by servants and the barn is full of field hands. No one will harm us.'

'It don't do no harm to take more care.' Leah nodded sagely.

Senara did not need her mother to remind her. She had been ill at ease since Peter had been attacked. That the smugglers had dared to strike at him in such a manner meant that they were becoming more dangerous to the whole community. She thought that St John had been foolhardy not to wait until Adam returned before acting against Sawle's henchman. But as usual he had been bent on proving himself a better man than his twin. And when had that ever resolved a matter satisfactorily? Certainly Adam would not view his brother's actions favourably and St John would resent any recrimination. She had hoped that family loyalty in this crisis had brought an end to the twins' rivalry, but as St John's rashness had caused Sawle to flee the district without being brought to justice for attacking Peter, then the rivalry would be even more intense than before.

Chapter Thirty-nine

For a moment Hannah thought the stranger must have been mistaken about Sam and that that was why they had been arguing. But the man had said he worked for Sam's family and would not have made such an error. She had placed so much trust in Sam, and to learn that he had lied to her over such a fundamental issue made her realise that she did not know him at all. And what was it the stranger had said about Sam hiding from his responsibilities? That did not fit with what she knew of him.

There were shouts from the children playing behind the farmhouse and she saw Charlie and Davey climbing the tree. Charlie was high in the branches for one so young and Hannah worried he would fall.

'Come down, Charlie, you are too high. Davey, do not encourage him,' she called to them.

Davey and Charlie waved to her and climbed down. Charlie was a plucky little chap and would match Davey in any dare. He was a loving child and adored Sam. Hannah had thought it commendable of her overseer that he had chosen to raise his sister's bastard child. Sam had told her that when his father had refused to acknowledge Charlie, he had walked out and not spoken to his father since. Did he hate him so much he would not even use his family name?

Or was it that he wished to keep his true identity secret? Again she realised how little she knew him. That both angered her and left her disillusioned. It wounded her that he did not trust her enough to tell her the whole truth. Sam was working with Mark Sawle mending the gate on the far side of the hayfield. She watched him with a growing pain in her heart. Even from this distance she could see the tension in his body as he sawed through a thick piece of wood. When he raised his voice to upbraid Mark for not holding the post steady, it was so unlike Sam she knew the stranger's visit had disturbed him. It made her own anger flare.

She needed men she could trust. If only Japhet were here. She had always turned to him for advice. The weight of her responsibilities for the farm and raising four children threatened to crush her. Peter's abduction had shown her how vulnerable anyone could be. Although Peter decried violence because he saw it as against the Lord's teachings, he had brawled with Japhet and his cousins when he was younger. He could handle himself in a fight and was certainly no coward. But if Peter could be overpowered, what chance did she have? She had been lucky so far in outwitting Sawle. But she had challenged him too often to feel safe.

She continued to watch Sam and Mark. At least with Mark she knew his background. Harry Sawle had frequently beaten his younger brother, but Mark had refused to work for him. Hannah respected him for that, which was why she had offered him employment.

She did not doubt that Sam would defend her against Sawle, but what if his responsibilities, that had been referred to in such emphatic terms by the stranger, took him away? She had come to rely on him and that possibility frightened her. She pressed a hand to her temple. She had been foolish to place her trust in a servant. Yet she had begun to regard Sam as more of a friend than a servant. That was why his deception over his name had affected her so forcefully.

Hannah despised weakness, especially within herself. Pride had made her refuse Adam's frequent offers of help. She had been stubbornly determined to run the farm alone after Oswald's death, but she had not been truly on her own. Sam had always been in the background, stalwart and protecting.

Another spate of angry words between Sam and Mark again showed her that Sam was affected by the visit from the stranger. Several whoops of joy from the children running across a field drew her attention. Little Luke was trailing behind on his short legs but he was determined to follow his siblings.

'Charlie, don't go too far,' Sam shouted.

He had never stopped the boy running wild before. Hannah marched towards her overseer. Both men were stooped over the gate, hammering the final wooden bar into place. 'Mark, there are some supplies I need from the kiddley at Trevowan Hard. Please hitch up the wagon and I will give you a list for Pru Jensen.'

'I thought we were collecting the supplies tomorrow,' Sam observed as Mark walked to the stables.

'I wanted Mark out of the way so that we can talk.'

He swung the gate shut before answering her. His expression was guarded. 'What do you wish to discuss?'

284

'The man you were speaking with earlier. Who was he?'

'No one important.'

'Yet he works for your family.'

'Is that what he told you?' It was as though a wall had been erected between them. Sam's eyes hardened. 'It has nothing to do with you, Hannah.'

'Does it not! Should I not be concerned that a friend is not who he has made himself out to be? He said your name was Deighton.'

'I prefer Deacon.'

Her temper erupted. 'And I prefer that you are honest with me. What are you hiding from that you have changed your name?'

He held the large hammer in his hand, his knuckles white around the handle, and stared across the fields to where the children were playing. His back was straight and his broad shoulders were squared. He had the commanding bearing of an officer though without the arrogance.

'You are not a man to hide from anything,' she amended, 'so why the mystery?'

'To protect Charlie. There is no mystery. My family are dead to me. I told you about Charlie and my sister. The rest is no one's concern but my own.'

The rebuke was like a slap. Her cheeks flamed with colour and anger flashed in her eyes. 'Forgive me for worrying that a friend was in trouble. Just make sure your past business does not affect your work here.'

She spun on her heel and strode away. To add to her fury, tears blinded her vision and she stumbled in the calf-high grass. A firm hand on her elbow steadied her. 'Your pardon, Hannah, I did not mean to upset you.'

'I am not upset.' She shook off his hand. 'I dislike deceit. I thought we were friends.' She drew a sharp breath to control her breathing and dashed the tears from her cheeks. 'This business over Peter has overset me more than I thought.'

Although she did not turn to look at him, she could feel his breath on her cheek. His voice was husky. 'Captain Charles Samuel Deighton at your service, dear lady. Formerly of the King's Own Hussars. Formerly of Merle Place on the eastern banks of the River Tamar. Formerly the third son of Sir Hugo and Lady Isabella Deighton.'

The day was sunny and warm and Hannah sank down on to the long grass and beckoned Sam to join her. 'Thank you for that, Sam. Your visitor made you angry. As a friend I was concerned. Did he bring disturbing news? Or is it none of my business?'

'You take your friendships seriously.' He sat with one arm resting on his knee and studied her for a long moment, 'You have accepted Charlie and allowed him to play with your own children. You did not condemn his birth as many would. Charlie has lived a good life here. It is what he needs. What he deserves.'

'You have been a good father to him, even though he is your sister's child and not your own.'

He shrugged. 'The family want to see Charlie, or rather his paternal grandfather does. I will not permit it. The man showed no compassion to my sister when his son cast her aside. Now he says he is blood. As I killed his son in a duel – his only child – he wishes to adopt Charlie and make him his heir. The man who came today is our family lawyer. He said I have no rights to Charlie. That his grandfather is his legal guardian. I will not allow them to take him. They will destroy all that is good in him. Uncle Robert was at my mother's funeral. He did not even appear to notice Charlie at the time.'

'So why his interest now?'

'Uncle Robert and my father have a mutual loathing for each other.' He gave an ironic laugh. 'You have despaired over St John's rivalry and resentment with Adam, but it is nothing compared with my father's hatred for his brother. Robert is the elder and inherited the family home. My father became an officer and married my mother, whose dowry was Merle. He received a head wound at Lexington when we lost the old colony of America. He may have survived, but each year he becomes more entrenched in old feuds and resentments. He saw my sister's love for my cousin as the ultimate betrayal.'

'And was your Uncle Robert the same?'

'If it is possible, he was worse. But he adored my mother, who had grown up with them as my grandfather's ward. Her funeral was the first time they had been in the same place for twenty years.'

Hannah's heart went out to Sam. It made her realise the importance of family loyalty, which had kept her family close despite their rifts and rivalries. She was puzzled by the complexity of the feud and sensed that Sam had told her only part of his background.

'The estate is entailed and Uncle Robert does not want my father to inherit,' Sam further explained. 'Charlie is of his son's flesh and blood and would therefore be next in line if he was legitimate. I do not want him used that way.'

'What can you do if they have right on their side?'

'Disappear as I have done in the past. There is no other way.'

The enormity of his words seared her like a branding iron. 'Then you will leave here and I shall never see you again?'

He did not look at her, continuing to stare into the far distance. His handsome face was taut with tension and his voice thick with suppressed emotion when he answered. 'I must go far away. Charlie is young and my uncle is arrogant enough to think I will abide by his request to spite my father. I may not be on speaking terms with him, but I would never be disloyal. Father, then my brother Richard, are the rightful heirs to my uncle's estate.'

The sun had gone behind a cloud and Hannah shivered. She did not know why her feelings were in such turmoil. Sam was a friend, nothing more. She still mourned Oswald with an acute intensity. But to lose Sam as well was almost too much to bear.

'What kind of life will it be for Charlie? He will make friends only to lose them because you feel you have to move on. Is it not better to fight your uncle in the courts?'

'He is a powerful man who has powerful friends.'

Hannah chewed her lip, uncertain how to word her thoughts so as not to antagonise Sam. 'What about your father? Has he influence and position?'

'He wants nothing to do with Charlie. And I would not want him to.' Sam dismissed her statement with suppressed anger in his voice.

'But how would he feel if he knew his brother wanted him?'

Sam jumped to his feet, his anger simmering, and stared down at her. 'I would not allow Charlie to be bartered in such a fashion.'

'Sit down, Sam, and listen.' She held out a hand to draw him down to her side. 'Our family upholds loyalty to each other. Uncle Edward often said, "Without loyalty we can be broken. United we will triumph." It healed many a rift during a family crisis. Show your father that loyalty to him and to your sister is your family strength. Charlie deserves to know his grandfather and his heritage.'

'You do not know what you are asking. My family is not as yours. They will tear each other apart.'

'And would your mother, or your sister, have wanted Charlie to grow up not knowing his ancestry? Sam, it is noble of you to sacrifice your life to bring him up, but it need not be a sacrifice. I am not saying the battle will be easy, or that I am right. But is it not worth a try?'

He knelt for a long time with his head bowed. She could feel the tension emanating from him. This was the hardest decision he would make in his life. When he spoke, his voiced was cracked with pain. 'I could never give up Charlie. He has become my son.'

'Then he is worth fighting for. I know you will succeed.' She came up on to her knees and placed both hands on his cheeks. 'You have proved you are the best father a son could have. You did not forget your loyalty to your sister. She was young, and foolishly fell in love with a blackguard. You will right the wrong done to her by triumphing over your uncle.'

His stare held hers. 'I know my father. He may fight his brother over this, but he will not accept my sister's bastard into his home.'

She wanted to tell him that there would always be a home here for Charlie and himself. But once Sam no longer had to keep his identity secret, he could build a better life for them both. He would call no man master.

'This has come at a bad time for you, Hannah. How can I leave you when Sawle is such a danger to your family?'

'Sawle will not beat us.'

Their gazes locked. There was such tenderness in Sam's eyes that Hannah felt her breath stop in her throat. Her blood was rushing through her veins. She did not want him to leave. She would miss him, ache for him to hold her as Oswald had held her. The passion in her Loveday blood had been long denied and her desire for him was suddenly all-consuming. His hands were on her shoulders, drawing her to him, and his mouth crushed her lips. She clung to him, returning his kisses with an ardour that was devastating in its magnitude.

The sound of Abigail and Florence singing a nursery rhyme brought her back to her senses with a jolt. How could she have so betrayed her love for Oswald? She pulled away and rose on trembling legs to shake out her skirts.

'I am sorry, Sam. That was madness. I am not ready to . . .'

He regarded her with sadness darkening his eyes. 'It was not madness, it was inevitable. It is as well I am leaving. You need time to continue your grieving for your husband and I have an uncertain future ahead of me. Charlie and I will leave at the end of the week. The harvest will be finished by then.'

He strode through the field, head held high and shoulders straight and proud. Hannah put out a hand to stop him but snatched it back. She had no right to delay him. Guilt and grief weighted her heart as she stared around the farm and remembered the plans she and Oswald had made when they married. When her gaze settled once more upon Sam, she knew she would never meet the likes of such a remarkable man again.

After a sleepless night Felicity still had not made her decision. She was frightened of being hurt again. She loved St John but she did not trust him. Once a gambler and wastrel, always a gambler and wastrel were the words that kept running through her mind. To delay her meeting with him as long as possible, she had her maid re-dress her hair twice, and spent another half-hour deciding what gown to wear. It was long past the time to break her fast and she had ordered her maid to bring her a drink of chocolate rather than eat in the dining room with her mother and St John.

She then called for her jewellery casket and tried on all her earrings, necklaces and bracelets, unable to settle on a choice.

'Felicity, why are you such a slugabed?' Her mother paraded into her chamber dressed in a flamboyant gown of pink and green silk. 'St John has been awaiting you in the orangery and now he has been called away to tend to a problem at one of the tenant farms.'

Felicity breathed a sigh of relief. 'I slept poorly, Mama.'

Sophia pouted and regarded her daughter with irritation. 'You are prevaricating, child. I know your ways. Has he proposed?'

Felicity pulled her earrings from her ears and searched for a simpler design. Sophia slapped her hand away from the trinket casket. 'He has proposed, hasn't he? And you have yet to give him an answer.'

'Mama, I do not know what to do. I was so sure he had changed on our first visit here. Then there was the gossip in Bodmin. He told me it was all exaggerated and he had not recklessly gambled away so much money. But . . .'

'No buts, child. St John is a fine catch. He can give you a life far grander than you have had before. He has important and influential friends. This beautiful house . . .' Sophia spread her hands. 'What is there not to decide upon? He is handsome and well mannered. You try my patience, daughter!'

'It is not that simple for me.' She resented her mother's interference. Sophia had been eager for her to choose Captain Barrett as a husband and she had finally given in to her pressure and been miserable for years.

'He adores you. Is that not enough?' Sophia persisted.

Felicity stared at her reflection in the mirror. 'I do love St John. There is something about the Loveday men that is irresistible. But will he make me happy?'

'Come with me.' Sophia took her arm and guided her along the upper corridor. They paused by a window overlooking the cliff. The sea was the colour of a kingfisher and threw up white spray as it crashed on to the black rocks of the cove. From the window they could see the church at Penruan and some of the houses on the higher reaches of the coombe. 'Daughter, all the land between here and Penruan is Loveday land.'

Sophia pushed open several doors, showing furniture draped in dust sheets. 'There must be a dozen bedrooms. Think of the house guests you can entertain.' They walked down the curving staircase to the entrance hall with its black and white marble floor and she gestured to the open doors of the oak-panelled dining room, the morning room, music room, drawing room, winter parlour and orangery. 'Look at this house. It is beautiful and Amelia has made some changes, but it is in need of a woman's loving touch. When Amelia was mistress here, the Lovedays were recovering from a financial crisis caused when they lost heavily on bad investments. They escaped ruin and some of Amelia's money was used to support the shipyard. Not much was spent on the house. You are a rich woman, Felicity. Think what you can do here to bring the house back to its full glory.'

'And what if St John is marrying me for my money?' She voiced her greatest fear.

'Then he is blind. You have poise and beauty. Many marriages within our class are not love matches at the start. St John is a passionate man. Give him a son and he will be your adoring slave.'

They walked out into the garden through a side door. The grounds were bathed in sunlight and the scent of roses from the walled garden drifted on the breeze from the sea. Water from a large fountain of Neptune cascaded with rainbow droplets. Horses were grazing in the paddock, a meadow contained the beef herd and several fields were planted with crops. Sophia took her daughter's arm and sighed. 'To be mistress of an estate like this is to be mistress of your own destiny.'

'Mama, you exaggerate.' Though Felicity could not deny that her mother was right about the splendour of the house and estate. To have such a home would make any woman proud. 'I do find Trevowan quite magical.'

'And Charlotte is happy here. She has found a friend in Rowena. Is that not also important? St John is an adoring father. And as you say, the Loveday men are charming and entrancing. If you do not marry St John, you will regret it for the rest of your life.'

Sophia dug her elbow into her daughter's ribs. 'There is your beau now, looking extremely handsome and debonair. Do not disappoint him.'

She left Felicity and sauntered towards the Dower House to persuade Amelia to ride to Trewenna and visit Cecily. She hoped that Joshua would be there. It would be diverting to flirt with him, for indeed she did find the Loveday men quite fascinating.

*　　*　　*

St John's manner was guarded as Felicity approached. He was suspicious that she had deliberately avoided him that morning. She smiled to reassure him. 'I have been enjoying the peace and charm of your home. But I have not seen Charlotte this morning.'

'Elspeth took her and Rowena to Hannah's farm.'

'Charlotte thrives here. She does not like the town.' She was carrying her parasol and opened it to keep the sun from her face. It also shaded her expression.

'Am I to have your answer this morning, Felicity?' St John sounded on edge. 'Will this day bring me the greatest of joys in your acceptance of my hand, or am I to be cast into despondency? I have waited many months for this moment. I love you. You are my perfect bride and companion.' That he was nervous and unsure and not taking her acceptance for granted overcame the last of her reservations. She could no longer deny how much she loved him.

'I will marry you, St John.'

He drew her close, holding her tenderly in his arms. The parasol hid their kiss from the curious stare of Sophia Quinton, who was grinning broadly.

Chapter Forty

At first Etta had not been unduly disturbed by her arrest. She had faith that Mordecai would find a way of ensuring her release. But as the days dragged into the second week and there had been no visits or word from her husband, a cold dread pervaded her. The cell in the lockup held two other women, Mary Blunt and Kitty Perkiss, both arrested for stealing. They were older than Etta and seasoned criminals. They mocked her when she spoke of her connections and how her arrest was all a misunderstanding.

'You were stupid enough to actually wear stolen goods,' Kitty jeered. 'Where's the misunderstanding in that?'

'I had no idea it was stolen. It was a gift.'

'And I'm the Queen of England,' Mary cackled. 'You bain't nothing but a thief, same as us.'

'I stole nothing. I am the landlady of a respectable inn.'

'That inn of yours is no better than a bawdy house, so I hear.' Kitty scowled.

Etta tried to ignore the other women. She thought herself above them, but her airs earned their greater animosity and they ganged up on her, fighting her for the meagre rations of food that were brought in. On the fourth night in the cell Mary held her down and Kitty stripped her fine gown and petticoat from her. When she clawed and kicked at them in outrage, they laid into her face so viciously that it was bruised and swollen. Kitty's foul-smelling rags were thrown at her to wear, and they were stiff with sweat and grime.

'You'll pay for this, you hags,' Etta screamed. 'My man has friends you don't want to cross.'

'Stupid bitch! How they gonna hurt us? We'll be tried and hanged or at the least transported, which is a living death so I hear. What they gonna do that's worse than that?'

Etta had not cried since she was child, when her brutal father had sold her to a laundry, where she had been forced to work fourteen hours a day in the steam, the skin on her hands rubbed raw from the rough soap and every bone in her body aching from the damp air and the heavy sheets she had to scrub. Now tears ran down her cheeks, her dreams of riches smothered by her despair. Mordecai had abandoned her to save his own hide. There was no other explanation.

Kitty and Mary often overpowered Etta to steal her food and she was constantly hungry. That no one had sent money to pay the turnkey for extra food or privileges added to her fears that her husband and Sawle would leave her to her fate.

After two weeks of misery the door to the cell was opened and the guards hauled the women to their feet and marched them out to a small courtyard. Heavy shackles were put on their ankles and wrists. Etta's first step made her bite her lip with pain and she almost fell headlong at the weight of the chains.

'Where you taking us?' she demanded as they were shoved towards a cart where two men sat, also in chains.

'To your new accommodation at Bodmin gaol to await trial.' A pock-marked turnkey with an ear missing from a knife fight laughed evilly. 'Then it will be riding the three-legged mare for you all, dancing on the end of a rope.'

Until now Etta had not believed she would face trial, having confidence that Nance or Sawle would save her. They had rescued their men before from the authorities. It would take several hours of travelling to reach the gaol, a great part of it across the bleak moor. Etta tossed back her matted hair and dug Kitty in the ribs to give her more room on the bench in the cart. Kitty lashed out at her, but Etta was expecting the blow and hit her across the mouth with her chains. Kitty screamed and cowered away. Her mouth was bleeding and she spat out two broken teeth. Mary was on the other side of the cart and could or would not aid her friend. The turnkey struck both of them with his cudgel.

'You cow, you'll pay for that,' Kitty whistled through her missing teeth.

'You long had it coming!' Etta made another strike at her but was hauled back into her place by the guard with such violence that her spine felt it would snap. She turned her back on the two women and cast a cursory glance over the men. At first she had hoped that they were part of Mordecai's escape plan. A closer inspection dashed her anticipation. They were old. One had the constant shakes and reddened face of a sot and the other nursed a broken arm in a splint.

The fighter in Etta would not let the sight of them dispirit her, and she drew the first fresh air into her lungs in nearly two weeks. It was like nectar after the fetid smells of the lockup. Four soldiers accompanied their party and again she was disheartened that they were all strangers to her. Mordecai had been generous with his free drinks for the militia who came to the inn. But that did not mean he had not bribed these men in some other way.

The ride through Fowey was humiliating. Several women recognised Etta and jeered, 'Hang the thief! Not so proud are you now, Etta Nance!'

She ignored them but made a mental note of their names. When she was free they would pay for those insults. Though the shackles bit cruelly into her flesh, she remained alert to the possibilities of escape throughout the day, her sharp eyes scanning the trees or rocky outcrops that could provide a place of ambush for her rescue.

When the late afternoon sun shone golden on the rooftops of Bodmin now only a mile distant, the old dread returned with crushing intensity. Had her husband abandoned her to her fate?

One of the men stared at her with hatred glittering in his small piggy eyes. 'You be Nance's wife, bain't you?'

'Yes.' Her head lifted proudly at the recognition. 'There is no way I'll stand trial. He'll see to that.'

'Like he poisoned those others who were taken, I shouldn't wonder. They were killed to stop them from talking.'

'My Mordecai never poisoned no one!' she defended.

'He's done worse than that. He's turned bad and you know it.' The man hawked and spat at her feet. 'Ale were sent into the gaol for the men taken by the revenue. They were all dead the next morning. One of them were my cousin.'

'That weren't Mordecai.'

'Then it were the devil he works for. Do you think they'll let you peach on them?'

Etta felt her stomach heave with a sickening dread. She knew that if she spoke out about Sawle she'd be a dead woman anyway. But she had not thought Sawle would cold-bloodedly murder his own men.

'My man will save me,' she flung back in defiance, but deep inside she cursed the day she had met Mordecai Nance. He was a bully when he had the power of Harry Sawle's name behind him, but in many ways he was weak. Once he had learned the goods had been found at the Dolphin he would make himself scarce to save his yellow hide.

Adam had been away from Boscabel for eighteen days. His mood was irritable as he kicked his heels, awaiting an interview with the Admiralty.

He had spent hours every day pacing corridors and anterooms, having been informed that he would be summoned shortly. There was much celebrating in Plymouth. The success of the Battle of Cadiz for the British fleet had raised the morale of all seamen. The people's hero, Nelson, had been promoted to rear admiral and given a knighthood for his bold actions.

But news of the war with France was not all good. General Bonaparte, now a figure of considerable influence and beyond the new directory's power to control, had shown he meant to dominate the Mediterranean. Britain was now France's only active enemy and the government feared that Bonaparte planned an invasion.

Adam had come to Plymouth anticipating that he would receive an order for another cutter. Instead in the last days he had witnessed the heart-rending sight of *Challenger* limping into harbour, a gaping hole in her quarter deck and the top half of her main mast shattered by cannon. *Challenger* was the first cutter his father had built for the revenue service.

It was mid afternoon and rain lashed the tiny windows of the gloomy corridor where he had been waiting for five hours. A door opened and he did not even trouble to look up.

'Loveday.' His name was rapped out in a terse voice.

He entered the room to find Admiral Thorpe and two other naval officers seated behind a large desk. They were all elderly, portly of build, their features wrinkled from the harsh elements endured at sea. Thorpe was in the centre, one sleeve of his uniform pinned to his waistcoat. He had lost an arm fighting pirates in the Caribbean before the war with France broke out.

'You've seen *Challenger* in port.' Thorpe eyed Adam sternly. 'A French frigate off the Isles of Scilly holed her. She had been on the tail of another cutter of yours, *Sea Mist*. She escaped in a bank of fog and *Challenger* ran into the damned Frenchie. We cannot afford to have her lying idle. How long will it take to get her seaworthy?'

'I would have to inspect her before giving you a precise time. But if she is sailed to Trevowan dry dock today, I would estimate a month before she can return to duty.'

'She'll need to be done at more or less cost.' Thorpe glowered. 'If *Sea Mist* had not been so fast, the chase would not have gone on so long and she would not have engaged the French frigate.'

'I am not responsible for the sailing speed of my ships. That is why they are commissioned. They are the fastest in their class. I cannot afford to do the work at cost.'

'It is your patriotic duty!' another officer barked out. He was a commodore, covered in gold braid and insignia.

Adam had faced enough censure from officers high above him in the navy that he was not intimidated by this man's bluster. 'With respect, I have every right to make a profit on my work. My charges are not extortionate for the quality of the ship you received. And I was under the impression I had been summoned to Plymouth to discuss the commission of a new cutter.'

'Our funds are limited,' Admiral Thorpe informed him.

'You know my price for one cutter. It has not changed. It will be built by the spring – a busy time for the smugglers you would pursue. I will need a one third down-payment for the new cutter, and if you wish me to inspect *Challenger* I shall send you my costing report tomorrow and require half payment for the work before I commence.'

'The navy will not be held to ransom.' The commodore banged a fleshy hand covered in liver spots on the table.

Adam rose. 'If you wish me to inspect *Challenger* I will do so now. If not, I have other business to attend to and customers to see.' He was angry that the commission for the cutter still eluded him. At least the repairs to *Challenger* had made his visit to Plymouth worthwhile.

'Inspect the cutter and deliver your costing report tomorrow,' Admiral Thorpe ordered. 'If it meets our approval she will sail to Trevowan Hard and you can return with her.'

Adam spent the rest of the day on *Challenger*. She had been worked hard since she had been built, but apart from this recent attack had remained sound. He suspected that she had not been in a dry dock since she was launched. If her keel was cleaned of barnacles she would be faster in the water. His inspection was thorough and it was dark as he walked along the quay and through the back streets of the port to his inn. The dockside taverns were not a place to loiter. Two naval ships were in port and the press gangs were indiscriminate in abducting able-bodied men to serve on them. Few such men returned to their homes, and their families suffered and often ended in the workhouse as a consequence. Adam hated the brutality of the press gangs, and in times of war they were more active than ever. The marauding gangs usually played on the drunks who were too far in their cups to put up a fight, but aware that even his fine clothes might not save him from attack, he walked swiftly with his hand on the dagger in his belt.

The narrow streets were dark and fetid. Unwashed beggars lay hunched in doorways and drunks were sprawled in their own vomit in the gutters. The central runnels were little better than open sewers and rats foraged for food amongst the accumulated debris. Half-naked gin-sodden hags haunted the doorways, offering their bodies to sailors, and the sounds of fights frequently broke out in the taprooms.

Adam turned into the street where he was staying. The windows of his inn were brightly lit, spreading pools of light into the thoroughfare. Inside was the sound of drunken revelry and someone playing a mournful tune on a mouth organ.

The sound of footsteps behind him alerted him to possible danger. He drew his dagger, clasping it tightly, ready to strike at an attacker. Then a foot shot out of a darkened doorway ahead of him, tripping him off balance. Adam was lithe as a cat and remained on his feet, but two men leapt from the shadows and pinned his arms before he could use the weapon to protect himself. His body slammed against the wall of a house, the window shutters closed against the noise of the port. A third man loomed in front of him and Adam kicked out, catching one of his assailants on the shin and loosening his grip of his shoulder long enough for him to lunge forward with his dagger.

'I bain't here to fight you, Loveday.' Harry Sawle's voice cut through the darkness. 'Leave him, men. Loveday and I need to talk.'

The smuggler moved into the dim light cast from an unshuttered window on the second floor of a coffin-maker's shop. His scarred face was made even more ugly and sinister by the partial shadows.

Adam shrugged out of the two men's hold and straightened his jacket. 'I do not conduct conversations skulking in shadows.'

'I could have you killed tonight and make it look like a robbery,' Harry goaded.

'You always did prefer to get your men to do your dirty work,' Adam jeered. 'You haven't the guts to face me man to man.'

'Your family be interfering in my business.' Sawle's tone was arrogant. 'St John got Etta Nance arrested and Mordecai is on the run from the law. Those two were fools, so happen he did me a favour there. Unfortunately it bain't something I can allow, or I lose the respect of my men. An eye for an eye, Loveday.'

'If you strike at my family I will hunt you down. You're vermin that must be eradicated.'

'Fancy words can't harm me,' Sawle mocked. 'I've got the upper hand here. I always will have. St John will pay. I've plans for him. But my first concern is the rumour I've heard that you've been given another commission to build a cutter. That would not please me. With *Challenger* out of commission, *Sea Mist* can outrun any revenue ship.'

'*Challenger* will be back patrolling our waters within a month.'

'I suppose you've been asked to repair her.'

Adam did not reply.

'I paid good money to ensure *Sea Mist* could outrun the excise vessels. You took my money. Go against my interests and you will regret it, Loveday. Your father nearly lost a ship through a fire in your yard. That weren't my doing. But men get careless – fires start easily and can burn everything around them to a cinder. Many of the houses at your yard are thatched. Nasty things, fires. As you found with your haystacks.'

Fire was every shipbuilder's nightmare. Some never recovered from such a financial disaster. But Adam would not weaken at such threats. His anger strengthened. '*Challenger* will be repaired and the new ship built. Accept it, Sawle. There is nothing I would like more than to see more revenue ships giving you a run for your money. Make the most of the next month.'

'You'll regret your actions, Loveday.'

'Your threats do not frighten me.' Adam brought the dagger up. His back was protected against the wall of the house and he had fought and won fights with greater odds against him in the past. 'Are you going to fight me man to man or show yourself to your men for the coward you are?'

'Maybe killing you would be too easy,' Sawle threw back at him. 'I'd rather see you ruined, a broken man, your proud family beggars. That be what your family did to my sister. As I said, an eye for an eye, Loveday. That be true justice.'

'You are no match for my family and you know it, Sawle. There is a warrant out for your arrest.'

'They have to catch me first. But I don't like unfinished business.'

Sawle let out an animal snarl and launched himself at Adam. The two henchmen who had accompanied the smuggler held back from joining the attack. There was enough light from the inn windows to show Adam the glint of steel in Sawle's right hand. Adam had fought the smuggler in the past. Sawle relied on brute strength rather than agility. He was thickset and laboured in his movements, and in recent years had done little physical work, relying instead on the men he employed. The carpentry work in the yard which Adam still took pride in, and his involvement with tasks on the home farm at Boscabel, kept him lithe and his muscles honed. His movements were smooth and lightning fast.

He sidestepped Sawle's bovine charge, ducked, spun round, and kicked out to catch the smuggler behind the knee. Sawle stumbled and fell on the cobbles, and before his men could act, Adam had pressed his dagger against Harry's throat.

'Kill 'im!' Sawle panted.

'They move and you die!' Adam vowed. 'I'll slit your throat before they get near me. And one of them will get the dagger in his belly before he touches me.'

The men hesitated. Sawle was breathing heavily, his face shining with sweat, yet he showed no fear. The two enemies held each other's gaze. Sawle grinned.

'You bain't gonna kill me in cold blood, Loveday. It bain't your way. It bain't honourable. And you be a man who puts honour first.'

'The law will deal with you,' Adam snarled. 'Get up, I will hand you over to the justices.'

Sawle did not move. His eyes were narrowed and cunning.

Then there was a shout and the sound of heavy boots. 'What's the disturbance?' a voice bellowed. 'Fighting, are you? The King needs men who can fight!'

The patchy light showed the white trousers of an officer and a dozen seamen hunting for recruits. They were still some distance away.

One of Sawle's associates yelped in alarm. 'It be the press gang. I'm outta here!'

'You bain't gonna kill me, Loveday. Not like this, anyways,' Sawle taunted, slithering backwards into the shadows. 'Not with witnesses. 'Sides, you won't escape them if they see you kill me. They'll press you into service rather than hand you over to the judge to hang.'

Adam knew the smuggler was right. 'There'll be another time, Sawle.' He cursed the press gang and all they stood for. A pressed man had no rights. No rank. He became a prisoner for life on his ship.

There was an alley immediately to his left, which he ran down, then darted through the kitchen of the inn, startling the cook, who was chopping meat. 'Press gang is outside.'

'Those bastards took my brother ten years back. He bain't bin heard of since.' The cook followed Adam into the packed taproom. The press gang rarely struck in such circumstances and the inn was more respectable than their usual haunts. The door to the kitchen was ajar and Adam watched it from the taproom. Four sailors entered with an officer and, finding it empty, backed out.

The officer was young and inexperienced and was reluctant to enter the taproom. 'They've run to ground. We'll try the taverns nearer the docks,' he ordered as he left the inn.

Adam went to his room to write out his damage report on *Challenger*, to be delivered the next day, but the figures were crowded from his mind by his confrontation with Sawle.

It rankled that he had missed his chance to bring him to justice. But the words that Sawle had used to mock him focused Adam on the fate of the smuggler. Killing him would have been too easy. Sawle was a coward at heart. He would suffer far more facing trial and eventually the hangman's rope. To kill him would have been to be no better than the smuggler himself. Sawle had escaped this time, but not for long. Justice would be served.

Chapter Forty-one

At the Rabson farm the harvest was finished. Two haystacks would feed the cows through the winter, the corn had been sold by Sam at the exchange for a good price and the barley field had been equally productive. The stalks had been burned and Mark was already ploughing a field for a winter crop of turnips and cabbages. As was customary, one field would be left fallow and the order of crops rotated next year. Oswald had liked a mix of arable and animal farming. Hannah, though unwilling to break the tradition of her late husband's farm, which had been owned by his family for four generations, now had to be practical. Arable farming was more labour intensive at harvest time and there was a resistance from many men to take orders from a woman. That had not been a problem with Sam as her overseer.

The last of the casual labourers had been paid off that morning. The harvest had provided the money for Hannah to improve her milk herd with ten more cows, and a prime bull had been purchased from Lord Fetherington and now grazed in the near paddock. Mark Sawle had spent a week on his lordship's home farm learning more about working with cattle and their ailments.

Hannah leaned on the paddock fence watching the bull with mixed feelings. Sam stood beside her.

'The last bull we had was the very devil to handle,' she observed. 'When Oswald became worse we sold him and had a bull brought in to service the cows. Lord Fetherington assured me this one is more mellow in temperament.'

'He is a fine beast,' Sam replied. 'But there is only one rule with bulls and that is never to trust them. Mark is doing well with the cattle. He was always good with the horses. There should be no problems.'

The last week had been strained between them. The harvest had kept them busy and then Sam had been away at the corn exchange. Hannah blamed herself for that moment of weakness when she had allowed him to kiss her. It was a kiss that haunted her dreams, awakening feelings of desire she had schooled herself to crush since Oswald had died. Often she would walk into a room and expect to find Oswald there, or look across the fields he loved and see him at work. In Davey's laughter was the echo of his father's ability to turn the most ardous job into fun. Somehow Sam had invaded that space where once Oswald had ruled. His advice had been invaluable and he had lifted many of the burdens from her shoulders, and it had come as a shock to acknowledge how much she relied upon him. Now that would all change.

The set of his body was tense as he continued to study the bull. He was an honourable man who took his responsibilities seriously. The way he cared for Charlie proved that.

'You've made a decision about your father, haven't you, Sam?'

There was a tightening to his lips and even now he seemed to be wrestling with his emotions.

'A life of constant change is not fair to Charlie. In a year or so he will need proper schooling if he is to make something of his life. You were right about family loyalty. You cannot escape it. I will not allow my uncle to have control over Charlie's life. It would be the ruin of him. My father must be made to see reason.'

They were the words she had dreaded, but she knew he had made the right decision. 'When do you leave?'

'You will need another man to work the farm. I shall hire one at the market fair. Many are seeking employment now that the harvest is all but over. There is also a new tenant to be found for Tor Farm. Once these matters are settled I will leave.'

'They are my responsibilities, not yours. The longer you delay, the more power your uncle will wield against you. My father believes he has found a tenant for the farm. He is the younger son of a farmer and recently married, and is eager to make a success of a place of his own. It's Walter, the cousin of Baz Tonkin, who has a tied cottage at Trevowan and who asked for work when he was here for the harvest.'

'Walter Tonkin was a good worker and sparing with his drinking, which is always a good sign.' Sam nodded approval. 'He's not one of Sawle's tubmen, is he?'

'St John spoke to Baz for me. He says not,' Hannah replied.

'He would be a sensible choice. And you have a good man in Mark. I will not be missed.'

'I would not go that far,' she laughed. Then, when he shot her an assessing look, she became flustered. She covered her hand with his. 'You have been the best of friends. I do not know how I would have managed this last year without you. And now you must put Charlie first and be reconciled with your father.'

There was concern in the way his brow wrinkled as he regarded her. 'I still do not like leaving you unprotected. What of Harry Sawle and his threats?'

'I have my family, and Sawle will be arrested if he shows himself in these parts. St John saw to that.'

'A warrant will not stop that knave from exacting retribution.'

Hannah jutted her chin in a way that showed her pride and belief in her family and a certain stubborn wilfulness not to be cowed. 'I will not allow fear to rule my life. It is not the Loveday way.'

His hand moved briefly over hers in a tender gesture before he withdrew it. 'And woe betide any foolish enough to challenge that way.' His expression sobered at seeing Charlie and Luke engaged in a mock sword fight with sticks. 'The boy will miss you and your family. We will leave early tomorrow. I have purchased a gelding from Squire Penwithick and would stop at Bodmin to have myself and Charlie fitted with new suits of clothes. My father sets much store by appearances.'

'Clothes do not a gentleman make. It is what is in the heart and the actions. Your father is a fool if he does not welcome you with open arms. I wish you every success, Sam. Charlie is a wonderful boy. You will write and tell me how you are, will you not?'

'I am not much of a letter-writer. I make no promises, Hannah. And I am not one for goodbyes either. We will be gone at first light.'

She felt herself rebuked; their roles of employer and servant were no longer appropriate. Sam was again his own master.

She rose early to ensure they had food enough for the journey, but there was no light in Sam's cottage. It looked so desolate she felt bereft and ran to check if he was still there. It was empty.

A hollow well of emptiness formed in her chest. Sam had been her rock through her grief. It was now time for her to stand alone.

The pink glow of dawn brightened the hill in the direction of Penwithick Manor. For a moment two figures were silhouetted against the sky. One large and one a small boy. For a moment the man paused. Was he looking back at the farm? Hannah raised her hand in farewell, not sure whether he would see her. He stood for some moments before disappearing from sight.

'God go with you, Sam. And if fate is kind, we may yet meet again.' She did not like to contemplate that he was gone for ever from her life. Yet she accepted that he had a very different future ahead of him once he was reconciled with his family.

With a sigh she surveyed her home: the milkmaids were emerging from their room above the barn rubbing sleep from their eyes, the cows gathering near the gate to be led into the milking shed. There was a light on in Mark and Jeannie's kitchen as the couple prepared to start another day, and a thin plume of smoke rose from the farmhouse, where Aggie had stoked the Cornish range and would be making breakfast for Hannah's children.

These were the sights she loved. This was her home and her destiny. Oswald had entrusted the farm to her and she would not fail him.

Clem Sawle had little love for his brother Harry. The latest incident with the smugglers and the attack on Parson Loveday angered him. For years his family had respected the Lovedays. It was foolish to antagonise them. In the end the gentry would win against their adversaries.

Neither did he approve of St John's high-handed manner. He did not care that the new master of Trevowan had instigated a warrant for Harry's arrest, but he did care that Sal was upset at how little she saw of her granddaughter. Clem knew his family would have no part in Rowena's upbringing, but Sal loved the girl and as her grandmother should be allowed to see her, especially as Rowena had shown that she cared for Sal.

There was no point in a confrontation with St John. Clem realised that would only make matters worse. But he had information the Lovedays wanted – information he had kept to himself until he could use it to advantage.

St John hated Clem's family, and with just cause after the way Meriel had treated him. Clem trusted Adam, but if he went to him it would only fuel the rivalry St John felt for his twin, and that would not further Clem's plan.

He decided to visit Joshua Loveday. It was a long walk to Trewenna and he waited until the day was fine and the weather would hold before he undertook the journey. Even Keziah and his ma did not know of his intent.

Clem was careful that no one saw him in Trewenna. He hid behind a yew tree in the churchyard until he saw Joshua Loveday leave the rectory. Checking that he was not observed by others, he walked quickly to approach him.

'Sir, I've news you've long sought. I would speak with you in the church where we'll not be seen.'

Joshua regarded him warily and anger was sharp in his voice. 'If this is to plead on behalf of your brother Harry . . .'

'It concerns your brother.'

'How is that possible? My brothers are dead.'

'Ah, but how did one of them die? Word be that you would like matters surrounding a certain disappearance cleared up.'

The preacher frowned, but there was also apprehension shadowing his eyes. 'You had better come into the vestry. We will not be disturbed there.' He led the way and gestured for Clem to be seated by the cupboard where the parish registers were held.

'What have you to say?'

'First I want something from you.'

'How much?'

A flicker of annoyance creased Clem's face. 'I don't want money. I want what be right. Ma grieves that she sees so little of Rowena. Happen it weren't right for her to visit at the inn, but Ma could see her in her cottage.'

'Her father is against it,' Joshua said regretfully. 'That is no reflection upon Sal. She is a worthy woman.'

'St John be right to be set against our family over Meriel. She shamed us all. But my information will benefit St John. It only be right there be some gain for us.'

'Then you must tell me this knowledge you deem so important and I will judge its value.'

'I saw what happened the day Captain William Loveday died.'

Joshua gripped his hands together to control his shock. 'Why have you said nothing before? Do you intend to blackmail us?'

Clem stood up abruptly, his features twisted in anger. 'So you think there be something suspicious about that day? I said nothing afore this because I didna think it were my affair. I bain't no blackmailer. I just be asking that you do what be right by Ma, if you think the information is of relevance.'

'Enough of this beating around the bush!' Joshua spread his hands in a gesture of supplication and again indicated that Clem should be seated. 'Speak out. I ask your pardon for suggesting you intended blackmail. But this matter has long troubled our family. Is it to do with the disappearance of Lisette?'

'I were fishing off Trevowan Cove just round the headland. I'd put out pots for crabs and there'd been several good catches.' Clem sat down and leaned forward in his chair, his stare assessing upon the preacher. 'I heard what I thought were a shot and angry voices. But I reckoned it were Loveday business. There were two horses tethered out of sight of the cove. They'd been there other days when I'd been tending my pots.

One was Captain Loveday's wife's mare and the other belonged to her brother. Though what those two got up to in that cave weren't nothing no brother and sister should be doing.'

'Good God!' Joshua turned a sickly grey and took several moments to recover his composure. 'What you imply is a serious offence before God and the law. Are you sure you were not mistaken?'

'Not when I saw them both run naked into the sea and they were kissing and cuddling. I be sorry, Reverend. Captain Loveday were a good man. He didn't deserve such ill from a wife.'

Joshua was stunned and found it impossible to speak as he digested this information.

'I reckon Captain Loveday must have caught them together,' Clem went on. 'I'd brought in all my pots when I saw the captain rowing out to sea in the dinghy kept at the cove. I were curious then. He rowed a fair way then tossed the oars overboard. What happened next, you're gonna find hard to believe, Reverend. Captain Loveday rolled the body of a woman over the side of the boat, and then one of a man. They both sank so they must have been weighted. Then he scuppered the boat, making it sink, and swam out to sea. I were going to sail after him but reckoned if he'd killed them then he did not want to live. Your family had had its fill of scandals in those days.'

Joshua wiped a shaking hand across his face. 'So you believe William killed them then drowned himself?'

'The Frenchies were lovers. That bain't natural and it bain't godly. But that were what I saw. I had no grudge against Captain Loveday. He were a man of honour. No one could blame him for what he did. I reckon he wanted to spare the Lovedays further shame.'

'You could destroy us if this became common knowledge,' Joshua said. He was still ashen and shocked by the news.

'I got no grudge against your family, Reverend. Except with St John over this business with Rowena. I bain't about to gossip about things that don't concern me. Especially if we have an understanding.'

'In the circumstances it is not much that you ask. I will speak to St John. I cannot see why Sal should not see her granddaughter as she no longer lives at the inn.'

Clem stood up. 'Then that will be an end to this matter.'

'Have you spoken to anyone else of this, Mr Sawle?'

'No.'

Joshua held his hand out to the fisherman. 'Thank you for telling me. I suppose we will never know the whole truth of what happened that day. And certainly we cannot use this knowledge to prove that

Lisette and her brother are dead. It is better that the incident is forgotten.'

After Clem had left, Joshua spent a long time in the church praying for his brother's soul, and for Lisette and Etienne. He felt a deep sadness for his brother. William, although a competent naval captain, had been the least worldly of the Lovedays. Lisette had ensnared him and then callously betrayed him.

He stopped briefly at Boscabel to inform Senara of the events of the morning. She was saddened but did not seem unduly surprised. 'Etienne always had an unnatural power over Lisette. She adored him even though he often treated her badly. Adam was shocked when he learned Uncle William had married her. She had no morals or scruples and had taken many lovers, while I thought him a confirmed bachelor. At least we now know something of the truth of Uncle's drowning and the disappearance of Lisette and her brother. Adam loved his uncle, he will take this hard.'

When Joshua called on St John later in the day, his nephew was equally shocked by the news.

'Should we tell Elspeth and Amelia?' he asked.

'It would only upset them. And of course you will grant Clem's request that Rowena see more of Sal Sawle.'

'I do not see that we have much choice, but I will insist a maid attend upon her. Can we trust Clem?'

'Clem is wise enough to know that he is better off without a feud between our two families. I would trust him.'

'Yet we cannot release the money from Uncle William's estate without Lisette's body. The lawyer will not accept that she simply drowned.'

'Once a person has been missing for seven years upon suspicion of drowning, I believe they will be declared dead. The estate will be released to the family then.'

Adam delayed his return to Boscabel for two more days, searching Plymouth for Harry Sawle. The smuggler was at none of the haunts he would have expected, and no one appeared to have seen him. If it was not for the bruise to his ribs, Adam would have wondered whether he had dreamed the encounter. The painful ache in his side proved it had been real enough.

On the second day he was summoned to attend upon Admiral Thorpe and was given the commissions to repair *Challenger* and build a new cutter on the same lines. Thorpe agreed to his prices providing that

Challenger returned to sea within six weeks. At least his time here had not been wasted, and with the yard books now filled for the next year, his immediate financial worries were solved.

Adam wanted *Challenger* seaworthy within a month. Without the cutter patrolling the inshore waters, *Sea Mist* would make her runs unhindered. There was no other revenue ship that could match her in speed. It would mean paying the shipwrights extra money for longer hours, but his reward would be to curb Sawle's dominance in these waters. *Challenger* would be ready to sail to Trevowan Hard on the early-morning tide. Adam would sail with her and draw up the work schedule on the voyage, and the yard would be ready to start work as soon as they got her into the dry dock.

Restless to be home and reunited with his family, Adam slept little and was on board *Challenger* two hours before they sailed. By the time the cutter limped out of Plymouth Sound and rounded Rame Head his paperwork was completed and he ventured on deck.

Captain Ambrose Pinsett came from Helston and had been a smuggler and fisherman himself for some years. That life had ended for him when a revenue vessel took his ship and he and his brother were pressed into service. His brother had died in the first year, but Pinsett's knowledge of the coast had won him release from the imprisonment of life at sea as a pressed man if he used his experience to help the revenue. He had never married and had no family in Helston to return to now that his brother was dead. He had never made much of a living from the trade, and working for the revenue brought not only his freedom, but also regular pay and a captain's portion from the sale of any ship confiscated and sold.

He had been a revenue man for the last seven years, and when *Challenger* had gone into service he had been promoted and made her captain.

'She be a grand ship and much afeared by the free-traders, Cap'n Loveday.'

Pinsett was a stout, barrel-chested man with a bushy white beard and bulbous red nose. He stood with his tree-trunk legs planted firmly apart, a real old Cornish seadog in Adam's book.

'Rightly so,' Pinsett went on with evident pride. 'She's captured more than two score in her time, the ships and cargo confiscated and sold. Her guns give her an extra edge but she were no match for that Frenchie that we come upon in a fog bank. Though we turned about and made a run for it, one of the frigate's cannon caught her across the bows and brought down her mast. The fog saved us. I don't like to see the old girl like this.'

'She will be back under your command in a month, Captain. And two small swivel guns will be fitted to her aft as an extra protection.' Adam surveyed the remaining mast with only its foresail unfurled. To use more canvas could make the ship unstable in the present crosswind. It was frustrating for him to witness her slow passage; the last time he had sailed in her was during her sea trials, when she had cut through the water with the grace and speed of a dolphin. Today she lumbered more like a whale. At least she responded well to the helm, and if they did not venture too close to shore would not drive herself on to the rocks.

There was little blue in the sky but the clouds were pearlescent and did not look to be building for rain. The wind was fresh and they should make the Fowey River before the harbour chains were lowered across the estuary for the night as protection from French attack. They would have to moor in the central river channel at Fowey and wait for the full tide the next morning to take them to the inlet at Trevowan Hard.

A skeleton crew handled the cutter well and Adam felt a catch in his throat to be at sea again on a ship he had designed. It was many months since he had last captained *Pegasus*. His life had changed with the responsibilities of the yard after his father's death and he had no regrets, but this feeling that came over him on board had been an entrenched part of his heritage. The sea was a seductive mistress and had never entirely got out of his blood.

He stood by the rail watching the familiar coastline as the afternoon passed. A few tall masted ships were moored along the quay at Looe, dwarfing the fishing fleet. Further along the coast the harbour arm of Polperro provided a haven for the fishermen, the village houses clustered around the water's edge or scattered like gull's nests clinging to the sides of the steep winding valley of the coombe. With Pencarrow Head behind them, the pull of the current carried them towards the Fowey estuary. Beyond that the coast turned to a purple hue as the crimson streaks of the sun dropped lower on the horizon. In the far distance the land curved like a lobster's claw past Falmouth and the headland at the Lizard; the open pincers of the claw sweeping round to Mullion, Porthleven, St Michael's Mount, Penzance and the rugged peninsula at Land's End. Beyond that was the Atlantic Ocean.

His eyes narrowed. The image of Harry Sawle intruded upon his reverie. The man was as elusive as the great beast legend said haunted Bodmin Moor. Fate had been against Adam in Plymouth when he had had the chance to bring Sawle to justice. It was likely that the smuggler had once more gone into hiding, having delivered his threat to the

Lovedays. Did Sawle really think they would be intimidated?

He smothered his frustration that by the time they sailed into Fowey the tide was too low to allow *Challenger* to continue upriver to Trevowan Hard. He did not want to stay another night from his home. He had already been absent during the harvest and the work on the new merchantman at the yard was at a crucial stage. He spoke briefly with Captain Pinsett.

'I will not stay aboard tonight. Sail upriver on the tide in the morning and dock at the landing stage of Trevowan Hard. My overseer Ben Mumford will come aboard and *Challenger* can be guided into the dry dock. If your longboat is lowered for me I will pay a ferryman to take me upriver tonight. I have been too long from my home.'

'Two of my men will row you to Trevowan Hard, Captain Loveday.'

'That is a kind offer, but it will be an hour and a half round trip. The ferryman has a skiff and he will sail in half the time.'

An hour later Adam stopped briefly at Trevowan Hard to speak with Ben Mumford. '*Challenger* will arrive in the morning for her repairs. And I was given an order for another cutter.'

'That is good news, Cap'n.'

The overseer's expression became more serious and he regarded Adam in an uncertain manner.

'Have there been problems at the yard, Ben? It was unfortunate that I was away so long, but at least we have the orders to secure our immediate future.'

'Best you get home to your good lady wife, Cap'n. There's been trouble with your family.' Ben sounded worried and seemed reluctant to go on, sending a ripple of alarm through Adam.

'What's happened?'

'It's been a sorry time, Cap'n. Parson Loveday fell foul of the smugglers, who took exception to his sermons against them. And there were the other trouble on Mr Japhet's land which Mrs Rabson dealt with.'

'What trouble is this?' Adam was appalled. 'Have any of the family been harmed?'

'All be sorted so I hear. Best Mrs Loveday tells you. I only heard bits of gossip and you know how the truth do get distorted. Mr St John may have acted a bit hasty calling out the military, but with respect, it bain't really my place to say.'

As Adam mounted Solomon and turned towards Boscabel, he had a terrible sense of foreboding.

Chapter Forty-two

It was twilight when he reached Boscabel. There was a light in the nursery and the old solar where Senara would be relaxing after getting the children settled for the night.

At the sound of his voice Senara ran to greet him in the old high-beamed hall. 'Thank God you are home, my love.' She threw her arms around him and hugged him tight.

'Have things been that bad? Mumford said there had been trouble. You are shaking.'

'There is much to tell you, but you must be ravenous.'

'I dined with Captain Pinsett on *Challenger*.' They walked arm in arm to the solar, where a small fire had been lit against the first chill of approaching autumn. 'I sailed with them from Plymouth. The cutter is moored awaiting the tide to sail to our dry dock. The French holed and demasted her. And I got the contract for another cutter.'

'That is wonderful news.' Her smile was strained. 'I fear you will be displeased with what has passed in your absence. But you must promise me not to lose your temper with St John. He did what he thought was best.'

The alarm bells in Adam's mind rang louder. He made an effort to keep his voice even and not jump to conclusions that his twin had caused some major disaster.

'Tell me what has happened. Mumford was unusually evasive. From his words I gather Sawle's men have been causing trouble for Peter and Hannah. Tell me everything.'

Senara waited until he sat down opposite her. She gripped her fingers tightly in her lap. 'First of all we are all delighted, as I am sure that you will be, that St John is to marry Felicity Barrett.'

'That is good news! She will be a far better wife than Meriel.'

She told him about the smugglers using Japhet's land and Hannah's intervention in informing the military, as well as the resulting arrest of some smugglers, their death in prison in suspicious circumstances, and the loss of Japhet's tenant.

'I knew Sawle was up to his old tricks. I met him in Plymouth and he ordered me to stop meddling in his affairs and told me that I would be unwise to repair *Challenger* too quickly. Mumford also mentioned Peter and Sawle's men, something about his sermons?'

'That was a worrying time. Your Uncle Joshua and St John were in Bodmin. After what happened on Japhet's land Peter took to sermonising about the wickedness of smuggling with greater virulence than before. He did not return one evening from a service at Polmasryn.' She continued to explain the details of his cousin's abduction and escape. 'Fortunately his injuries were not serious. He was left to die in the cave, tied up without food or water. He showed everyone his true mettle in the way he escaped. Since then he has been helpful with our harvest and has also been working in Hannah's fields.'

'Sawle will not get away with attacking our family.' Adam leapt to his feet, pacing the floor with long, angry strides. 'And where does St John come into all this? You cannot have thought I would be angry at his pending marriage.'

'He discovered a horde of valuables taken on the day of Tamasine's wedding. That cleared Caleph's men of the crime, and for that I am grateful.'

'That at least is good news.' He waited for his wife to continue, his chest constricted with the feeling that at last he would be told what Mumford and Senara feared would again set him at odds with his brother.

'The valuables were found at the Dolphin. St John told the revenue officer of a secret room in the cellar. There was also brandy hidden there. Etta was arrested and is now in Bodmin gaol. There has been no sign of Mordecai Nance or Sawle since then.'

Adam was indeed angered at his twin's rash action. 'They can feel the noose tightening about their necks and have flown the coop. Why did St John not wait until he could lay a trap to catch Sawle? The fool!' His fists clenched in his frustration that the smuggler could now have escaped them. 'It could be months before he shows his face in these parts again.'

'There is a warrant out for Nance and Sawle's arrest. St John has put up a reward of one hundred pounds for their capture.'

'The goods found at the Dolphin condemn Nance, not Sawle. He will have wasted his money if Nance is caught. He will not speak against his leader.' Adam slammed his fist into his open palm, then slumped in a chair and put his head into his hands. 'I should have been here.'

'You cannot be everywhere, my love.' Senara moved to sit on her husband's lap and wrap her arms around his neck. 'The contract for the new cutter was too important for the yard. It is not wrong to put our needs first in times of crisis. Besides, Sawle will not stay away for ever. He has too many business interests in these parts.'

Adam remained tense. She kissed his mouth and along his jaw, whispering against his cheek, 'Do you intend to allow your foolish brother to spoil our first night together after so long apart? I have missed you so very, very much.' She interspersed her words with kisses, and when she felt him respond she laughed softly and hoisted her skirts higher and sat astride him. 'You really do not want to talk about the family now, do you?'

'Seductive minx!' he chuckled and kissed her with passion.

She sighed and her hands became impatient on his clothing. Then a loud banging was heard on the front door and a frustrated curse replaced Adam's murmured endearments. By the time the maid tapped discreetly on the door to announce their visitor, Adam stood by the fireplace and Senara had smoothed the creases from her crumpled gown, though both their faces were still flushed from their ardour.

The maid dropped a curtsey. 'Begging your pardon, Cap'n Loveday, it be a messenger from Polruggan.'

'Ma could be ill,' Senara gasped.

'Show them in,' Adam ordered.

Gert Wibbley's oldest boy hesitated in the doorway. The maid snatched his cap off his head and slapped it against his chest. 'Show proper respect to your betters, lad.'

The cap was twisted in grimy hands and the youth looked down at his feet as he stumbled out his words. 'Parson says for Mrs Loveday to come right away. His wife be taken bad.'

'Bridie must be in labour.' Senara cast a stricken look at her husband. 'She's had one or two false alarms recently with worry over Peter.'

'I'll come with you,' Adam said as he flipped a silver coin towards the youth. 'It's been a fair run from Polruggan. I'll take you back on my horse, lad.'

When they arrived at the parsonage, Peter was slumped in the chair by the kitchen range. A scream of agony from upstairs sent a shudder through Senara. Bridie was indeed in labour, but it was too early.

Peter glanced up, his expression haggard. 'Go to her, Senara, and for the love of God ease her suffering.'

Senara hurried to the bedchamber, where Leah was holding her daughter's hand and Gert Wibbley was bent over the straining woman.

'I've done all I can, Mrs Loveday.' Gert was clearly relieved to see Senara. 'I bain't got your skills. Not only is the child early, it be breech. You make the decision if it be the child or the mother you save. I don't reckon either of them will survive.'

'That is nonsense,' Senara protested. 'Bridie is strong and the child can be turned.' She knew it would be an ordeal for the mother and she had spoken the words with a confidence she was far from feeling.

'Has Dr Yeo been summoned?'

Leah nodded. 'No disrespect to your skills, daughter, but I thought it best.'

'You did right, Ma. Mrs Wibbley, I will still need your help until the doctor comes. Make sure there is plenty of hot water. Ma cannot get up and down the stairs too well since her fall last year.'

Gert ambled out of the room and Senara turned to her mother. 'Peter is taking this badly. Get him out of the house. He does not need to hear her suffering. Bridie and the child will need all their prayers. Ask Adam to take him into the church.'

Bridie's back arched at another contraction and she pulled on the sheets Leah had tied to the bedposts. Her lips were bleeding where she had bitten into them. When the pain passed, she moaned, 'Save my child, Senara. If you have to make a choice, save the child.'

'There will always be other children, Bridie. I shall do my best to save you both.' She examined her sister between pains. Unfortunately, Gert Wibbley had been right in saying the child was breech. Senara could feel its buttocks where the head should be, and the feet were doubled up high in the womb. It was going to be a difficult birth and a long night for them all. Her examination also showed her that the child was small, which would enable her to turn it more easily, but it was clearly coming before its time.

Senara found this the hardest birth she had attended. She loved Bridie dearly and was reluctant to submit her to the terrible pain of turning the child, which could not always be achieved anyway. After an hour she heard a knock on the door and was relieved that Dr Yeo was here. Gert Wibbley appeared and shook her head. 'Doctor were already out on another delivery, a woman having twins and another difficult birth. His wife has sent him word to come here as soon as he can. Do you want me to send my boy to Dr Chegwidden in Penruan?'

'Chegwidden is a butcher.' Senara feared he would kill Bridie with his bungling ineptitude.

Two hours later, exhausted, Bridie passed out, and fearing that the baby was also growing weaker, Senara tried to turn the baby again. If she failed this time, she knew it was likely that both child and mother would die.

'It's moved of its own accord,' she said at her next examination, her body drenched in sweat from her efforts. 'I can feel its feet.'

Her sister remained unconscious, and with the next pain the baby was delivered.

Bridie groaned and opened her eyes, her voice hoarse. 'My baby.'

A thin cry carried to them. Leah came to the side of the bed, holding a tiny bundle. 'You have a son, my dear.' She laid the baby in her daughter's arms, wrapped tightly in a fine woollen shawl. 'I'll call your husband. This is a proud moment for you both.'

The new mother moved aside the shawl that partly covered his face. 'Is he not beautiful, Ma?'

Leah wiped a tear from her eye. 'He be an angel, my sweet.'

Senara knelt at her sister's side and kissed her cheek. 'He has a cloud of dark hair – a real Loveday – but he has your tenacity and courage for life. May the gods bless him.'

Bridie frowned. 'Do not let Peter hear you say such things.'

'Peter and I will always differ on matters of religion. But we both have the love and welfare of this child at heart. And you will now need plenty of rest. I will not hear of your rising from this bed until the end of your six-week lying-in period.'

'You never stayed abed so long.'

'I never had such a difficult birth.'

'But the children's schooling . . .'

'Adam will find a temporary teacher and you will need a maid to help Ma with the work. I am sure one of the women from the village will come for a few hours a day.'

'But without my wages from the school we cannot afford a servant.'

'Stop worrying. You must put your health first. Adam has another contract to build a revenue cutter and for repairs to be made on *Challenger*. We can afford to pay these wages. Nothing must stand in the way of your full recovery.'

Peter could be heard taking the stairs two at a time. Senara rose to congratulate him. 'Bridie is exhausted,' she said softly.

Adam grinned at her as she entered the kitchen. He was holding a glass of brandy; he had been toasting the baby's health. 'A fine boy. Peter is so proud.'

Senara bowed her head and laid a hand on her husband's arm. 'Peter should baptise the child as soon as possible. He is weak and may not survive. Bridie has lost a lot of blood but she is not haemorrhaging. I would not have her worried about the baby until she is stronger.'

'Will he live?'

'He needs special care. I will wrap him in a blanket and he must be placed in a drawer on top of the range to keep him warm through the night. Care must be taken that no one with a cold or infection goes near him until he has gained more weight. He is lucky to be alive.'

Dr Yeo arrived before Peter had come down from the bedchamber, and after examining Bridie and the baby he took the proud father aside and also advised that the child should be baptised without delay. 'Have you chosen a name?'

'Michael. After the Lord of all the Angelic Hosts who stands on the right hand of God. He will protect his namesake from harm.' Peter challenged the doctor with a defiant stare. 'I thank you for attending on my wife and son this night. But Michael will live. God will not so forsake us as to answer our prayers only to snatch something so precious away again.'

Chapter Forty-three

The next day Adam was up at dawn. He and Senara had stayed all night at the parsonage and he left before anyone else had stirred. He spent an hour with Eli Rudge, who reported on the success of the harvest and told him that three calves had been born to the beef herd and another dozen or so were due in the next ten days. By the time he had finished his rounds on the home farm, his children were awake and, having learnt of his return, clamouring for his attention, and he spent a half-hour in the nursery before leaving for the yard.

When he arrived there the shipwrights were already at work and Ben Mumford informed him of the current work being undertaken on the merchant ship. The outer planking was now complete and they had begun on the internal struts and deck supports. Adam spent another hour selecting wood from the seasoned piles at the rear of the yard to be used both for *Challenger's* repairs and for the laying-down of the keel for the new cutter. After he had chosen what was needed for the repairs to *Challenger*, he saw the revenue ship being guided into the dry dock. Only then did he leave the yard to return to Polruggan. Peter had sent word to the family that Michael would be baptised that afternoon.

With the school closed, Hannah's children were playing blind man's buff in the parsonage garden. Joshua and Cecily's horses were tethered by the fence. The smell of baking bread and saddle of lamb roasting in the kitchen reminded Adam that he had eaten nothing that morning. Leah was peeling potatoes and carrots and Senara had made an apple pie. There was a cheese and a large jug of cream supplied by Hannah. A feast would follow the baptism.

'It is all very hurried.' Senara came down the stairs carrying a tray of used teacups. 'Cecily, Hannah and Joshua are upstairs with Bridie and Peter. St John, Elspeth and Amelia should be here soon. And please, Adam, let there be no dissension with your twin. The baptism must go smoothly.'

'There will be time enough for me to talk with St John. And not when all the family are around,' he said ominously. 'I want all the facts before I confront him. Are Mrs Barrett and her mother still at Trevowan?'

'They returned to Truro two days ago. Felicity is insisting on a quiet wedding, which will take place next month at Trewenna. She has much to put in order before then.'

'Is there anything I can do to help? You and Leah look tired.'

'We are nearly finished. Go and see your family. They have been asking after you.' Senara glanced anxiously up the stairs. 'Though Bridie should have rest, she was upset at the thought of missing the service. So it will take place upstairs. It will be rather crowded but Peter will keep the blessing and baptism simple.'

Peter was next to enter the kitchen. He was grinning with pride. 'I thought I heard your voice, Adam. You left before I had a chance to properly thank you for all you and Senara did last night.'

'I did nothing,' Adam said, 'except enjoy wetting Michael's head. How are he and Bridie this day?'

'Bridie is tired. I will chase my family away from the bedside soon to give her time to rest. Michael is suckling, which Senara says is a promising sign.'

'He is a Loveday. He will be a fighter. And what of yourself? We did not speak of your ordeal with the smugglers. You look as though you are still suffering from the effects.'

Peter had a cut across his eye and yellowing bruises on his cheek and temple. His figure was slightly hunched and he was clearly still in pain. He gestured for Adam to follow him into the parlour. 'A few bruises will not stop me from the Lord's work.'

'Things have been bad here, so I understand,' Adam remarked. 'Did Sawle think we would let him get away with using Japhet's farm to hide his contraband?'

Hannah appeared at the doorway and answered his question. 'He frightened the new tenant into agreeing. The poor man has since left, though Sam Deacon helped protect his family when the smugglers returned. The farmer did not want to be involved in such matters and his wife was badly frightened by the incident.'

Adam kissed her cheek in greeting. 'I should have been here. At least you had Deacon watching out for you. He would not be scared of facing up to Sawle.'

'He was exemplary. But he has now left my employ. He has family business to attend to elsewhere.'

Adam hid his misgivings. Sam had shouldered the responsibility of protecting Hannah. She could be vulnerable now that he had left. 'I'm sorry, he was a good man. A strong, reliable man. I thought he was loyal to you.'

Hannah's head tilted with a proud defiance as she quickly defended him. 'Sam had to put loyalty to his family first. You would do the same, would you not?'

Adam had not expected such a strong rebuke from his cousin. Hannah had dark circles under her eyes and her cheeks were sunken and drawn. He suspected she was not sleeping well. He did not like to think of her on the farm with Mark as the only man to protect her. 'Have you engaged someone to replace him?'

'Yes Toby Keswick, his family work at Traherne Hall.'

'There is still the matter of Mordecai Nance to deal with,' Peter said. 'He was the one responsible for using Tor Farm. He escaped that night. And since the raid on the Dolphin he has not been seen in Penruan.'

Adam stifled a surge of anger at his twin's incompetence. 'I heard St John ordered a warrant for Nance's arrest and insisted on the raid. Why did he not wait until we had more evidence and knew Nance was at the inn?'

Peter shrugged. 'Nance is wanted for the thefts on the day of Tamasine's wedding. They found the goods at the inn. That is a hanging offence.'

'But it does not link him to Sawle,' Adam protested. 'St John was a fool to act so rashly. After the service today I shall have it out with him.'

'Adam, is that wise?' Hannah counselled. 'St John thought he was acting for the best. He was not to know Nance was not at the inn.'

Adam absently rubbed the nagging ache in his ribs. 'Even if Nance had been there, there was no evidence to condemn Sawle. That is the point I am making. I had an encounter with Harry Sawle in Plymouth. It must have been after you were attacked, Peter. He warned me to back off from interfering in his business or he would strike at us. An eye for an eye, he threatened.'

Adam glanced at Hannah, and seeing her swallow nervously, he regretted his outburst in front of her. He had not meant to alarm her, but she must realise that her actions at Tor Farm would have placed her in danger. 'Sawle's bluffing for the most part. He knows that if anything happens to any of us, he will be the first the authorities look to.'

'But he'd strike and run, same as he always does,' Peter protested. 'Hannah, perhaps you should get Father to stay at the farm until Sawle is caught. I would do so myself but Bridie should be resting here without family worries to trouble her.'

Adam nodded. 'I am sure Joshua will agree. I do not like to think of Hannah and the children unprotected.'

'And what about what I want?' Hannah folded her arms across her chest and there was a dangerous light in her eyes. 'I can look after myself. Papa has his parish duties. It is not practical for him to live at the farm.'

Adam knew from the stubborn tilt of her chin that she would not listen to reason. He suspected that Sawle's real grudge was against himself and St John and that Hannah was not in any immediate danger. Hannah was greatly respected. If any harm came to her there would be public outrage and the law would not stop until Sawle was brought to trial. Sawle would not risk so much by striking at a woman. He would do so only to gain revenge upon the Loveday twins.

'Hannah is not Sawle's quarry,' he stated. 'He suspects I have been given a contract for another revenue cutter and he threatened to set the yard on fire if I built it. If Sawle is to be brought to justice it will take planning and tactics to get solid evidence against him. St John could ruin everything by his rash action. But I doubt Sawle will do much for the moment. He knows we are on our guard. There must be no delay in getting the evidence we need.'

'And I shall work with you,' Peter insisted. 'I have my own score to settle with that fiend.'

'Then speak to St John of the matter after the service,' Hannah counselled, 'but do not antagonise him. He did what he thought was best. None of us can fight Sawle alone and win. But we can triumph over him if we are united.'

Japhet knew he could not afford to wait for the next ship of Adam's to arrive before he confronted Haughton. He had always believed in meeting any sign of trouble head on. There were more ways than one to win an enemy over. Sometimes it took the form of an open challenge; at other times diplomacy was the better course. Japhet had made his living as a gambler for many years and knew how to play on another man's greed and ambition.

He dressed with care in the quality clothing Gwendolyn had brought for him from England. The intricately tied stock and embroidered waistcoat proclaimed his status as a gentleman. He was not given to ostentation, but such attire set him apart from the rags of the convicts or the work clothes of the settlers. Today he needed all the subtle tools he could muster at his disposal.

His only weapon was a dagger hidden inside his fine leather riding boots. He arrived at the barracks in Sydney and sent a messenger to present Japhet's compliments to Captain Haughton and request that he meet him by the partially built church. He was kept waiting for the best part of an hour, but his patience was rewarded when Haughton finally deigned to appear. He had guessed the officer's curiosity would bring him, if nothing else.

'I do not take kindly to being summoned like a common lackey, Loveday,' Haughton sneered. Even from several feet away Japhet could smell the rum on his breath.

'That was not my intention. I have a proposition to make to you and thought you would prefer to hear it alone rather than in front of your fellow officers.'

'I do not have dealings with convicts.'

Japhet ignored the baiting and stood relaxed, with one leg bent and his thumbs hooked into the front pockets of his waistcoat. 'You are a man of foresight and perspicacity. You have shown that by your enter-prising ventures here.'

The officer's eyes narrowed. Obviously he was not sure if that was intended as a compliment or an insult.

Japhet smiled, his manner remaining relaxed. 'This is a land of bound-less opportunities. Look around you. What do you see?'

Haughton scowled. 'A ramshackle town peopled by the dregs of society.'

'But what do you see of its future?'

The officer shrugged. 'It's no better than a prison camp. How will it change?'

'It will change by the vision of those bold enough to risk all for the highest rewards.'

'Is this a way of you trying to get more goods to sell in your store? It is not going to happen, Loveday. You are wasting my time.' He turned to leave.

'How long will it be before you are recalled to England, Captain?'

'Three years. What of it?'

'That is about the time I would seek to make my fortune in. When I look at this town I see houses, shops, taverns built by experienced men. More ships are sailing here. My cousin is not the only private investor. Once banks and merchants learn of the profits to be made here, a steady fleet will arrive. I will certainly write to another cousin,

Thomas Mercer, a partner in Mercer and Lascalles bank in London, to advise his clients to become investors.'

'Is there no end to your illustrious connections?' Haughton was sarcastic.

Japhet laughed. 'I am fortunate to be so blessed. You do not have a high opinion of the convicts, but every month more of them become emancipated. They will want employment, better homes. The more we prosper, the more settlers will arrive. Within a dozen more years you will not know the place for its industry.'

'And I shall be in England by then. What is your point, Loveday?'

Japhet bit back his irritation at Haughton's lack of vision. 'Sydney and Parramatta are expanding. Land is the key to success, and what goes on to such land – buildings. Not all ticket-of-leave convicts want to work their land grants. They can be cheaply bought. I can train carpenters into skilled builders and supply the wood from my sawmill when it is fully manned and working. I am suggesting a partnership.'

The officer scratched his wide side-whiskers. 'And how would this partnership work?'

'To make it a success, we need as much convict labour as possible to clear the land. You are in a better position than myself to learn where and when land can be cheaply purchased. I supply the cut wood and will train the men as carpenters. Fifty-fifty partnership in the expenses and the profits.'

'And the trading vessels?' Haughton remained guarded.

'I want no trouble when my cousin's ship brings goods and merchandise. If, as I believe will happen, many ships start to trade here, then it will be time for renegotiation. For now the Corps still has the monopoly of the government stores.'

'It is not just for me to say. The other officers will want their cut.'

'Then the deal would not be worth my while, or yours.' Japhet had noted the interest in the captain's eyes, although the officer tried to hide it. He played a trump card. 'One more thing, Haughton. My family is not without its connections. As my partner you could have some very influential introductions when you return to England.'

He walked to where he had tethered his horse. 'Sleep on it, Captain Haughton. I doubt you will find a better way of making your fortune in so short a time as three years.'

As he swung into the saddle, the officer reached up to hold the bridle. 'As you say, we would not want to split our profits with others. We will talk more of this, Loveday.'

Japhet rode away certain that Haughton would take the bait. He still did not like the man and certainly did not trust him. He would rather know his enemy and keep him close than be constantly on guard against a knife in his back. It was now in Haughton's interests for Japhet to prosper. The officer would keep the rest of the Corps off their backs and their riches would be assured.

Chapter Forty-four

Clem Sawle had turned his back on the smuggling trade when he married Keziah and he had never taken much interest in the family inn. He had been out two hours before dawn on the early morning tide. The wind had been bitter cutting through his oilskin to bite deep into his bones. After mending his nets after a poor catch, he arrived at his home Blackthorn cottage that was built halfway up the steep slope of the coombe. His mother Sal was seated at the kitchen table watching Zach forming his letters on a slate. Since the death of her husband, Sal had left the inn to live in a cottage further down the coombe from them. She had regained some of her weight and the hollows in her cheeks were filling out; her grey hair was pulled back tightly into a neat bun.

'He will go far with his reading and writing.' Sal smiled, her meaty arms giving the boy a hug. He squirmed with embarrassment in her embrace. 'I were never much good at it meself and you and your brothers refused to attend any lesson given by Mrs Snell. You'd rather be out fishing or up to no good with Reuben. Your pa did wrong by you not making you attend to lessons.'

Clem shrugged and winked at Keziah who was hand feeding one of the kids from her goat herd. Her hair corkscrewed over her shoulders in long tresses hiding her expression from him. 'It never stopped me doing what I wanted and I married a woman with learning enough for the two of us.'

'Aye, it was a proud day for me when you brought Kezzie home and told me you'd have nothing more to do with your father's free-trading. You never had much time for the inn either.'

'I did my share when I were younger.' Clem lowered his thickset figure on to a stool and scowled. 'I took to fishing to get away from Pa. He were always too free with his beatings. He near worked you to death, Ma.'

'Inn keeping were a respectable trade. I could hold my head high working there. The fishermen needed their beer to bring a bit of cheer into their lives. Thirty-five years we ran the Dolphin. It bain't right it be shut because that no good Mordecai Nance has fallen foul of the law.'

'That be our Harry's business. The inn be his,' Clem grunted.

'It be mine and don't you forget it,' Sal said with a burst of vigour. 'And Harry bain't in no position to look after it. He be gone to ground rather than get himself arrested.'

Keziah cut in and nodded a warning to Sal about her son. 'Zach, go and play with the Biddick boys.'

The boy ran gleefully out of the house and as soon as the door closed behind him, Keziah said, 'I don't like Harry's business discussed in front of the lad.'

'Aye, you be right in that,' Sal conceded. She then continued to berate her son, 'That St John Loveday has took against us after what our Meriel did to him. He's offered a reward for our Harry and for Nance.'

'But bain't he allowed Rowena to visit you this week?' Clem tried to deflect his mother's anger. 'He won't like you getting involved in Harry's business. Not if you want to see your granddaughter.'

'The inn be mine. It were once a place to be proud of,' Sal countered.

'That apart, Ma. I don't want to get involved in St John's feud against Harry. My brother be too greedy and he takes too many chances.' Clem tossed a string of mackerel on the kitchen table and pulled off his oilskin before adding, 'When Pa were in charge of the free-trading, we didn't do a third of the runs Harry deals in.'

'But the inn were what kept us respectable,' Sal dabbed at her eyes. 'You've got to keep the inn open, Clem.'

It was not like his mother to get so upset but Clem was tired and aching from his long hours battered by the wind and the sea. 'I'm out fishing every day.'

'But the catches have been poor these last weeks,' Sal would not drop the matter. 'Some loyalty to your family would not go amiss.'

'I promised Kezzie I would have nothing to do with Harry's business.'

'But the inn be different,' Sal insisted.

'No, Ma,' Clem declared and went to stand by the kitchen range to warm his back. He eased his shoulders against a twinge of rheumatism that had been plaguing him in recent months. Most of the fishermen in the village ended up bowed and their joints stiff and twisted.

325

Sal pushed herself up from the table and stared at Keziah. She had stopped feeding the black and brown kid and was ruffling its ears as it nuzzled its head against her chest. 'I don't know about you, Kezzie, but I were brought up where family loyalty meant something.'

Keziah flicked back her hair and stood up to tower over the smaller woman, 'I don't hold with Harry's ways. Clem has made a new life for himself.'

'I'm not saying you have to live at the inn or even that you work there, Kezzie.' Sal eyed her with stony resilience. 'Clem can run it. There be two tavern wenches.'

'They be whores.' Keziah put her hands on her hips and stared hard at her husband. 'I'll not have my man in their company. The Dolphin is no longer a respectable place, Etta Nance saw to that.'

Sal folded her arms across her chest, her feet planted firmly apart. The two women squared up to each other. 'Then get rid of them. Get a couple of decent women from the hiring fair. Now the harvest be over, servants are desperate for work.'

When Keziah did not reply Sal turned to her son. 'In Penruan the Sawles were always a name to be reckoned with. St John had your sister's body moved after her burial in the Loveday vault. She were his wife and though she did him wrong, she were still the mother of his child. What he did were an insult to his daughter and to us.'

'Meriel never did know her place, Ma. She also shamed us when she ran off with her fancy lover.' Clem was weary of his mother's nagging and, to change the subject, nodded at the mackerel on the table. 'Take a couple of those back with you, Ma.'

Sal was undeterred. 'Don't try and sidetrack me. I be the first not to want a feud with our betters, but St John wed Meriel and she only led him a dog's life because he was not strong enough to stand up to her. Are you gonna let him walk all over us now? We would be a laughing stock in Penruan. Do you want to lose the respect you hold over the other fishermen? Respect you earned because no one got the better of you? If you bain't man enough to run the Dolphin, I shall go back to working there.'

'Ma, you can't do that!' Keziah was horrified. 'The work is too much for you now.'

'It were my life for long enough. Reuban weren't always the brutal man you knew him to be. When we first wed he were so proud of the inn. We made it a success and it provided well for us. It were only in later years when the drink got the better of him that it all went wrong. I'd like to show our neighbours that the Sawles can rise again. Not by brute force but by hard work. If the inn goes under because of this rift with the Lovedays and strangers take it over, the Sawles won't be nothing in this village. They'll say you be too craven to take up the fight. Then how will Rowena look us in the eye when she be all grown.'

Clem picked up two mackerel and handed them to his mother. 'You've said enough, Ma. It be best if you go now. Take your joy in Rowena while she be young.'

Sal eyed him sourly. 'I don't want her ashamed of her Sawle blood. I'll be off to the inn. You can support me or not.' She lumbered towards the door and paused to glare at Keziah. 'You can move my stuff out of the cottage for me today. The Lovedays believe in loyalty. That be what made them what they be today. We may be poor but are we less of a family than they be?'

When she left, Clem slammed his fist down on to the table. 'Why must Ma be so pig-headed! But she be right.'

Keziah saw his pain. He was a good man. She knew he would not break his word to her, but she would be abusing his loyalty to her if she stopped him doing what he clearly thought was right. 'Go and help your ma, Clem. Keeping the inn open is just making a stand, showing the world that the Sawles bain't afraid to hold their heads high and defend what be theirs by right. Sal were upset when the Nances took over and by what they did to the inn. It be Sal who owns the inn not Harry. He took the profits when you showed no interest in it.'

'I be a fisherman not an innkeeper.'

Keziah studied him for a long time before saying, 'Is that the life you want? Four men from the village have drowned in the last two winters. Wouldn't it be a more settled way of life to run an inn? You could make it respectable. There bain't no need to be involved in the free-trading. Sal were saying she thought it should be your birthright not Harry's.'

'Harry sees it as his.'

'Well if you have no mind to make a stand over it and prefer the uncertainties and income of life as a fisherman . . .' She shrugged and picked up the mackerel from the table and began to gut them.

Clem sat down on the chair his mother had vacated. 'Fishing be a hard life. I had'na given much thought to the inn. It were always Ma and Pa's.'

'So why should Harry benefit now Reuban be dead? He don't even live there,' Keziah pressed.

'Bain't you happy living here?'

'This could still be our home.' She did not look up from her work.

She knew any decision Clem made would be after he had mulled it over for some time. She had been upset by the four drownings. Raised on a farm she had not realised how dangerous a life at sea could be. She loved Clem. She worried each time he went out in his sloop that he may not return. 'We could make the Dolphin a proper inn again. Take in lodgers. I'd cook them meals but we don't have to sleep there. We'd give a room to a potman in the stables and I would still keep the goat herd and sell my cheeses. It would be a better life for Zach – a better inheritance than a fishing sloop.' She glanced at her husband who was listening intently to her words and added, 'You may forget that Zach be Rowena's cousin. She will marry well and be a grand lady. She be loyal to her own. She would help Zach if he wanted to be a man of standing in the community. The inn would provide well for us. We could pay for Zach to have proper schooling. He could become a physician or a lawyer. Wouldna that be something to be proud of?'

Clem did not answer but it was a good sign he had not dismissed her idea. She pressed on, enthusiastic with her plans for the future. 'The inn is but a start. The place would need some money spent on it. But it be the only inn in Penruan now.'

Clem rubbed his chin. 'You've been talking to Ma.'

'Sal talked of nothing else all morning. She be ashamed of Meriel and Harry. The Sawles have got a bad name in recent years. Harry be worse than ever Reuban were. Do you want Zach to grow up proud of his name or ashamed?'

There was a long silence from her husband as she finished cleaning the fish and started to cook them on the range. By the time they were ready and they sat down with Zach to eat, Clem had considered the matter.

'I reckon we've as much right to the inn as Harry. If he bain't working there why should he get the profits. I'd get a good price for my sloop. It would pay to make the place more presentable. A coat of lime wash on the walls, perhaps even a new sign. You be a good cook Kezzie and renting the rooms to lodgers would be a darn sight easier than getting up at godforsaken hours to catch the tide or spend hours battling the elements through another stormy winter.'

'So what will you do about Harry?'

'He bain't here, is he? And with a warrant out for his arrest he bain't likely to show his face round here for many a month. I can handle Harry when the time comes. I'll get Ma to sign the Dolphin over to me, legal like, and we'll pay for her cottage.'

'Sal hinted she would not mind living here and helping me out with

Zach. I think she be lonely in the cottage and, if we take over the inn, someone will have to be with Zach of an evening.'

'She wouldn't live here when I asked her afore,' Clem frowned.

'She thought she'd be imposing. She's not one to want to be idle and she'd like nothing more than to care for Zach.'

'I'll speak with Ma.' Clem got up from the table. 'Happen I'll be moving her things here instead of the inn, if that be alright with you?'

Keziah breathed a sigh of relief. She did not want Clem to risk his life at sea. The Dolphin would be made respectable again. It would give her and Clem a safer more secure life and she did not want Zach growing up with people reviling him for being a Sawle and mixed up with violence and smuggling.

Chapter Forty-five

Unwilling to spoil the baptism and celebrations of Michael's birth, Adam curbed his anger towards his twin. Yet St John was insufferably smug, bragging to Joshua how he had proved Nance was behind the robberies and that there was contraband at the Dolphin Inn, which would implicate Sawle as a smuggler.

To stop accusing St John of being a short-sighted idiot, Adam sought out Senara who had been tending Bridie. Once the baptism was over the family had withdrawn from her bedchamber to the parlour to allow the young mother to sleep. Senara was in the kitchen wrapping some warmed bricks in a woollen shawl.

'We must keep these placed under Michael in his crib and changed every hour,' she explained. 'And he must be kept tightly cocooned in a shawl. He is a frail little mite but at least he is suckling. That bodes well. He is a fighter.'

'I will take those upstairs,' Leah took the covered bricks from her daughter sensing by his frown that Adam needed to talk with his wife.

'You look troubled, my love,' Senara addressed him as she pushed back a lock of hair from her brow.

'It is St John. He is so puffed up with his own importance over those warrants. But what good are they? Sawle will not venture near these parts for months until the furore has died down. Nance also has slipped the net. All it achieved was putting Etta in gaol. She may be a misguided adventuress but she did not plan the robberies or Peter's abduction. It is her no good husband who should be in prison.'

'Etta is not so innocent,' Senara reasoned, 'but it does seem unfair that she was taken whilst Nance remains free. He wanted Peter dead and Peter had done nothing but preach against the smugglers. And he sacrificed the success the Bradstocks could have made at Tor Farm to get back at your family.'

'Nance has not the intelligence to be so devious.' Adam selected from

330

a bowl an apple picked in Joshua's orchard and bit into it. 'He followed Sawle's orders. But let us not spoil this day with thoughts of our enemies.'

Senara took up the beaded reticule she had laid on a dresser, pulled out a crumpled letter and passed it to her husband. 'This is more good news. It came from Tamasine while you were away. I've been carrying it round to show Hannah and Cecily.'

Adam scanned the half page of writing and laughed. 'Not much of a missive is it? Unlike Aunt Margaret who can write a dozen pages at a time. She writes of her happiness and the splendour of her new home and that she has made many new friends. And Max has promised that they will visit Cornwall soon.'

'I am so happy for her.' Senara put her arms around Adam's waist. 'She is very much in love and a whole new and exciting world has been opened to her. She is indeed blessed. As am I to have won your love.'

Adam kissed her and Hannah, entering the kitchen, teased, 'You are a staid old married couple, control yourselves.'

Adam stepped back from his wife with a grin. He was glad to see how much brighter Hannah looked. He sensed her grief was lifting. She was still a young woman with so much vigour and life ahead of her. 'Not so staid and not so old, if you do not mind, cousin.'

Mordecai Nance had been watching Polruggan Parsonage all day. He had seen the Loveday family arrive in ones and twos until they had all gathered to celebrate the birth of the parson's child.

Nance sat in the churchyard hidden from view of the house by a large oblong tomb. He squatted on the grass and drank from a bottle of brandy he had stolen from the Dolphin inn that morning. Thinking the place deserted, he had hidden in the cellar and nearly been discovered by Clem Sawle. He had come back to search for anything of value that may have been missed by the soldiers. He had been furious to discover they had taken all the stolen trinkets and the small stash of money he had hidden away. He had taken up a bottle of brandy to drown his sorrows and fallen into a drunken doze to be awoken by voices.

He had recognised Clem's deep tones and the old woman Sal was with him. Nance had listened at the trap door of the cellar while Clem and the old woman spoke of their plans for the inn. Clearly they thought Harry would not be around for some time. The smuggler had told Mordecai to leave Cornwall while he could and if he was arrested, he should keep Harry Sawle's name out of any trial if he knew what was good for him.

Abandoned by his leader, Nance was bitter about his fate. He had committed murder for Sawle and where had it got him? He was on the run without money or friends. He gave little thought to his wife. Etta had been playing him false with an officer since they had taken over the inn. He also suspected that St John Loveday may have been her lover and, when he had spurned her, she had concocted the story of his attack on her. Etta could rot in gaol. Though knowing her, she would lie, cheat and give her favours to any man who could help her to escape justice.

Mordecai was no sailor or he would have stolen a fishing sloop and risked sailing to the Scilly Isles. There were too many revenue men and soldiers around for the roads to be safe for him. He had spent two weeks in hiding and his future seemed bleak unless he could get safely out of Cornwall. The brandy soured his mood. He blamed his misery on St John Loveday. He would not leave Cornwall until he had his revenge on his enemy.

Once Clem and his mother left the inn, he wrapped a muffler around his face and stole away through the back streets of Penruan. Two women returning to their cottages made him dart behind an outbuilding storing nets. He heard the women talking of the new Loveday child born to the parson and how it was to be baptised later that day.

The family would all be at the parsonage. That would be the time for him to strike. The brandy bottle had been his only companion all day and his hatred for the family had grown with each hour that he waited for a chance to strike at them. He would wait for St John to leave and then waylay him. He would be alone, for his aunt and step-mother had left earlier.

Another hour passed and he drained the dregs from the bottle and threw it away. He was finding it hard to stay awake. Then St John emerged from the parsonage and went into the stable to bring out his horse. Mordecai edged around the perimeter of the graveyard to the road. He carried a primed pistol.

A spate of angry words drifted to him and Nance peered over the top of the boundary wall to see that Adam was arguing with his brother, but their words were indistinguishable. St John was mounted on his horse and Adam circled the mare goading his brother to dismount and face him.

'You cannot bear it that I was right to act as I did,' St John raised his voice. 'Nance will be brought to trial because of me, not anything you did.' He then kicked his horse and it cantered away down the lane. It had to turn a corner before it would be level with Nance. He had the pistol steady and aimed at the rider as he appeared in his vision. St John Loveday would pay for his arrogance. He fired and saw St John reel in the saddle. His mare reared from the sound of the gunshot and tossed its rider to the ground.

Nance chuckled, vaulted back over the boundary wall and darted across the cemetery to take cover in a nearby wood. There was a yell behind him and the pounding of running feet. Nance stumbled over a fallen gravestone and had trouble keeping his balance. His gait was unsteady, the brandy making his movements clumsy.

Other cries were taken up from the direction of the parsonage and he glanced over his shoulder to see Adam and Peter Loveday bearing down on him.

He turned the spent pistol round to use its handle as a cudgel. His body was weaving and he collided with a grave stone and stumbled. The world around him was spinning crazily from the effect of his drinking. Then Adam threw himself at him, his arms catching him around the knees to bring him down. Nance was winded but swung wildly with his arms at his assailant. Adam rolled on top of him and slammed his fist into his face. Pain exploded in his skull and he passed out.

Peter caught up with his cousin, dagger in hand. 'I'll deal with him, Adam. I'd take great pleasure in beating him senseless if he comes round after how he attacked me. There is some rope in the stable to bind him.'

Adam reckoned that Peter was owed his time with Nance, though he doubted his cousin would touch the man whilst he was unconscious. He ran back to the stable and passed Joshua and Senara helping St John back into the parsonage. He was relieved to see his brother was able to walk and did not appear too badly injured.

Peter was wrestling with Nance when Adam returned to the cemetery. Though lighter and more wiry, Peter had delivered several punches before the innkeeper again collapsed and was unable to rise. Adam threw the rope to Peter who tied Nance's arms to his sides and then, pressing the dagger to his throat, ordered him to march to the stable.

'Good work, Peter,' Adam praised. 'Shall we escort him to Fowey ourselves or call out the militia?'

'Hannah suspects he bribed Tregare.' Peter was breathing heavily from his exertion but there was a glow of triumph on his usually austere countenance.

Adam grinned. Peter was proving himself not so pious after all.

His cousin continued, 'We will take him in ourselves. That way we know he will not escape. He can stand trial with his wife in Bodmin at the next Assizes.'

Joshua came out to the stable as Adam was saddling Solomon. He saw Nance tied on to the back of the dog-cart pony and nodded approval.

'How is St John?' Adam asked.

'The shot glanced the top of his arm. Senara is tending to him. It was no more than a scratch and for that I thank the Lord.' Joshua placed his hand over Adam's fingers. 'You two quarrelled again. Go and make your peace. I will accompany Peter to the lockup.'

Adam was about to protest but realised that if he took Nance into custody, St John would see it as him trying to claim the glory and again get one better over him. He was too old for such petty rivalry. St John may have acted rashly over Nance, but he had paid the price by luring the innkeeper to attack him. His brother was lucky that Nance had been too drunk to shoot straight. St John deserved to be commended that Sawle's henchman would now be brought to justice.

He found his twin in the parsonage kitchen being tended by Senara. She had bandaged his shoulder and fashioned a sling for his arm.

'You had a lucky escape, St John. Peter and Uncle Joshua are taking Nance to the Fowey lockup. He will hang for this attack and his involvement with Sawle. How is your arm?'

'It is nothing serious. Though what Felicity will make of it . . .' He seemed worried about her opinion.

'Because of you we have apprehended a violent villain,' Adam stated. 'She should be proud of you.'

'But the real villain remains free,' St John said with heat. 'He's fled the district because I was too hasty in getting a warrant for his arrest.'

'You did what you thought was right. The authorities have the evidence against Nance. Sawle will not escape justice. We will hunt him down if we have to, will we not?'

'We will do whatever it takes to bring that fiend to justice,' St John vowed and his stare was heartfelt as he continued, 'But we will work together next time to ensure he pays for his crimes.'

'No more talk of retribution.' Senara packed away the bandages in a wicker basket. 'Today we are celebrating. It is good Nance will face trial but let us rejoice that Bridie and Peter have a son. That is a wonderful blessing. St John is to be wed next month; that will be another wonderful occasion.'

St John moved stiffly, his leg bruised from the fall from his horse. 'I must return to Trevowan. I would welcome you all at my home this Sunday to dine after Uncle's service at Trewenna.'

'It will be our pleasure,' Adam accepted.

Chapter Forty-six

Adam was determined to put his differences with his twin behind them. St John had been less antagonistic since Nance's attack and today the family were to celebrate the couple's engagement at Trevowan. The occasion promised to be even more special as Tamasine would be there to celebrate with them.

From the moment she stepped from the Deverell carriage, it was obvious to everyone that Tamasine was blissfully happy. Since her marriage she had changed in subtle ways; her manner and dress were more sophisticated and though her love of life and fun still emanated from her, there was also a deeper confidence that came from her having found her sense of place.

She had brought gifts for all the children. There were forts and toy soldiers for Nathan, Joel, Davey and Luke, with a smaller version for Rafe. Rowena, Abigail, Florrie, Rhianne and also Charlotte Barrett had dolls with china faces, and Sara a rag doll with bells inside that jingled when she shook it. Michael had a silver rattle and a coral teething ring. Adam, St John, Peter and Joshua received cricket bats; Senara, Hannah, Bridie and Felicity backgammon sets, Elspeth a gold-topped riding whip and Amelia and Cecily Indian shawls.

The family were startled by her generosity. 'These gifts are too expensive to accept,' Senara protested. 'You should have saved them for Christmas.'

'I wanted to thank you all for your kindness. And to show Felicity and Charlotte how they are already part of our family. I could not resist the children's toys or indeed the cricket bats and backgammon. I had no toys as a child. It is a great joy for me to give gifts that will bring pleasure and relaxation to others.'

Adam ran his hand over his cricket bat admiring its workmanship. 'The gifts are most thoughtful. We will have many picnics and matches on the lawn.' He grinned at St John. 'Perhaps we should raise two teams for an annual match in the summer between Trevowan and Boscabel.'

'Not if it encourages any rivalry between the pair of you,' Elspeth snorted. 'Thank you for the riding whip, Tamasine. It is a most thoughtful gift.'

'And my wife and I will take much pleasure in our backgammon when Bridie recovers from her lying-in,' Peter observed.

'I suspect the generosity is all Max's,' Amelia said on a cooler note, momentarily falling back on her old animosity towards her late husband's child.

'My wife has a warm and giving nature, it is my pleasure to indulge her.' Max replied. A frown creased his brow as he regarded Tamasine's stepmother. 'Tamasine took great care in selecting your shawl, that particular shade of blue embroidery is, I believe, your favourite colour, Amelia.'

The reserve that had tempered Amelia's manner since their arrival dissipated. Clearly the shawl had been chosen with care and she was acting ungraciously. It was time to bury her old resentments. Her smile was sincere as she regarded her stepdaughter. 'The shawl is beautiful, my dear, and Rafe delights in his soldiers. I can hear the boys enjoying themselves in the nursery from here. Come, let me kiss you and thank you properly.'

Tamasine kissed her cheek and Amelia clasped her hand and whispered. 'Forgive me for being a foolish, jealous woman. Edward would be so proud to see you now.'

'There is nothing to forgive,' Tamasine assured her. 'It was wilful of me to thrust myself upon my guardian when I ran away from school. It was a great joy to learn that he was my father, but it must have caused you a great deal of pain. I regret that.'

The older woman's reconciliation made Tamasine's reunion with her family perfect. Finally she felt accepted by them all and though she had a new life with a man who adored her, the love and respect of her family would always be important.

St John surveyed the dining room. It was good to hear the house filled with laughter and animated voices. Amelia and Elspeth had ensured that the servants had worked hard to bring the rooms back to their former glory. The mirrors, chandeliers and furniture shone in the candlelight. The silver candelabra and three-tiered fruit dish and serving dishes had been taken from their chests and polished to adorn the table. There had been some caustic comments from his aunt, when she discovered many items of the family silver were missing, as he had sold them to pay his gambling debts. His conscience had troubled him and he was now eager to make amends.

He had come to an understanding with Clem Sawle that Rowena could visit her grandmother in Penruan once a week. In exchange, Clem had repeated to Sir Henry Traherne, as the local magistrate, the events he had witnessed in Trevowan cove concerning Uncle William and his wife. Sir Henry had written to William's lawyer informing him that he was satisfied that Lisette Loveday had drowned in a boating accident with her husband and that the money should be apportioned to the beneficiaries of Captain William Loveday's estate. Sir Henry had proved a true friend and the circumstances of the sordid affair and suicide had been kept confidential.

Relieved that no knowledge of the jewels of Lisette's he had sold had come to light, St John had informed his family that he would use his share of the inheritance to replace the crystal chandelier in the hall that had been smashed the previous year during a drunken weekend with his friends, and several rooms in the house would be redecorated.

He smiled now at Felicity who was conversing with Peter. For the first time in many months his cousin was not discussing religion but the importance of family ties. The birth of his son had taken the fervour from Peter's faith and that was a blessing. St John studied all the guests from his place at the head of the table. Adam was listening to an anecdote related by Max. His twin was in a good humour and had been effusive in his greeting on his arrival. There had been no condemnation in his attitude and he had been solicitous of St John's health. The wound in his shoulder had been infected for a week but Senara's remedies had drawn out the poison and it was almost healed. Though it still pained him, with Felicity staying in his home he was careful to drink sparingly of the brandy that would have eased the ache in his shoulder.

On his left he noted that Joshua was unusually silent. He was seated next to Sophia who was flirting outrageously with him but he seemed abstracted and Sophia pouted and turned her attention instead upon Cecily.

'Is it not wonderful that our families are united, Cecily?' she gushed. 'We shall see so much more of each other in the future.'

Her words deepened his uncle's frown and St John sensed that Joshua was uneasy at such a prospect. That was surprising as his uncle was usually so affable and now he looked almost haunted. St John himself had no great liking for his future mother-in-law whom he found brash, overbearing and somewhat predatory. He did not intend for Sophia to be a regular guest, his home was already overfull of formidable women.

'You appear distracted, Uncle Joshua,' he observed. 'Do you not approve of my engagement?'

'I am delighted you have chosen such a worthy bride,' Joshua rallied his thoughts with a visible effort. 'Your pardon if I gave you the wrong impression. I was thinking of those who are not here to celebrate with us.'

'Of course, you must miss my father and also Japhet.'

He nodded. 'I was also thinking of William. At least something of the mystery of his death and his wife's disappearance has been cleared up. It has been a difficult year, but we have remained steadfast and come through it. Peter and yourself have suffered no lasting ill-effects from your wounds. And Mordecai Nance will hang for his crimes. He has been sent to Newgate to face trial. His wife will fare little better. For all she tried to win a pardon by turning king's evidence against her husband, she was still sentenced to transportation and has been sent to the prison hulks in Plymouth to await the next sailing.'

'At least the people of Penruan no longer face the tyranny imposed by Nance and Harry Sawle. Clem is determined to make a success of the Dolphin Inn and have no dealings with the smugglers. But his brother remains free . . .' St John stared into his wine glass and a muscle pumped along his jaw showing his displeasure. 'Harry Sawle cannot be trusted. I fear he will seek retribution for his losses. It is a travesty that he escaped justice.'

'Let there be no more talk of retribution and justice,' Joshua warned. 'The vendetta between the Lovedays and the Sawles must end.'

Adam heard his uncle's words and frowned. He caught his brother's eye and knew that St John would not let the matter rest any more than he would.

Joshua saw the exchange between them and spoke sternly. 'I want your word, St John, and yours also, Adam, that you will not pursue this folly.'

'If Sawle stays away he has nothing to fear from us,' Adam returned.

Hannah overheard the conversation and saw the tightening of her father's face and the stubborn set to her cousin's chin. She had seen those expressions too many times and was warned that an argument was brewing. Joshua expected too much from his nephews. The twins would not rest until their father's death was avenged, and Sawle never backed down from a threat. But Harry Sawle had many enemies and she prayed that the law would catch up with him before there was an inevitable confrontation involving her family.

'Let us have no talk of such an objectionable man today of all days,' she interceded. 'This is a joyous occasion. Let us speak only of your wedding plans, St John. When is the happy day?'

Grateful to Hannah for diverting a dangerous conversation, St John smiled at her. Very often he felt like he was walking on thin ice in Felicity's presence. His fiancée had grown very pale at Joshua's outburst and her eyes had narrowed with a reproving light. She had been upset at Nance's attack on him and had been appalled when she learned the full story of Sawle's hatred for his family. She abhorred violence and had threatened to call off their betrothal if he did not agree to end the feud with the smuggler. To placate her he had agreed. After their marriage she would realise that family honour demanded that Sawle be brought to justice.

For now he could be magnanimous. He raised his glass to his fiancée. 'My dear Felicity has no wish for a grand affair as we have both been wed before. We will marry at Trewenna next month and a banquet will be held for the family and a few friends.'

'I hope you will chose your friends wisely, St John,' Elspeth commented. 'Who is to be your best man? I trust not the objectionable Basil Braithwaite. He is a bad influence.'

'There is only one man I would wish to stand at my side on such a joyous occasion and though I have as yet not asked him, I do so now. Adam, I would be honoured if you would be my best man. It is time to put our past differences aside.'

Adam was taken aback and wondered if the gesture had come at Felicity's instigation. Nevertheless it was a turning point. It would show the world that the Lovedays were again united and invincible in their loyalty.

'I shall be honoured to accept, St John.' Adam stood up and raised his glass. 'A toast to St John and Felicity for their future prosperity and happiness.'

The family raised their glasses and said in unison, 'To St John and Felicity.'

Adam hoped that this sign of reconciliation from his twin meant that their rivalry was over. It was something that should have been laid to rest years ago.

ROGERSTONE 31.3.06

PILLGWENLLY 4.10.07